Beautiful Day

Elin Hilderbrand

D1493961

HODDER &
STOUGHTON

First published in the USA in 2013 by Reagan Arthur Books
An imprint of Little, Brown and Company
A division of Hachette Book Group, Inc.
First published in Great Britain in 2013 by Hodder & Stoughton
An Hachette UK company

1

A CIP catalogue record for this title is available from the British Library

Hardback ISBN 978 1 444 72398 4
Trade Paperback ISBN 978 1 444 72399 1
Ebook ISBN 978 1 444 72401 1

Printed and bound by the CPI Group (UK) Ltd, Croydon, CR0 4YY

Hodder & Stoughton policy is to use papers that are natural,
renewable and recyclable products and made from wood grown in sustainable
forests. The logging and manufacturing processes are expected to conform
to the environmental regulations of the country of origin.

Hodder & Stoughton Ltd
338 Euston Road
London NW1 3BH

www.hodder.co.uk

Beautiful Day

Also by Elin Hilderbrand

Summerland
Silver Girl
The Island
The Castaways
A Summer Affair
Barefoot
The Love Season
The Blue Bistro
Summer People
Nantucket Nights
The Beach Club

About the author

Elin Hilderbrand: novelist, mother of three, sports enthusiast, avid fan of Bruce Springsteen, Veuve Cliquot, and four-inch heels. She serves on the Board of Directors of the Nantucket Boys & Girls Club and Nantucket Little League and is a founding member of Nantucket BookFest. Her resting pulse is 65. Elin is a graduate of John Hopkins University and the graduate fiction workshop at the University of Iowa.

You can follow Elin on Twitter @elinhilderbrand or find out more on her Facebook page www.facebook.com/ElinHilderbrand.

You want a love story?
This novel is dedicated to my grandparents,
Clarence Watt Huling Jr. and Ruth Francis Huling,
who were married from June 19, 1943,
until my grandfather's death on June 2, 2012.
Sixty-eight years, eleven months, and two weeks.
That's a love story.

Jennifer Bailey Carmichael and Stuart James Graham, along with their families, invite you to share in the celebration of their wedding.

Saturday, July 20, 2013, 4:00 p.m.

St. Paul's Episcopal Church, Fair Street

Nantucket Island

Reception to follow at the Carmichael home, 34 Orange Street

RSVP by June 1.

THE NOTEBOOK, PAGE 1

Dear Jenna,

I have finally reached the point with my prognosis where I accept that there are certain things I will not live to see. I will not see the day your father retires from the law firm (he always promised me he would retire on his 65th birthday, safe to say that promise was only made to appease me); I will not live to see my grandchildren ride roller coasters, get pimples, or go on dates—and I will not live to see you get married.

This last item pains me the most. As I write this, you are a senior in college and you have just broken up with Jason. For my sake, you are pretending like it's no big deal, you said you knew he wasn't "the One"; his favorite politician is Pat Buchanan and yours in Ralph Nader. So it won't be Jason you end up with—dishy though he was (sorry, true)—but there will be someone, someday, who will light you up. You will get married, and you have said that you would like a big, traditional wedding with all the bells and whistles. Since you've been a little girl, you've had your heart set on getting married on Nantucket, and although marriage is probably

5

further from your mind now than it was when you were six, I hope that is still true.

That's where this notebook comes in. I won't be here to encourage or guide you when the time comes; I will, sweet Jenna, probably never meet the man you're going to marry (unless it's the delivery man from FTD who has been here three times this week. I can tell he has a crush on you). My hand aches knowing that it will not be squeezing your hand just before you walk down the aisle.

But enough feeling sorry for ourselves! I will, in these pages, endeavor to bestow my best advice for your big day. You can follow it or ignore it, but at the very least you will know where I stand on each and every matter.

I wish for you a beautiful day, Jenna, my darling. You alone will make it so.

Love, Mom

OUTTAKES

Finn Sullivan-Walker (bridesmaid): I can't wait to see Jenna wearing her mother's gown. It's vintage Priscilla of Boston, silk bodice with a sweetheart neckline and lace column skirt. There used to be a picture in the Carmichael house of Jenna's mother, Beth, wearing the dress. I was obsessed with that picture when I was younger, even before Beth died. Seeing Jenna in that dress is going to be surreal, you know? Like seeing a ghost.

Douglas Carmichael (father of the bride): I can't stand the thought of giving Jenna away. She's my last one. Well, I guess technically Nick is my last one, but Nick might never get married.

Nick Carmichael (brother of the bride): My sister has extremely hot friends.

Margot (sister of the bride, maid of honor): Can I be honest? I really just want this weekend to be over.

THURSDAY

MARGOT

They were on the ferry, the hulking white steamship that was properly named the *Eagle,* but which Margot had always thought of as *Moby-Dick,* because that was what their mother used to call it. Every year when the Carmichael family drove their Ford Country Squire into the darkened hold of the boat, Beth used to say it was like being swallowed by a whale. She had found the ride on the steamship romantic, literary, and possibly also biblical (she would have been thinking of Jonah, right?)—but Margot had despised the ferry ride then, and she despised it even more now. The thick, swirling fumes from the engines made her queasy, as did the lurching motion. For this trip, Margot had taken the Dramamine that Jenna offered her in Hyannis. Really, with the seven thousand details of her wedding to triage, the fact that Jenna had remembered to pack pills for her sister's seasickness was astonishing—but that was Jenna for you. She was thoughtful, nearly to a fault. She was, Margot thought with no small amount of envy, exactly like their mother.

For Jenna's sake, Margot pretended the Dramamine was working. She pulled down the brim of her straw hat against the hot July sun, which was blinding when reflected off the surface of the water. The last thing she wanted was to freckle right before the wedding. They were outside, on the upper deck. Jenna and her best friend, Finn Sullivan-Walker, were posing against the railing at the bow of the boat. Nantucket was just a smudge on the horizon; even Christopher Columbus might not have said for sure there was land ahead, but Jenna was adamant that Margot take a picture of her and Finn, with their blond hair billowing around their faces, as soon as Nantucket was visible in the background.

Margot planted her feet at shoulder width to steady herself against the gentle and yet nefarious rocking of the boat and raised the camera. Her sister looked happy. She looked excited-happy that this was the beginning of her wedding weekend, which was certain to be the most fun-filled and memorable weekend of her life — and she also looked contented-happy, because she was confident that marrying Stuart James Graham was her life's mission. Stuart was the One.

Stuart had proposed to Jenna on a park bench across the street from Little Minds, the progressive, "sustainable" preschool where Jenna was the lead teacher, presenting her with a ring featuring Sri Lankan sapphires and ethically mined diamonds from Canada. (Stuart was a banker, who made money buying and selling money, but he knew the path to Jenna's heart.) Since that day, Margot had cast herself as devil's advocate to Jenna's vision of a lifetime of happiness with Stuart. Marriage was the worst idea in all of civilization, Margot said. For two people to meet when they were young and decide to spend the rest of their lives together was unnatural, Margot said, because everyone knew that human beings changed as they got older, and what were the chances — honestly, *what* were the *chances* — that two people would evolve in ways that were compatible?

"Listen," Margot had said one evening when she and Jenna

were having drinks at Cafe Gitane in SoHo. "You like having sex with Stuart now. But imagine doing it four thousand times. You'll lose interest, I promise you. You'll grow sick of it. And the enthusiasm that you used to have for having sex with Stuart will migrate—against your will—to something else. You'll develop an unhealthy interest in cultivating orchids. You'll be *that* mother on the baseball field, harassing the umpire over every pitch that crosses the plate. You'll start flirting with the cashier at Whole Foods, or the compost guru at the local nursery, and the flirting will turn into fantasies, and the fantasies will become a fling, then perhaps a full-blown affair, and Stuart will find out by checking your cell phone records, and your life will be ruined, your reputation will end up in shreds, and your children will require expensive therapy." Margot paused to sip her sauvignon blanc. "Don't get married."

Jenna had stared at her levelly. Or almost. Margot thought that this time, maybe, somewhere deep inside those clear blue eyes, she detected a flicker of worry.

"Shut up," Jenna said. "You're just saying that because you're divorced."

"Everyone is divorced," Margot said. "We owe our very livelihood to the fact that *everyone is divorced.* It put food on the table, it paid for our orthodontia, it sent us to college." Margot paused again, more wine. She was under the gun to get her point across. It was nearly seven o'clock, and her children were in the apartment without a babysitter. At twelve years old, Drum Jr. was okay to be left in charge until it got dark, then he would panic and start blowing up Margot's phone. "Divorce, Jenna, is paying for your wedding."

Margot was referring to the fact that their father, Douglas Carmichael, was the managing partner at Garrett, Parker, and Spence, a very successful family law practice in midtown

Manhattan. Technically, Margot knew, Jenna would have to agree with her: divorce had always paid for everything.

"There is no man on earth better suited for me than Stuart," Jenna said. "He traded in his Range Rover for a hybrid for me. He and two of the guys on his trading desk showed up last weekend to fix a hole in the roof at Little Minds. He brings me coffee in bed every morning when he stays over. He goes with me to foreign films and talks with me about them afterwards at the fondue place. He likes the fondue place and doesn't mind that I always want to eat there after the movies. He doesn't complain when I listen to Taylor Swift at top volume. Sometimes he even sings along."

This was a litany Margot had heard many times before. Famously, after only three dates, Stuart had showed up at Jenna's apartment with a bouquet of yellow roses and a screwdriver, and he had fixed the towel bar in her bathroom, which had been broken since she'd moved in two years earlier.

"What I'm saying is that you and Stuart are tra-la-la now, everything is sunshine and lollipops, but it might still fail down the road."

"Shut up," Jenna said again. "Just shut the eff up. You're not going to talk me out of it. I love Stuart."

"Love dies," Margot said, and she snatched up the bill.

Now Margot tried to center Jenna's and Finn's shining faces in the viewfinder. She snapped a picture, all hair and toothy smiles.

"Take another one, just in case," Jenna said.

Margot took another as the boat pitched side...to...side. She grabbed one of the plastic molded chairs that were bolted to the deck. Oh, God. She breathed in through her nose, out through her mouth. It was good to be gazing at the horizon. Her three children were down in the hold of the ship, sitting in the car, playing Angry Birds and Fruit Ninja on their iDevices. The movement of the boat didn't faze them; all three had their father's ironclad constitution. Nothing made them sick; physically, they were warriors. But Drum Jr. was afraid of the dark, and Carson, Margot's ten-year-old, had nearly failed the fourth grade. At the end of the year, his teacher, Ms. Wolff, had told Margot—as if she didn't know already—that Carson wasn't stupid, he was just lazy.

Like his father. Drum Sr. was living in San Diego, surfing and managing a fish taco stand. He hoped to buy the stand and possibly turn it into a franchise; someday he would be a baron of fish taco stands up and down the coast of California. The business plan sounded hazy to Margot, but she encouraged him nonetheless. When she met him, Drum Sr. had had a trust fund, which he'd frittered away on exotic surfing and skiing trips. His parents had bought Drum and Margot a palatial apartment on East Seventy-third Street, but his father offered nothing more in the way of cash, hoping that Drum would be inspired to get a job. But instead Drum had stayed home to care for the kids while Margot worked. Now she sent him a support check for $4,000 every month—the trade-off, along with a lump sum of $360,000, for keeping the apartment.

However, after the phone call she had received last night, she supposed the palimony payments would end. Drum Sr. had called to tell her he was getting married.

"Married?" Margot had said. "To whom?"

"Lily," he said. "The Pilates instructor."

Margot had never heard of Lily the Pilates instructor before, and she had never heard the kids—who flew to California the last weekend of every month, trips that were also financed by Margot—mention anyone named Lily the Pilates instructor. There had been a Caroline, a Nicole, a Sara, pronounced

"Sah-RAH." Drum had women moving through a revolving door. From what Margot could tell, girlfriends lasted three to four months, which aligned with what she knew to be his attention span.

"Well, congratulations," Margot said. "That's wonderful." She sounded genuine to her own ears; she *was* genuine. Drum was a good guy, just not the guy for her. She had been the one to end the marriage. Drum's laid-back approach to the world—which Margot had found so charming when she met him surfing on Nantucket—had come to drive her insane. He was unambitious at best, a slacker at worst. That being said, Margot was astonished to find she felt a twinge of—what? jealousy? anger? resentment?—at his announcement. It seemed unfair that news of Drum's nuptials should arrive less than forty-eight hours before Jenna's wedding.

Everyone is getting married, she thought. *Everyone but me.*

Jenna and Finn were as young and blond and pretty as a couple of milkmaids on a farm in Sweden. Finn looked more like Jenna than Margot did. Margot had straight black hair, the hair of a silk weaver in Beijing—and she had six inches on her sister, the height of a tribeswoman on the banks of the Amazon. She had blue eyes like Jenna, but Jenna's were the same color as the sapphires in her engagement ring, whereas Margot's were ice blue, the eyes of a sled dog in northern Russia.

Jenna looked exactly like their mother. And so, bizarrely, did Finn, who had grown up three houses away.

"We need to get a picture of the three of us now," Jenna said. She took the camera from Margot and handed it to a man reading the newspaper in one of the plastic molded chairs.

"Do you mind?" Jenna asked sweetly.

The man rose. He was tall, about Margot's age, maybe a little older; he had a day or two of scruff on his face, and he was wearing a white visor and sunglasses. He looked like he was going to Nantucket to sail in a regatta. Margot checked his left hand — no ring. No girlfriend in the vicinity, no children in his custody, just a folded copy of the *Wall Street Journal* now resting on his seat as he rose to take the picture. "Sure," he said. "I'd love to."

Margot assumed that Jenna had picked the guy on purpose; Jenna was on a mission to find Margot a boyfriend. She had no idea that Margot had allowed herself to fall in love — idiotically — with Edge Desvesnes, their father's law partner. Edge was thrice married, thrice divorced, nineteen years Margot's senior, and wildly inappropriate in half a dozen other ways. If Jenna *had* known about Margot and Edge, she would only be more eager to introduce Margot to someone else.

Margot found herself assigned to the middle, pegged between the two blond bookends.

"I can't see your face," Regatta Man said, nodding at Margot. "Your hat is casting a shadow."

"Sorry," Margot said. "I have to leave it on."

"Oh, come on," Jenna said. "Just for one second while he takes the picture?"

"No," Margot said. If her skin saw the sun for even one second, she would detonate into a hundred thousand freckles. Jenna and Finn could be cavalier with their skin, they were young, but Margot would stand vigilant guard, despite the fact that she must now seem rigid and difficult to Regatta Man. She said in her most conciliatory voice, "Sorry."

"No worries," Regatta Man said. "Smile!" He took the picture.

There was something familiar about the guy, Margot thought. She knew him. Or maybe it was the Dramamine messing with her brain.

"Should I take one more, Margot?" he said. "Just to be safe?"

17

Regatta Man removed his sunglasses, and Margot felt as though she'd been slapped. She lost her footing on the deck and tipped a little. She looked into Regatta Man's eyes to be sure. Sure enough, *heterochromia iridum* — dark blue perimeters with green centers. Or, as Margot had thought when she first saw him, he was a man with kaleidoscope eyes.

Before her stood Griffin Wheatley, Homecoming King. Otherwise just known as Griff. Who was, out of all the people in the world, among the top five Margot didn't want to bump into without warning. Didn't want to bump into at all. Maybe the top three.

"Griff!" she exclaimed. "How *are* you?"

"I'm good, I'm good," he said. He cleared his throat and nervously shoved the camera back at Margot; the question of the second photo seemed to have drifted off on the breeze. Margot figured Griff was about half as uncomfortable as she was. He would be thinking of her only as the bearer of disappointing news. She was thinking of him as the worst judgment call she had made in years. Oh, God.

He said, "Did you hear I ended up taking the marketing job at Blankstar?"

Margot couldn't decide if she should pretend to be surprised by this, or if she should admit that she had been Googling his name every single day until she was able to reassure herself that he'd landed safely. The job at Blankstar was a good one.

She changed the subject. "So why are *you* headed to Nantucket?" She tried to recall: Had Griff mentioned Nantucket in any of his interviews? No, she would have remembered if he had. He was from Maryland somewhere, which meant he had probably grown up going to Rehoboth or Dewey.

"I'm meeting buddies for golf," he said.

Ah, yes, golf — of course golf, not sailing. Griff had spent two years on the lower rungs of the PGA Tour. He'd made just enough money, he said, to buy a case of beer each week and have enough left over for the Laundromat. He had lived out of the back of his Jeep Wrangler and, when he played well, at the Motel 6.

These details all came back unbidden. Margot couldn't stand here another second. She turned to Jenna, sending a telepathic message: *Get me out of here!* But Jenna was checking her phone. She was texting her beloved Stuart, perhaps, or any other of the 150 guests who would gather on Saturday to drink in the sight of Jenna wearing their mother's wedding gown.

"I'm here for my sister's wedding," Margot said. She chewed her bottom lip. "I'm the maid of honor."

He lit up with amused delight, as though Margot had just told him she had been selected to rumba with Antonio Banderas on *Dancing with the Stars.* "That's great!" he said.

He sounded far more enthusiastic than she felt.

She said, "Yes, Jenna is getting married on Saturday." Margot indicated Jenna with a Vanna White flourish of her hands, but Jenna's attention was glued to her phone. Margot was afraid to engage Jenna anyway, because what if Jenna asked how Margot and Griff knew each other?

Thankfully, Finn stepped forward. "I'm Finn Sullivan-Walker," she said. "I'm just a lowly bridesmaid."

Griff shook hands with Finn and laughed. "Not lowly, I'm sure."

"Not lowly at all," Margot said. This was the third time that Finn had made reference to the fact that she *wasn't* Jenna's maid of honor. She had been miffed when Jenna first announced her decision to Margot and Finn, over dinner at Dos Caminos. Finn had ordered three margaritas in rapid succession, then gone silent. And then she had gotten her nose out of joint about it again at the bridal shower. Finn was upset that she had been stuck writing down the list of gifts while Margot the maid of honor fashioned the bows from the gifts into a goofy hat made from a paper plate. (Jenna was supposed to wear that hat tonight, to her bachelorette party. Margot had rescued it from the overly interested paws of Ellie, her six-year-old daughter, and had transported it here, more or less intact, in a white cardboard box from E.A.T. bakery.)

Margot had told Jenna that it would be fine if Jenna wanted to ask Finn to be the matron of honor. Margot was eleven years older than Jenna; Finn had always been more like Jenna's sister. Now Jenna and Finn were both in the throes of the nuptial era; everyone they knew was getting married. For the two of them, being the maid of honor was an actual *honor*—whereas Margot had been married and divorced and, quite frankly, couldn't care less.

But Margot knew the reason why Jenna would never ask Finn to be matron of honor. It was because of the Notebook. It had been assumed by their mother that Margot would serve as Jenna's maid of honor.

Margot said, "Finn just got married last October."

"Oh, really?" Griff said.

Finn gazed out at the water. "Yeah."

"Her husband is a golfer, too," Margot said. "Scratch!"

Finn's husband, Scott Walker, had been on the golf team at Stanford, where Tiger Woods had played. Now Scott was a hedge fund manager making a bajillion dollars a quarter.

Finn made a face like she had just eaten snail and vinegar stew, and Margot wondered if something was awry in her seemingly perfect marriage. Scott, Margot knew, wasn't coming to the wedding because of one of the inevitable conflicts for those mired in the nuptial era: *his* best friend, his roommate from Stanford, was having *his* bachelor party this very same weekend. Scott was in Las Vegas.

Probably Finn just missed him, the way that Margot missed Edge. The way that Margot lived in a perpetual state of missing Edge. She had sex with Edge, she had conversations with Edge, some more meaningful than others, she occasionally had dinner with Edge—but never the movies, never theater, never ever any kind of benefit or dance or party where other people they knew would be in attendance. Those kinds of events Margot attended alone or with her brother, Nick, who was always sure to leave with someone else.

"Well!" Margot said. She was dying to put the small talk with Griffin Wheatley, Homecoming King, to bed. She would have excused herself to check on the children below, but she wasn't feeling well enough to even step inside the cabin in the name of such a bluff. "Have fun playing golf! Birdie, birdie, eagle!"

"Thanks," Griff said. He took a step toward the chair where his *Wall Street Journal* awaited, and Margot thought, *Okay, that's over. Good-bye, Griffin Wheatley, Homecoming King!* Jenna could have asked Idi Amin to take their picture and Margot might have been less flustered.

"See ya," Margot said.

"Have a great wedding," Griff said. And then to Finn, "Nice meeting you, lowly bridesmaid."

Finn scowled at him, but undeterred, Griff called out to Jenna, "Congratulations!"

Jenna raised her eyes from her iPhone long enough to offer the quick, impersonal wave of an Oscar winner.

Finn said, "I'm going down below."

Margot nodded, and with a glance at Griff and another awkward, unnecessary "See ya!" she took Jenna by the arm and led her to the railing on the side of the boat opposite from Griff.

"Look," Margot said. She pointed past the hovering seagulls and the scattered sailboats. They could both see clearly now: the north and south steeples of the churches, the column of Brant Point Lighthouse.

Nantucket Island, their summer home.

Jenna squeezed the heck out of Margot's hand. Just as Jenna had helped Margot with her seasickness by remembering to bring the Dramamine, so now Margot would forget about the unnerving interaction with Griffin Wheatley, Homecoming King, and focus on helping Jenna with her surfeit of overwhelming emotion.

"I miss her," Jenna said.

Margot's eyes stung. The longest, most excruciating weekend of her life had officially begun.

"I know, honey," she said, hugging her sister close. "I miss her, too."

THE NOTEBOOK, PAGE 4

The Reception

The reception can be held under a tent in the backyard. Call Sperry Tents and ask for Ande. I worked with him on the benefit for the Nantucket Preservation Trust and he was a dream. I do here want to insert a warning and I hope you won't find it trivial: I would be heartbroken if anything happened to my perennial bed. By "perennial bed," I mean the narrow garden that runs along the eastern edge of the property from the white gate all the way to Alfie's trunk. The blue hardy geraniums, the moonbeam coreopsis, the black-eyed Susans, the plum pudding Heuchera, the coneflowers—all of these I planted in 1972, when I was pregnant with Margot. That bed has bloomed reliably for decades because I have taken good care of it. None of you children seem to have inherited my love of gardening (unless you count Nick, and the pot plants in the attic), but trust me, you will notice if one summer those flowers don't bloom. Please, Jenna, make sure the perennial bed remains unmolested. Do not let the tent guys, or anyone else, trample my blue hardy geraniums.

DOUGLAS

Somehow, he had ended up with the Notebook.

It was Thursday afternoon. Doug had left the office early and had taken the 3:52 to Norwalk, Connecticut, where he lived with Pauline, in a house across the street from the Silvermine Tavern. But when the conductor announced the stop for Darien, Doug grabbed his briefcase and stood halfway up before remembering.

Remembering that the life he had lived for thirty-five years—married to Beth, father of four, in a center-entrance colonial on the Post Road—was over. Beth was dead, she'd been dead seven years, the kids had all moved out, they had lives of their own, some of which they'd already managed to screw up, and Doug was now married to Pauline Tonelli, who had, once upon a time, been his client.

This wasn't the first time he'd nearly stood up at the Darien stop. But it seemed more meaningful today because today wasn't just any Thursday. Today was the Thursday before his youngest child got married.

The girls, as far as Doug knew, were already on Nantucket. They had a reservation for Margot's car on the afternoon ferry, which meant they would be arriving right about now, driving up Main Street to their home on Orange Street. They would pull the key from under the stone turtle in the garden, where the key had always been kept, despite the caretaker. They would walk into the house, they would throw open the windows and unstick the back screen door, they would turn on the water heater, they would make a shopping list. They would hasten to get all the suitcases inside, but they would be arrested by the view of the sparkling harbor below. Margot's kids would head out to the backyard to see Alfie, the two-hundred-year-old oak tree, and sit in the swing. Or at least Ellie would; the boys might be beyond that now.

Of course, Doug remembered when it was Jenna in that swing.

Pauline's car wasn't in the driveway, which came as a relief. For the past twelve months, maybe longer, Doug had found he was happier without Pauline around. This was a bad sign. For his entire professional life, Doug had sat on one side of his partners desk and listened while the person on the other side shared the details of his or her disintegrating marriage. Doug had heard it all—He cheated with Her best friend, She cheated with the tennis pro, there was wife swapping, He hit the kids, She had Munchausen's, She had a drinking problem, He gambled away the kids' college funds, He was addicted to pornographic websites, She abused prescription drugs, He lost his job and sat around the house all day in his bathrobe, She weighed three times what She had when He married Her, He was an asshole, She was a bitch, He wasn't giving Her one red cent, She was going to take Him for all He was worth. For thirty-five years,

Doug had nodded along, pretending to be feeling his clients' angst, but really, he had no idea. He was happily married; he flat-out adored his wife. Even after twenty-five years of marriage, he had sat on this very train and looked forward to the moment he would walk into the house and see Beth.

It was only in the past year that Doug had finally understood what his clients were feeling. He didn't recognize himself in the dramatic scenes—there was no abuse in his marriage to Pauline, no derelict behavior, no destructive habits, no special needs children, no financial woes, no infidelity—rather, Doug identified with his quieter, sadder clients. The marriage no longer provided any joy. They got on each other's nerves, there was a constant buzz of low-level bickering, they were happier and more comfortable when they were apart from each other.

Yes, that was him. That was him exactly.

Pauline was out somewhere, she had probably told him where, but he had forgotten; it went in one ear and out the other, just as she always said. He didn't care where she was, as long as she wasn't home. Lately, Doug had even had fantasies of Pauline driving on Route 7 while talking on the phone to her daughter, Rhonda, and having a fatal accident. He couldn't believe it. He had heard similar sentiments come out of his clients' mouths—*I wish he/she would just die!*—but he never believed himself capable of such a thought. And yet it did now occasionally cross his mind. He nearly always amended this fantasy. Pauline didn't have to *die* to set him free. She might, one day, wake up and decide that she wanted to go back to her ex-husband, Arthur Tonelli. She might climb into the car, get Rhonda immediately on the phone, as was her annoying habit, and announce to Rhonda that she was driving to the Waldorf Astoria to see if Arthur would take her back.

Doug shed his suit coat and his briefcase and loosened his tie. He'd skipped lunch so he could get out of the office early. Edge was going to court first thing in the morning to deal with the shitshow Cranbrook case (Mr. Cranbrook, investment banker, leveraged to the hilt because he was keeping a woman on the side in an apartment on East Sixtieth Street and had bought her a Porsche Carrera, all with his secret credit card, the fate of three children under seven, one of them with extreme special needs, hanging in the balance)—and thus Edge wouldn't get to Nantucket until six o'clock tomorrow evening at the very earliest. He would miss the first round of golf, and Doug felt guilty about that. The Cranbrook case was Doug's case, and it was a hot, steaming mess. Edge was helping Doug out by taking over tomorrow. Doug obviously couldn't do it himself and risk missing his daughter's wedding.

He was starving and went into the kitchen for something, anything, to eat. Pauline, like a housewife from the Depression era, liked to leave the fridge and cupboards all but bare before they went away. In the crisper, Doug found one apple and a few stalks of celery. He bit into the apple and dragged the celery lavishly through a jar of peanut butter that he pulled out of the pantry.

Then he saw it on the kitchen counter, next to the prep sink where Pauline was defrosting a couple of sad-looking lamb chops that were probably going to be their dinner.

The Notebook.

His mouth was sticky with peanut butter, but he let a garbled cry escape: *Oh, shit!*

The Notebook.

That *was* it, right? The spiral-bound notebook with the kelly green cover and the word in black Sharpie written in Beth's handwriting: *WEDDING*. The notebook itself had probably cost $1.69 at Staples, but it was no less precious than the Magna

Carta. That notebook contained all of Beth's hopes, wishes, and suggestions for Jenna's wedding. She had written it in the eight months between the time she was diagnosed with ovarian cancer and the time she died. She had written it not to interfere or be prescriptive but because more than anything she wanted Jenna to feel like she had a mother during that time when she most needed a mother.

Beth had filled the notebook hoping that she would be part of the special day, even though she would be gone. She planned the details of Jenna's wedding even though Jenna had not yet met the man who was to be her husband. Beth had confidence in Jenna. She would meet someone wonderful, and she would want a lavish, traditional wedding.

In the summertime, of course.

At the house on Nantucket, of course.

Their older daughter, Margot, had gotten married to a fellow named Drummond Bain on a cliff in Antigua with just the immediate family in attendance—Doug and Beth, Nick and Kevin, Kevin's wife, Beanie, and Jenna. From Drum's side, only the Bain parents had attended because Drum was an only child. That was half the problem with Drum, or maybe that was the whole problem. He had been handed things without having to earn them. Mitchell Bain was a big shot with Sony, always back and forth between New York and Tokyo. He had set up a trust fund for Drum on his twenty-first birthday. The kid had done nothing with his life but surf, ski, and zip carelessly through his money. Why had Margot fallen for *him?* Doug and Beth had gently expressed their reservations about Drum, but then Margot got pregnant. Doug had been sure Drum would say sayonara and run for the hills. Doug and Beth had actually wished for this to happen; they would help Margot raise the baby themselves. But Drum had done the unthinkable and proposed.

Margot had worn a flowing maternity dress to the ceremony, in a color Beth called "blush."

Doug remembered lying in bed with Beth after Margot's wedding. He and Beth, and Drum's parents, Mitchell and Greta Bain, had heedlessly plowed through six bottles of wine at the reception. Kevin and Nick had pulled Drum off to the bar, and Margot had been left behind with Beanie, who was also pregnant, and Jenna, who had been only sixteen at the time. The three of them sipped sparkling water.

"She looked absolutely miserable tonight," Beth said.

"I wouldn't say *miserable*," Doug said.

"What word would you use to describe her, then?"

"Resigned," Doug said.

"Well, that's perfectly awful!" Beth said. "I wanted more for her. I wanted more than a shotgun wedding, even if it is in the Caribbean."

"Honey, she loves him."

"It'll never last," Beth said.

Drummond Bain Jr. had been born, and then Carson. When Beth had died, Margot hadn't been pregnant with Ellie yet. When Beth died, things were still okay between Margot and Drum Sr. But Beth had ended up being right, of course. The marriage didn't last.

Doug touched the front cover of the Notebook. He opened to the first page. *I wish for you a beautiful day, Jenna, my darling. You alone will make it so.*

Doug closed the Notebook. The rest of it was filled with information, ruminations, suggestions: Where in the closet to find Beth's wedding dress should Jenna want to wear it (of course Jenna would wear it) and the names of places to get it dry-cleaned and altered. Which flowers to use, which florist, what hymns were Beth's favorites, what to say when Jenna called Reverend

Marlowe and asked him to perform the ceremony on Nantucket. The Notebook contained menu suggestions and an invitation list and poems Beth had clipped that would make excellent readings. Doug knew there were more than a few "DO NOTS," such as "*Do not, under any circumstances, use Corinthians 13 as a reading. If you use Corinthians 13, you will hear a collective groan.*"

Doug hadn't read the Notebook, although he had started out with that intention. He had meant to read the pages closely, as he would have a legal brief, before presenting it to Jenna, just after Stuart proposed. But Doug had found even reading the opening letter painful. Beth's voice was too vivid on the page, and the emotion was too raw. *My hand aches knowing that it will not be squeezing your hand just before you walk down the aisle.* Doug realized there were stories and memories, bits of Carmichael family lore—some of which he might have forgotten—interspersed throughout. It would be excruciating for him to read the pages that he'd watched Beth furiously scribbling, right up until the very end, when hospice arrived and the morphine made it difficult for her to hold a pen, much less write anything. Furthermore, the Notebook hadn't been meant for his eyes. It had been meant for Jenna; it was a mother-daughter document.

Doug had, however, stumbled across the following lines: *Your father is going to be a cause for concern. Margot is married, Kevin is married, and who knows if Nick will ever get married. So you're it, the last one, his baby flying from the nest. He will take it hard. But Jenna, he will have no prouder moment than escorting you down the aisle. I saw him with Margot before they walked out onto that cliff in Antigua. He could barely hold back the tears. You must promise me that you will (A) check to see that his tie is straight (B) pin his boutonniere and (C) please make sure he has a clean white handkerchief. He will need it. Even if your father has Another Wife, I want you to do those things. Do them for me, please.*

Doug had welled up when he read that paragraph. Jenna had been present when this happened. She had said, "If you think that's sad, you should skip ahead and read the last page."

"What's on the last page?" he asked.

"Just read it," she said.

"I can't. It's too hard."

"I think Mom would want you to see it."

"No," he said. And then he had closed the Notebook.

Now, Doug thought to panic. The Notebook was here, on the counter, at Pauline's house (even now, five years after moving in, he still always thought of it as Pauline's house). Jenna was on Nantucket. It was the Thursday before the wedding. Two days before.

He pulled his cell phone out of his briefcase. He had an iPhone, purchased for him by his children, all of whom used iPhones themselves. Doug had been a BlackBerry user for years, Edge was a BlackBerry user, all self-respecting attorneys were BlackBerry users. iPhones were *toys.* But the children had bought him this iPhone, and Margot had shown him how to use it and demonstrated how easy it was to text. Then Drum Jr. had gotten one, and Kevin's oldest son, Brandon, had gotten one, and Doug liked the idea of being able to communicate with his grandsons. He found the iPhone made him feel younger than sixty-four.

The face of his phone was an emergency crash site. He had four missed calls from Margot, three missed calls from Jenna, a missed call from Pauline, two texts from Margot, two texts from Jenna, a text from Edge, and a text from Drum Jr. Doug didn't know where to look first. He decided to just call Margot.

"I have it," he said peremptorily.

"Dad?" Margot said. "We have a crisis."

"No, you don't. I have it."

"Yes," she said. "We do."

"I have it," he said. "It's here. The Notebook. I have it here, I'm looking right at it. I'll bring it with me tonight. She'll have it in her hands by nine a.m."

"Dad has it!" Margot shouted. To Doug, she said, "Thank God, oh, thank God you have it. Jenna thought she left it in a cab because the last time she remembered having it was at dinner with you and Pauline at Locanda Verde, when she took a cab all the way uptown. *Yes, he has it, he has it!* Can you imagine how catastrophic that would have been? Okay, Dad, I've gotta go, because now she's having a reverse nervous breakdown that strongly resembles the nervous breakdown she's been having for the past thirty minutes. She's crying hysterically, but they're tears of relief, I'm happy to say." Margot paused, and Doug did indeed hear sounds of female hysteria in the background. "Jesus, can you imagine what would have happened if she'd left it in a cab? And it was gone forever?"

Doug swallowed. The thought was too awful to contemplate. *Please make sure he has a clean white handkerchief.* Had there ever been a purer declaration of love? he wondered.

"No," he said.

"What is the Notebook doing there, anyway?" Margot asked.

"I..."

"Forget it, Daddy, I have to go. This place is a madhouse."

"Okay, I'll—"

"See you in the morning," Margot said. "Don't forget to bring it!"

"I won't," he said.

He carried the Notebook upstairs and slid it into the pocket of his suitcase right away, just to put his mind at ease.

What *was* the Notebook doing there?

*   *   *

Doug lay down on the bed, still in his shirt and tie and suit pants and Gucci loafers. He was suddenly tired. He and Pauline would be rising at 3 a.m. to make his 10:30 a.m. tee time at Sankaty; the mere thought was exhausting. Plus, Pauline set the air conditioner lower in the bedroom the way he liked it; the cool room was begging him to nap.

What *was* the Notebook doing there?

Jenna had brought it to dinner at Locanda Verde. Doug remembered her setting it on the table next to the platter of crostini with house-made herbed ricotta. He remembered Jenna saying, "There's a cheat sheet in here, Daddy, an index card with the names of all of Mom's cousins and their spouses and children. I memorized it, and you should, too."

"Sure," Doug had said automatically. He then wondered what it would be like to see Beth's cousins, people he hadn't seen since the funeral. He was grateful when conversation turned to another topic.

If the wine had gone to her head, Jenna might have left the Notebook at the restaurant. But she *hadn't* left it at the restaurant. It had ended up here.

How, though? He certainly hadn't carried it out.

So there was only one answer: Pauline had taken the Notebook and brought it home. However, Doug didn't remember Jenna offering to show the Notebook to Pauline, nor did he remember Pauline asking to see the Notebook. If that had happened, he would have remembered. Pauline was jealous of the Notebook, which really meant that Pauline was jealous of Beth. Beth, who had been dead seven years, who had died in a matter of months under excruciatingly painful circumstances, leaving behind the family she'd loved more than anything. How could Pauline be jealous of Beth? How could she begrudge Jenna a missive filled with motherly love and advice? Well, Pauline hadn't been granted access to the Notebook, a fact that bugged the shit out of her, but as Doug pointed out, the Notebook was private. It was Jenna's choice to share it or not share it. Pauline was further bothered because she had offered to take Jenna shopping for a wedding dress and Jenna had informed Pauline that she would be wearing Beth's dress (per the Notebook). Pauline had suggested calla lilies in the bridal bouquet; Jenna was going with limelight hydrangeas and tight white peonies (per the Notebook). Pauline had wanted herself and Doug listed on the invitation by name, but Jenna had gone with this wording: *Jennifer Bailey Carmichael and Stuart James Graham, along with their families, invite you to share in the celebration of their wedding* (per the Notebook).

Doug had gently advised Pauline to back off where the wedding was concerned. Pauline had a daughter of her own. When it was Rhonda's turn to get married, Pauline could interfere all she wanted.

"When Rhonda gets married?" Pauline had exclaimed.

"Yes," Doug said.

"She'll never get married!" Pauline said. "She's never had a relationship last more than six weeks."

This was true. Rhonda had pretty, dark hair like her mother, and she was very thin. Too thin, if you asked Doug. She spent something like five hours a day at the gym. Going to the gym was Rhonda's *job,* and freelance graphic design was a hobby from which she received the occasional paycheck. She was thirty-eight years old, and Arthur Tonelli still paid her rent and gave her an allowance. At thirty-eight! The reason Rhonda's relationships didn't last was because she was impossible to please. She was negative, dour, and unpleasant. She never smiled. The reason Rhonda worked freelance was because she'd lost her last three office jobs due to "problems cooperating with coworkers" and "insufficient interpersonal skills with clients." Which meant: no one liked her. Except, of course, for Pauline. Mother and daughter were best friends. They told each other everything; there was *absolutely no filter.* This fact alone made Doug uncomfortable around Rhonda. He was sure that Rhonda knew how frequently he and Pauline made love (lately about once a month), as well as the results of his prostate exam and the cost of his bridgework.

Pauline was right: Rhonda would never get married. Pauline would never become a grandmother. And so could Doug really blame her for clinging to his family with such desperation?

Pauline burst into the bedroom, and Doug sat straight up in bed. He had fallen asleep; his mouth was cottony and still tasted faintly of peanut butter.

"Hi," he said.

"Were you *sleeping?*" she asked. She was wearing her tennis clothes but had removed her shoes and socks, and so Doug smelled, or imagined he could smell, her feet.

"I took a nap," he said. "I was tired, and I thought it would be a good idea, considering the drive." Doug studied his wife. She was an ample woman with large breasts and wide hips; she was the despondent possessor of what she called a "muffin top," which kept her constantly dieting. Food wasn't just food with Pauline; it was a daily challenge. She always started off well—power walking along the Silvermine River with two other women from the neighborhood and coming home to eat a bowl of yogurt with berries. But then there was a thick sandwich with fries at the country club, followed by the two pieces of pound cake she ate at book group, and not only would Doug have to hear about it when he got home from work, but he would have to share in

Pauline's punishment: a dinner that consisted of grilled green beans and eggplant or a bowl of Special K.

Beth had been such a good cook. Doug would kill to taste her creamy mac and cheese or her pan-fried pork chops smothered with mushroom sauce. But he didn't like to compare.

He was glad to see Pauline had actually gone to play tennis. Her dark hair was in a ponytail, and her forehead had a sheen of sweat that gave her a certain glow. The short, pleated skirt showed off her legs, which were her best feature. Sometimes Pauline went to the club to "play tennis," but the courts would be booked, so instead she would sit at the bar with Christine Potter and Alice Quincy and drink chardonnay for two hours, and Pauline would come home feeling combative.

Pauline was a prodigious drinker of chardonnay. Doug remembered that during the divorce proceedings, Arthur had referred to her as "the wino." Doug had found that mean and unnecessary at the time, but he realized now that Arthur had not been complaining for no reason.

"How was tennis?" Doug asked.

"Fine," Pauline said. "It felt good to work out some of my anxiety."

Anxiety? Doug thought. He knew an attentive husband would ask about the source of his wife's anxiety, but Doug didn't want to ask. Then he realized that Pauline had anxiety about the upcoming weekend. He remembered the Notebook, now safely tucked into his suitcase.

He swung his feet to the floor and loosened his tie. "Pauline," he said.

She pulled her top off over her head and unhooked her sturdy white bra. Her breasts were set free. Had they always hung so low, he wondered?

"I'm going to shower," she said. "And then I have to finish packing. We're having lamb chops for dinner." She wriggled out of her skirt and underwear. She stood before him naked. Pauline was not an unlovely woman; if he touched her, he knew her skin would be soft and smooth and warm. Once upon a time, Doug had been very attracted to Pauline; their lovemaking had always been a strong point between them. He allowed himself to think about having wild, ravishing sex right now, maybe up against the closet door. He willed himself to feel a stir of arousal. He envisioned his mouth on Pauline's neck, her hand down his pants.

Nothing.

This was not good.

"Pauline."

She turned to face him, panicked. She sensed, maybe, that he was after sex—which she explicitly did not allow during daylight hours.

"What?" she said.

"Did you take the Notebook from the restaurant last night?"

"What notebook?"

Doug closed his eyes, wishing she hadn't just said that. He lowered his voice, the way he would have for a hostile witness or a client who insisted on lying to him despite the fact that he had been hired to help.

"You know which notebook."

Pauline's forehead wrinkled and her eyes widened, and she did, at that moment, resemble Rhonda very strongly, which did not improve her case. "You mean the green notebook? Jenna's notebook?"

"Yes," Doug said. "Jenna's notebook. I found it downstairs. Did you take it?" The question was ridiculous—of course she'd taken it—but Doug wanted to hear her admit to it.

"Why are you being so weird?" she asked.

"Define 'weird,' " he said.

" 'Define weird.' Don't harass me, counselor. Save it for the courtroom." Pauline took a step toward the bathroom, but Doug wasn't going to let her escape. He stood up.

"Pauline."

"I need to get in the shower," she said. "I'm not going to stand around *naked* while you *accuse* me of things."

Doug followed Pauline to the bathroom. He stood in the doorway as she turned on the water. This was the master bath she had shared with Arthur Tonelli for over twenty years. Pauline and Arthur had built this house together; they had picked out the tile and the sink and the fixtures. For the first few years of their marriage, Doug had felt like an impostor in this bathroom. What was he doing using Arthur Tonelli's bathroom? What was he doing sleeping with Arthur Tonelli's wife? But by now Doug had grown used to it. He and Beth had renovated their 1836 colonial on the Post Road until it was exactly to their taste, but after Beth died, it occurred to Doug that material things—even entire rooms—held no meaning. A bathroom was a bathroom was a bathroom.

"Did you take the Notebook?" Doug asked.

Pauline tested the water with her hand. She did not answer.

"Pauline…"

She whipped around. "Yes," she said. "Jenna left it on the table at the restaurant last night and I picked it up." She widened her brown eyes at him. When they'd first met, her eyes had reminded Doug of chocolate candy. "I *rescued* the Notebook. Now, if you'll excuse me, I'd like to take a shower. In peace."

"No," Doug said. "I will not excuse you. Why didn't you give it back to Jenna? What is it doing here?"

"She was in a hurry, remember? She and Stuart raced away in that cab."

What Doug remembered was standing out on Greenwich Avenue trying to hail Jenna and Stuart a cab, but having no luck. That far downtown, cabs were impossible to find. What Doug remembered was considering asking the maître d' to call a car service for the kids, but then at the last moment a cab appeared, and Jenna and Stuart hopped in it. But there had been a full ten minutes, maybe longer, with the four of them outside on the sidewalk. And Pauline had had the Notebook; she had probably stuffed it into one of the enormous purses she liked to carry.

"She wasn't in a hurry," Doug said. "We waited around for goddamned ever for that cab. I'm not wrong about that, am I?"

"I forgot to give it back to her," Pauline said. "I meant to, but then we were so caught up in trying to get them a cab, I forgot."

"You forgot?" Doug said.

"Yes."

"Really?"

Pauline nodded once, with conviction. That was her story and she was sticking to it. As Arthur Tonelli's bathroom filled with steam, Doug realized something. He realized that he did not love Pauline. It was possible that he had never loved Pauline. On Monday, once the wedding was over and they were safely back home, he was going to ask Pauline for a divorce.

He turned and walked out. It felt good to have made that decision.

Pauline must have sensed something dire because she shut off the water, wrapped herself in a towel, and followed him out.

"I need you to believe me," she said.

Doug watched her clutch the towel to her chest. Her thick, dark hair, out of its ponytail, fell in damp ropes over her shoulders.

"I do believe you," he said.

"You do?"

"Yes," he said. "You've presented a plausible argument. Jenna left behind the Notebook, you wisely scooped it up, and amidst all the brouhaha of trying to flag a taxi, you forgot to return it to her."

Pauline exhaled. "Yes."

"My question now is, did you read it?"

As Pauline stared at him, he watched conflicting emotions cross her face. He was an attorney; he dealt every day with people who wanted to lie to him.

"Yes," she admitted. "I read it."

"You read it." He had no reason to be surprised, but he was anyway.

"It was driving me crazy," Pauline said. "The Notebook this, the Notebook that, what 'Mom' wrote in the Notebook. Your daughters—and you, too, Douglas—treated the thing like the fifth gospel. Jenna wouldn't accept one suggestion—*not one*—from me. She only wanted to follow what was in the goddamned Notebook. And I wanted to see exactly what that was. I wanted to see what Beth had to say."

Doug didn't like hearing his second wife speak his first wife's name. This had always been true.

"So you read it?" Doug said. "You read it today? While I was at work?"

"Yes," Pauline said. "And I have to say, Beth covered all the bases. She let Jenna know exactly what she wanted—down to the pattern of the silver, down to the song you and Jenna should dance to, down to the earrings Jenna should wear with 'the dress.' It was the most blatant exercise in mind control I have ever seen. Beth planned her *own* wedding. She didn't leave anything for Jenna to decide."

Doug wondered if Pauline had read the last page. He wondered what the last page said.

"I think those were meant to be suggestions," Doug said, feeling defensive.

"*Suggestions?*" Pauline said. "Beth flat-out *told* Jenna what to do."

"Jenna is a strong person," Doug said. "If she had disagreed with something Beth wrote, she would have changed it."

"And go against the wishes of her dead mother?" Pauline said. "Never."

"Hey now," Doug said. "That's out of line."

"I offered to take Jenna out to try on wedding dresses," Pauline said. "To try them on, that was all, to see what else was out there, to see if there was anything that suited her better than Beth's dress—and she wouldn't go. She wouldn't even *try.*"

"I'm sure she looks lovely in Beth's dress," Doug said.

"You know," Pauline said, "I thought it was a good thing that you were widowed instead of divorced. I was *glad* there wasn't an ex-wife I had to see at family functions or that you were paying alimony to. But guess what? Beth is more intrusive than any ex-wife could have been."

"Intrusive?" Doug said. "Define intrusive."

"She's everywhere. Especially with this wedding. She is a palpable presence in the room. She is an untouchable standard by which the rest of us have to be judged. She has taken on sainthood. Saint Beth, the dead mother, whose memory grows more burnished every day."

"Enough," Doug said.

"I just can't compete," Pauline said. "I'll never come first, not with the kids, not with you. You are, all of you Carmichaels, obsessed with her."

Doug thought that hearing such words might anger him, but he merely found them validating. "Listen," he said. "I don't think you should come to Nantucket this weekend."

"*What?*" Pauline said.

"I guess what I'm really trying to say is that I don't *want* you to come to Nantucket this weekend. It's my daughter's wedding, and I think it would be best if I went alone." Doug heard Pauline inhale, but he didn't wait around for what she was going to say. He left the bedroom, shutting the door behind him.

Down the stairs, through the kitchen. His cell phone was on the counter. He snatched it up and saw the two meager lamb chops sitting in a pool of bloody juices.

He wasn't going to eat them. He was going out for pizza.

THE NOTEBOOK, PAGE 6

The Wedding Party

I assume you will ask Margot to be your Matron of Honor. The two of you have such a close relationship, and whereas at times I worried about the large age gap between you and the older three, I think that in Margot's case, it was for the best. She was your sister, yes, but she was also a surrogate mother at times, or something between a sister and a mother, whatever that role might be called. Remember how she did your makeup for the ninth-grade dance? You wanted green eye shadow and she gave you green eye shadow, somehow making it look pretty good. And remember how she drove you down to William & Mary your sophomore year so that Daddy and I could celebrate our thirtieth anniversary on Nantucket? Margot is the most capable woman you or I will

ever know. And to butcher the old song: Anything I can do,
she can do better.

I assume you will also ask Finn. The two of you have been
inseparable since birth. I used to call you my "twins." Not
sure that Mary Lou Sullivan appreciated that, but the two of
you were adorable together. The matching French braids,
the playground rhymes you used to sing with the hand clap-
ping. Miss Mary Mac Mac Mac, all dressed in black, black,
black.

As far as your brothers are concerned, I would ask Kevin
to do a reading, and ask Nick to serve as an usher, assuming
your Intelligent, Sensitive Groom-to-Be doesn't have nine
brothers or sixteen guys who served in his platoon who can't
be ignored. Kevin has that wonderful orator's voice. I swear
he is the spiritual descendant of Lincoln or Daniel Webster.
And Nick will charm all the ladies as he escorts them to their
seats. Obviously.

The other person who would be terrific as an usher is
Drum Sr. Of course if Margot is your Matron of Honor, she
might need Drum to watch the boys.

And then there's your father, but we'll talk about him later.

MARGOT

It felt so good to be back in the house of her childhood summers
that Margot forgot about everything else for a minute.

The house was two and a half blocks off Main Street, on the
side of Orange Street that overlooked the harbor. It had been
bought by Margot's great-great-great-grandfather in 1873, only

twenty-seven years after the Great Fire destroyed most of downtown. The house had five bedrooms, plus an attic that Margot's grandparents had filled with four sets of bunk beds and one lazy ceiling fan. It was shambling now, although in its heyday it had been quite grand. There were still certain antiques around—an apothecary chest with thirty-six tiny drawers, grandfather and grandmother clocks that announced the hour in unison, gilded mirrors, Eastlake twin beds and a matching dresser in the boys' bedroom upstairs—and there were fine rugs, all of them now faded by the sun and each permanently embedded with twenty pounds of sand. There was a formal dining room with a table seating sixteen where no one ever ate, although Margot remembered doing decoupage projects with her grandmother at that table on rainy days. One year, Nick and Kevin found turtles at Miacomet Pond and decided the turtles should race the length of the table. Margot remembered one of the turtles veering off the side of the table and crashing to the ground, where it lay upside down, its feet pedaling desperately through the air.

In the kitchen hung a set of four original Roy Bailey paintings that might have been valuable, but they were coated in bacon grease and splattered oil from their father's famous cornmeal onion rings. At one point, Margot's mother had said, "Yes, this was a lovely house until we got a hold of it. Now it is merely a useful house, and a well-loved house."

Margot was shocked at how well loved. She felt euphoric at the sight of the dusty brick of the kitchen floor, the old wooden countertops scarred by 140 years of knives coarsely chopping garden tomatoes, the sound of the screen door slamming as her children ran out back to the green lawn, the seventy-foot oak tree named Alfie—after Alfred Coates Hamilton, the original owner of the house—and the wooden swing that hung from Alfie's lowest branch.

Margot had lived in the city all her adult life. She loved Manhattan—but not like this. Her adoration of Nantucket was matched only by her adoration of her children. She wanted to be buried here, in the shade of Alfie's leaves, if possible. She would have to write that down somewhere.

No sooner had Margot entered the house and allowed herself those sixty seconds of appreciation than crisis struck. Jenna stood in front of Margot, holding open her Mielie bag, handmade by a woman in Cape Town, South Africa. Jenna was sobbing.

"What?" Margot said. She had certainly expected tears from Jenna this weekend. Jenna was an idealist, and the world was constantly falling short. But so soon? Ten minutes after their arrival? "What is it?"

"The Notebook!" Jenna said. "It's *gone!*"

Margot peered into the depths of Jenna's bag—there was her wallet made from hemp, the handkerchief Jenna used like a character from a Merchant Ivory film because, unlike Kleenex, handkerchiefs could be washed and reused, her Aveeno lip balm, the package of Dramamine, and her cell phone. There was no Notebook.

"Maybe you put it somewhere else," Margot said.

"I keep it here," Jenna said. "Right here in my bag. You know I keep it right here."

Yes, Margot did know that; she had seen Jenna remove and return the Notebook from that bag a hundred times. Jenna was the kind of person who had a place for everything, and her place for the Notebook was in that bag.

Margot laid her hands on Jenna's shoulders. "Calm down," she said. "Let's think. When was the last time you remember having it?"

Instead of this question focusing Jenna, it caused her to

become more scattered. She cast around the kitchen, her eyes frantic. Jenna was the kindest, most nurturing soul Margot knew; the students and parents at the Little Minds school adored her. As the youngest by such a large span of years—there were eight plus years between Jenna and Nick—Jenna had been raised in the warm bath of their parents' love. Her childhood and adolescence had involved little conflict. The downside to this was that Jenna wasn't great with crises.

"Think," Margot said. "Stop and think. Did you have it on the boat?"

"No," Jenna said. "I haven't seen it at all today. I had it last night at . . . Locanda Verde." Her face dissolved.

"Whoa, whoa," Margot said. "No big deal. We can *call* Locanda Verde."

"Then Stuart and I got into a cab!" Jenna said. "What if I left it in a cab?"

Margot's heart sank. What if Jenna had left it in a cab? Margot would go through the motions of calling the dispatcher's office, but they wouldn't have it. Once you left something in a New York City cab, it was gone forever. How many pairs of sunglasses lost each day? Margot wondered. How many cell phones? How many copies of *Fifty Shades of Grey*? A massive redistribution of personal belongings took place every day across the five boroughs because of what people left behind in cabs. The Notebook! Like Jenna, Margot had read the Notebook front to back and back to front, focusing most intently on the passages that mentioned her; she felt a piercing loss at the thought of never seeing it again.

Jenna was on her phone.

Margot said, "Who are you calling?"

"Stuart!" Jenna said.

Stuart, of course. Margot thought, with a glimmer of hope,

that maybe Stuart had the Notebook. If he didn't, he would fly out the door of his office and drive to godforsaken who-knows-where-Brooklyn-or-Queens to personally dig through the lost and found at the dispatcher's office. Stuart would be able to offer Jenna comfort; he was the only one who mattered.

Margot didn't have anyone like that. She could never call Edge about something like the Notebook. Instead she called her father. No answer. She called again and left a voice mail.

"Hey, Dad, it's Margot. Jenna has misplaced the Notebook. She had it last night at dinner, she said? She thinks maybe she left it in the cab? Any thoughts? Call me back."

Margot then sent her father a text: *Jenna lost Notebook.*

And another: *Please call me.*

Jenna, meanwhile, was still on the phone with Stuart. In the Notebook, their mother had referred to Jenna's future husband, whoever he may be, as her Intelligent, Sensitive Groom-to-Be— and Stuart fit the bill. Jenna had already calmed down; she had stopped crying.

Margot marched upstairs. Jenna's luggage was in the hallway, and Margot started to look through it, thinking, *Please appear, please appear.*

What appeared were a pair of shapely, tanned legs. Finn's legs. Margot used to have legs like that, back in her surfing days, before she worked sixty-five hours a week trying to support three kids and an ex-husband.

Finn said, "Why are you going through Jenna's things?"

Her voice was accusatory, but Margot didn't even both looking up.

Finn said, "Oh, shit."

"Exactly," Margot said. A second later, her cell phone buzzed in her pocket. Involuntarily, she thought: *Edge.*

But it was her father.

"I have it," he said.

Margot filled with giddy relief, and Jenna sobbed with tears of joy. One of the best feelings in the world was finding something you were sure you'd lost forever.

A little while later, a white van pulled into the driveway behind Margot's LR3. She poked her head out the side door. The Sperry Tent Company. She hoped she didn't have to sign anything or decide anything. She hoped the four guys who hopped out of the truck knew exactly what they were doing. She hoped that Roger, the wedding planner, had reminded the tent guys about her mother's perennial bed.

Beth had been a fanatical gardener, and some of those perennials were over forty years old, which made them heirloom. Or maybe not. Margot knew nothing about gardening; every year, she killed one store-bought herb garden by placing it on her fire escape and forgetting to water it.

Out the back screen door, which faced the yard, Margot called to her children, "The gentlemen are here to set up the tent! Either make yourself useful or get out of the way!" Ellie was lying on her stomach on the swing, spinning in circles until the ropes were twisted to the top.

"Eleanor, come in, please!" Margot called.

"No!" Ellie said.

Margot sighed. Was it too early for wine?

Upstairs, Margot heard Jenna and her maidens milling around; she caught the occasional burst of laughter. The hysteria over the missing Notebook had subsided—THANK GOD— and shortly thereafter, Autumn Donahue had arrived in a cab from the airport. Autumn had been Jenna's roommate at the College of William and Mary. She had beautiful copper-colored hair and freckles and brown eyes and was the visual antidote to Jenna's and Finn's uncompromising blondness. Autumn swore like a sailor, and she could turn any situation pornographic in seconds. At the bridal shower, which had been attended by Pauline, as well as Jenna's future mother-in-law, Ann Graham, Autumn had seen fit to give Jenna a two-headed vibrator and a tube of lubricant.

"Just turn that thing on for Stuart," Autumn had said. "He'll love it."

Autumn always dated three men at the same time; she called these men her "lov-ahs," and she sometimes threw a random one-night stand into the mix. She had never been in love; she had no intention of ever falling in love.

Quite frankly, Margot admired this about Autumn.

Margot was waiting for a text from Edge. She had texted him the night before to tell him that Drum Sr. was getting married. What she'd written was: *Drum Sr. is getting married to someone named Lily the Pilates instructor.*

When, after thirty minutes, she hadn't received a response, she had written: *No, seriously, Drum Sr. is getting married.*

Margot had fallen asleep with the phone in her hand, waiting for a response. But in the morning there was still nothing from Edge. Margot found this silence perplexing. He often let one or more of her texts go without a response, but a text about her ex-spouse remarrying? That was real *news.* It deserved *something.* Then Margot began to worry that Edge wasn't responding because he thought Margot was fishing for a proposal herself. Ha! The mere idea of a proposal from Edge was ludicrous. He had allowed her to spend the night at his apartment only once — and then only because he'd had a favor to ask of her.

She wouldn't let herself think about that night, Picholine for dinner first, then the unprecedented invitation to sleep over, then the ask, like a cold hand on her throat. Griffin Wheatley, Homecoming King. She *couldn't* think about it.

Maybe Edge was just busy. He had been preparing for court all week; he was taking over something called the "shitshow Cranbrook case" for Margot's father. Margot had asked what that meant, but he hadn't told her; he couldn't tell her about any of his cases — not only because it was privileged information, but because Edge didn't want Margot to accidentally slip up in front of her father.

The result of this was that Margot knew next to nothing about Edge's work life or how he spent his days. She almost preferred the way things had been with Drum Sr. Drum Sr. had done nothing for work, but at least that nothing had been reported to Margot in excruciating detail. *Going for run in park. Back from run. ATM, $80. Warren Miller film — off the hook! Thinking about enchiladas for dinner — ok with u? Store. Sale on canned tomatoes, buying 3. Picking up Ellie now. Walking. What is name of Peyton's mom? And what is wrong with her face?* Margot used to sit in her office at Miller-Sawtooth, which was the most prestigious executive search firm in the world, and receive these texts and think, *Don't you understand that I am too busy for this piddly-shit?*

Now, with Edge, Margot would kill for some piddly-shit. She would kill to know what he had for breakfast. But he told her nothing. If he was feeling expressive, he would text, *In court.* Or, *With Audrey,* who was his six-year-old daughter.

Margot checked her phone: nothing. It was quarter to six. Maybe Edge was in a meeting with a new client; those could take a while. Maybe he was so busy preparing for court — with his favorite paralegal, *Rosalie* — that he simply hadn't had time to check his phone. But Edge checked his phone compulsively. The red light blinked, and he salivated as though the next text or e-mail was going to offer him a million free dollars or a house on the beach in Tahiti. With clients, he prided himself on responding within sixty seconds. But Margot he let languish for days.

Most of Margot and Edge's relationship had taken place via text, which had started out seeming modern and sexy. They would go back and forth for hours—and unlike in actual conversation, Margot could take her time to compose witty responses. She could text things she was too shy to express in person.

But the texting now was frustrating beyond all comprehension. It made Margot want to tear her hair out. It made her—late one night when she and Edge had been going back and forth and then she texted *I miss u* and heard nothing back—throw her phone across the room, where it, thankfully, landed in her laundry basket. She both hated the texting and was addicted to it. She despised her phone—the seventy-two times a day she checked to see if Edge had texted were torturous—and then if she did have a text from him, she went to absurd lengths to answer it, no matter what she was doing. She had answered texts from him under the table in big client meetings. She had stood up and left Ellie's kindergarten play (*Stone Soup*) to text Edge from the school corridor. She had texted while driving, she had texted him drunkenly from the bathroom while she was out with her girlfriends, she had texted him from the treadmill at the gym. The texting with Edge was keeping her from being present in her real life. It was awful, she had to stop, she had to control it somehow, to keep it from destroying her.

Because now, on Thursday, July 18, instead of focusing on her sister's bachelorette party, which she, Margot, had organized and which was due to begin shortly, Margot was thinking: *I texted him nineteen hours ago and he hasn't responded. Why not? Where is he and what is he doing? He isn't thinking about me.*

Margot remembered when she had stood in this very house waiting for the mail to arrive because she was expecting a letter from her high school boyfriend, Grady Maclean. That had been stressful in the same sort of way, except then all of Margot's anxiety had been focused on one moment of the day, and once she got a letter—Grady Maclean had been pretty devoted for a fifteen-year-old boy—she didn't have to sweat it out until the following week.

At that moment, a text came into her phone, and Margot thought, *There he is, finally!* But when she checked, she saw it was a text from her father. Okay, that was absolutely the worst: she had waited and waited for a text, and then a text came in, but from the wrong person.

The text read: *Pauline isn't coming to the wedding.*

Margot stared at her phone. She thought, *WTF?* Her mind was whizzing now. This was family drama, exactly the type that was supposed to happen at weddings. Pauline wasn't coming!

Why did this news make Margot feel so buoyant? Was it because deep down she didn't *like* Pauline, or was it because Margot was grateful for something to think about other than Drum Sr. getting married to Lily the Pilates instructor or Edge's nonresponse to Drum Sr. marrying Lily the Pilates instructor, or . . . Griffin Wheatley, who was still irritating a part of Margot's mind. (He had looked *great* with the scruff on his face—like Tom Ford or James Denton. Margot had always seen him within an hour of his last shave.)

Margot decided she was simply grateful for the distraction. She had nothing against Pauline, Pauline was harmless, Pauline was devoted to their father. So then *why* wasn't she coming to the wedding?

And what about Rhonda? Margot wondered. Would Rhonda still come to the wedding? Rhonda Tonelli, Pauline's daughter, was serving as Jenna's fourth bridesmaid. Jenna hadn't wanted Rhonda, but their father had asked (okay, begged), and since he was paying well into the six figures to make this wedding happen, Jenna had acquiesced.

It would be much better if neither Pauline nor Rhonda came this weekend. Margot felt a space open up in her chest where, apparently, anxiety about Pauline and Rhonda had been residing like an undiagnosed tumor.

There would be an uneven number of bridesmaids and grooms-men. Roger might fret about that, but who cared?

Maybe they could find someone to fill in for Rhonda. Jenna had a group of fellow teachers from Little Minds coming.

Margot's thoughts were interrupted by a knock on the side door. Margot spun around, phone in hand. It was Roger.

"Roger!" Margot said. "I was just thinking about you."

Roger blinked. Something was wrong. Had he already heard they might be down a bridesmaid?

"The tent guys have an issue with the tree," he said.

"What tree?" Margot said. "You mean Alfie?"

Roger swallowed. He was uncomfortable, she knew, calling the tree by a person's name.

"I thought we went over all of this," Margot said. "I thought they could fit the tent under Alfie."

"They thought so too, Margot," Roger said. "But that one branch has dropped since we measured it in April. It's dropped a lot."

"Shoot," Margot said. She didn't have time to deal with another unforeseen snafu. It was already six o'clock, she needed to unpack her suitcase and hang up her bridesmaid dress, she needed to run to the store for groceries, feed her children, take a shower, change, and she had hoped to open a bottle of champagne here with Jenna and the girls before their dinner reservation at eight. "I'm sure you guys will figure out what to do."

"I'll tell you what we need to do," Roger said. "If you want the big tent to go up, you are going to have to let them cut that branch."

"Which branch?" Margot asked. She was relieved that the problem had a solution. Maybe. She and Roger walked to the back door together and peered out at Alfie. Margot's chest, which had for a few short, sweet minutes been a wide-open breezeway, now felt like it was clogging with cement. "Which branch are you talking about? *Not* the..."

"The branch with the swing," Roger said.

Ellie was still on that swing, twisting then spinning out—just as Margot used to do.

"No," Margot said.

"It's the only way."

"It can't be the only way."

"Look how low that branch is," Roger said. "Compare it to the rest of the branches. The tent guys have a chain saw; they can take it down in ten minutes. It's really not that big, compared to the rest of the tree. The tree will survive."

"No," Margot said. "That branch is...the swing is...they're important. They're not going anywhere."

Roger brought his hand to his mouth. He had been a smoker for thirty years, he'd told Margot back in October, when she and Jenna first met him, but he'd quit cold turkey after his brother-in-law died of lung cancer.

"Okay, then," Roger said. "No tent."

"No *tent?*" Margot said.

"Not the big one you and Jenna picked out," he said. "It won't fit. Now, I can ask Ande if he can put up a smaller tent closer to the edge of the bluff. That will cover the bar and dance floor, maybe the head table. But everyone else will be exposed."

"What are we going to do if it rains?" Margot asked.

"I think you know the answer to that," Roger said. "You're going to get wet."

Margot couldn't look at Roger because she couldn't stand to see the stark truth on his face. Roger had lived on Nantucket all his life. He had graduated from Nantucket High School in 1972—which made him, Margot had realized, the same age as Edge. Fifty-nine. He had worked for years as a carpenter and a caretaker, and then in 2000, a dot-com bazillionaire had thrown the wedding-to-end-all-weddings at Galley Beach. There wasn't a dance floor big enough on the island, so the family had hired Roger to build one. In this way, he had stumbled into the wedding business through the back door.

He wasn't like any wedding planner Margot had ever met or imagined. He wasn't anal or super high-energy. He wasn't stylish, young, or hip. He was no-nonsense, he was reliable, he knew everybody you needed to know on the island. He exuded authority, he showed up early, worked hard, got things done. He had been married for thirty-five years to a woman named Rita; they had five children, all grown. Roger and Rita lived in an unassuming house on Surfside Road. Roger used the apartment over the garage as his office. Roger wrote everything down on a clipboard; he kept a pencil behind his ear and a phone on his hip. He drove a pickup truck. When Jenna and Margot had first met him, they'd thought, *This* is the most sought-after wedding planner on Nantucket? Now that they'd seen him in action, they knew why. He could talk canapés and floral arrangements and price per head with the best of them. But his company—if that was what it was—didn't even have a name. When he answered his phone, he said, "This is Roger."

Roger was what they were paying for, and Roger was what they got. And now here was Roger telling Margot that they had to cut down the branch that supported the tree swing, or 150 guests would be without a tent.

They couldn't go without a tent. So Margot would have to let them cut the branch.

She checked the weather for Saturday on her phone. This was the only thing she'd been more compulsive about than checking for texts from Edge. The forecast for Saturday was the same as it had been when she'd checked it from the ferry: partly cloudy skies, high of 77 degrees, chance of showers 40 percent.

Forty percent. It bugged Margot. Forty percent could not be ignored.

"Cut the branch," she said.

Roger nodded succinctly and headed outside.

Margot had fifty million things to do, but unable to do any of them, she sat at the kitchen table. It was a rectangular table, made from soft pine. Along with everything else in the house, it had been abused by the Carmichaels. The surface held ding marks, streaks of pink Magic Marker, and a half-moon of black scorch that came from popcorn made in a pot on a night when Doug and Beth had been out to dinner at the Ships Inn and Margot had been left to babysit her siblings.

Margot remembered her mother being distraught about the scorch mark. "Oh, honey," she'd said. "You should have used a trivet. Or put down a dish towel. That mark will never go away."

At age fourteen, Margot had thought her mother was over-reacting to make Margot feel bad. She had stomped up to her room.

But her mother had been right. Twenty-six years later, the scorch mark was still there. It made Margot wonder about per-manence. She had just given the okay for the tent guys to ampu-tate Alfie, a tree that had grown in that spot for over two hundred years. The tree had been there since colonial times; it had a majesty and a grace that made Margot want to bow down. The branch would never grow back; a tree wasn't like a starfish, it didn't regenerate new limbs. Margot wondered if twenty-five years from now she would walk her grandchildren out to that tree and show them the place where the branch had been sliced off and say, "We had to cut that branch down so we could put up a tent for my sister Jenna's wedding."

Generations of their descendants would go without a tree swing in the name of this decision.

Margot heard the whine of the chain saw. She covered her face with her hands.

Her mother hadn't written anything about the tree swing in the notebook.

Cut Alfie's branch? Margot asked her.

The sound of the chain saw raised goose bumps. It felt as if the guy was about to cut out Margot's own heart.

She ran out the back door.

"Stop!" she cried.

The wedding was taking on a life of its own. It was the damnedest thing. A person could plan for months down to the tiniest detail, a person could hire someone like Roger and have a set of written blueprints such as their mother had left—and still things would go wrong. Still the unexpected would happen.

"I can't let you do it," Margot said to Roger. "I can't let you cut it."

"You understand this means no tent?" he said.

Margot nodded. No tent. Partly cloudy, 40 percent chance of showers. A hundred and fifty people, tens of thousands of dollars of tables, chairs, china, crystal, silver, floral arrangements, food, and wine—all with a 40 percent chance of getting drenched.

Margot fretted as she thought about the antique, hand-embroidered table linens, most of which were the same linens Margot and Jenna's grandmother had used for her wedding in this very same backyard in 1943. What if those linens got rained upon? (Their grandmother had hosted ninety-two guests at her wedding, under a striped canvas tent supported by wooden poles. Back in 1943, Alfie's branches would have been younger, stronger, and higher.)

Margot knew she should confer with someone, get a second opinion: Jenna, or her father. But Margot felt that her primary duty as maid of honor was to shield Jenna from the treacherous obstacles that would pop up over the next seventy-two hours. On Sunday afternoon, as soon as the farewell brunch was over, Jenna would be on her own. She would have to face her life as Mrs. Stuart Graham. But until then, Margot was going to make the tough decisions. She might have called her father, but her father, obviously, had issues of his own.

Plus, Margot felt confident that no one in the Carmichael family—not Doug, not Jenna, not Nick or Kevin—would want to see that branch cut down.

"No tent," Margot said.

"I'll see about the smaller tent," Roger said.

"Thank you," Margot said. She paused. "I don't expect you to understand."

"Pray for sun," Roger said.

Margot was staying in "her room," sharing the double bed with Ellie, who was a flopper and a kicker. Drum Jr. and Carson would sleep in the attic bunk room with Kevin and Beanie's three boys, and their uncle Nick—who, if he remained true to form, wouldn't make it home to sleep at all. Jenna and Finn and Autumn were all cramming into Jenna's room, which had one twin bed and one trundle bed; this was their choice, but it was also true that neither Finn nor Autumn had wanted to share with Rhonda, who had the proper guest room—with two double beds—all to herself. Kevin and Beanie would sleep in Kevin and Nick's room (on the Eastlake twins), and Doug (but apparently not Pauline) would sleep in the master.

Margot hadn't texted her father back yet because she didn't know what to say, and she hoped that her silence would prompt more information.

She unpacked her suitcase and Ellie's. Ellie had stuffed hers with trinkets, homemade bracelets, a ball of string, a stuffed inchworm that someone had brought to the hospital the day she was born, the tape measure from the junk drawer, an assortment of dried-out markers and broken crayons, and a tattered paperback copy of *Caps for Sale*. Ellie, Margot realized with weary concern, was becoming a hoarder. This was probably a result of the divorce, another thing for Margot to feel guilty about. She sat on the bed, letting the broken crayons sift through her fingers. Was it too early for wine?

In the way of clothes, Ellie had packed two mismatched socks, a white T-shirt with a grape juice stain down the front, a pair of turquoise denim overalls, her black-and-silver Christmas dress that she'd worn to *The Nutcracker* last year and had complained about the whole time, her favorite purple shorts with the green belt, and a seersucker sundress embroidered with lobsters that was two sizes too small. And hallelujah—a bathing suit. Margot should have checked Ellie's packing job—really, who trusted a six-year-old to pack for herself?—but she'd been too busy. At least Margot had packed Ellie's flower girl dress and her good white sandals in her own suitcase.

Margot hung up the white eyelet flower girl dress and then her own grasshopper green bridesmaid dress, thinking, *God, I do not want to wear that.*

But she would, of course, for Jenna. And for her mother.

Grocery store, liquor store. She was racing the clock, there was no time to think about Edge, or Drum Sr. getting married, or about Griff with his kaleidoscope eyes and the two days of growth on his face. But the three of them were in her brain. How to exorcise them?

She took an outdoor shower under the spray of pale pink climbing roses that her mother had cultivated and that still thrived. The roses alive, her mother dead. Was the fact that Margot didn't like gardening a character flaw? Did it mean she wasn't nurturing enough?

In the worst days of their divorce, Drum Sr. had accused Margot of being a coldhearted bitch. Was this true? If it *was* true, then why did Margot feel everything so keenly? Why did life constantly feel like being pierced by ten thousand tiny arrows?

She had been a coldhearted bitch to Griffin Wheatley, Homecoming King. He didn't realize it, but it was true.

Guilt.

But no, there wasn't time.

Margot fed her children a frozen pizza and grapes, serving them in her bathrobe, her hair still dripping wet.

Carson said, "Are you going out tonight?"

"Yes," Margot said.

The three of them started to squeak, squeal, and whine in chorus. They hated it when Margot went out, they hated Kitty, their afternoon babysitter, they hated their afternoon activities regardless of what they were—because they sensed that these activities were also babysitters, substitutes for Margot's time and attention. Margot had hoped that as they got older, they would come to see her career as one of the wonderful things about her. She was a partner at Miller-Sawtooth, where she did valuable work, matching up top executives with the right companies. She had a certain amount of power, and she made a lot of money.

But power and money meant little to her twelve-year-old and even less to the ten and the six. They wanted her warm body snuggled in the bed between them, reading *Caps for Sale*.

"It's your auntie's wedding," Margot said. "A sitter named Emma is coming tonight and tomorrow night. Saturday is the wedding, and it will be held here in the backyard, and Sunday we're going home."

"Tonight *and* tomorrow night!" Drum Jr. said. Of the three of them, he was the one who needed Margot the most. Why this was, she couldn't quite explain.

"Who's Emma? I don't know Emma!" Ellie said.

"She's nice," Margot said. "Nicer than me."

It was nearly seven, and the light outside was still strong. The smaller tent had been raised, and now the guys were laying the dance floor. The grass would be matted, but Roger had assured them it wouldn't die. The smaller tent looked good, Margot thought. It was bigger than she'd expected, but it wasn't big enough to shelter 150 people. Maybe between the tent and the house. Maybe.

Forty percent chance of showers.

Emma Wilton showed up right at seven. She was a girl whom Margot used to babysit, now twenty-five years old and between years of veterinary school. She and Margot hugged, then remarked on how their relationship had circled around, and Margot said, "And ten or fifteen years from now, Ellie can babysit *your* kids." They laughed, and Margot excused herself for the blow-dryer.

She checked her phone. Nothing from Edge. What was *wrong*

with him? Margot was tempted to text, *Is everything okay?* But that might come across as sounding nagging or needy—or worst of all, wifely. Another problem with texting: it was nearly impossible to express tone. Margot wanted to let him know that she was concerned without having him think she was asking, *Why the hell aren't you texting me back?* Which was, of course, exactly what she was asking.

There was a text on her phone from Rhonda. Margot opened it eagerly, expecting more drama. It said: *My plane arrives at 8:20. What time dinner?*

Margot deflated a bit. It sounded like Rhonda was still coming. This was bad. This was, in so many ways, the worst-case scenario. To have Rhonda, but no Pauline? Unthinkable. Who would Rhonda talk to, who would Rhonda hang out with, if not Pauline? There were no other Tonellis coming to the wedding, and none of Pauline's friends.

Margot typed back: *Dinner is at 8.*

Rhonda responded right away: *Who picking me up?* Rhonda always, in Margot's experience, responded right away because—Margot suspected—Rhonda had nothing to do but text back right away. She had no proper job, no other friends.

Margot typed: *Pls take a cab.*

Rhonda replied: *?*

Margot looked at the question mark, then burst out laughing. Of course Rhonda had texted a question mark. She was probably wondering why Mr. Roarke wasn't picking her up in a white stretch limo.

Margot had sent a handful of detailed e-mails about tonight's bachelorette party to all involved. She had listed the name and address of the restaurant and the time of their dinner reservation—8:00—in each message. That Rhonda had then booked a flight that landed at 8:20 wasn't Margot's problem.

Was it?

Guilt.

But no, there wasn't time.

Although Jenna's bedroom was the smallest—the "spinster aunt bedroom," their mother had always called it, since for decades it had belonged to Doug's spinster aunt, Lucretia—it was also the best appointed because it had a deck that overlooked the backyard and the harbor. It was on this deck that Margot and the other maidens opened the champagne.

Autumn took charge of popping the cork, since she waited tables at a beachfront seafood restaurant in Murrells Inlet, South Carolina. The cork sailed into the yard, and Margot watched Jenna's eyes follow it as it landed in the grass.

Then Jenna said, "I guess I thought the tent would be bigger."

Autumn expertly filled four glasses, and Margot reached for one. She wanted to drink the whole thing down in one gulp, but she had to make a toast. She smiled at Jenna, and Jenna smiled back. Jenna wouldn't care about the tent or about Margot making a unilateral decision about Alfie's tree branch. All Jenna cared about was Stuart, who would be arriving tomorrow with his people.

"To an amazing, wonderful...and *sunny* weekend!" Margot said.

The four of them clinked glasses.

Jenna said, "There *is* another tent going up, right? The one the people are sitting under?"

"Yes," Margot said. Drink drink drink. "Tomorrow."

"Oh," Jenna said. "I thought it was going up today."

"Nope," Margot said. Drink drink drink. "It's tomorrow."

Jenna frowned. Margot thought maybe the issue would explode right then and there. Instead Jenna said, "I miss Stuart."

Finn was frowning also. She said, "At least he's not in Vegas, getting a *lap dance.*"

Margot recalled Finn's expression on the ferry when Scott's name came up. So that was why: Vegas, lap dances, strip clubs, cocktail waitresses with large, enticing fake breasts. Margot remembered how things like that could seem threatening to a new marriage. But that kind of jealous anxiety faded away, just like everything else. At the end with Drum Sr., Margot had found herself thinking, *Why don't you go to Vegas and get a lap dance?*

Autumn said, "Lap dances are harmless. I get them all the time."

For the first time all day, something struck Margot as funny. "*You* get lap dances?"

"Yeah," Autumn said. "Guys love it."

"Oh," Margot said. She wondered for an instant if Edge would love it if she, Margot, got a lap dance. She decided he most definitely would not.

Autumn filled her glass with more champagne, and Margot watched the golden liquid bubble to the top. The kids were playing Frisbee with Emma in the yard below. Margot remembered when it had been she and her siblings playing in the yard, while her parents drank gin and tonics on this deck and turned up Van Morrison on the radio. Her mother used to wear a blue paisley patio dress. Margot would hug Alfie's trunk, her arms not even reaching a third of the way around. A tree wasn't a person, but if a tree *could* be a person, then Alfie would be a wise, generous, all-seeing, godlike person. She couldn't let the tent guys cut the branch. The cut would be a wound; it might get infected with some kind of mung. Alfie might die.

Margot stood up and leaned over the railing. She felt dizzy. She felt like she might drop.

"We should go," she said.

*　　*　　*

Jenna was driving.

They bounced across the cobblestones at the top of Main Street. Town was teeming with people who had come to Nantucket to celebrate summer. Margot loved the art galleries and shops, she loved the couple carrying a bottle of wine to dinner at Black-Eyed Susan's, she loved the dreadlocked guy in khaki cargo shorts walking a black lab. She noticed people noticing them—four pretty women all dressed up in Margot's Land Rover. Jenna and Finn were wearing black dresses, and Autumn was wearing green. Margot was wearing a white silk sheath with a cascade of ruffles above the knee. She loved white in the summertime. The city was too dirty to wear white—one cab ride and this dress would be trashed.

Jenna took a right onto Broad Street, past Nantucket Bookworks and the Brotherhood and Le Languedoc, and then a left by the Nantucket Yacht Club. Margot tapped her finger on the window and said, "That's where we'll be tomorrow night!"

No one responded. Margot turned around to see Finn and Autumn pecking away at their phones. Then Margot looked at Jenna, who was skillfully navigating the streets, despite that fact that pedestrians were crossing in front of them without looking. Margot felt bad that Jenna was driving to her own bachelorette party, but Jenna had insisted. Margot should have hired a car and driver, and then all four of them would be sitting in the backseat together. And Margot should have made a rule about no cell phones. What was it about life now? The people who weren't present always seemed to be more important than the people who were.

Margot picked her clutch purse off the floor of the car and, against her better judgment, checked her phone. She had one text, from Ellie. *I miss you mommy.*

Margot decided not to be disappointed that her only text was from her daughter, and she decided not to be horrified that her six-year-old knew how to text. Margot decided to be happy that someone, somewhere in the world, missed her.

When she looked up, Jenna was pulling into the restaurant parking lot. Margot knew this was the time to muster her enthusiasm and rally the troops. The group was low-energy; even Margot herself was flagging. A glass and a half of champagne might as well have been three Ambien and a shot of NyQuil. If Jenna turned the car around, Margot would happily sleep until morning.

But she was the maid of honor. She had to do this for Jenna.

And her mother.

The Galley was a bewitching restaurant. It was the only fine dining on Nantucket located on the beach. Most of the seating was under an awning with open sides bordered by planters filled with red and pink geraniums. There were divans and papasan chairs and tiki torches out in the sand. There was a zinc bar. The crowd was buzzing and beautiful. Over the years, Margot had seen an assortment of powerful and famous people at these tables: Martha Stewart, Madonna, Dustin Hoffman, Ted Kennedy, Michael Douglas and Catherine Zeta-Jones, Robert DeNiro. The Galley was see and be seen. It was, always, on any given night, the place to be.

They were seated at a table for four in the main dining room, but in the part of the room that was closer to the parking lot. Autumn didn't sit down right away; she was scanning the surroundings. Finally, she settled in her chair. She said, "I think we should ask for a better table."

Margot felt something sinking and rising in her at the same time. Spirits sinking, ire rising. She said, "A better table, *where?* This place is packed!"

"Out in the sand, maybe," Autumn said. "Where there's more action."

Margot couldn't believe this. She'd had a hell of a time even getting *this* reservation for eight o'clock on a Thursday night in July. She had called on the Tuesday after Memorial Day and had been told, initially, that the restaurant was *booked,* but her name could be added to the wait list. And now Autumn—the so-called restaurant professional—was *complaining?* Insinuating that Margot hadn't been important or *insistent* enough to score a better table? It was Autumn's fault that the bachelorette party was being held tonight, at the very last minute, instead of weeks or months earlier, which was more traditional. There were five people's schedules to accommodate, and so Margot had put forth options, all of them enticing. A ski weekend in Stowe, or a spring weekend out at the spa in Canyon Ranch. But Autumn hadn't been able to make either one. *Weekends are really hard for me,* she'd written.

Well, it was nearly impossible to plan a bachelorette party *during the week,* but Margot gave it a shot and threw together something in Boca Raton the week of Jenna's spring break from Little Minds, but again Autumn couldn't attend, so Margot canceled.

Then Jenna told Margot she thought the real problem with Autumn was money. She was, after all, waiting tables.

Margot wondered *why* Autumn was waiting tables. She had a degree from the College of William and Mary, where she had majored in political science. She could have done anything with that—grad school, law school, think tanks. She could have taught like Jenna or gone into business, an Internet start-up, anything. Margot was impatient with people who didn't live up to their potential. This, she supposed, was the result of having been married to Drum Sr. Drum Sr. was so unambitious, it was like he was moving backward.

Margot ignored Autumn's dissatisfaction with their table. She asked the waiter (who was a woman, but one of the things Margot had learned over the years from Autumn was that the term "waitress," like the term "actress," was outdated) for a wine list. The wine list appeared, and Margot asked Jenna, "White or red?"

Jenna waved a hand. "I don't care. Either."

Margot didn't ask Finn or Autumn for input, even though she could *feel* Autumn staring at her. Probably Autumn wanted the wine list. Well, too bad, Margot was going to exercise her sovereign right as maid of honor and pick the wine.

One white, one red. Margot preferred Sancerres and Malbecs. Sancerres reminded her of Drum Sr. (he had wooed her the first summer they dated by taking her to a restaurant called the Blue Bistro—which had since closed—and plying her with Sancerre), and Malbecs reminded her of Edge (that night at Picholine, which she could *not* allow herself to dwell on). Margot wished she could look at a wine list and not think of men at all. She wished she could look at a wine list and think about herself.

She handed the list to Autumn. "Would you mind picking the wine?"

Autumn looked so happy that Margot immediately felt petty for denying her this tiny pleasure in the first place. "I'd love to!"

Margot leaned back in her chair and tried to relax. Jenna and Finn were talking between themselves sotto voce, which Margot found rude, if completely predictable. Finn seemed to still be in foul humor. She had always been petulant and spoiled. When Finn was seventeen, she had landed a job on Nantucket, nannying for the Worthington family, who were friends of Beth and Doug Carmichael. Finn had lasted thirty-six hours before she quit. She missed Connecticut, she claimed, and she missed her parents. What Finn *really* wanted was to return to Darien in order to have sex with her boyfriend, Charlie Beaudette, while her parents—the ones she purportedly missed—were on vacation for two weeks in the south of France. Beth and Doug had tried to talk Finn into staying—she would outgrow her homesickness, she would have a wonderful summer—but Finn was determined to go, and the Carmichaels were powerless to make her stay. Margot had been on Nantucket that same week and had a front-row seat for the drama. Back then, Drum Jr. was less than a year old, and Margot was working as an associate principal at Miller-Sawtooth. As a new mother and a placement professional, Margot had determined that Finn lacked character, had no sense of responsibility, and no hustle. Margot could not abide people without hustle. Finn's inner core, Margot suspected, was as soft as a rotten banana.

Thankfully, the wine arrived, and they ordered their meals. Jenna turned to include Autumn and Margot in the conversation, although Margot couldn't keep track of what they were talking about from one minute to the next. Her mind was on other things. She had ordered the crab cake to start, Autumn had the chowder, Jenna and Finn had both gotten the foie gras. Margot thought, in no particular order: It was funny the way Jenna and Finn always ordered the same thing, and they had dressed alike. Had they ever had a fight? If so, Margot didn't know about it. They had been friends for more than twenty-five years, and it had always been harmony. The summer of the nanny job, Jenna had supported Finn's decision to go home. She was the one who had confided to Margot that the real reason Finn wanted to go home was to screw Charlie Beaudette. Jenna had found it romantic—instead of stupid, immature, and shortsighted.

Margot allowed that her bitterness regarding Finn might have been born of jealousy. Margot herself had never had a friend the way Jenna had Finn. She had had friends, of course, some casual, some closer, but Margot and her friends had bickered and switched alliances; this had been true in high school, and then again in college. As an adult, Margot and Drum Sr. had become friends with the people whose children went to school with their children, and did the same sports and activities as their children—which was, Margot realized, an insufficient litmus test for friendship. Few of those friendships had survived her divorce. None of the couples she and Drum used to hang out with called her for dinner parties anymore. Now, when Margot saw those people, they scheduled the children's playdates like business transactions.

If Margot needed to talk to someone, she called Jenna, or her sister-in-law, Beanie, or her father. She sometimes talked to Edge. At the start of their relationship, he had been sweet and attentive, but lately the sweet attentiveness had dwindled. For the past four or five months, he had sounded like a man of fifty-nine who had been married and divorced three times, who had seen it all, survived it all, and could barely conceal his impatience that Margot was still in the life stage where she cared what other people thought.

Margot eyed Jenna and Finn with envy. Then she worried that the fact that she had never had a best friend was another indicator—like the fact that she didn't garden—that there was something wrong with her. And her marriage had failed! Was that due to some inability to connect in a meaningful and permanent way with others? *Was* she a coldhearted bitch? Jenna would, no doubt, be just as devoted to Stuart as she was to Finn. Margot wondered if all family wedding weekends were doomed to be exercises in painful self-examination.

She turned her attention to Autumn.

Autumn had ordered the chowder, which was the least expensive thing on the menu, and Margot wondered if *that* was why she had ordered it. Maybe Autumn really *was* financially strapped.

Of course, she wasn't rich; she was waiting tables and living in a rented bungalow. At that moment, Margot decided that she would pay for dinner. She had a great job, she could afford it, she was the maid of honor: she would pay.

She took a bite of her crab cake. It was drizzled with a lemony sauce. More wine. She was starting to feel a little drunk, but this came as no surprise. Anytime she had thought about the wedding in the past twelve months, she had thought, *When I don't know what else to do, I'll get drunk. I'll just stay drunk all weekend, if need be.* And here she was.

Finn got up to use the bathroom. She hadn't even touched her foie gras, and Margot eyed it covetously. Margot loved foie gras, but she hadn't ordered it because it was bad for you, and it was a travesty the way they force-fed the poor French geese. But it looked so yummy—plump and seared golden brown, topped with ruby red pomegranate seeds.

Margot noticed Jenna watching her with a concerned expression on her face. She realized that she had to tell Jenna about Alfie's tree branch; she had to tell Jenna that the second tent wasn't coming tomorrow. The second tent wasn't coming at all.

Forty percent chance of showers.

Margot lifted the bottle of white wine out of the ice and found it empty. She flagged the waiter.

"Another?" she said.

Jenna bit her bottom lip, and Margot didn't like the way that looked. She wanted to ask Jenna if she was having fun. She wanted to ask Jenna if this night was memorable. It was too early to tell, they had barely started, but Margot feared it wasn't memorable enough. What could she do? Should she suggest a game? Some kind of bachelorette game? In general, Margot found bachelorette parties distasteful—the penis lollipops, the ludi-

crous sashes the bride-to-be was forced to wear, the hot pink
T-shirts with lewd sayings. And at that moment, Margot realized
she had forgotten to bring the hideous bow-and-paper-plate
"hat" that Jenna was supposed to wear. Jenna would most definitely be thrilled that Margot had forgotten the hat, but Margot
still felt like she was failing at her maid-of-honor duties. Finn
would have remembered to bring the hat.

Forty percent chance of showers. Griffin Wheatley, Homecoming King. He had taken the job at Blankstar; he was happy
there. Margot could relax. No harm, no foul.

The restaurant was loud. The other tables were talking and
laughing, and under all that, Bobby Darin sang "Beyond the
Sea," and champagne corks popped, and knives and forks scraped
plates. Margot thought of her mother, wearing the blue paisley
patio dress. She had seemed like the most beautiful woman in all
the world, and Jenna looked just like her.

Margot said, "Is it me, or has Finn been gone a long time?"

Jenna said, "I'm sure she's texting Scott."

"Oh," Margot said, collapsing back in her seat. She wondered
if she should take her phone to the ladies' room and check her
texts. She knew the answer was no. She was determined to be present. She would eat her crab cake. She wouldn't worry about Alfie's
tree branch or about what Edge was doing, or about whether or
not Carson needed to repeat fourth grade or about whether it had
been rude to pick such an expensive restaurant for this dinner. She
wouldn't feel the weight of her age, even though it had been difficult to see Emma Wilton all grown up. A blink of an eye ago,
Emma had been six, and Margot had been twenty-one. Forty was
too old to be a maid of honor, Margot thought. And yet that was
what their mother had wanted.

There was a tap on Margot's shoulder. She thought it was Finn returning from the ladies' room, or the waiter with their wine, but when she pivoted in her seat, she saw Rhonda. Rhonda Tonelli.

Oh, shit, she thought.

Margot struggled to push her chair away from the table and stand. She thought, *What do I do? What do I say?* She'd had too much to drink to handle this graciously, but at least she was sober enough to realize it.

She said, "Hey, Rhonda!" She moved in to give Rhonda a hug and a peck on the cheek, and Rhonda bobbed away to avoid this gesture, so Margot ended up with her hand on the side of Rhonda's neck, and her lips landed on Rhonda's bare shoulder. It all happened quickly, but the embarrassing fact resonated through Margot's mind like a gong. She had kissed Rhonda's shoulder.

Oh, God, awkward.

Rhonda said, "I didn't know the address of the house, so I called my mother, but she wasn't answering her phone, so then I called you, like, fifty times, and you didn't answer. So then the cabdriver had pity on me—I mean, here I am, just landed on this island and there's no one to meet me and I don't know where the hell I'm going. So we pulled out the phone book and looked up Carmichael, but there were two Carmichaels so I picked one and I was *wrong*—the other Carmichaels were at home, I interrupted their dinner—and then finally I found the right house. The babysitter was there with your kids, she had no idea which room was mine, so I put my stuff in the blue room with the twin beds…"

Kevin's room, Margot thought.

"And thank *God* the babysitter knew where you guys were eating because I lost the e-mail you sent me with the name of the restaurant. It was like, 'Welcome to Nantucket, Rhonda!'"

Margot laughed. She said, "Welcome to Nantucket, Rhonda!"

She stood with her back to the table, hoping to disguise the fact that there was no chair for Rhonda. Margot had completely forgotten Rhonda was coming. Margot had made a reservation for five people, but when they'd arrived, the hostess had said, "Four?" and Margot had said, "Yes, please," and they were seated at a table for four.

Now Autumn was up out of her chair, using her professional skills, informing the waiter that there would be one more joining them and they needed a chair. But then Finn returned to the table, her face streaked with tears, and Jenna hopped up to see what the matter was. In the process, she upended her wineglass, and Margot's white silk sheath dress was splattered with burgundy, and Margot's gut reaction, which she was not quick enough to suppress, was to shriek. The dress was ruined.

Jenna said, "Oh, Margot, I'm sorry!"

Rhonda said, "White wine will get that out. Use white wine."

Autumn said, "That's a myth."

Rhonda said, "I've seen it done."

Margot watched Finn and Jenna, who were now hugging. Jenna rubbed Finn between the shoulder blades. "What happened?" she said. "What's wrong?"

The waiter came back with the fifth chair, and then there was the big production of squeezing it in and moving the plates, all of them still filled with very expensive uneaten food. Then the waiter noticed the spilled wine and Margot's dress, and she ran to get fresh linens and a dish towel and seltzer for the stains. The wine looked like blood, and Finn was crying with gusto now. It probably seemed like there had been a murder at their table. Margot thought it would be best if they all sat down, and she said so.

Finn said, "I have to go home."

Margot said, "What? Why? What happened?"

Finn shook her head and pressed a streamer of toilet paper to her nose.

Jenna said, "I'll go with you."

"No!" Margot said. "You can't. This is your party!"

"Your sister's right," Finn said. "You stay. It's your party."

"Don't be absurd," Jenna said. "If you're going home, I'm going with you."

Finn cast her eyes to the ceiling in a look of mock surrender that Margot had seen a thousand times in the past twenty-five years. Margot thought, *You can't ask Jenna to leave her own party! Pathetic!* Finn was upset because Scott was in Las Vegas having fun. Why wasn't Finn willing to just have fun herself, here? But Margot knew there was nothing she would be able to say, no guilt trip she would be able to lay, that would make either of them change their minds.

Jenna wrapped herself in her pashmina. "I'm going to take the car," she said to Margot. "You guys can get a cab, right?"

"Right," Margot said. She smiled at Jenna, willing herself to pretend like this was all okay for the next sixty seconds, until they were out of the restaurant. "We'll see you in the morning."

Jenna returned Margot's smile, and Margot saw her gratitude and relief. She kissed Margot on the cheek and said, "Thank you for understanding. I'm not feeling very fun, either. I just want Stuart to get here."

"Okay," Margot said. Jenna and Finn left, and a second later the waiter approached with the seltzer and a rag, and Margot blotted the stains on her dress until she looked like a watercolor canvas. It was not okay, of course, not okay that the evening she had planned for months had been sabotaged by Scott Walker, of all people. In fact, if Margot looked back on the last six hours, nothing had been okay. If Margot let herself think about it another second, *she* might break down in tears and go home.

But no, she wouldn't capitulate. She was the maid of honor, and that word, *honor,* meant something. She wasn't sure just what, but she knew it didn't mean going home. She had an evening to salvage.

She turned to Autumn and Rhonda. "So," she said.

They decided to move to the bar. This was Autumn's idea, and it was brilliant. Instead of the three of them sitting forlornly at a table set for five, they had their wine and food moved to three stools at the zinc bar. It was a fresh start. Margot sat in the middle, with Rhonda to her right and Autumn to her left. Rhonda ordered dinner, and Autumn finished her chowder, and Margot managed to eat her crab cake, then she and Autumn split Finn's untouched foie gras. Margot began to feel a little more like a human being. She was hosting a bachelorette party without a bachelorette, but that wasn't true because both Autumn and Rhonda were bachelorettes, and for that matter, so was Margot.

Autumn and Rhonda had never met, which turned out to be a good thing because Rhonda, once she had gotten a glass of wine and taken a few deep breaths, did something Margot had never seen before: she turned on the charm.

She said, "I can't believe Jenna asked me to be a bridesmaid. I am so thrilled."

"Thrilled?" Autumn said. "Really? I agreed because I love that girl to pieces, but I wouldn't call myself thrilled."

"No," Margot said. "Me either."

"I've been a bridesmaid eleven times," Autumn said.

"How many of those couples are still married?" Margot wondered aloud.

"Eight couples still married, two divorced, one separated," Autumn said.

"More will fall," Margot predicted.

"I've never been a bridesmaid before," Rhonda said.

"You're kidding!" Autumn said. "How'd you manage to escape?"

Rhonda shrugged. "No one ever asked me."

Autumn sat with that a moment, and Margot thought, *No one ever asked you because up until ten minutes ago you presented yourself to the world as a miserable bitch.* Right? Rhonda was the same woman who had refused to eat anything other than celery sticks at Thanksgiving dinner because she was newly vegan—although she hadn't bothered to inform her mother—and then she picked a fight with Margot's sister-in-law, Beanie, about what being a vegan actually entailed, and the whole time she had pronounced the word "veg-an," with a short "e," so that it rhymed with "Megan." Rhonda was the same woman who had gotten a flat tire in the Bronx and had called Doug in the middle of the night, begging him to come help her change it, then screamed at him for taking so long to get there, saying he was lucky she hadn't been gang-raped. Rhonda was the same woman who announced unsolicited that her body fat was a mere 4 percent, then asked Margot to feel her biceps, then pulled up her shirt so that Margot could view her six-pack abs. Rhonda openly admitted that her favorite show was *Jersey Shore* and that she had a celebrity crush on Mike "The Situation."

Margot said, "Well, I'm glad you're thrilled. It's going to be a lovely wedding."

Rhonda said, "I love the dress."

"Ha!" Autumn said. "You're kidding!"

Rhonda said, "I'm not kidding. I love it."

"Grasshopper green," Autumn said. "I'm sorry, but those two words spoken together are fingernails down a chalkboard."

Margot pressed her lips together. On the one hand, she agreed with Autumn. The color did not thrill Margot. Nor, really, did anything else about the dress. The dress was, undeniably, a *bridesmaid* dress—silk shantung in a reptilian green, off-the-shoulder, cinched-at-the-waist sheath skirt to the knee. To Margot, the dress felt dated. These days, everyone got bridesmaid dresses at J.Crew or Ann Taylor, or women were given a color and then they were free to find their own dresses, ones they might actually wear again. But on the other hand, Margot was grateful that Rhonda liked the dress. The suggestion of this green had come from the Notebook. It was their mother's idea, because their mother's vision was one of an elegant woodland, all green and white. The green should be "the color of new leaves," the Notebook stated, but it had ended up as a shade the woman at the bridal salon called "grasshopper." Reminiscent of classroom lizards and sour-apple Jolly Ranchers. Their mother had also suggested dyed-to-match pumps and opera-length pearls—and Jenna had fully subscribed to both of these things, even though Margot had advised rethinking both. Dyed-to-match pumps and pearls were fine a decade ago—*maybe*—but not any longer.

Margot had said, *You don't have to follow Mom's advice to the letter, Jenna. If she were alive now, even she might second-guess the pearls.*

But Jenna wouldn't budge.

To Rhonda, Margot said, "I'm glad you like the dress."

Autumn said, "But just so you know, bridesmaids are *supposed* to complain about the dress. It's in the Bridesmaid Handbook."

"Handbook?" Rhonda said.

"She's kidding," Margot said.

Their entrées came, Margot's steak, Autumn's chicken, Rhonda's sole. Rhonda had obviously given up being a Megan-vegan, but Margot decided not to mention it. Why rock the boat? She sipped her wine and then drank some water. Her steak was seared on the outside and pink and juicy on the inside, and it came with some kind of creamy potato thing and lemony sautéed spinach, and as Margot ate, her mood improved. She realized she was sort of glad that Jenna and Finn had left because the pressure of making sure the evening was perfect and that Jenna was having fun had been lifted.

Rhonda said, "So . . . I have a new boyfriend."

"Really?" Margot knew next to nothing about Rhonda's personal life, but from certain things Pauline had said, Margot had gleaned that Rhonda's career was abysmal and her dating situation even worse.

"Wanna see a picture?" Rhonda whipped out her phone and scrolled to a photo of a behemoth man wearing a tight black T-shirt that showed off his oiled, rock-hard muscles. He reminded Margot of Arnold Schwarzenegger from his bodybuilding days. He had a full head of hair and a nice smile.

"Wow," Margot said.

"His name is Raymond," Rhonda said. "He's a trainer at my gym." She dropped her voice to a whisper. "He has an eleven-inch penis."

"Really?" Autumn said, perking up. "Eleven inches? You're sure you're not exaggerating? Eleven inches is BIG."

"Eleven inches," Rhonda confirmed.

Margot nodded appreciatively, guessing that Raymond and his prodigious member might be responsible for the transformation of Rhonda's personality.

"What about you, Margot? Are you dating anyone?" Rhonda asked. "You must have men all over you. You're so pretty and smart."

Smart? Margot knew Rhonda meant book smart, but when it came to men, Margot was as big an idiot as anyone else. A bigger idiot, in fact.

Before she could stop herself, Margot said, "Actually, I'm dating my father's law partner."

She sat for a second, stunned that she had spoken those words out loud. She was scandalized with herself. She looked at her glass of red wine and thought, *Damn you.* Nobody, and she meant *nobody,* knew about her and Edge—except for her and Edge. But she found it felt cathartic to say it aloud. To finally tell someone.

"He's fifty-nine years old," she said.

"Whoa," Autumn said.

"You can't say a word," Margot said. "It's a secret." She looked at Autumn first. Autumn might whip out her phone any second and text Jenna. Then Margot looked at Rhonda, who was a bigger security threat. Rhonda, Margot knew, told her mother *everything,* and if Rhonda told Pauline about this, Pauline would most certainly tell Doug. What had Margot *done?* She had blown it. She might as well have changed her status on Facebook to read, *Dating my father's law partner,* so that all 486 of her "friends" knew the truth. She had just sabotaged her relationship. If Edge knew that Margot had spilled the beans, he would end it.

Margot said, "I'm dead serious. You can't tell a soul. I'll know if you've told anyone, and I will find you, and I will kill you." She was using what Drum Jr. called her "scary mom voice." This was the only weapon she had in her arsenal, and she wasn't certain it would be effective. She didn't trust either of these people.

"I won't tell," Autumn said.

"I won't tell," Rhonda said.

They sounded earnest, but Margot was forty years old, and she had learned that human beings were incapable of keeping secrets. When handed a privileged piece of information, the first thing a person wanted to do was share it.

"My father would die," Margot said. Or at least this was Edge's position. He believed that Doug would be appalled, their friendship would be strained, and their working relationship ruined. Margot believed her father would take the news in stride. He might even be happy. Doug had *not* been fond of Drum Sr. He thought Drum Sr. was a spoiled ne'er-do-well. Doug liked and respected Edge; they had been law partners for thirty years. True, Edge's track record with women wasn't great. He was paying alimony to three wives; he had four children, the oldest of whom was thirty-six, and the youngest of whom was six. Audrey.

That was how Margot and Edge had ended up together: Ellie and Audrey, both six years old, had taken ballet class at Mme Willette's studio on Eighty-second and Riverside. Mme Willette's ballet school was expensive, rigorous, and impossible to get into, but Margot had heard excellent things about it. Mme Willette held her girls to high standards — perfect posture, perfect French pronunciation, not a strand of hair escaping the bun. At the open house, Margot had been captivated by Mme Willette and became determined that Ellie should study with her. She had mastered the admissions game after getting three kids into Ethical Culture Fieldston, and she pursued the prestigious ballet class relentlessly.

Ellie had thrived under Mme Willette's discipline. She quickly bonded with all the girls in her class, and her favorite ballet friend was a tiny girl with black hair and Asiatic eyes named Audrey. Margot had glimpsed the mother a few times — an elegant, lean woman of indeterminate ethnicity. Ellie begged for a playdate with Audrey, and she claimed that Audrey wanted a playdate with her, but the odd and awkward thing about socializing children in

Manhattan was that none of the parents knew each other. And quite frankly, Margot was intimidated by Audrey's mother. She looked like she lived downtown, although it just as easily could have been Sutton Place. Margot didn't know if she was a Little Red Schoolhouse mom or a Bank Street mom or a Chapin mom. She might have asked, but she didn't have the energy, the *output,* required to forge any new alliances.

And then, one week, Margot went to pick up Ellie from Mme Willette's—and there, in the foyer, waiting for the class to be let out, was Edge Desvesnes.

"Hi!" Margot had said, her voice containing amazement and confusion. Edge was way out of context here; it was like seeing her dentist at the Union Square Greenmarket, or her childhood minister, Reverend Marlowe, at the hardware store.

Edge had turned to look at her, but she could tell he was having a hard time placing her, as well.

She said, "Margot Carmichael."

"Oh, my!" he said, and they embraced.

Margot had known Edge Desvesnes since she was a teenager. He and his first wife, Mary Lee, used to come to barbecues at the Carmichael house in Darien. There had been a time when Margot was still in braces and glasses and bad-hair-and-worse-skin when she had a terrible crush on Edge Desvesnes. She remembered once passing hors d'oeuvres at a party that her parents were throwing. After she had served Edge, he had turned to Doug and said, "That's a beautiful girl you've got there, partner. Those eyes."

And Doug had said, "Don't I know it."

Margot had blushed hot and retreated to the kitchen. No one had ever called her "beautiful" before. The boys in Margot's class were ruthless about her looks. That Mr. Desvesnes, who was cool and funny and cute, had called her "beautiful" was enough to turn Margot's world upside down.

Beautiful. She had looked at herself in the mirror for months after that, wondering: *Am I beautiful?* And what had he meant about her eyes?

Margot had seen Edge Desvesnes periodically in the years that followed. He came to dinner to celebrate her parents' twentieth anniversary, he pulled into the driveway to honk for Doug when they went golfing, he attended Kevin and Beanie's wedding. Before she ran into him outside the dance class, the last time Margot had seen Edge Desvesnes was at her mother's funeral. Edge had served as a pallbearer. In Margot's memory, he had been with a woman, but Margot had been too racked with grief and swarmed by people to notice which woman. She had heard through her father that Edge had divorced, then married, then divorced, then married—but amid the drama of her own life, Margot hadn't been able to keep up.

Seeing him again so unexpectedly, Margot felt as flushed as she had been at fourteen. She said, "You're not here for..."

"Waiting for my daughter," he said.

"Your daughter?" In Margot's memory, Edge had sons. Two with the first wife, one with the second, or the other way around. Did she remember hearing about a daughter?

"My youngest," he said. "Audrey."

Margot said, "Audrey is your daughter? Ellie *loves* Audrey." Margot swallowed. She thought of the Indochine beauty. "So your wife..."

"My ex."

"Oh," Margot said. "Well, I've been meaning to approach her about getting the girls together. I had no idea...I mean, I didn't know she was *your* daughter."

At that moment, the door to the studio opened, and the girls filed out in graceful silence. Ellie reached for the cold water bottle in Margot's hand. Audrey wrapped her arms around Edge's waist and squeezed.

"My daughter," he said.

"Fifty-nine," Autumn said now. "That's old. That's Viagra territory."

Rhonda laughed at this.

Margot said, "Not quite."

Things had turned romantic right away. At that very first encounter, they had exchanged cell phone numbers, and by that evening, Margot had a text from Edge that said, *You are a knock-out, Margot Carmichael.*

And she had said, *Moi?*

Two Saturdays later, when Edge was back to pick up Audrey, they made plans to have coffee. A few days after the coffee date, they met for drinks, and drinks had turned into the two of them making out on a dark street corner in Hell's Kitchen. Edge had said, "Your father would kill me if he saw us now."

And Margot said, "My father will never find out."

Those had been the words that they'd lived by; those had become the chains that strangled their relationship, made it clunky, and kept it from growing. Doug could never find out.

"Whatever," Margot said now. "It's kind of a mess."

"Is he coming to the wedding?" Rhonda asked.

"Yes," Margot said. "Tomorrow."

"Well, then, we still have tonight," Autumn said. "Let's get out of here."

That's a beautiful girl you've got there, partner. Those eyes. Margot had asked Edge if he remembered saying that.

He had shaken his head, baffled. *No,* he said.

Margot flagged the bartender for the check. "This is my treat," she said.

"Oh, Margot, come on," Autumn said. "It's too much."

"I insist," Margot said, and she could tell Autumn felt relieved.

"Thank you!" Rhonda said. "That's really generous."

Margot looked at Rhonda. Rhonda's face was fresh, smiling, sincere. This *was* the same woman who had once told Margot she bought dresses at Bergdorf's, wore them with the tags on, and returned them the next day?

"You're welcome," Margot said. She was done trying to predict what would happen next. This wedding had taken on a life of its own.

THE NOTEBOOK, PAGE 9

The Service

Religion is tricky. Think of Charlemagne and Martin Luther and the Spanish Inquisition and the Gaza Strip. I don't know if you'll marry a man who is Muslim or Jewish or a happy agnostic, and I will tell you here that I don't care what religion your Intelligent, Sensitive Groom-to-Be practices, as long as he is good to you and loves you with the proper ardor.

I am going to proceed with this portion of the program as though you will be married at St. Paul's Episcopal. I fell in love with St. Paul's the first time I passed it on Fair Street, and I convinced your father to attend Evensong services one summer night in June. Who wouldn't love Evensong in a church with that glorious pipe organ and those Tiffany windows?

I have been to weddings where the officiant didn't know the couple getting married, and he was therefore forced to deliver a canned sermon. For this reason, I suggest you ask Reverend Marlowe to come to Nantucket to perform the service. Harvey is a sedentary being, and he won't like the idea of traveling to an island thirty miles offshore. But ask him anyway. Beseech him. He has never been able to resist you, his little Jenna who went on the Habitat for Humanity trip to Guatemala at the tender age of fifteen. I think he believed you would grow up to be a missionary. You single-handedly changed his mind about the Carmichael family — you (nearly) made him forget that it was Nick who set off a smoke bomb in the church basement during coffee and doughnut hour.

Reverend Marlowe is fond of his creature comforts, so be sure to mention that your father will fly him to the island and pay for a harbor view room at the White Elephant, where a bottle of fifteen-year Oban will be waiting for him.

But the Scotch and the turndown service are just window dressing. Reverend Marlowe would do anything for you.

DOUGLAS

He drove to Post Road Pizza, which was a place he used to go with Beth. He asked to sit at the two-person booth in the front window, which was where they always sat. He ordered a draft beer, a pizza with sausage and mushrooms, and a side order of onion rings with ranch dressing for dipping, which was what he and Beth always used to order. Doug took a couple of swills off his beer and walked over to the jukebox. It still took quarters. He dropped seventy-five cents into the jukebox and played "Born to Run," "The Low Spark of High Heeled Boys," and "Layla." These were all Beth's favorite songs; she had been fond of the rock anthem. If Doug asked Pauline to name one song by Eric Clapton or Bruce Springsteen, she would be stumped.

There had been a time—six, seven years ago, right after Beth died—when Doug had come into this pizza place and ordered this food and played these songs and occupied this booth as a way of wallowing in his misery. Now, he felt, he was doing it as a show of strength. This was who he really was—he *liked* this restaurant, he loved these songs, he preferred a cold draft beer to even the finest chardonnay. When the waiter brought his food, he thought with enormous satisfaction: *Not a fresh vegetable in sight!* Pauline would look upon the onion rings with disgust. When he dragged the golden circles through the ranch dressing, she would say, "Fat and more fat." Secretly, she would be dying to take one—but she wouldn't, because she was obsessed with calories. The only way she felt in control was when she was depriving herself. And that was the reason, or part of the reason, why she had become so miserable.

Doug lifted a piece of pizza, and the cheese stretched out into strings. He gloried in the fact that he was not at home eating lamb chops.

In his back pocket, his phone was buzzing away. Pauline, Pauline, Pauline. She didn't know how to text, and so she would just call and call, leaving increasingly hysterical messages until he answered. He imagined her stumbling around the house, bouncing off the furniture, drinking chardonnay, calling Rhonda—who, by this time, would be on Nantucket—saying the rosary or a Hail Mary or whatever Catholic ditty was supposed to fix the things that went wrong. Sometimes, when things were really bad with Rhonda or her ex-husband, Arthur, Pauline would tell Doug that she was going upstairs to "take a pill." Doug didn't know what pills those were; he had never asked because he didn't care, but he hoped now, anyway, that she would take a pill, just so she would stop calling.

He could practically *see* Beth in the seat across from him—wearing one of her sundresses, her hair long and loose, with a little hippie braid woven into the side. She had liked to wear the braid to let the world know that although she was married to a hotshot lawyer and worked as a hospital administrator and was the mother of four children and lived in a center-entrance colonial on the Post Road in a wealthy Connecticut suburb, she still identified with Joni Mitchell and Stevie Nicks, she was a Democrat, she read Ken Kesey, she had a social conscience.

Beth, he asked. *How did I end up here?*

Beth had left the Notebook for Jenna, but she hadn't left any instruction manual for him. And oh, how he needed one. When Beth died, he had been lost. The older three kids were all out of the house, and Jenna had stayed with him for a few weeks, but then she had to go back to college. He only had to take care of himself; however, even that had proved challenging. He had buried himself in work, he stayed at the office for ridiculously long hours, sometimes longer than the associates who were trying to make partner. He ordered food in from Bar Americain or the Indian place down the street, he kept a bottle of Johnnie Walker Black in his locked drawer, he didn't exercise, didn't see the sun, and he dreaded nothing more than the weekends when he had no choice but to return to his house in Darien and the bedroom he had shared with Beth, and the well-meaning neighbors who drove by, wondering when he was going to call the landscapers.

He had loved her so much. Because of his line of work — day in, day out, divorce, divorce, divorce — he knew that his union with Beth was a rare and precious thing, and he had treated it as such. He had revered her; she always knew how much he loved her, at least he could say that. But that assurance didn't fill the hole. It couldn't mend the ragged edges of his loneliness. Nothing helped but the oblivion that work and whiskey provided.

To this day, he wasn't sure how Pauline had gotten through to him. Probably, like everything else in life, it was a matter of timing. Pauline had come to see him eighteen months after Beth's death, when the acute pain was subsiding and his profound loneliness was deepening. He had gained thirty pounds; he was drinking way too much. When Margot paid an unannounced visit to Darien and saw the state of his refrigerator (empty), his recycling bin (filled with empty bottles), and his house (an utter and disgusting mess), she had a fit. She said, "Jesus, Daddy, you have to *do* something about this!" But Doug didn't know what that something was. He was proud that he managed to get his shirts and suits back and forth from the dry cleaners.

At first, Pauline Tonelli had been just another fifty-something woman who had been married for decades and was now on the verge of becoming single. Doug had seen hundreds of such women. He had been hit on — subtly and not so subtly — by clients for the entirety of his career. Being propositioned was an occupational hazard. Every woman Doug represented was either sick of her husband or had been summarily ditched by him (often in favor of someone younger), and most, in both cases, were ready for someone new. Many women felt Doug should be that man. After all, he was the one now taking care of things. He was going to get her a good settlement, money, custody, the yacht club membership, the second home in Beaver Creek. He was going to stand up in court on her behalf and fight for her honor.

Doug knew other divorce attorneys who took advantage of their clients in this way. His partner—John Edgar Desvesnes III—Edge, had taken advantage of at least one woman in this way: his second wife, Nathalie, whom he had fooled around with in the office before she had even *filed,* then dated, then married, then procreated with (one son, Casey, age fifteen), then divorced. There were still other attorneys who, it was rumored, were serial screwers-of-clients. But Doug had never succumbed to the temptation. Why would he? He had Beth.

Pauline had been on a mission. Doug knew that now because she had confessed to it. She had told him that she had chosen him as her divorce attorney because she knew he was recently widowed and she wanted to date him. The Tonellis and the Carmichaels both belonged to Wee Burn Country Club in Darien, although they weren't well acquainted. Doug and Arthur had been paired together once for a golf tournament. Pauline and Beth had met a couple of times side by side at the lipstick mirror in the ladies' room during a dinner dance. Doug didn't remember Pauline from the club. However, she mentioned their mutual membership at Wee Burn within the first three sentences of their meeting. She threw out names of friends of his—Whitney Gifford, Johnson McKelvey—and then she expressed her condolences for his wife ("such a warm, lovely woman") and hence established a personal connection and common ground.

She started bringing things to their meetings. First it was a hot latte, then a tin of homemade blueberry muffins, then a bottle of green chile sauce from a trip she'd taken to Santa Fe. She touched him during these meetings—she squeezed his arm or patted him on the shoulder. He could smell her perfume, he admired her legs in heels or her breasts in a sweater. She said things like "I really wanted to go to the movies this weekend, but I didn't want to go alone."

And Doug thought, *Yeah, me too.* Then he cleared his throat and discussed ways to negotiate with Arthur Tonelli.

On the day that Pauline's divorce was final, Doug did what he had never agreed to do with any client before: he went out for drinks. He had planned to say no, just as he always said no, but something about the circumstances swayed him. It was a Friday in June, the air was sweet with the promise of summer; the victory in the courtroom had been a good one. Arthur's attorney, Richard Ruby, was one of Doug's most worthy adversaries, and Doug, for the first time in his career, had beaten Richard Ruby on nearly every point. Pauline had gotten what she wanted; she had divorced well.

She said, "Shall we celebrate?"

And for the first time in nearly two years, Doug thought another person's company might be nice.

"Sure," he said.

She suggested the Monkey Bar, which was the kind of spot that Doug's partners always went to but Doug had never set foot in. He was charmed by Pauline's confidence. She knew the maître d', Thebaud, by name, and he whisked them through the after-work drinks crowd to a small round table for two, which was partially concealed by a curved banquette wall. Pauline ordered a bottle of champagne and a plate of gougères. The waiter poured their champagne, and Doug and Pauline toasted their mutual success.

Pauline smiled. Her face was glowing. Doug knew her to be fifty-four, but at that moment, she looked like a girl. She said, "I'm so glad that's over. I can finally relax."

Doug let his own deep breath go; he was still experiencing the winded euphoria particular to conquering his opponent. It was not unlike a good game of squash. Doug thrived on the competition. He wanted to win. His job was to liberate people from the stranglehold of an unsatisfactory union. Many times when a divorce was declared final, his client would spontaneously burst into tears. Some clients saw their divorces as an ending, not a beginning; they saw their divorces as a failure, not a solution. It wasn't Doug's job to put a value judgment on what was happening, only to legally facilitate it. But he had to admit that he felt much better about his profession when he was faced with a client as buoyant as Pauline.

Drinks at the Monkey Bar had been a success. Doug had headed home on the train feeling nourished by actual human interaction. He had not fallen in love with Pauline, but he had appreciated the hour drinking champagne and eating golden, cheesy gougères, admiring the wall murals by Ed Sorel, regarding the well-heeled crowd, and enjoying the presence of a convivial, attractive woman. He realized, as he and Pauline parted ways outside the restaurant on Fifty-fourth Street, that he would miss her.

And then the universe had worked its magic. A few weeks later, on the Fourth of July, Doug had played golf at Wee Burn, and then he'd stayed to swim some laps at the pool, where he met up with the Drakes, who invited him to join them on the patio for dinner. Doug had nearly declined—he no longer socialized with any of his and Beth's couple friends because he couldn't abide being a third wheel—but it was a holiday, and if Doug went home, he was looking at an evening of drinking whiskey and watching a recap of Wimbledon on TV. And so he stayed and ate dinner with the Drakes and met up with more friends whom he hadn't seen since the funeral. These friends all mentioned how wonderful he looked (he did not look wonderful) and how much they'd missed him (though what they meant, he suspected, was that they missed Beth), and Doug realized how limited his life had become.

It was at the end of the night that he'd bumped into Pauline. He was sitting at the bar finishing a nightcap when she walked through the room with Russell Stern, who was the president of Wee Burn's board of directors. Russell Stern was divorced himself; he'd endured a rather high-profile split from his wife, Charlene, who sang with the Metropolitan Opera. Doug wondered for a second if Pauline and Russell Stern were dating. He had to admit, the thought irked him.

Pauline caught sight of Doug at the bar and said to Russell, "You go ahead, Russ, I'm going to stay for a minute. Thanks for everything."

Russell eyed Doug and waved, then said to Pauline, "You sure you're okay getting home? I can wait, you know."

"I'm fine," Pauline said. "Thanks again!"

Russell Stern lingered for a moment, and Doug felt both a surge of macho triumph and a flicker of worry that, as president of the board, Russell might inflict some kind of institutional retribution—a raise in Doug's dues, perhaps, or revocation of Doug's front-row parking spot. Then Russell left, and Pauline fluttered over.

She said, "Hey, stranger."

He had ended up taking her home that night to the house in Silvermine that he had helped her wrest from Arthur Tonelli's grip. They had kissed on the front porch, then in the foyer like a couple of teenagers. Doug had been amazed by his level of arousal. He hadn't even allowed himself to think of sex in years. But with Pauline, his body asserted its natural instincts. He had thought they might do it right then and there up against the half-moon mail table, or on the stairs—but Pauline stopped him.

He said, "Are you dating Russell Stern?"

She paused for what seemed like a long time. "No," she said. "We're old friends."

"Really?" Doug said. "Because he seemed a little miffed that you came over to talk to me."

"Just friends," Pauline said.

Doug asked Pauline to dinner the following week. He picked a place on the water in South Norwalk, where neither of them had ever been before. This was important, he thought, for both of them. They had a fine time, and during the dinner conversation, it came out that Pauline and Russell had gone to high school together in New Canaan. They had dated their senior year, Russell a football star and Pauline a cheerleader. They had stayed together for two more years while Pauline went to Connecticut College and Russell went to Yale. They had talked of getting *married*.

"Wow," Doug said.

"Then I met Arthur at the Coast Guard Academy, and Russell met Charlene, and that was that. Now, we're just friends."

As "Layla" ended, Doug went to the counter to pay his bill. In retrospect, he could see that he had been dazzled by Pauline's ease out in the world alone; he had been comfortable with her, and he had been intrigued by her relationship with Russell Stern. Pauline was nothing at all like Beth, and so Doug was free from feeling like he was replacing her. Pauline was someone else entirely—a friend, a lover, someone to enjoy. Doug had never fallen in love with Pauline, he'd never had the sick, loopy, head-over-heels feeling that he'd had from start to finish with Beth. And that, he saw now, had been preferable. Pauline wasn't threatening. She wasn't going to break his heart. She was someone to do things with, someone to talk to, someone to hold at night.

The problems had started when he agreed to move into Arthur Tonelli's house with her. Why had he ever agreed to that? At the time, the real estate market had been good, and Doug had been anxious to get rid of his house. The kids were grown, Beth was dead, the house was far too big for him alone, it was filled with memories, nearly all of which were excruciatingly painful, and he didn't want to take care of the house anymore. And so it had been wonderful to have another place to go, a place he wasn't responsible for. But he had never thought of the Silvermine house as anything but the Tonelli house.

The bigger mystery was why Doug had married Pauline. More than anyone in the world, Doug knew how dangerous marriage could be. Why not just cohabitate without the messy business of binding their union? The answer was that Doug was old-fashioned. He was nearly sixty years old, he had been married to Beth for thirty-five years, he was used to being a married man. He was comfortable with a ring on his finger and a joint checking account, and one way of doing things. He was comfortable in a union. The thought of him and Pauline "living together," referring to her as "my partner" or worse still "my girlfriend," and keeping two memberships at the country club and two sets of finances (his money, her money, most of which arrived in the form of Arthur Tonelli's alimony checks) was absurd to him, bordering on distasteful.

And so he and Pauline had made it official in a very small civil ceremony followed by a lunch at Le Bernardin.

At the time, Doug could never have imagined the way he felt now. Disenchanted, trapped, eager for his freedom. He had thought that he would live out his days with Pauline in comfortable companionship. He had not predicted that his needs and desires would announce they wanted something more, something different.

When Doug got back to the house, it was only eight o'clock, and the sun was still up. He would have preferred to wait until dark when he could be sure Pauline was asleep, but he had nowhere else to go. He didn't want to drink anything more with the long, middle-of-the-night drive ahead; he didn't want to go to the club and get sucked into inane conversation about Mickelson's chances at Oak Hill. He didn't have a single person he could talk to. In a pinch, he supposed he could call Edge, but Edge lived in the city, and he had endured so much personal drama of his own that Doug would feel terrible heaping on more. Plus, Edge wasn't particularly fond of Pauline, and so if Doug told Edge he was thinking of leaving Pauline, Edge might give him too much encouragement. Furthermore, Edge had been distant lately, and increasingly vague about his own romantic life. He was dating someone, Doug was sure of that. Edge had the measured calm and patience these days that he only displayed when he was having sex on a regular basis. But Edge didn't talk about the girl, whoever she was, and the one time Doug had asked about the lucky woman who was keeping Edge on an even keel, Edge had shaken his head and turned away.

Doug had been puzzled by this reaction. He'd said, "Okay, sorry, not up for discussion, then?"

And Edge had said, "Not up for discussion."

Doug entered the Tonelli house, afraid of what he might find. But everything appeared to be normal. The kitchen was quiet and undisturbed; the lamb chops still lay in the sink. Doug got himself a glass of ice water. His alarm was due to go off at 3 a.m.; he needed to get to sleep.

He crept up the stairs, feeling spooked by the silence. He had half expected Pauline to meet him at the front door with a frying pan in her hand. He had expected to hear her crying.

The door to their bedroom was closed. Doug thought: *Go to the guest room. Sleep for a few hours, then hit the road.* But that was the coward in him speaking. Plus, his suitcase was in the bedroom.

He cracked open the door enough to see rays of the day's last sunlight striping the floor. Pauline lay on the bed, still wrapped in her towel. She was awake, staring at the ceiling, and when she heard him, she turned her head.

"Hey," she said.

"Hey," he said. He paused, waiting to see if there was going to be a scene, but she was quiet. Doug sat on the bed and took off his shoes and socks, unbuttoned his shirt and slacks, and stuffed them into the dry cleaning bag. He thought briefly of work and the shitshow Cranbrook case, which was going to trial in the morning. Then he thought about Nantucket and the house and the 150 guests, his children and grandchildren, his daughter's future in-laws, his wife's cousins. He had a wedding to host, a wedding his dead wife had planned and he had paid for. He couldn't let the turmoil of his personal life get in the way of this weekend. In the hottest moment, as he was climbing into the car, he had sent Margot a text message that said, *Pauline isn't coming to the wedding.* Now he regretted sending that message.

He climbed into bed next to Pauline, the way he had for the past five years. He had done something truly egregious, he realized, in marrying a woman he didn't love.

"Pauline," he said.

"I'm so sorry," she said. "I shouldn't have read the Notebook."

The Notebook, right. Doug had forgotten about the Notebook.

"It's okay," he said.

"You forgive me?"

"I forgive you for reading the Notebook," he said. "Your curiosity was only natural. But Pauline..."

"And I can go to the wedding with you?" she said. "I mean, obviously, I knew you were speaking in anger when you said you wanted to go alone. I knew you would never, ever go without me."

But he would. In his mind, when he pictured himself seven

hours from now in the car, he was alone, windows down, singing to the radio.

"Pauline," he said. But he was stuck. He couldn't get the words out. Every single client he represented had endured a version of this conversation. Doug had heard about hundreds of them in minute detail, he knew which words to say, but he couldn't make himself say them. Was it the courage he lacked, or the conviction?

Pauline laid her hand over his heart. She said, "You should get some sleep. We have to get up early."

THE NOTEBOOK, PAGE 17

Hors d'Oeuvres at the Reception

Nothing with spinach (stuck in teeth) and no smoked salmon (bad breath).

Trust me.

Everyone loves a raw bar. Call Spanky—he invented the raw bar on Nantucket—and he is so in demand that he should be your first call once you say yes.

Your father loves anything wrapped in phyllo. He simply cannot resist a pillowy golden triangle—biting into one, for him, is as good as Christmas. What is he going to get?

Anything but spinach!

MARGOT

Outside the Chicken Box, there was a line a million people long. Margot felt herself filling with despair. All the people in front of them were kids in their twenties, and Margot's feet were beginning to hurt in her four-inch heels, and she couldn't stop worrying that either Rhonda or Autumn was going to spill the beans about her and Edge.

What had she been thinking?

Autumn said, "This line is pretty long."

"I know," Margot said. She wondered if they should cut bait and go home. It was after eleven now, and they had a big weekend ahead of them. She had already lost Jenna and Finn; she was only sailing with half a crew. Her dress was blotched with pink stains; it looked like the dress had hives. And yet Margot still felt there was fun to be had, if they stuck it out. They would go inside and dance, goddamn it.

She said, "Let's go to the back door. I know someone."

"I'm game," Autumn said.

They stepped through the sand-and-gravel parking lot to the back of the bar, past the Dumpster and a silver tower of empty kegs. Margot marched up the back steps in her stilettos and knocked on the door.

She turned to Rhonda and Autumn. "I used to..."

The door swung open, and a dark-skinned man with wire-rimmed glasses stood looking at them.

Margot said, "Pierre? It's Margot. Margot Carmichael."

Pierre smiled. "Margot." He enveloped her in a bear hug. "I would recognize you anywhere."

He would recognize her here, half drunk, trying to avoid the line out front. This was the only place she'd seen him, approximately once each year, since 1995, when they'd dated.

They had only gone out three times, then Margot had met Drum and dropped Pierre like a hot potato. She had felt badly about it until she learned that Pierre had had a girlfriend the whole time they were dating anyway.

He said, "You're down for the weekend? Or all summer?"

"Just the weekend," Margot said. "Some of us have to work."

Pierre laughed. He said, "I work, girlfriend. Believe me, a full house every night is hard work." He ushered them into the back room and pulled three Coronas out of a cooler. He said, "You ladies have fun!"

"Thanks!" Margot said. "My sister's getting—"

But her words were drowned out by the sound of the band and the writhing mass of humanity gyrating on the dance floor.

Autumn said, "Whoo-hoo, SCORE, girl, this is awesome!"

It was awesome, in a way. Margot had just capitalized on her long-ago quasi-romance with the bar's owner to get them inside. The band was playing "Champagne Supernova." Margot swilled from her cold beer.

"Let's dance!" Autumn said.

Margot said, "I have to go to the ladies'. I'll meet you up there."

Autumn grabbed Rhonda by the hand, and the two of them threaded their way through the crowd, toward the stage.

Margot wandered to the back of the bar, where there were three pool tables and the crowd was thinner. The Chicken Box used to be the place she came to dance every night of the summer. When she was only nineteen, she sneaked in using her cousin's ID to see Dave Matthews play. She had seen Squeeze, and Hootie and the Blowfish, and an all-girl AC/DC tribute band called Hell's Belles, and a funk band called Chucklehead who frequented the same coffee shop that she did back in New York. Margot couldn't decide if being at the Box made her feel younger or older.

She stepped into the ladies' room. The girls waiting in line in front of her were all in college, with long hair and bare midriffs and tight jeans. Even when Margot was young, she hadn't dressed that way. She'd worn hippie skirts and tank tops, or surf dresses with bright, splashy flowers. Her hair had always been in a bun because invariably she would show up here straight from a beach party where she would have been thrown into the ocean by one of her drunk brothers or one of her drunk brothers' drunk friends.

Yes, she felt a hundred years old. She mourned her youth and lost innocence. She thought, *I'm a divorced mother of three with a fifty-nine-year-old lover.*

Imagine!

From her stall, Margot listened to a girl out by the sinks, talking on her phone.

"You've got to get here. The band is off the chain! Come right now..."

Margot pulled her phone out of her bag. How she hated the damn thing. But she was feeling okay, she had survived the evening, or mostly. She would just check her texts, and then, regardless of whether or not there was a text from Edge, she would go out and dance.

She steeled herself. It didn't really matter if there was a text from Edge; she would see him tomorrow night. They were going to spend the weekend in the same place, although not together. It would be stressful keeping their relationship hidden from Doug and everyone else. In their last conversation, which had taken place on Monday night at 11 p.m., Edge had said, "I'm worried you won't be able to handle it."

This had infuriated Margot. Would she not be able to handle it because she felt more for Edge than he did for her? Or because she wasn't as emotionally mature as he was at fifty-nine, after three marriages and three divorces?

She said, "I'll be fine."

And he had said, cryptically, "Well, let's hope so."

She checked her phone.

And there, glowing like a single golden nugget among smooth gray river rocks, was his name.

Edge. Text message (2)

Not one message, but two! Margot's heart suddenly had wings. She felt a surge of molten energy like a silver river that could not be mistaken for anything else: it was love. She had done the unthinkable and fallen in love with John Edgar Desvesnes III.

She wasn't sure how she dropped the phone. One minute it was in her hands, and the next minute it was gone. The strap of her purse slipped, and she had her beer wedged between her elbow and her rib cage, and to keep her beer from falling, she had loosened her grip on her phone and it dropped. She reached out to catch it, but she was too late. It landed in the toilet with a splash.

Margot reached into the toilet to snatch it out. The phone had been submerged for less than one second. Less than one second! She tried to dry the face of the phone on the front of her stained silk dress, then she swabbed at it with a wad of bunched-up toilet paper. She pushed the button repeatedly, like a person performing CPR. But she knew it was no use. The phone was dead, cold, inert. The two text messages from Edge were lost.

What had he said? Oh, what had he *said?*

Margot shoved the lifeless phone in her purse. She exited the stall, washed her hands, and examined herself in the mirror. She should have sensed a disaster like this; everything about this night had gone wrong, starting when Jenna had realized the Notebook was missing.

Now Margot understood Jenna's hysterical reaction: a person's words, a personal message to you, lost forever. What could be more devastating?

Margot stepped out of the bathroom. She was going to find Rhonda and Autumn and tell them she was going home. Her spirit had been sapped; she was all done. Some nights had good karma, and some nights were cursed. Tonight was a fine example of the latter.

Margot fought her way through the crowd by the pool tables until she found her way blocked by a man in a striped polo shirt.

"Excuse me," she said.

But the man didn't move.

Margot looked up.

The man said, "Hey, Margot."

Margot swallowed. It was Griffin Wheatley, Homecoming King.

He laughed. "You should see your face," he said. "Am I really that bad? It's my eyes, right? They still freak you out."

"I never said they freaked me out," Margot said. "Those were not my words."

"You said they unsettled you."

Unsettled. He was right; that was what she'd said. Maybe because everyone had always commented on the startling ice blue of Margot's eyes, she was more deeply attuned to other people's eyes. Griff's eyes had been hard to stop looking at once she noticed them. The intense blue on the outside and green on the inside drew her in and made her feel like the earth was spinning the wrong direction.

"I have to go," Margot said. She sounded rude, even to herself.

"I'm sorry. I dropped my phone in the toilet, and I'm not sure what to do about it."

"In the toilet?" Griff said. "Really?"

Margot nodded. She made a mental note not to tell anyone else she had dropped her phone in the toilet. It was disgusting.

"Let me see it," he said.

"No, there's nothing you can do."

"Please," he said, holding out his hands. "Let me see it."

Margot dug the phone out of her purse. It was nice that he'd offered to help. That was one of the things her life was missing: someone to help. In her marriage to Drum Sr., she had been the one who had taken care of everything. And Edge was too busy putting out fires with his three ex-wives and four children; he didn't have any spare time or energy to problem-solve for Margot, and for this very reason, Margot didn't ask him.

Griff looked at the phone, shook it, pressed all the buttons in various combinations. "It's dead," he said.

"I know," Margot said. It physically hurt to hear someone else say it. "I drowned it."

"Well, can I buy you a drink?" Griff asked. "We can toast the passing of the phone."

"No, thank you," Margot said. "I'm leaving."

"Oh, come on?" Griff said. "Just one drink? My buddies left, and the other women in this bar are far too young for me."

Great, Margot thought. He was offering to buy her a drink because she was old.

Homecoming King. Just standing this close to him made her feel guilty. If he knew what she'd done to him and why she'd done it, he would never have offered to buy her a drink. Or he would have bought her a drink and thrown it in her face. That was what she deserved.

"I'm sorry, Griff," Margot said, and she was sorry. *Sorrysorrysorry.* She took her phone back and crammed it into her purse. Even though it was useless, she liked having it tucked safely away.

"Come on," he said. "I don't want you to feel awkward about the other stuff... signing me off..."

Margot raised her palm. She couldn't bear to stay another second.

"Not tonight," Margot said. *Not any night.* She erupted in crazy-hysterical laughter. She was losing her mind. "I'm really sorry, Griff. I have to go."

"I'd ask for your number," he said, "but something tells me you wouldn't answer when I called."

She cackled some more, then clamped her mouth shut. She couldn't encourage him.

"Just take my card," he said. "And when you get a new phone, you can call me, how about that? There's no reason why we can't be friends."

Margot stared at his card: Griffin Wheatley, V.P. Marketing, Blankstar. *Friends?* No, she couldn't take it, but he was handing it to her, and she couldn't *not* take it. She slipped it into her purse.

"I'm serious," Griff said. "Call me. In fact, why don't you call me tonight when you get home?"

"Tonight when I get *home?*" she said.

"From your land line," he said. "I've heard homes on Nantucket are so quaint that they still have such things."

"My land line?" she said. "What for?"

He shrugged. "I don't know. The one thing I miss about being married is having someone to talk to late at night. Someone to tell all the stupid stuff."

"Oh," Margot said.

He said, "I'm sure I sound like an idiot."

"No," Margot said. "You don't. You sound perfectly sane, actually." She wanted to say that she agreed with him—more times than she could count, she had lain alone in bed, wishing that Edge was the kind of boyfriend she could call up to talk to about the pointless minutiae of her day. But he wasn't that kind of boyfriend; he wasn't a boyfriend at all. However, confessing this to Griff would just be another double fault. She looked up at him. He was gazing at her with earnest blue-and-green Homecoming King goodness—and all Margot could think was that the final injustice of her night was that Griff was Griff and not someone else. Anybody else.

She said, "I'm not going to call you, Griff. I can't, you know I can't."

He said, "You signed me off. Why not start over?"

She smiled sadly, then weaved through the bar traffic for the door.

The bouncer said, "Have a good night!"

Ha! Margot thought. It was far too late for that.

When Margot got home, the house was dark and quiet. Jenna must have sent Emma Wilton home. Margot checked on her children. The boys were two lumps in the attic bunk beds, and then Margot spied a third lump in another of the beds, an adult-sized lump, snoring loudly. She pulled back the covers to find the shaggy golden head of her brother Nick.

Nick!

Nick, in general, was completely useless except when it came to procuring tickets to baseball games. He was the in-house counsel for the Washington Nationals, he was a confirmed bachelor, he partied his ass off and ran through women the way Margot ran through sandwich bread. He had never offered a single emotional insight that Margot could recall, and yet at this instant she was tempted to wake him up and spill her guts. He might have some useful advice; it was possible she wasn't giving him enough credit.

But no. Nick wasn't the answer.

Downstairs, in her own room, she checked on Ellie, who was spread-eagled in the bed meant for them both. She was still in her clothes (since she had packed no pajamas) and had a smear of chocolate around her mouth from the Fudgsicles Margot had bought. She probably hadn't brushed her teeth. On the dresser was a pile of twigs, stones, acorns, and three blue hardy geraniums, chopped off at the head. These were the flowers that Beth Carmichael had worried about the tent guys trampling. They had survived the tent guys, but not Ellie the hoarder, who had felt the need to add the flowers to her collection of backyard detritus.

Margot swept the stones and sticks and flowers into her palm, hoping that by morning Ellie would have forgotten about them and would not wake up wailing over her missing treasure. Margot checked Jenna's room—lights out—and then headed downstairs. She tossed the handful of collected nature out the back screen door, poured herself a glass of water, and picked up the house phone.

She dialed the number; she had called it so often during the past few months that she had it memorized. It was late, she knew, but this couldn't wait.

He picked up on the second ring. Of course he did.

"This is Roger."

"Roger, Margot Carmichael," she said. "The branch has to come down."

"Yes," he said. "I know it does. I've been waiting for you to call."

"You have?" Margot said.

"You're doing the right thing," Roger said. "There is no other way."

"No other way," Margot repeated. "You're sure?"

"I'll see you bright and early," Roger said.

OUTTAKES

Jim Graham (father of the groom): I am a man who has lived and learned. I married the right woman, but I didn't know it, I married the wrong woman and I did know it, I married the right woman a second time. My advice to all four of my sons has been "Look before you leap." This may be a cliché, but as with most clichés, it contains a hard kernel of truth. I like to think that advice was what kept Stuart from making a mistake several years ago. But he's got the right idea now. Jenna is a beautiful girl and she brings out his best self. Really, what more can you ask?

H.W. (brother of the groom, groomsman): Open bar all weekend long.

Ann Graham (mother of the groom): I was born and raised in Alexandria, Virginia, I attended Duke University, I have served in the North Carolina General Assembly for twenty-four years. When Jim and I take vacations, we go to Savannah or the Outer Banks or Destin. Once to London, once on a cruise in the Greek islands. But I can't tell you the last time I crossed the Mason-Dixon Line. It might have been New York City, 2001, when Jim and I went to the funeral of one of his fraternity brothers who worked for Cantor Fitzgerald. It will be nice to head north this time for a happier occasion.

Jethro Arthur (boyfriend of the best man): Unlike Martha's

Vineyard, Nantucket is no place for a black man. I told this to Ryan and his response was that Frederick Douglass spoke on the steps of the Nantucket Atheneum in 1841. Frederick Douglass? I said. That's what you've got? Yes, he said. And you know who else spent time on Nantucket? Who? I said. Pip and Daggoo, he said. Pip and Daggoo? I said. You mean the characters from *Moby-Dick*? Yes! he said, all proud and excited, because literary references are usually my territory. I said, Pip and Daggoo are fictional black men, Ryan. They don't count.

FRIDAY

ANN

There were only a few ills in life that a five-star hotel on a bright, sunny day couldn't fix. This was what Ann Graham told herself at ten o'clock on Friday morning when she and Jim arrived at the White Elephant resort on Nantucket Island. Ann had personally seen to it that they would be able to check in right away; nothing would have driven her battier than having to sit around — possibly for hours — waiting for their room to be ready. And so, less than thirty minutes after arriving on Nantucket, Ann was standing on the balcony of their suite, overlooking the harbor, which was as picturesque as she had imagined. The sailboats, the ropes, the bobbing red and white buoys, the two blond teenagers in a rowboat with fishing poles, the lighthouse on the point. This was the real thing. This was East-Coast-Yankee-blue-blood-privilege-and-elitism at its very finest.

Jim came up behind her and placed his hands on her shoulders. "Should we order up champagne and get naked?"

Ann willed herself not to shrug him off. He was being funny; he wanted her to relax. He did not want her to become the woman she was dangerously close to becoming: a woman who alternately expressed bitterness and hysteria because her son was getting married in a place where she exerted no influence.

The groom's side of the family, Ann had learned over the past thirteen months, were second-class citizens when it came to the planning and execution of the wedding ritual in America. Maybe it was different in some far-flung tribe in Papua New Guinea or Zambia, and if so, Ann would gladly move there. She was the mother of three sons. She would have to endure this humbling social position at least twice—with Stuart now, and later with H.W. She had no idea what would happen with Ryan.

She and Jim weren't even throwing the rehearsal dinner, which it was customary, in the wedding ritual in America, for the groom's parents to do. Jenna had insisted on holding the rehearsal dinner at the Nantucket Yacht Club—apparently this was a suggestion drawn straight from the blueprints her deceased mother had left behind. The Carmichaels had been members of the yacht club since forever; Ann and Jim couldn't have paid if they'd wanted to. They had, initially, offered to do just that, however— Doug Carmichael could let the Grahams know the cost of the yacht club party, and Jim would write Doug a check to cover it. Doug had graciously refused the offer, and Ann was glad, not because of the expense—she and Jim could easily have afforded it—but because if Ann was going to host a party, she wanted to put her stamp on it. She wanted to pick the location and the flowers and the menu. If the rehearsal dinner had to be held at the Carmichaels' club, she agreed that the Carmichaels should pay. After Ann's insistence that she and Jim do *something,* Jenna had suggested that the Grahams host the Sunday brunch. This felt like a consolation prize to Ann. The Sunday brunch? Half the guests would skip the damn thing because of early departing flights or boats, and the other half would show up exhausted and hung over. Ann nearly rejected the Sunday brunch idea, but then she realized that doing so would make her seem like a spoiled child who hadn't gotten her way, rather than the six-term North Carolina state senator, devout Catholic, and mother of three that she was. So she said yes and made up her mind that the Sunday brunch was going to be the best part of the whole weekend. Ann had arranged for the White Elephant to set up a tent on the lawn facing the water, and under this tent would be a little piece of the Tar Heel State. The menu would include barbecue flown in from Bullock's in Durham, as well as two kinds of grits, hush puppies, collard greens, coleslaw, buttermilk biscuits, and pecan pie. Ann had asked the head bartender at the White Elephant, a guy named Beau who actually hailed from Charleston and had worked at Husk, to make ten gallons of sweet tea and order Kentucky bourbon for juleps and whiskey sours. Ann had hired a Dixieland band, who would wear straw boaters and candy-striped vests. They would show Stuart's new family some genteel southern hospitality.

Still, Ann felt like the runner-up in this particular beauty pageant, and it brought out the worst in her—much the way a nasty campaign did. During her third term, when the scandal with Jim was breaking at home, Ann had battled against the reprehensible Donald Morganblue. She had been sure she was going to lose. The race was close, Morganblue had gone after Ann about a certain failed development project near Northgate Park that had cost Durham County millions of dollars and nearly five hundred promised jobs, and Ann had spent a string of months convinced that both her personal life and her professional life were going to go up in flames. She had, very nearly, become addicted to Quaaludes. The pills were the only way she had made it through that period in her life—the victory by the narrowest margin in the state history of the Carolinas (requiring two recounts) and her divorce from Jim. Ann remembered how the pills had made her feel like a dragonfly skimming over the surface of these troubles. She remembered more than one occasion when she had held the pill bottle in her sweating palm and visualized an easy descent into sweet eternity.

She told herself now that she had never seriously considered suicide back then. Stuart had been ten years old, the twins barely six, Jim had moved to the loft in Brightleaf Square; the boys needed Ann to pack their lunches and transport them to the Little League fields. At night that year, Ann had read the boys *Charlie and the Chocolate Factory*. Their addiction to that book (at the kids' behest, Ann had ended up reading it three times in a row) was the only outward reaction they had to their father's departure. Or possibly they were addicted to the quiet minutes with her, curled up on the sofa, her voice always evenly modulated despite her inner turmoil.

There could be no killing herself. Plus, Ann was Catholic, and suicide was a sin for which there was no repenting.

Every once in a while, however, she still yearned for a Quaalude.

Now, for instance. She could use one right now.

She let Jim kiss the side of her neck, a move that always preceded sex. What if they did just as he suggested? What if they ordered up champagne, and strawberries and cream? What if they slipped on the white waffled robes and tore open the scrumptious bed and laid across the ten-thousand-count sheets and enjoyed each other's bodies? Even now, fifteen years after their reconciliation, Jim's sexual attention felt precious, like something that could be, and had been, stolen away from her. What if they drank champagne—the more expensive, the better—then ordered another bottle? What if they found themselves giddily drunk by noon, then fell into a languorous sleep with the balcony doors open, sunlight streaming over them in bed? What if they treated this not like their eldest son's wedding weekend but like a romantic getaway?

"Let's do it," Ann said, pivoting to kiss her husband full on the lips. "Call for the champagne."

"Really?" he said, his eyebrows lifting. He was fifty-six years old, a senior vice president at GlaxoSmithKline but just under the surface was the boy Ann had first married—president of Beta at Duke, the ultimate bad boy, for whom fun would trump responsibility whenever possible.

She was surprising him. He thought she would be in anal-Ann mode, spinning with the hundred things she thought she had to do, the thousand thoughts whirling through her mind. But instead she unbuttoned her crisp white blouse, bought at Belk's for her arrival on Nantucket. She slid off her navy-and-white gingham Tory Burch capri pants. In just her bra and panties, Ann threw herself across the bed.

"Wow!" Jim said.

"Call!" Ann said.

She was surprising herself.

It was only later, after they had enjoyed the kind of sex particular to really good hotel rooms—Jim had actually clamped his hand over her mouth to stifle her cries—that Ann let herself admit the real reason for her anxiety. She didn't care about the wedding hierarchy or her position in it; she was too big and too busy a woman to worry about such things. She was only concerned about how she appeared, about how she and Jim appeared as a couple, because Helen was coming.

Helen Oppenheimer—who had, for a period of twenty-nine months, been Jim's wife.

Ann's best friend, Olivia Lewis, had nearly inhaled her

cell phone when Ann informed her that Helen was on the invite list.

"But *why?*" Olivia said. "Why why *why?* Why did you let Jim talk you into it? You're a strong woman, Ann. Why didn't you stand your ground?"

"Jim was dead set against it," Ann said. "It was my idea."

"What?" Olivia said.

"Stuart asked Chance to be a groomsman," Ann said.

"So?" Olivia said. "That does *not* require you to invite Helen to the wedding."

Ann didn't know how to explain it to Olivia, or to Jim or to anyone. When she was sitting on her sunporch the previous summer, composing a list of people to invite to the wedding, she had simply added the name Helen Oppenheimer, and it had felt... right. It had felt *Christian*—but if she told Olivia or Jim this, they would cry bullshit. Jim had cried bullshit anyway. When he saw Helen's name, he said, "No way. No fucking way."

"But Chance is in the wedding party," Ann said.

"I don't care," Jim said. "Doesn't matter."

"She won't come anyway," Ann said. "We can look good for inviting her, we can look like the bigger people, and she'll decline."

Jim had stared at Ann for a second. "I'm not quite sure what you're trying to do here."

What *was* Ann trying to do here? When Ann was very young, her mother had explained the reason behind the spelling of her name: Ann was the saint; Anne with an "e" was the queen. Ann had felt the burden of her nomenclature since then. She yearned to be queenly rather than saintly. After all, no one liked a saint. Saints weren't fun at parties; saints weren't good in bed. Saints were altar girls, as Ann had been. Saints devoted themselves to a life of service. Ann had spent her entire adult life in service— first to Jim and Stuart and the twins, then to the population of

Durham, North Carolina. Her acts of self-sacrifice bugged Jim and Olivia and her sons to no end, and yet she couldn't help herself. Her spirit yearned to do the selfless thing, the right thing, the worthy, admirable thing.

Was inviting Helen Oppenheimer to the wedding just another example of Ann flaunting her innate goodness?

She didn't think so. Deep down, it felt like the opposite. Deep down, Ann despised Helen Oppenheimer, hated her with a dense, black force. Helen Oppenheimer had seduced Jim right out of his marriage to Ann, Helen had allowed herself to get pregnant, she had forced Jim's hand. Jim had divorced Ann and married Helen Oppenheimer. Helen Oppenheimer had massacred Ann's family as surely as if she'd entered the living room with an AK-47 and gunned them all down. She had turned the Graham family—once a paragon of the community—into a mockery of a family.

And so admit it: the reason why Ann had written Helen Oppenheimer's name on that list was because she wanted to prove something. Jim had come back to Ann a scant three years later. Jim had married Ann a second time, and this time they were far, far happier. They treated their marriage with care; they were vigilant about guarding its sanctity. Ann wanted Helen to see her renewed, nearly perfect union with Jim firsthand. Ann wanted to force Helen to gaze upon them operating in unison on this happy occasion, the marriage of their eldest son.

Ann wanted to gloat.

Jim had relented. He was powerless to overturn any of Ann's decisions once she made up her mind. He had said, "She'd *better* decline. The last person I want to see on Nantucket on July twentieth is Helen Oppenheimer."

Ann had thought, *Well, then, you shouldn't have climbed into bed with her, buster.*

*   *   *

Even more shocking than issuing the invitation was Helen Oppenheimer accepting it. For all of Ann's big ideas about showing off to Helen, she had never believed for one second that Helen would actually *come.* But she had responded yes. She was coming to Nantucket for the weekend, all the way from Chattanooga, Tennessee, where she now lived with a man ten years younger than herself. But she was coming alone.

"Shit!" Jim had shouted.

He'd said, "There's still time to renege."

"We can't renege," Ann had said, although she was tempted. God, just the thought of Helen Oppenheimer among them all weekend long, and *alone,* was enough to make Ann physically ill. And she had no one to blame but herself.

"I'll do it," Jim said. "I'll call and tell her you were temporarily insane."

"No," Ann said. "If she's comfortable with it, then I'm comfortable with it."

Jim had shaken his head and paced the room; she could see him doing battle in his mind. He had created this insufferable situation, and in the thousands of times the topic had arisen over the past fifteen years, he had never once denied the blame.

Finally, he'd taken Ann in his arms and said, "You're amazing, you know that?"

Now here it was: showtime. Neither Ann nor Jim had been in contact with Helen about her arrangements, but she had RSVP'd yes for the rehearsal dinner, the wedding, and the brunch. They would see her tonight.

Ann wished like hell that Helen could see her and Jim right now: propped up against the pillows of the bed, covered by just a white sheet, sipping champagne at eleven o'clock in the morning.

"To Stuart," Ann said.

"To Stuart and Jenna," Jim said, and they clinked glasses.

Ann was experiencing typical mixed feelings about watching her oldest son marry. She had known from the beginning that Stuart would be the first, not only because he was the oldest but because he had always seemed like the marrying kind, sweet and devoted. He had had a girlfriend in high school — darling Trisha Hamborsky — and then in college and a few years after, a girlfriend named Crissy Pine, whom the family now referred to (like Voldemort) as "She Who Shall Not Be Named." Stuart had very nearly married Crissy. Ann still rued the loss of her grandmother's Tiffany-cut 2.5-carat diamond ring, although over the years Ann had reminded herself that it was only a ring, a physical object, which was a small price to pay for Stuart's freedom and future happiness. He and Jenna were a far superior match. Jenna was a wonderful young lady, if perhaps a little liberal leaning with her devotion to Amnesty International and her extreme eco-consciousness. (She had once scolded Ann for throwing away her cardboard coffee cup from Starbucks.) Jenna would never have worn Grand-mère's ring anyway, Stuart had said. She would have called it a blood diamond.

Blood diamond? Ann had thought. Good grief.

"We're losing our little boy," Ann said to Jim.

"Now, now," Jim said. He took Ann's champagne flute from her hand and set it on the night table next to his own. Then he came after Ann again.

She pretended to protest, but she couldn't resist him. She didn't want to think about Helen Oppenheimer, or She Who Shall Not Be Named. Ann wasn't going to let either of them take anything away from her ever again. Ann was going to shine.

THE NOTEBOOK, PAGE 14

Table Linens

There are ten antique tablecloths in the attic of the Nantucket house in a box marked "Antique Linens." These are the tablecloths that Grammie used for her wedding to Pop-Pop in 1943. They are ivory with exquisite, delicate twists of ivy along the border. Your great-grandfather J. D. Bond brought them home from Ireland as a gift for Grammie. They are handmade, classic, and elegant. They are family heirlooms. I have seen them, touched them, ogled over them, dreamt of them. Inanimate objects can't express wishes, but I know in my heart that if those linens could talk, they would ask to be aired out and used again.

MARGOT

The mood in the backyard was funereal. At quarter to nine, Margot stood in her ersatz pajamas—an old blue oxford shirt of Drum Sr.'s and a pair of cutoff gray sweatpants—holding a cup of coffee that Rhonda had thoughtfully made at seven o'clock before she left for her twelve-mile run. Margot was in her bare feet, they were all in their bare feet—Margot, Jenna, the three kids, and her brother Nick. They were gathered in a semicircle a safe distance away from where the men were clipping the ropes of the swing. Ellie was crying.

The tent guys were young, handsome El Salvadorans. The one

named Hector clipped the ropes, and the wooden plank of the swing crashed to the ground. Margot felt her heart drop.

Jenna hid her face in her hands. "Oh, God," she said. "I can barely stand to watch. This is all my fault."

Nick was wearing nothing but a pair of red Hawaiian-print swim trunks. His hair was overgrown and sunbleached, and his torso was tanned golden brown. He did have a *job,* right? He looked like he'd just spent two months in California surfing with Drum Sr. He turned to Margot.

"I don't know about this, Marge," he said. "Marge" was his nickname for her, bestowed in 1989 with the first season of *The Simpsons,* and Margot detested it, which only made Nick's enjoyment of it more profound. "This is Alfie we're talking about. This tree should probably be listed in the historic registry. It's two hundred years old."

"I know," Margot snapped. She was impatient with Nick and everyone else who was lagging behind; she had traveled this emotional highway yesterday. "It's just one branch! There's no other way, believe me."

Ellie sobbed into Margot's leg. Margot watched Nick pick the swing up off the ground and loop the rope around his arm. The plank of the swing was worn smooth. Margot was forty years old, and the swing had been there as long as she could remember. Who had put it up? She thought it might have been Pop-Pop; she would have to ask her father. *Forty percent chance of showers,* she thought. There was no doubt in Margot's mind that now, because the branch was coming down, there wouldn't be a cloud in the sky all day tomorrow.

Hector and his associates indicated that they should all back up even farther. He set up a stepladder, and one of the other guys brought out the chain saw.

"I can't watch," Jenna said.

It did seem morbid, all of them standing around, gawking like witnesses at an execution. Margot reminded herself that it could be worse. Alfie might have been struck by lightning. As it was, he would still stand guard over their property, still shade them; birds would still sing from their unseen perches in his upper branches. They were only taking off one limb—and Roger was right, that branch was hanging awfully low. It might have snapped on its own with the next nor'easter.

There was a honking, and Margot turned to see a silver mini-van pull into the driveway.

"It's Kevin!" Jenna said. "Oh, thank God!"

Margot made a face. Their whole lives it had always been "Thank God for Kevin." Kevin was eleven months younger than Margot—an oops baby, Margot was certain, although neither of her parents had ever admitted to it—but because Kevin was a boy, he had often been treated as the oldest. And to boot, he had been born with the unflappable calm and unquestioned author-ity of an elder statesman. He had been class president all through high school, then had attended Penn, where he'd been the head of the Student Society of Engineers. While in college, he had performed CPR on a man who collapsed on the Thirtieth Street subway platform, and he'd saved the man's life. Kevin had been awarded a medal by the mayor of Philadelphia, Ed Rendell. Kevin Carmichael was, literally, a lifesaver.

He unfolded himself from the minivan—he had no shame about driving the thing, despite ruthless teasing from both Mar-got and Nick—and stood, all six feet six of him, in the sun, grin-ning at them.

"We're here!" he said. "The party can start!"

Beanie materialized at his side, all five foot two of her, and slid her arm around Kevin's middle so that the two of them could be frozen in everyone's mind for a second, posed like a photograph captioned "Happily Married Couple," before the three boys busted out of the back of the car and all hell broke loose.

Kevin strode forward, shielding his eyes from the sun as he gazed at the tree and the stepladder and Hector with the chain saw. "What's going on here?" he asked.

God, his tone drove Margot *insane*. Was it normal, she wondered, to have your siblings grate on you like this? As much as she was dreading the amputation of Alfie's branch, she now wished it had already happened, just so she didn't have to stand by and watch Kevin weigh in on it. Kevin was both an architect and a mechanical engineer; he had founded a company that fixed structural problems in large buildings, important buildings— like the Coit Tower in San Francisco. Like the White House.

"They have to cut that branch," Margot said. "Otherwise the tent can't go up."

Kevin eyed the branch, then the upper branches of the tree, then the yard as a whole. "Really?" he said.

"Really," Margot said.

At that moment Roger appeared, holding his clipboard; Margot hadn't heard his truck, so he must have parked on the street. Plus, that was Roger's way: he appeared, like a genie, when you most needed him. He could explain to Kevin about the branch.

Margot turned her attention to Beanie and gave her sister-in-law a hug. Beanie had looked exactly the same since she was fourteen years old, when she and her family moved to Darien from the horse country of Virginia. Her brown hair was in a messy bun, her face was an explosion of freckles, and she wore horn-rimmed glasses. She never aged, never changed; her clothes were straight out of the 1983 L.L. Bean catalog—today, a white polo shirt with the collar flipped up, a madras A-line skirt, and a pair of well-worn boat shoes.

Beanie had probably worn this very same outfit on her first

date with Kevin in the ninth grade. He had taken her to see *Dead Poets Society.*

Beanie said, "You look great, Margot."

Beanie was a true golden good person. It was her MO to start every conversation with a compliment. Margot adored this about Beanie, even as she knew the compliment to be a lie. She did *not* look great.

"I look like a dirt sandwich," Margot said.

"Last night was fun?" Beanie said.

Margot raised her eyebrows. "Fun, fun!" she said. She thought briefly of her sunken phone, Edge's lost texts, and the reappearance of Griff. Oh, man. It was quite a story, but Margot couldn't confide it to anybody, not even Beanie.

The Carmichael boys—Brandon, Brian, and Brock—were racing around the yard, chasing and tackling Drum Jr. and Carson. Ellie was perched above the fray on her uncle Nick's shoulders. Nick came over to kiss Beanie, and Margot turned her attention to Roger and Kevin, who were deep in conversation. Then Kevin started speaking to Hector in fluent Spanish—what a show-off!—and pointing up at the tree branches.

Roger came over to Margot with an actual smile on his face, and Margot shivered, despite the warm sun. She had never seen Roger smile before.

"Your brother has an idea," Roger said.

Margot nodded, pressing her lips together. *Of course he does,* she thought.

"He thinks we can lift the branch with a series of ropes that we would tie to the upper branches," Roger said. "He thinks we can lift it enough to clear the height of the tent."

"How is he planning on reaching the upper branches?" Margot asked. The upper branches were high, a lot higher than Kevin standing on top of the ladder.

"I have a friend with a cherry picker," Roger said.

Of course you do, Margot thought.

"I'm going to call him right now," Roger said. "See if he can come over."

"Will a cherry picker *fit* through here?" Margot asked. Alfie dominated the eastern half of the backyard. Beyond Alfie was Beth Carmichael's perennial bed and the white fence that separated them from the Finleys' next door. Any kind of big truck would mow right over the flower bed. "My mother was very clear that no one was to trample her blue hardy geraniums."

But Roger was no longer listening. He was on his phone.

"Isn't it *great?*" Jenna said. "Kevin found a way to fix it! We don't have to cut Alfie's branch."

"Maybe," Margot said. She wondered why she didn't feel happier about this breakthrough news. Probably because it had been Kevin who came up with the answer. Probably because she now looked like a knee-jerk tree-limb amputator who would have lopped off a piece of Carmichael family history if Kevin hadn't arrived in time to save the day.

Margot smiled. "Thank God for Kevin," she said.

She knew she sounded like sour grapes, and Jenna kindly ignored her.

Margot heard the back screen door slam, and she turned, expecting to see Finn or Autumn emerging—but the person who came through the door was her father. And behind her father, Pauline.

"Daddy!" Margot said.

Doug Carmichael was dressed in green golf pants and a pale pink polo shirt and the belt that Beth had needlepointed for him over the course of an entire summer at Cisco Beach. The outfit said "professional man ready for a day of good lies and fast greens," but his face said something else.

For the first time in her life, Margot thought, her father looked old. He was a tall, lean man, bald except for a tonsure of silver hair, but today his shoulders were sloping forward, and his hair looked nearly white. His face held the same hangdog expression that he'd worn for the two years after Beth died, and it broke Margot's heart to see it now.

As he approached, Margot held her arms out for a hug, and they embraced, and Margot squeezed extra hard. He still felt solid and strong, thank God.

"Hi, sweetie," he said.

"You made it," Margot said. "Is everything okay?"

He didn't answer. He couldn't, he had to move on to Beanie and Nick—and Jenna, whom he picked clear off the ground. Margot felt a crotchety old jealousy. How many times had she wished that she was the little sister instead of the big sister, the youngest instead of the oldest? She never got coddled; she never got *picked up.* Jenna was the Carmichaels' answer to Franny Glass, Amy March, Tracy Partridge. She was the doll and the princess. Margot used to comfort herself with the knowledge that she had been their mother's confidante, her right hand. In the weeks before Beth died, before things got really bad and hospice and morphine were involved, she had said to Margot, "You'll have to take care of things, honey. This family will need to lean on you."

Margot had promised she would take care of things. And she had, hadn't she?

"Hello, Margot."

Margot snapped out of her self-indulgent bubble to see Pauline standing before her. Usually, Pauline was breezy and officious, as though Margot were a woman at a cocktail party whom Pauline knew she had to greet and give five minutes of small talk before moving on to mingle. And Margot liked things that way.

She had never discussed anything personal with Pauline. On the occasion of Doug and Pauline's wedding at City Hall in Manhattan, Margot had kissed Pauline on the cheek and said congratulations. She had meant to say, "Welcome to the family," but she couldn't form the sentence. She always referred to Pauline as "my father's wife," never "my stepmother."

Something about Pauline's demeanor and her tone of voice was different now. It was apologetic, nearly obsequious.

Pauline isn't coming to the wedding.

Margot realized that Doug and Pauline must have had a fight, a fight big enough to warrant the sending of that text. She had never once considered that her father and Pauline were a *couple,* who might have *problems.* At their age, Margot assumed, the drama would be all dried up. She didn't like thinking about their intimate life—sexual or emotional.

"Hi, Pauline," Margot said. She gave Pauline a hug, smelled her familiar perfume, wondered if Doug had wanted Pauline to stay home, or if Pauline had been the one who hadn't wanted to come. She wondered what the issue had been.

"What's going on here?" Doug asked.

At that second, Margot felt the weight of the late night and the drinks. The weekend had only just begun, and she was already exhausted. She didn't want to explain about the tree to anyone else, she would let Kevin explain it; she needed to go upstairs and lie down, just fifteen minutes and she would be fine.

But once she headed upstairs to the relative peace of her bedroom, she felt ill at ease. It was a well-known fact that once you left the room—or in this case the yard—the rest of the family would start talking about you. Margot lay across her bed, feeling as though her head was filled with pea gravel. She could hear the voices and laughter coming from the yard, and she thought, really, this was the best part of any wedding, not the ceremony or the cake or the dancing but the downtime when they were all together without the lights shining on them. Her mother, if she had been alive, would be snapping pictures, asking the kids to pose, deadheading flowers, pulling weeds. Her mother would have had a platter of bacon and eggs ready, a pitcher of juice, and boxes of doughnuts from the Nantucket Bake Shop.

The problem, Margot realized, with having had a wonderful mother was that it was impossible to live up to the standards she had set.

Margot couldn't sleep. She knew they were all down in the yard, calling her a tree killer.

She stood up, and seeing that the door to Jenna's bedroom was open and the room was empty, she walked through and stepped out onto the deck. From this vantage point, she could see everything. Nick had his arms wrapped around both Finn and Autumn. Okay, that was dangerous: Autumn and Nick had had a not-so-secret fling during the weekend of Jenna's college graduation eight years earlier. (They had nearly broken the bed at the Williamsburg Inn; everyone had heard them, including Margot and Drum Sr., and in the morning over the breakfast buffet, Drum Sr. had given Nick a high five.)

Next Margot's attention was drawn to Pauline and Jenna, who were standing apart from everyone, alone. They seemed to be engaged in the kind of deep conversation that Margot studiously avoided having with Pauline. Pauline was doing most of the talking, and Margot wondered what she was saying. Then Pauline pulled the Notebook out of her enormous handbag and handed it to Jenna, and Jenna and Pauline hugged, and Margot thought, *Ohhhhhh. Pauline had the Notebook.* And Margot thought, *Ohhhhhhhhhh. Oh, boy.* Had Pauline taken the Notebook from the dinner on Wednesday night? Had she *absconded* with it? Maybe that was what the fight with Doug was about. He had banned her from the wedding. Or she had said she didn't want to come.

Margot was flushed with high emotion. She wondered if Pauline had read the Notebook. She bristled at the thought. Pauline had only met their mother once or twice, a thousand years earlier. The Notebook was none of Pauline's business.

Jenna accepted the Notebook graciously, then hugged it to her chest. She didn't seem the least bit ruffled by the exchange. She was their mother reincarnated. She had probably thanked Pauline for returning it, instead of asking why she had taken it in the first place, which was what Margot would have done.

At that moment, heads swiveled, and Margot knew someone had just entered the yard, but she couldn't tell who. It was Rhonda, back from her half marathon. Pauline ran toward her daughter, and in the middle of the Carmichael chaos, the two Tonellis embraced, and Pauline's shoulders heaved. She was sobbing. Doug took no notice of this, nor did Nick or Kevin or Beanie or any of the kids—they were either oblivious, or too consumed with Alfie's branch, or willfully ignoring the teary scene. Rhonda wisely shepherded Pauline inside. A moment later, Margot could hear them in the kitchen. She couldn't hear what they were saying, only the sounds of their voices. If Margot had moved to the staircase, she would have been able to hear every word of their conversation, and while it was tempting to eavesdrop, Margot refrained. When it came to weddings, all people were not created equally. There were insiders, and there were outsiders. There were people like Finn, who had been Jenna's friend since diapers, and then there was a couple attending whom Stuart and Jenna had just met in their premarital counseling. Jenna admitted they barely knew the couple, but she felt like they would be friends going forward, and she wanted to include them. Edge was coming to the wedding, but there were law school friends of Doug's coming who had never even met Jenna. Pauline and Rhonda must have felt like outsiders, too, although Pauline was Doug's wife and Rhonda was a bridesmaid. Or maybe they didn't feel like outsiders, but neither did they feel like insiders. They were family...but not family. It was no secret that Pauline didn't like the Nantucket house; she only let Doug visit the island once or twice a summer. Pauline found the house dusty and moldy and decrepit; she didn't appreciate its charm, she hadn't bothered to learn its nooks and crannies, she hadn't experienced it as a summer haven for decades the way the rest of the Carmichaels had. Maybe she sensed that although the house was the ancestral abode of Doug's family, it had really been Beth's home. Beth had planted the perennial bed and cultivated the climbing roses; Beth had chosen the artwork and sewn the slipcovers. Pauline wouldn't give two hoots about Alfie's branch or the swing, but at the same time, she yearned for a connection. She wanted to *be* a Carmichael. She must have thought the Notebook would provide a secret clue, the elusive key to understanding. *How do I fit in here? How do I become one of them?* What Margot knew and Pauline must have figured out was that the membership was closed; Pauline had arrived too late in the game. The Carmichaels were incapable of forming any meaningful new memories because the old memories—the ones with Beth in them—were too precious to replace.

This weekend would be difficult for Pauline. Really difficult. Margot decided to forgive her for taking the Notebook.

Margot, Jenna, Finn, Autumn, and Rhonda were due at the RJ Miller Salon at ten o'clock for manicures, pedicures, and facials— but it was such a splendid day that Margot decided to cancel her appointment. She was going to hang out at the house for a while and then take her children to Fat Ladies Beach. Margot thought

Jenna might be bummed about this — really, Margot was proving to be the lamest maid of honor in the history of weddings — but Jenna just grinned wickedly and said, "Great idea. I'm canceling, too. I'm going to go kayaking with Stuart in Monomoy Creeks."

"Wait," Margot said. "*You* can't cancel. You're the bride."

"So?" Jenna said.

"Don't you want your nails done?" Margot said. "Don't you want your skin to glow? Tomorrow, all eyes are on you, angel bear."

"I couldn't care less," Jenna said. "Do you mind calling the salon?"

Margot didn't mind calling the salon at all. First she checked with the other bridesmaids to see if there would be any other truants.

Autumn wanted to keep her appointment.

Rhonda wanted to keep her appointment, and she asked if there was a tanning bed.

"Tanning bed?" Margot said. She studied Rhonda, whose skin was evenly bronzed — possibly, if Margot was being super critical, even a little orange. Rhonda must have used a tanning bed in New York; the thought struck Margot as amusing. She had thought that tanning beds went out in the 1980s with perms and Loverboy. "If you want to get some sun, come to the beach with me and the kids," Margot said.

"No, that's okay," Rhonda said quickly. "I was just wondering."

Finn opted to cancel her appointment — not because she planned on wallowing in misery in her room, and not because she was tagging along with Jenna and Stuart's kayaking expedition. She canceled because she was going to the beach with Nick. He was going to teach her to paddleboard.

Oh, boy, Margot thought.

131

"Nick is coming to Fat Ladies with us," Margot said. "So we'll all go together."

Beanie and Kevin and the kids were also coming to the beach, so there would be eleven people headed to Fat Ladies.

"I'll make sandwiches," Margot said.

"Since when do *you* make sandwiches?" Kevin said. "Call Henry Jr.'s and order sandwiches. Nick and I will go to Hatch's and get chips and soda and beer."

"I am capable of making sandwiches, Kevin," Margot said. "It's not always takeout at my house, you know."

Beanie patted Margot's arm. "You have a job," she said. "It's okay."

"*What's* okay?" Margot said. "I can make sandwiches! I bought deli stuff yesterday and Portuguese bread at Something Natural. I can do peanut butter and fluff. I bought fluff! I can cut the crusts off."

"You don't have to prove anything," Kevin said. "We know you're capable of making sandwiches, but it will be easier for us to call them in." He handed her a notepad. "Here, take everyone's order."

"Why don't *you* take everyone's order?" Margot said. She was inexplicably furious. She didn't care if they made lunch or ordered it from Henry Jr.'s, but she didn't like Kevin's insinuation that Margot was incapable of making sandwiches and his further insinuation that in offering to do so, she was trying to prove something. Prove what? Prove that she didn't subsist on pizza from Lombardi's and Thai takeout? Prove that she was like their mother—she could have a career *and* make sandwiches?

At that moment, her father stuck his head in the back door. "Margot?" he said.

Margot thought their father was going to weigh in on the sandwich decision. Everyone had an opinion. Even Beanie had said, *You have a job. It's okay.* What had *that* meant? Beanie could normally be counted on to side with Margot, but apparently not today.

"What?" Margot snapped.

"Can I chat with you a second?" Doug asked.

Margot stormed out the back door. Roger was directing the cherry picker into the side yard. Miraculously, the big machine steered clear of the perennial bed. The five boys stood a few yards away, their mouths agape as the cherry picker rose up and Hector clambered with the ropes into Alfie's upper branches.

By the time they all got back from the beach, Alfie's lowest branch would be lifted, and the tent would be up. All these emergency services would cost her father an arm and a leg, but although the Carmichael family had loads of problems, money wasn't one of them.

"There's an issue with the cars," Doug said.

"The cars?" Margot said.

"You and Kevin will need your cars to get everyone to the beach," Doug said. "Pauline will need my car to take the girls to the salon."

"Oh," Margot said. The logistics had eluded her. "What is Pauline going to do?"

"She's going to the salon as well," Doug said. "She wants to be with Rhonda."

"Okay," Margot said. "She can take my appointment."

Doug nodded. "Thank you, that's very nice. But what I really need is for you to drive me out to the golf course."

"Okay," Margot said. Was this okay? Hadn't she just committed to making eleven sandwiches, or had she been overruled? She was so addled that she couldn't remember how the disagreement had ended. "When?"

Doug looked at his watch, the Submariner that Beth had bought him for his fiftieth birthday. "Right now."

"Right *now?*"

"My tee time is at ten thirty. I'm playing at Sankaty."

Margot nearly said, *Can't Kevin take you? Or Nick?* But that was ridiculous. Her brothers were never summoned to onerous tasks such as shuttling their father out to his golf game. Kevin probably felt he had to be here to supervise the branch tying or the sandwich ordering. Nick was either flexing his muscles for Finn or waxing his paddleboard. Margot's mood grew darker. But then it occurred to her that this was exactly what she wanted—some time alone with her father. He must have wanted it, too, and that was why he'd asked her.

"Okay," she said. "Let's go."

Margot negotiated Doug's Jaguar through town, around the rotary, and out the Milestone Road. Every year as children they had ridden their bikes to Sconset to get ice cream at the market and traipse across the footbridge.

"You and Mom were such good parents," Margot said. "You gave us a lot of great memories."

Doug didn't respond to this. When Margot looked over, she saw him gazing out the window.

"Kevin is probably right," Margot said. "The only memories I'm giving my kids are ones of me arriving home late from work and calling up samosas from Mumbai Palace."

Margot could hear her father breathing. He said, "Your mother always worried that you were too hard on yourself. The curse of the firstborn."

"Sometimes I'm glad she can't see the ways that I've failed."

"Oh, Margot, you haven't failed."

"I'm divorced."

"So what," Doug said. "Didn't work out, nobody's fault."

"Carson is in danger of repeating the fourth grade," Margot

said. "Drum Jr. is twelve years old and afraid of the dark. Ellie is a hoarder."

Doug laughed, and even Margot cracked a smile. But she hadn't wanted her father alone so she could bemoan the missteps of her own life.

"So what's going on with you?" she asked. "That text you sent me was pretty startling."

Doug leaned his head back against the seat and let out a sigh. "Long story," he said.

"We've got a few minutes," Margot said. It was easy to break the law in the XJ, so she made a point to slow down. "I figured out that Pauline took the Notebook."

"She didn't *take* it," Doug said. "At least she says she didn't. Jenna left it on the table at Locanda Verde and Pauline picked it up, then she just forgot to return it."

"Oh," Margot said. Was she a horrible person for feeling skeptical about that story?

"I've decided to believe her," Doug said. "It's easier."

"Right," Margot said. "Did you ask if she read any of it?"

"She read it," Doug said. "She claimed it was making her crazy, not knowing what was in it."

"Wait," Margot said. "Did she read the last page?"

"I don't know," Doug said. "I would assume so?"

Margot said, "Have *you* read the last page?"

"No," Doug said.

"Well, you should," Margot said. "Make a point of it. Today, when you get home from golf, ask Jenna."

"I don't know about that, honey," Doug said.

Margot said, "I can't believe *Pauline* read it. I'm sure you were pissed."

"I was pissed," Doug said. "If Jenna had wanted her to read it, she would have offered."

"So you were pissed enough to tell Pauline not to come?"

"I didn't want her to come," Doug said.

"Oh."

"But as you may have noticed, she came anyway."

"Yes, I did notice that."

"She thought I was just angry. She thought I would change my mind back."

"Weren't you just angry?" Margot said. "Didn't you change your mind back?"

"No," Doug said. "I didn't want her to come—for a whole host of reasons, really—but she insisted, and I wasn't brave enough to press the issue."

"Oh," Margot said.

"It's Jenna's weekend," Doug said.

"Right, I know. But what...? What are the host of reasons? What are you not saying?"

"I don't love Pauline," Doug said. "When we get back to Connecticut, I'm going to ask her for a divorce."

Margot gasped. "You're not!"

"I am."

Margot clenched the leather band that swaddled the steering wheel. Her father was sixty-four years old. She had thought him too old for this kind of upheaval. When she thought about Doug's life, she imagined him retiring from the firm and doing a little pro bono work on the side. She imagined him golfing, she imagined him and Pauline eating at the country club and the two of them taking a vacation to Maui each February. But he might live another thirty years. Thirty years was a long time to be saddled with a woman he didn't love.

"Wow," Margot said.

"I'd appreciate it if you didn't say anything."

"Of course not," Margot said. "What will you do? Where will you live?"

"Oh, maybe in the city," Doug said. "I've been toying with getting a suite at the Waldorf like Arthur Tonelli. Or maybe I'll live on the Upper West Side near Edge. I could walk to work, subscribe to the philharmonic, spend more time with you and the kids."

The thought of her father as a sixty-four-year-old single man alarmed Margot. The thought of her father and Edge living in the same neighborhood and going out to bars, or even to the philharmonic, together made her tongue swell to twice its normal size. She couldn't speak. And, thankfully, she didn't have to — because here they were at the Sankaty Head Golf Club.

Margot pulled up in front of the clubhouse. Her father's family had belonged to Sankaty since its founding in 1923, but nowadays her father was the only one who played. Nick hated golf, and Kevin didn't have time. Stuart played golf — the membership might pass on to Stuart and Jenna, and the children they would someday have.

"Just think," Doug said. "Once I'm single, I can come to Nantucket for the whole summer. I can play golf every day."

"Just think!" Margot said. She tried to smile as he unloaded his clubs from the trunk.

Once he was single.

Doug waved to Margot, and she thought, Yes, now she was supposed to drive away, burdened by an impossible secret. She put down the passenger side window. "Am I coming back to get you?" she asked.

"Pauline will come," he said.

"Oh," Margot said. "Okay. Does she know how to get here?"

"No," he said. "But she'll use the GPS."

Margot nodded and watched her father head up the stairs into the clubhouse. She sat for a long moment after he was gone, thinking, *Okay, wow, who knew. Wow.*

She had an overwhelming desire to text Edge. It was a good thing her phone was dead.

There was a tap on the driver's side window, and Margot jumped, inadvertently hitting the horn. Standing next to the Jaguar in a pair of stone white pants and a navy golf shirt and that damn white visor was Griff.

Margot thought, *This just isn't happening.*

She had half a mind to drive away without a word, but she didn't have it in her to be rude. Unprofessional and unprincipled—yes. But not rude.

He said, "I *thought* it was you, but then I asked myself, 'What are the chances?' Three times in twenty-four hours?"

"Hi," Margot said.

"I think we both know what this means," Griff said.

Margot thought, *It means I'm destined to be haunted by my worst mistake.*

Griff said, "It means you're stalking me."

Margot smiled. The guy was charming, there was no denying that.

She said, "I was dropping my father off."

Griff said, "I just finished my first round. We teed off at six this morning, and I think I was still drunk."

"Nice," Margot said.

"I stayed at the Box until close," Griff said. "Drowning my sorrows after you rejected me."

"I didn't *reject* you," Margot said. Then she realized she needed to be careful about her wording. "I was just tired, and the thing with my phone bummed me out. I needed to get out of there."

"You can make it up to me now," Griff said. "Come on."

"Come on *where?*" Margot asked.

"Have a drink with me at the bar," he said.

"It's ten thirty," Margot said. "In the morning."

"So?" he said. "You're on vacation, right? This is your sister's wedding weekend, right? You can't tell me there isn't a part of you that's dying for a drink. You can't tell me you wouldn't love an opportunity to vent your frustration with your family to a friendly acquaintance."

"I don't feel any frustration with my family," Margot said.

"Now you're lying to me."

Margot smiled at this. "So what if I am? I can't just drink my morning away. My kids want to go to the beach. They're at home, waiting."

"Drum...Carter...and Ellie?"

Margot was flabbergasted.

"Carson," she said. "But wow, good memory." She recalled having asked Griff about his children at his first interview; his children were similar in ages to her own, but she would never have been able to come up with their names. And Griff, in turn, had asked about Margot's kids, which wasn't really standard protocol—she was interviewing him, not the other way around—but she had told him their names and ages. That he remembered was astonishing. If pressed, Edge probably wouldn't be able to produce any name but Ellie's, because she was the one in Audrey's ballet class. Margot mentioned the boys all the time, but Edge never seemed to be listening.

"Well, I'm not a man who would deny three kids the company of their mother," Griff said. "You should go, although I wish you'd stay."

"I can't stay," Margot said.

"But I'm getting to you, right?" Griff said. "Just admit it, you're starting to like me."

"I like you just fine, Griff."

"I mean, *like me* like me. Come on, I'm nice," he said.

Margot allowed herself a glance at him. He was nice. If things were different, if she didn't have a horrifying history with him, she would be willing, possibly even eager, to go for a drink with him. He was attractive and smart and personable, and he'd remembered her children's names. But she had wronged him. And how.

"I have to go," she said.

"What are you up to tonight?" he asked.

"Rehearsal at the church at five o'clock. Rehearsal dinner, six o'clock at the yacht club."

"I'll be at the Boarding House tonight," he said.

"You'll like it there," Margot said. "The food is terrific."

"Come meet me," Griff said.

"I'll be too busy getting frustrated with my family," Margot said. "But thanks for the invite."

"Tell me something," Griff said. "Do you have a date for this wedding?"

Margot blinked. It was none of his goddamned business if she had a date or not. Then she considered the question. *Did* she have a date for the wedding? Edge would be in attendance— tonight and tomorrow and Sunday—but Margot wouldn't be able to kiss him or hold his hand or claim him as anything more than a friend of her father's. Margot had asked Edge if they might be able to dance together to just one song, and Edge had said he didn't think that was a good idea.

"Not really," Margot said.

"Not really?" Griff said.

"No," Margot said.

Griff looked off into the green distance, then crouched down by Margot's window so that his face was right by her face and her stomach did a funny, inside-out flippy thing. His blue-and-green eyes were spellbinding. What was going *on* here? This was very bad.

In a low voice, he said, "I don't believe in love anymore, and I'm never getting married again...but I'm free tomorrow if you need me." He held up his palms. "Just saying."

Margot couldn't tell if the guy was earnestly pursuing her or if he was batting her around like a cat with a mouse because she'd signed him off. She, with her perfect instincts, could not tell.

She said, "Okay, thanks. I'll keep that in mind."

OUTTAKES

Autumn Donahue (bridesmaid): Fingers, *Mademoiselle.* Toes, *Black cherry chutney.* I needed something edgy to offset the grasshopper green.

Rhonda Tonelli (bridesmaid): Fingers, French. Toes, French. Some people get one color on their fingers and another on their toes, but I think that looks tacky.

Douglas Carmichael (father of the bride): The green on sixteen gave me trouble, but overall, I was happy with my short game. I shot an 80. After a few drinks tonight, I will tell anyone who asks that I shot a 79.

Pauline Tonelli (stepmother of the bride): I'm wearing blue tonight, nothing flashy, just a St. John suit I got at Bergdorf's that does a good job of camouflaging my midsection. I let the nail technician at the salon talk me into a color for my fingers called "Merino Cool," which is a sort of purplish gray. Very au courant, she said. They can barely keep it stocked, she said. I think it looks like the color my nails will turn naturally after I'm dead.

Kevin Carmichael (brother of the bride): Tree branch lifted! I can't believe Margot was going to let them chop it off.

Nick Carmichael (brother of the bride): I think Finn has gotten hotter since she got married. I've seen this happen before. Women get married, they get hotter. Then they have kids, and... (motion with finger indicating downward spiral). Then — some of them — bounce back. These are the ones who have affairs with their personal trainers...or some lucky guy who happens to be in the right place at the right time.

THE NOTEBOOK, PAGE 10

Readings

When Daddy and I were in our late twenties, there was one six-month period when we attended eight weddings, and it nearly bankrupted us. I was a bridesmaid in three, and your father was an usher in two. At nearly every one of these weddings, the readings were Corinthians 13 and a selection from Kahlil Gibran's The Prophet.

I beg you, avoid these choices. If you use Corinthians 13, you will hear a collective groan.

I am, as you know, a fan of song lyrics. You are the only one of my children who inherited my taste in music. Your sister and brothers listened to the punk stuff — the Dead Kennedys, the Violent Femmes, the Sex Pistols, Iggy and the Stooges, the Ramones — oh, how I wearied of the Ramones! But you were a Rolling Stones fan from a young age, you loved Springsteen, Clapton, and Steppenwolf, especially

"Magic Carpet Ride." Remember Halloween in sixth grade when all your friends dressed up like Courtney Love or the girl in the bumblebee costume from the Blind Melon video, and you went as Janis Joplin? They made fun of you, and you came home from trick-or-treating a little weepy, but I explained that you couldn't help it. You were my daughter.

This is a long way of saying that song lyrics often make good readings. Try the Beatles. No one has ever gone wrong with the Beatles.

MARGOT

When Margot pulled into the driveway at a quarter to five with her three sand-encrusted children in the backseat, she let out a shriek of awe and amazement. The backyard of their house had been transformed into a wedding wonderland.

"Look!" she said to her kids.

No response. When she turned around, she saw all three kids absorbed in their iDevices. She couldn't complain, however. It had been a magical afternoon at the beach, the exact kind of afternoon Margot remembered having as a child. Drum Jr. and Carson had boogie-boarded with their cousins like fiends all afternoon; Margot could barely get them out of the water to eat their sandwiches from Henry Jr.'s. Ellie had collected shells in a bucket, and then she sat on the shoreline and constructed an elaborate sandcastle. Margot, who was exhausted, drifted off to sleep under the umbrella. When she awoke, Beanie was sitting with Ellie, helping her mosaic the walls of the castle with shells. Margot watched them, and though she felt a twinge of guilt, she knew that Beanie loved spending time with Ellie because Beanie had only boys, and a little girl was a treat for her. Furthermore, Margot didn't want to sit in the sand; she had never been the kind of mother who got down on her hands and knees to play with the kids, and if she left the shady confines of the umbrella, there would be the issue of freckles. Margot was vain and lazy; she wasn't as nurturing as Beanie, perhaps, but she reminded herself that her own mother had never been a castle builder, either. Beth used to sit in her striped canvas chair and needle-point and dole out pretzel rods and Hawaiian Punch from the thermos.

Margot had enjoyed the beach immensely, even as she spooled the conversation with her father and the conversation with Griff through her mind. She decided that it was a blessing she'd sunk her phone because it freed her from worrying about whether or not there would be any texts from Edge. And she wouldn't worry herself about what the text from Edge last night had said. She would ask him tonight when she saw him at the yacht club.

It was only as Margot got out of the car and took in the staging for the wedding that she appreciated what a very special day tomorrow would be. She and Jenna had been talking about the backyard wedding for over a year, but that didn't prepare Margot for the excitement she felt now.

The tree branch had been lifted so that the ropes were barely visible. And under the tree was the large, circular center-pole tent, which was bigger in square footage than the Manhattan apartment where Jenna and Stuart would live. Inside, the tent was decorated with ivy, entwined branches, and white fairy lights. There were hanging baskets of limelight hydrangeas and hanging glass bowls filled with sand and one ivory pillar candle. There were fifteen tables, ten of which were swathed in the antique linen tablecloths, embroidered at the edges with green ivy, that their grandmother had used at *her* wedding, and five were the replica tablecloths that Margot and Jenna had hired an exceptional Irish seamstress in Brooklyn to make. Margot could barely tell the difference. She and Jenna had set the new table-cloths out in the sun for three weeks to get them to age properly. The Irish seamstress, Mary Siobhan, had also made 150 match-ing green linen napkins, which were tied with strands of real ivy. The centerpieces were white and limelight hydrangeas and the pink climbing roses, cut from the house, nestled into large glass jars encased in a mesh of woven twigs. The bone-white china was set over dark rattan chargers, and Roger had found 120 Water-ford goblets in the Lismore pattern, which was the pattern Beth and Doug had collected, and Stuart and Jenna would now col-lect. The overall effect was one of simplicity and beauty; the white and the green evoked the house and the yard, and the entwined branches and wooden baskets evoked Alfie. The pink of the climbing roses was the softest of accent colors. All of this had been her mother's vision, and Margot had doubted it; she had cursed the grasshopper green dress, but now she saw how the green dresses and Jenna's white dress would all make perfect aesthetic sense once they were under this tent.

"You're a genius," Margot whispered.

She peered up into the funneled pinnacle of the tent, where she imagined her mother's spirit residing. She heard someone clear his throat, and she turned to see Roger enter the tent.

"It looks beautiful," Margot said.

He moved a fork in one of the place settings a fraction of an inch. "I've done a lot of weddings," he said. "But this is one of the prettiest. I always say to my wife that there is no accounting for taste. But you girls knocked it out of the park here."

"Oh," Margot said. Why was it always in the face of kind words that she felt like crying? "It wasn't us."

*   *   *

When she entered the kitchen, Margot was met with chaos. There were people everywhere. Margot's kids and the Carmichael boys were still in their wet bathing suits, tracking sand with each step.

"I thought I told you to go to the outdoor shower!" Margot said.

"No, you didn't," Ellie said.

Margot allowed that maybe she had forgotten that instruction, but didn't her kids know they should always head to the outdoor shower after the beach?

"Go now," Margot said. "Be fast."

Autumn, Rhonda, and Pauline were sitting in the breakfast nook, eating crackers with smoked bluefish pâté. The people from the catering company were trying to work around them, moving between the kitchen island, where they were prepping food, to the dining room, which was serving as a staging area, to their refrigerated truck out in the street.

Then Margot noticed a new face.

"Stuart!" she cried.

Stuart was standing just outside the screen door with three other men, who were all wearing coats and ties.

Margot stepped out to greet them.

"Hey, Margot," Stuart said.

He looked terrible. He was pale, and he had bruise-colored circles under his eyes, and he'd gotten a haircut that was too short. He worked ridiculously hard in a stressful industry. He was a food and beverage analyst for Morgan Stanley; he never took time off. He had gone twelve months without a vacation to take today off, and the next two weeks for his honeymoon to St. John. It looked like he hadn't left his office in twelve months — or rather, it looked like he had left it only once, to visit a really incompetent barber.

And yet there lived in Stuart a kindness so pure that it caused Margot to marvel. He wasn't flashy, he wasn't slaying the market like Finn's husband, Scott Walker, he would never buy a thousand-dollar suit, he would never, probably, own a car as nice as her father's Jaguar, but Stuart was devoted to Jenna. He sent her flowers at the school "just because," he lit candles for her bath, he stood at the finish line with hot tea and a muffin whenever she ran a race in Central Park. In the five seconds that Margot spent taking in the sight of him, she felt badly for all the times she'd tried to talk Jenna out of marrying him.

"You remember my brothers," Stuart said. "H.W. and Ryan, and...Chance."

Margot studied the other three men. H.W. and Ryan were identical twins, impossible to tell apart until they opened their mouths. H.W. was an overgrown frat boy, and Ryan was gay. Margot deplored stereotyping, but she knew right away that the one who was better dressed was Ryan. Ryan came over to kiss Margot's cheek. He smelled divine; he was wearing Aventus, Margot's favorite scent, which she had bought for Edge but he had not, to her knowledge, even opened.

"How are you, Margot?" Ryan asked. "Tell me everything."

Margot laughed. "Oh, believe me, you don't want to know everything."

Ryan slid an arm around her waist and leaned her back into a dip. He was one of those men whose every move was smooth and elegant. "I've been bragging about how lucky I am to be escorting the maid of honor."

Ryan was Stuart's best man. Margot wondered if it had been difficult for Stuart to pick between his brothers, but Jenna said they had shot rock-paper-scissors for it.

H.W. raised his beer bottle in Margot's general direction. "Hey," he said.

Margot smiled. H.W. was paired up with Autumn. They would have sex before the weekend was over, Margot was sure of it.

Margot had seen the twins on numerous occasions—at Stuart's thirtieth birthday celebration at Gramercy Tavern, and then more recently at the engagement party in a private room at MoMA. But Margot had never met this other brother. Chance. Whereas the other three Graham brothers were square jawed and dark haired and built like hale and hearty tobacco farmers, Chance was tall and lean and had strawberry hair. Really, his hair was nearly pink, and he had a matching pinkish skin tone. *One of these things is not like the others.* Chance was Stuart's half brother, the product of an affair Stuart's father had in the nineties. He was nineteen years old, a sophomore at Sewanee, the University of the South, a math whiz, apparently, a good kid if a bit socially awkward.

Well, yeah, Margot thought. It was bad enough that he was a love child, the product of a midlife crisis, but then someone— Stuart's father? the other woman?—had thought it would be acceptable to name him "Chance." No wonder the kid was socially awkward. The other woman—Margot had never learned her name—had been married to Stuart's father for a few years, then they had split, and Stuart's father married Stuart's mother a second time. It was the kind of story that people had a hard time believing, except for the Carmichael children, who had been hearing bizarre divorce-and-marriage stories their whole lives.

Jenna found the story of Stuart's parents romantic.

Margot thought, Yeah, romantic—except for the living, breathing, six-foot-four reminder of when things had not been so romantic.

But this was a wedding, what had happened in the past could

not be undone, and so everyone would simply have to roll with it—smile, chitchat—and then gossip about the darker reality later.

"Hi, Chance," Margot said. Oh, how she would love to rename him something normal, like Dennis or Patrick. "I'm Margot Carmichael, Jenna's sister."

"Nice to meet you," Chance said. He had an elegant southern accent; he sounded—and looked—just like Ashley Wilkes from *Gone with the Wind*. He gripped Margot's hand and gave it a nice, strong shake. Margot's line of work caused her to evaluate everyone's handshake and eye contact. *Eight,* she thought. *Not bad.*

"Can I get you a beer?" Margot asked.

"I..." Chance said. He swallowed. "I'm only nineteen."

"Who cares?" H.W. shouted, momentarily animated by his favorite topic. H.W. had a twangy accent straight out of *The Dukes of Hazzard*. "Grab a beer, Chancey, come on!"

Chance turned even pinker. Margot had never seen anyone with such unusual coloring. It was almost a birth defect, perhaps indicating the murky circumstances of his conception. And with this thought, Margot suddenly felt protective of Chance. Clearly he was a darling, scrupulous kid. It wasn't his fault that Jim Graham had made an atrocious error in judgment.

"How about a Coke?" Margot asked.

Chance nodded. "A Coke would be great, thanks." He tugged at the collar of his shirt. "It's, uh, kind of hot out here."

"It is hot," Margot agreed. "And look at you guys, all ready to go." She stepped back into the kitchen to grab Chance a Coke from the fridge and narrowly missed hitting a woman holding a tray of empty vol-au-vents. At the breakfast nook, Autumn, Rhonda, and Pauline were telling stories about the incompetent masseuses they had known; they were getting along like a house on fire. Jenna would be pleased about that, wherever she was. Probably upstairs, putting on the showstopper backless peach dress.

Margot handed Chance the Coke. She said, "It's nearly four thirty." *Four thirty!* Margot wondered if Edge was on island yet. She got a Mexican jumping beans feeling in her belly. "I've got to get cracking!"

THE NOTEBOOK, PAGE 3

The Dress

You should feel no compunction or sense of duty to wear my dress; however, it is available to you. I fear you might find it too "traditional"—as I watch you now, you are twenty-one years old and you primarily wear clothes you sew yourself or that you get at Goodwill. I'm guessing it's a phase. It was for me, too. I wore the same prairie skirt for five weeks in the spring of 1970.

The dress will fit you, or nearly. You seem to be losing weight. I'd like to believe that's because you're away from the dining hall food of college, but I fear it's because of me.

My mother and I bought the dress at Priscilla of Boston, which was where every bride on the East Coast wanted to buy her dress back in those days, much like Vera Wang now. My mother and I argued because I wanted a dress with a straight skirt, whereas my mother thought I should choose something fuller. You don't want everyone staring at your behind, she said. But guess what? I did!

The dress has been professionally cleaned and is hanging up in the far left of my cedar closet. If you need to get it altered, go to Monica at Pinpoint Bridal on West 84th Street.

I have to stop writing. I am growing too sad thinking about how captivating you will look in that dress, and how seeing you wear it might undo your father.

I am crying now, but they are tears of love.

DOUG

He wanted to say that golf had calmed him. He had played with a couple about his age named Charles and Margaret and their friend Richard, who was a decade younger and had a very, very fine drive. Doug had a wonderful time chatting with them about the elite courses they had all mutually played—Sand Hills in Nebraska, Jay Peak in Vermont, and Old Head in Ireland. They spent four delightful hours of talking about nothing but golf, and Doug couldn't ask for a more appealing course than Sankaty Head on July nineteenth. The sun illuminated the rolling greens, the Atlantic Ocean and Sesachacha Pond, the red-and-white peppermint stick of Sankaty Lighthouse. Doug had joined his companions for lunch at the turn; he drank a cold beer and ate chilled cucumber soup and a lobster salad sandwich as they talked about the formidable prairie wind at Sand Hills. After lunch, Doug went out and slew the back nine.

He'd enjoyed another celebratory beer after the eighteenth, and then, not wanting to bother Pauline (which really meant not wanting to hear Pauline bitch about the GPS—she could never get the damn thing to work, she took it personally, as if the woman whose voice gave directions was an enemy of hers), he took a cab back to the house. Even the cab ride had been relaxing. Doug put the windows down and gazed out at the pretty cottages with their lovely gardens, their gray shingles and neat white trim, their sturdy widow's walks. He felt better than he had in months. Spending the day by himself playing golf was just what he needed.

He had believed, during the fifteen minutes in the cab, that everything would correct itself. He didn't need to make any drastic changes. He had been frazzled the day before with his own version of prewedding jitters. Nothing more.

But the second he entered the master bedroom—a bedroom he remembered his grandparents sleeping in, then his parents, then him and Beth—and saw Pauline sitting at this grandmother's dressing table, fixing her hair, he thought, *Oh, no, no, no. This is all wrong.*

She must have noticed his expression because she said, "You hate the suit."

"The suit?" he said.

She stood up and yanked at the hem of her jacket. "I didn't want anything too flashy. They're so conservative at the yacht club. All the old biddies with their pearls and their Pappagallo flats."

Doug looked at his wife in her blue suit. It was a tad matronly, true, reminiscent of Barbara Bush or Margaret Thatcher, and Doug could never in a million years imagine Beth wearing such a suit—but the suit wasn't the problem. It was the woman inside the suit.

"The suit looks fine," he said.

"Then why the long face?" Pauline asked. "Did you hook your drives?"

Doug sat on the bed and removed his shoes. He had a house full of people downstairs and more people coming to the yacht club. He had to get in the right frame of mind to play host. He had to follow the advice he had glibly given so many of his clients: fake it to make it.

"My drives were fine," he said. Pauline said things like "Did you hook your drives" to make it sound like she understood golf and cared about his game, but she didn't. He had never hooked a drive in all his life; he was a slicer. "I played pretty well, actually."

"What did you shoot?"

"A seventy-nine," he said. He wasn't sure why he fudged the number for Pauline's sake; he could have said he'd shot a 103, and she still would have said:

"That's wonderful, honey."

She sat next to him on the bed and started kneading the muscles in his shoulder. She must have realized something was very wrong, because unsolicited touches from Pauline were few and far between. But he wasn't in the mood to be touched by Pauline. He might never be in the mood again.

He stood up. "I have to get ready," he said.

It was only the rehearsal, but as they stood in the vestibule of the church, it felt like a big moment. Everyone else had processed before them — first Autumn on the arm of one of the twins, then Rhonda and the tall, nearly albino half brother, then Kevin and Beanie, who were standing in for Nick and Finn, who apparently were still at the beach although they had each been texted and called forty times in the past hour, then the other twin and Margot. Then Kevin and Beanie's youngest son, Brock, as the ring bearer, alongside Ellie, the flower girl.

Ellie was still in her bathing suit. Doug, who made a point never to interfere with his kids' parenting, had said to Margot, "Really? You brought her to *church* in a bathing suit?"

Margot had instantly gotten her hackles up, as Doug expected.

"I'm doing the best I can, Dad," she said. "She refused to change. I think it's a reaction to the D-I-V-O-R-C-E."

Really? Doug thought. Margot and Drum Sr. had been divorced for nearly two years. That sounded suspiciously like an excuse.

Roger, the wedding planner, was the director of this particular pomp and circumstance, despite the presence of the pastor of St. Paul's and their pastor from home, Reverend Marlowe, who were co-officiating. Roger had his clipboard and a number two pencil behind his ear; he was wearing a pair of khaki shorts, Tevas, and a T-shirt from Santos Rubbish Removal. Doug had an affinity for this fellow Roger that bordered on the fraternal. He appreciated that sense and order and logic were prevailing in the planning of this nuptial fete. Whatever Doug was paying the guy, it wasn't enough.

Roger had an old-fashioned tape recorder that was playing Pachelbel's Canon; tomorrow there would be two violinists and a cellist. Pachelbel's Canon was a piece of music Beth had loved even more than Eric Clapton or Traffic. She had loved it so much that she had asked Doug to play it over and over again in the days before she died. It would ease her passage, she said. Naturally, it was also the piece she had suggested for the processional, not realizing that as Doug stood, linked arm in arm with his youngest child, he would be suffused with the memory of sitting at Beth's bedside, helplessly watching her die.

Tears stung Doug's eyes, and he pinched the bridge of his nose. He took a few deep breaths. Next to him, looking as soft and lovely as a rose petal, Jenna said, "Oh, Daddy," and from some unseen place, she pulled a pressed white handkerchief.

That did it: Doug started to cry. It was all too much—giving his baby girl away, the confusion about Pauline, and his longing for Beth. She should be here. *She should be here, goddamn it!* In the seven years since her death, he had missed her desperately, but never as much as he did right this instant. Her absence physically pained him. He realized then that he had forgotten to read the last page of the Notebook, although he had decided, while overlooking the eleventh green at Sankaty, that today would be the day to do so. Now he was glad he hadn't read it. He couldn't handle it.

Doug blotted his face with the handkerchief, mopping up the tears that were now flowing freely. He caught Roger looking at him with concern. Doug didn't have an issue with grown men crying; he saw it week in and week out at his office—a college president had cried, an orthopedic surgeon had cried, a famous TV chef had cried. The loss of love could undo anyone.

And so, when the music switched to Jeremiah Clarke's Trumpet Voluntary and he and Jenna took their first matched steps down the aisle, everyone who rose saw him weeping.

He didn't try to stop himself. *Beth,* he thought. *Beth, look at our baby.*

Because it was the rehearsal, the only people in attendance were the wedding party and, seated in the front pew, Pauline, and Stuart's parents, Ann and Jim Graham. Doug figured he might as well get all the tender thoughts out of the way now; that way tomorrow he might have half a chance of remaining composed.

He allowed himself to remember the first moment that Jenna was placed in his arms. She had been the smallest of the four children at birth—a mere six pounds, twelve ounces—and she fit comfortably in both his upturned palms. He remembered her eyes, round and blue, and her head covered with baby chick fuzz.

"She's a little darling," Beth had said. "A precious sweetheart. She is our dessert."

Jenna had been exactly that. The other three kids had been born in such rapid succession—Margot first, Kevin eleven months later, Nick fourteen months after that—that they had all blended together. Then seven years passed, and both Beth and Doug had assumed they were done having children. The older three were too much to handle most of the time. Margot was bossy, Kevin scrappy, Nick messy. Beth had relaxed on her birth control; some nights she was simply too tired to put in her diaphragm, and most times their lovemaking was too urgent, squeezed into rare moments of privacy, for Doug to remember to pull out. They had gotten pregnant again, and they surprised themselves by feeling happy about it. They had Jenna, a baby girl they could relax and enjoy; she was the one they could spoil. And Jenna had given back every bit of their love. She had been a snuggler and a kisser, and in many ways a uniting force among the children. In seventh grade, Doug remembered, she had been learning calligraphy, and she had made a sign that said: *Only family matters.* Beth had insisted that Doug take the sign to work and display it in his office. He had hung it on the wall behind his desk. And then, when Beth died, he had brought the sign home and put it on Beth's nightstand.

Tears, tears. Doug couldn't meet anyone's eyes—not Pauline's, not Kevin's, not Margot's. He gazed straight ahead at the altar and the magnificent east and west Tiffany windows. He could remember the weight of Jenna in his hands the first time he held her, and now here she was firmly gripping his arm as though *she* were walking *him* down the aisle and not the other way around. This was going to be the next-to-last time he held on to her. Right now, she was still his.

Reverend Marlowe was standing before them; they had come to the end of their journey.

Doug didn't want to let her go.

Your father will be a cause for concern.

He kissed Jenna and gave Stuart a look.

You're a lucky bastard, he thought.

Take care of her, he thought. *She is so precious to us.*

And then he stepped aside.

Reverend Marlowe raised his hands and, in his melodious voice, said, "Dearly beloved."

THE NOTEBOOK, PAGE 21

My Cousins

You will need to invite all the Bailey cousins and their children. I'm sorry! But you know how tightly knit the Baileys are and how they will feel slighted if you don't invite each and every one of them. As you may or may not remember, Beanie's mother, Pat, only allotted Daddy and me forty invites, and so only five Bailey cousins made the cut and there was hell to pay. My cousin Linda STILL holds a grudge. And then NO ONE was invited to Margot's wedding in Antigua. So, you see, these invitations to your wedding are non-negotiable. I'm sorry, sweetie.

The full list follows below.

ANN

The sight of Doug Carmichael openly weeping as he walked Jenna down the aisle was the only thing all day that had managed to get Ann out of her own head. Ann thought, The poor man, he lost his wife; now he is giving away his daughter, whom he clearly adores. A man was different with daughters than with sons. Ann wondered for a second how Jim would have fared with a daughter. Ann hoped he would have been just like Doug Carmichael. Of course, they would never know.

The rehearsal was unremarkable except for that show of emotion. Ann's part was small and completed early—she would be walked in after the other guests were seated, escorted by Ryan.

Fine.

"Dearly beloved," followed by the readings. Jenna's brother Kevin read the lyrics to "Here, There and Everywhere," by the Beatles. And Jenna's sister-in-law, Beanie, read the Edna St. Vincent Millay poem "Love Is Not All":

I might be driven to sell your love for peace,
Or trade the memory of this night for food.
It may well be. I do not think I would.

Ann closed her eyes. Jenna and Stuart said their vows, then Jenna's childhood minister would give a short homily, although tonight, thankfully, they were spared. He was Episcopalian. It would have been nice if Jenna had been Catholic, but Ann couldn't complain. Episcopalians were close, and most of the girls whom Stuart had dated before had been Southern Baptists, including She Who Shall Not Be Named. Then there was a moment of silence to remember Jenna's mother, Beth Carmichael, during which Ann bowed her head and reminded herself to be grateful that she was whole, present, and healthy to see her son get married. Then the kiss. Then "I now pronounce you man and wife." Then the wedding planner hit the button on his funny old tape recorder, the strains of Mendelssohn played, and everyone filed out of the church in the reverse order, only this time Ann was escorted out by Jim.

It may well be. I do not think I would.

At the bar at the yacht club, Ann ordered a double vodka martini.

Jim looked at her sideways. "You?" he said. "Vodka?"

"Let me know the second you see her," Ann said. "And please, don't leave my side."

Jim cupped Ann's face with his big, strong hands and kissed her on the lips, a real kiss, the kind of kiss that, all these years later, could still make her weak with desire, especially since he tasted like his first sip of bourbon. During the four years of their separation and divorce, Ann had dated seven men and slept with two, but none of those men had made her dizzy with lust the way Jim did. Even now, in public, under such stressful circumstances, she felt a hot pulse. It wasn't fair.

"Nice party," Jim said.

Ann could do nothing but agree. The Nantucket Yacht Club was the kind of place that thrived on understatement and quiet privilege. The sloops on buoys, the grass tennis courts, the spectacular location on the harbor, the shabby genteel furnishings, the trophy cases displaying the same dozen Mayflower names.

Cocktails were being served on the patio. The college-age servers (all attending colleges like Mount Holyoke and Williams, all with names like Lindsley and Talbot) passed trays of bacon-wrapped scallops and phyllo filled with melted Brie and apricot preserves. They had ripped the recipes for this occasion right out of the official WASP cookbook.

It was exactly as Ann had imagined it.

In the ballroom, round tables were set with navy and white linens and napkins folded to look like sailing ships. Dinner was to be a traditional clambake—lobsters and potatoes and corn—served buffet style. Guests could sit wherever they pleased. Ann would have preferred assigned seating, with Helen Oppenheimer placed on the opposite side of the ballroom, preferably in the corridor outside the ladies' room. As it was, Ann had made her first priority—after acquiring her vodka martini and downing three healthy sips—rounding up Olivia and her husband Robert and the Cohens and the Shelbys and making sure that they were all planning to sit at the table with Ann and Jim.

"Absolutely," Olivia said. "I would never abandon you. Is the bitch here yet?"

"Not that I can see," Ann said. Olivia was the only person who knew about Helen; the Cohens and Shelbys had become close friends of Ann and Jim's the second time around. Jim's sister Maisy was here with her husband, Sam. Ann and Maisy had never hit it off—quite frankly, Ann couldn't stand the woman. She lived in Boone, North Carolina, and wore prairie dresses and had homeschooled her five children. When Jim left to move in with Helen, Maisy had condoned it. She and Helen became friends. Maisy had helped Helen with Chance when he was a baby. Ann pointedly did not ask Maisy and Sam to sit at her and Jim's table. Maisy could sit with Helen in social Siberia.

Ann finished her cocktail and got herself another. A young man named Ford who attended Colgate (it said so right on his name tag; it must have been yacht club tradition to let people know how well educated the staff was) offered Ann a deviled egg, but Ann declined. She couldn't possibly eat anything.

She wanted to find Jim and walk down the docks and admire the sailboats, but Jim was off mingling somewhere; he had not heeded her plea to stay within arm's reach. Ann knew she should introduce herself to some of the other guests instead of spending the whole evening within the cozy ring of her Durham friends. As it was, those six were circled together, talking and laughing, having a fine time. They felt no compunction to meet Jenna's mother's cousins or Stuart's boss, here with his wife and new baby.

But Ann was a politician, and it was in her nature to connect with as many new people as humanly possible. She was good at introducing herself; she should just do it. Helen would get there when she got there; Ann couldn't fritter the whole evening away worrying about when.

She decided she would start with Doug Carmichael and tell him how touching she had found the rehearsal. But Doug was all the way out by the cannon and the flagpole, talking to a young woman with dreadlocks, whom Ann guessed was one of Jenna's fellow teachers at the sustainable preschool. Then Ann spied Doug's wife, sitting alone at one of the patio tables, drinking a very large glass of chardonnay and attacking a bowl of cashews. Ann approached. The woman's name was Pauline, though Ann always had the urge to call her Paula.

"Hi, Pauline," Ann said. "Mind if I join you?"

"Please," Pauline said. She had the demeanor of someone sitting at home alone, rather than smack in the middle of a party, but she snapped to attention with Ann's words and pulled her hand out of the cashew bowl.

"Lovely party," Ann said. "This is such a beautiful club."

"Is it?" Pauline said. "I hate it here."

Ann tried not to appear startled. "Oh," she said.

"Nantucket in general, I guess," Pauline said. "So precious, so...I don't know, self-satisfied."

Ann had been thinking the same thing only that morning; she had about as much love for the North as General Lee. But Nantucket had grown on her over the course of the day. There had been the leisurely morning at the hotel, then Ann and Jim had strolled into town. They had shopped at galleries and antique stores. Ann had bought a painting of the ocean, all swirling blues and greens; it wouldn't exactly blend in with their sprawling Victorian—which had once been owned by a nephew of the tobacco baron W. T. Blackwell, and Ann had painstakingly decorated with help from *Southern Living*—but it would be a nice reminder of Stuart's wedding. Ann had also bought a straw hat with a black grosgrain ribbon, exorbitantly priced, but when she tried it on, Jim declared she had to have it. They had eaten a lunch of clam chowder and Caesar salad on the wharf, and Ann had tanned her legs in the sun.

"People seem to love it," Ann said neutrally. She wished she hadn't committed to sitting down. She cast about the party, looking for someone else she knew, somewhere else she could go. She saw Ryan with his boyfriend, Jethro; they were standing so close to each other that their foreheads were nearly touching. Ann was a Republican in a southern state, but parenting Ryan had given her an advanced degree in tolerance and acceptance. Jethro had become one of Ann's favorite people in all the world. He had been raised in the Cabrini-Green housing projects on the south side of Chicago, a fact that had shocked Ann at first. Jethro's manners were as elegant as if he'd been raised at Buckingham Palace. He was smart and funny, he spoke fluent Italian and French, he was the editor in chief at *Chicago Style* magazine. But right this instant, Ann wished that Ryan and Jethro would not announce themselves as so openly gay. They were at the Nantucket Yacht Club. The place was as straitlaced as a Junior League event at the Washington Duke back home. But Jethro had never been one to hide. Black and proud—the only person of color at this entire party, except for a Korean gal whom Jenna had gone to college with. And gay and proud.

Ann turned back to Pauline and smiled. Pauline's nose was deep in her wineglass. Ann scrambled for something else to say, something that would lead her organically to an exit.

Pauline set her wineglass down with a sharp *ching!*

"Do you ever feel like maybe your marriage isn't exactly what you thought it was?" Pauline asked.

Ann's mouth fell open. She was wearing a sleeveless shell-pink sheath, but at that moment, she felt completely naked. Exposed. She turned her head away—she couldn't meet Pauline's intense, questioning gaze—and at that very second she saw Helen Oppenheimer enter the party. The crowd seemed to hush; something about Helen's presence demanded it. She was a six-foot blonde, still as statuesque as ever, wearing a flowing, one-shouldered dress that was the brightest yellow Ann had ever seen. It was canary yellow, the yellow of a bushel of lemons, a juicy sunburst yellow. She was blinding and beautiful. Ann realized then what a terrible, terrible mistake she had made.

She shifted her gaze back to Pauline. "Yes," she said. "I do sometimes feel that way."

Ann stood up. Where was Jim? Just as she was about to curse him, she felt a pressure on her elbow. He was right next to her.

He said, "Okay, let's get this over with."

"Get *what* over with?" Ann said.

"We have to say hello," Jim said.

Of course they had to say hello, but Ann didn't want to. She wanted Helen to stand alone, ostracized, gawked at—because soon people would figure out who she was. Furthermore, Ann hadn't rehearsed a greeting in her head. She might say, "Hello, Helen. *So* glad you could come." Or "Oh, Helen, hello. Lovely to see you." Both lies—Ann wasn't glad Helen had come, she had been certain Helen would decline, and it was *not* lovely to see her, in fact it felt like having an ingrown toenail. Ann hadn't allowed for the possibility that Helen would look so...amazing. It was devastating to admit, but Helen Oppenheimer looked better than ever. The dress was magnificent, and she was wearing a very high pair of nude patent leather heels that made her legs look a mile long. It was so unjust. Helen was the home wrecker. How *dare* she choose to flaunt her height and her beauty *here,* at Ann's son's wedding! Ann squeezed Jim's hand until she was sure it hurt. It was also unjust that the person she needed to support her was the person who had caused this catastrophe in the first place.

Across the patio, Ann caught Olivia's eye. Olivia mouthed the words *Oh, shit.*

"All right," Ann said. This was her own fault. She had been intent on gloating. Now she understood why pride was a deadly sin. "Let's do it."

"Short and sweet," Jim said.

Together, they approached yellow Helen. Ann's molars were set. Chance appeared out of nowhere to kiss his mother and take her arm. Helen beamed at him and touched his face. With his height and his transparent complexion, Chance was all Helen; there was almost nothing of Jim in him.

Helen was so enraptured by the sight of her son that she didn't seem to notice Ann and Jim until they were at her feet. She towered over Ann like a queen over a royal subject, and Ann rued her decision to wear flats.

"Hello, Helen," Ann said. There was something else she'd meant to add, but further words escaped her. She found herself scrutinizing Helen now that she was closer to her. Helen's skin was smooth and tanned. Had she had work done? She had almost no makeup on—just a little mascara and something to make her lips shine.

"Oh, hey therrrrrrre," Helen drawled. She acted as if Ann and Jim's presence at this function had caught her by surprise.

Then there was the quandary of how to physically greet her. Ann held out her hand, and Helen leaned forward and executed a double-cheek kiss. Ann thought, God, how pretentious. This was Nantucket, not the Cap d'Antibes.

Jim said, "Helen." That was all, just her name, the barest acknowledgment of her presence. They did not kiss or shake hands.

Helen said, "I'd just luvvvvvvv a drank." Ann had lived in Durham since her freshman year at Duke; she had heard many a variation on the southern accent, and had even developed a slight one herself. But Helen's syrupy Scarlett O'Hara irked the hell out of her. Helen was originally from Roanoke, Virginia. She had been painting her nails and wearing hot rollers since she was six years old.

Ann said, "We're so glad you could come."

Helen smiled. Ann waited for a response. She waited for Helen to say, *You were so kind to invite me. Thank you.* But instead Helen said, "How about y'all point me to the bar?"

Ann was rendered speechless.

Helen said, "Never mind, Chance will help me find it. Won't you, Chancey?"

"Sure, Mama," Chance said.

Helen took Chance's arm, and the two of them strolled off.

"There," Jim said. "We don't have to speak to her again for the rest of the weekend."

"I guess not," Ann said. She knew she should be relieved that the interaction was over, but instead she felt cheated. Where was the thank-you? Where was Helen's acknowledgment of Ann's largesse?

THE NOTEBOOK, PAGE 24

The Photographer

Abigail Pease. Accept no substitute.

MARGOT

For some reason it was Margot who had been chosen to go back to the house and wait for Nick and Finn to return from the beach while everyone else headed to the yacht club. Margot understood that her father and Pauline and Jenna and Stuart all had to get to the club pronto, but why couldn't Kevin and Beanie go back to the house to wait for Nick? It was Kevin's premise that since Ellie had to be walked back to the house, Margot should be the one to go.

"Brock has to be walked back, too," Margot said.

"We're taking the Grahams and the groomsmen to the club,"

Kevin announced. "The pleasures of minivan ownership: seating for eight." He patted Margot's shoulder in the most condescending way possible and said, "We'll see you in a few minutes."

It would be more than a few minutes, everyone knew that, because once Nick and Finn did return, they would have to shower and change. Margot wanted to go to the yacht club to see Edge. She had been patient, she hadn't been a sourpuss about the mortal damage to her phone, she hadn't gotten drunk with Griff at ten thirty in the morning—but now she wanted her reward. She wanted to see Edge.

Back at the house, Emma Wilton was waiting. Margot gave her money to take all six kids down to the Strip for pizza, then to the Juice Bar for ice cream, then to the playground at Children's Beach.

"Please," Margot said, "try to get Ellie out of her bathing suit. She might listen to you, since you're not her mother."

At eight o'clock, Emma was to bring the kids home to watch a DVD. With the wedding tents set up, there could be absolutely no roughhousing in the backyard.

Once Emma and the kids took off down Orange Street, Margot was left to sit and stew alone. She realized it might be a good thing if she wasn't at the yacht club exactly on time. If Edge got there first, he would wonder where she was; *he* would be the one waiting while *she* made an entrance. This thought calmed Margot for a few minutes until she grew antsy again. She allowed herself to grow infuriated first with Kevin, then with Nick. Nick was thirty-seven years old, he was an adult, he had an advanced degree, he negotiated player contracts worth millions of dollars, he was quoted all the time in the *Washington Post* and even occasionally on ESPN. How could he allow himself to completely *miss* the rehearsal—and not only him but Finn, as well. How irresponsible!

It had crossed everyone's mind that something had gone awry. Nick and Finn had been at least a hundred yards offshore on their paddleboards. When Margot had corralled the kids to leave, she'd shouted to Nick, and he had waved and pointed to his wrist—indicating, she thought, that he would be along in a few minutes. Maybe either he or Finn had fallen off the paddleboard; maybe they'd gotten swept out to sea, maybe they'd drowned. Jenna had tried calling and texting Finn, and Kevin had tried Nick, with no response. But of course their phones would be on the beach. Margot knew in her heart that they weren't in any danger. Nick was too much of a competent asshole to meet with tragedy.

You can't tell me you wouldn't love an opportunity to vent your frustration with your family to a friendly acquaintance.

The grandfather and grandmother clocks announced the quarter hour in brassy unison. Margot closed her eyes and tried to achieve a Zen moment. She had always loved the mellow, honeyed chiming of those clocks; it was a sound particular to the Nantucket house. It was the sound of summertime; it was the sound of her childhood.

Six fifteen. Margot was the least Zen person on earth. She went to the fridge and poured herself a glass of wine.

She thought about Griff. He had come into the offices at Miller-Sawtooth in the second week of March. Griff's first interview with Margot—for the head of product development with a pre-IPO tech firm called Tricom—had gone so well that she knew he would end up on the final slate. Griff's third interview with the powers that be at Tricom, including Drew Carver, the CEO, had taken place on the morning after Margot had spent the night at Edge's apartment for the one and only time. Margot had been a flustered, sex-exhausted, lovesick mess. She had spent time in the ladies' room, trying to pull herself together—makeup for under her eyes, perfume to mask the smell of pheromones, her inner voice reflecting on what Edge had asked of her. *It would really mean a lot to me,* he'd said, tracing his finger along her jawbone. When Margot emerged from the ladies' room, Harry Fry, her managing partner, had asked if she was okay. Harry had served as Margot's champion within the company; he believed she had been blessed with "perfect instincts." Harry must have known to look at Margot then that she was *not* okay, but she had stared him dead in the eye and said, "Yes, I'm fine," because to be a woman in this business was already a disadvantage, but to be a louche, trashy woman who would be willing, perhaps, to compromise her principles for her lover was unacceptable. Harry Fry's number one mandate—indeed, Miller-Sawtooth's number one mandate—was that personal lives did not come into the boardroom. No individual prejudices. Ever.

Edge had asked Margot for a favor.

Edge, you know I can't, she had said.

But once Margot had gotten into the office and reflected on the evening at Picholine and the deliciousness of waking up in Edge's bed, she had decided that she would do anything for the man. She would have wrestled an alligator, she would have tattooed his name on her lower back.

But she had done worse.

The grandfather and grandmother clocks announced six thirty, and Margot thought, *I've had it, I'm leaving. They do not deserve a personal chauffeur. They can walk to the yacht club.* The wine had buoyed Margot a little, and she thought, *I'm going to see Edge!* She then wished that thinking about Edge brought her more happiness and less self-doubt.

As she stood to go, collecting her wrap and cocktail purse, she heard voices and laughter. A moment later, Nick and Finn walked into the house. Nick was carrying Finn on his back; Finn was resting her head on Nick's shoulder.

Margot, unable to leave personal prejudice out of this particular boardroom, said, "Oh, for fuck's sake!"

They both gazed at her, startled. Caught. Margot felt like an ugly, mean headmistress, holding a switch.

Nick set Finn down. Finn was...wow...wickedly sunburned. Her face, her chest, her back—she was *fried.* Margot thought about the following day when Finn would have to wear the grass-hopper green dress. She would look awful in the photographs, like a frog that had been through the blender, and no amount of makeup would hide it. This was Finn at her worst, silly and care-less; she was still the same seventeen-year-old girl who had left the Worthington family high and dry without a nanny after sticking it out for only thirty-six hours. But Finn's weak charac-ter wasn't Margot's primary concern.

She said, "Where the fuck have you two been? You *missed* the rehearsal!"

Nick put a hand up. "Marge," he said. "Don't be like this."

"Be like *what?*" Margot said, although she knew he meant shrill, strident, bitchy. She hated that she had been left to play the heavy. As the older sister, she had *always* played this role—babysitter, taskmaster, disciplinarian. She never got to be the goof-off or the princess. "It's six thirty! The rehearsal started at five! We were all at the church *waiting* for you!"

"We got left at the beach without a car," Nick said.

"You could have called a cab!" Margot said. "You could have taken the shuttle!"

"I ran into a buddy of mine," Nick said. He grinned. "Do you remember Tucker? Because he remembers you."

Margot glowered. She didn't care about anyone named Tucker. He was probably one of the asinine idiots who used to toss her into the ocean with her clothes on at the beach parties out at Dionis.

"Tucker said he'd give us a ride," Nick said. "But he wanted to stop for a beer at the brewery first."

Of course, Margot thought.

"And as we were leaving the brewery, Tucker got a call from his wife, something about their new baby, the wife was freaking out, so Tucker had to boogie home, and he lives out in Sconset. He had to drop us off at the rotary."

"I really don't care," Margot said.

"Finn lost her shoes," Nick said. "And the sidewalk was hot, so I had to carry her. It was slow going."

Margot glared at Finn. Lost her *shoes?*

"I'm gonna hop in the shower," Finn said. She disappeared out the back screen door.

Nick faced Margot. "I'm sorry, Marge."

"You suck," Margot said. "It's Jenna's weekend. She and Stuart asked you to stand up for them, and you let them down."

"It was the *rehearsal*," Nick said. "I'll be there tomorrow. Obviously."

"And what the hell is going on between you and Finn?"

"Um," Nick said. "Nothing? She's just, you know, *Finn,* our neighbor, Jenna's best friend, known her forever."

"She's married, Nick."

"I'm aware of that, Marge."

Margot shook her head. She could see right through him.

"I'm leaving," she said. "I've wasted enough time waiting for you. You two will have to walk."

"Okay," Nick said. "Fine."

"Yeah, I'll bet you think that's fine. The two of you will have the house all to yourselves."

"What's happened to you?" Nick asked. He shook his bush of

golden hair and brushed sand from his torso all over the bare wood floors—never mind that 150 guests were coming the next day. "You used to be so cool. Now you're just…I don't know what you are, but you're not like you used to be."

"I grew up," Margot said. "I'm an adult."

Nick studied her for a second. He had gotten a lot of sun; his face was darkly tanned, and his eyes seemed very green. Of the four Carmichael offspring, Nick was the only one with green eyes. Of the four of them, Nick was the free spirit. He had been a clown in school. He had once skipped class to go to the beach in a Volkswagen bus filled with girls; he had once gotten suspended for streaking during a Friday night football game. He had managed to make it through college and law school while closing the bars every weekend and bedding what Margot was certain was hundreds of women.

Their mother had always stepped in when Nick was about to be punished. Margot remembered their mother constantly saying to their father, *Douglas, please, don't clip his wings.*

"You grew up," Nick said. He nodded once, then headed upstairs. "That's too bad."

When Margot reached the yacht club, the party was in full swing. The band was playing, and a number of couples were already dancing—Doug's friends from East Brunswick, the Appelbaums, as well as the Riggses and the Mitchells, who were longtime family friends from Nantucket. Everyone else was still out on the patio, enjoying cocktails as the sun pinkened in the sky.

Margot's shoulders were tight, and her stomach was making unseemly squelching noises. *Edge.* She would *not* drink too much. She would *not* say anything silly or inappropriate. She would *not* touch Edge under the table, no matter how much she wanted to. She would be cool, maybe even a little aloof. Her dress was a knockout, she thought—lavender silk, very short, with spaghetti straps, and she had worn the silver heels with silver strings that wrapped around her ankles, strings that Edge had once dangled from his teeth. She wore long silver earrings and a touch of perfume. She looked good, she was the maid of honor, she was an adult, a grown woman. Nick could go to hell. Nick and Finn could go to hell together.

Margot scanned the crowd. She saw her father talking to Everett and Kay Bailey, her mother's cousins. She saw Kevin and Beanie with Autumn and the two Carolines (called Asian Caroline and Caucasian Caroline behind their backs), who had also gone to the College of William and Mary. She saw Stuart's brother Ryan with a very handsome black man. He and Asian Caroline added much-needed ethnic diversity to this event. Margot saw a statuesque blond woman in a buttercup yellow dress. She saw Pauline sitting at a table alone, mauling a bowl of cashews. She saw a gaggle of the crunchy-granola womyn whom Jenna taught with at Little Minds—Hilly and Chelsea and Francie. She noticed blandly handsome Wall Street types in good suits, who must have been the men who worked at Morgan Stanley with Stuart. She saw Stuart's parents with several other couples, definitely southern, judging by the hairstyles and the pantyhose on the women. Margot watched H.W. hand Autumn a shot. A shot during cocktail hour, Margot thought. *Really?* And it looked like bourbon. Autumn threw it back without hesitation and chased it with a sip of her wine. *Stay classy, Autumn,* Margot thought. She caught sight of Stuart and Jenna, arm in arm, parting the crowd as they moved through. Jenna looked striking in her peach dress, and Stuart seemed finally to be relaxing. His face had a little bit of color. He was wearing the peach silk tie that Jenna had bought to match her dress.

Margot did not see Edge.

She surveyed the room again, checking every single face. Edge was only about five foot ten, with a head of close-cropped silver-gray hair. He had that Roman nose, lovely hazel eyes, and an elegance—hand-tailored suits, polished Gucci loafers, a Girard-Perregaux watch. His deportment oozed importance and self-confidence. It was incredibly sexy. If he were in the room, Margot would have homed in on him in a matter of seconds.

She checked the time: it was five of seven.

He wasn't here.

Maybe the texts he'd sent last night were texts saying he wasn't coming. Edge was a habitual canceler. More than half the time they had plans, something came up: Audrey had the flu, or one of his sons had gotten his car impounded, or a client had been threatened by her soon-to-be-ex-husband, or his most famous client—a legendary rock star—had ended up back in rehab and needed Edge to deal with the custody arrangement for his children. But it had never occurred to Margot that Edge might cancel on Jenna's *wedding*.

There was only one person she could ask.

But no, she couldn't. It would send up a red flag.

But she had to.

Margot threaded her way through the crowd and reached her father just as he was excusing himself from Everett and Kay Bailey. Margot would have liked to talk to Ev and Kay—all her mother's cousins were fun, good-natured people—but Margot didn't want to do it right now. She would talk to them tomorrow at the wedding. She waited until Doug and the Baileys parted, then she snatched her father's arm.

"Oh, good," he said. "You're here. Where are Nick and Finn?"

"At the house," Margot said. "Getting ready."

"I thought you were going to wait for them and drive them down."

"They wanted to walk," Margot lied.

"Well, they'd better hurry up, or they're going to miss dinner," Doug said. "They're serving in five minutes."

"Right," Margot said. She took a breath. Launch? Or abort mission?

She had to know.

"So," she said. "Representation from Garrett, Parker, and Spence seems a little light. Isn't Edge coming?"

"He thought he'd be here tonight," Doug said. "But I got a call from him about an hour ago. Today in court was a disaster, I guess, and he and Rosalie were still finishing the paperwork, and he didn't want to fight Friday night traffic on I-95. Can't blame him for that."

He and Rosalie finishing paperwork, Margot thought. Or he and Rosalie screwing on top of his partners desk. Or he and Rosalie taking advantage of an empty city to snare seats at the bar at Café Boulud.

"So he's coming tomorrow?" Margot asked. She sounded panicked, even to her own ears.

Doug gave her a quizzical look. "That's what he told me, honey," he said.

THE NOTEBOOK, PAGE 2

The Invitations

Mail them six weeks in advance. (You don't need your mother to tell you that, although it appears I just did.) Classic white or ivory—maybe with one subtle, tasteful detail, such as a starfish, sand dollar, or sailboat at the top. Maybe a small Nantucket? Pick a traditional font—I used to know the names of some of them, but they escape me now. Matching response card, envelope stamped.

I get the feeling you may have issues with this vision. I see you sending out something on recycled paper. I hear you claiming that Crane's kills trees. I imagine you deciding to send your invitations via e-mail. Please, darling, do not do this!

My preferred wording is: Jennifer Bailey Carmichael and Intelligent, Sensitive Groom-to-Be, along with their families, invite you to share in the celebration of their wedding.

In my day, it was customary to list the bride's parents by name, but my parents, as you know, were divorced, and Mother had remarried awful Major O'Hara and Daddy was living with Barbara Benson, and the whole thing was a mess, so I used the above wording, which diffused the whole issue.

No e-mail, please.

ANN

She was standing behind Chance in the buffet line when it happened. She had positioned herself there on purpose, like a sniper, waiting for Helen. Contrary to her earlier expectations, Ann wanted another shot at conversation; she wanted that thank-you, goddamn it.

Ann tapped Chance on the shoulder. "Hey, sweetie."

Chance said, "Hey, Senator."

Ann smiled. He always called her "Senator," which was a good, neutral moniker—better than "Mrs. Graham" or "Ann." Ann's relationship with Chance had always been a tender question mark. What *was* their relationship, exactly? Technically, she was his stepmother, and she was the mother of his three half brothers. He was her husband's son from another union. She had grown to know and love him, but there was a certain barrier.

The buffet included clam chowder, mussels, grilled linguiça, corn on the cob, and a pile of steaming scarlet lobsters served whole. Ann had doubts about her lobster-cracking ability; she worried about lobster guts messing the front of her dress. There were plastic bibs on the tables, but the last thing Ann wanted was to be seen wearing one.

Ahead of her, Chance loaded his plate with mussels. He turned to Ann. "I've never had mussels before."

"They're yummy, you'll love them," she said, which was a glib thing to say, as, living three hours from the coast, she ate mussels about once every decade.

Chance pulled one from its shell and popped it into his mouth. He nodded his head. "Interesting texture," he said.

Ann searched the party for the yellow of Helen's dress. She spied Helen out on the patio, talking to Stuart.

Ann had been forced to swallow a whole bunch of unpleasant facts in the past twenty years, but the worst thing was that, for a time, Helen had been a stepmother to her children. Helen had coparented them every third weekend with Jim. Ann used to question the boys when they got home from weekends with their father and Helen. What had they done? What had they eaten? Had they gone out or stayed in? Did Helen cook? Did Helen read to them at night? Did Helen let them stay up late to watch R-rated movies? Did Helen kiss them good-bye before they piled into Jim's car at seven o'clock on Sunday evening?

What Ann had gleaned was that, in those years, Jim took on most of the duties pertaining to the three older boys, while Helen cared for Chance. Chance had been a colicky baby, Helen carried him everywhere in a sling, Chance didn't sleep in a crib, he slept in the bed with Helen and Jim. Chance had walked early, and Helen was forever chasing him around. Helen had made chicken with biscuits once, but the biscuits were burned. (In Roanoke, Ann knew, Helen had grown up with a black housekeeper who had done all the cooking.) Jim often took the boys to McDonald's for lunch, which was a treat for them, since Ann was sponsoring an initiative for healthier eating habits for Carolina schoolchildren and hence did not allow the kids fast food. Helen bought the boys Entenmann's coffee cake for breakfast and let them eat it straight from the box in front of the TV on Saturday mornings. Helen sometimes yelled at the boys—or even at Jim—to help out more. Jim took the boys to the Flying Burrito for Mexican food on Sunday nights before bringing them back to Ann, and Helen and Chance always stayed home.

Ann tucked every piece of information away. To her credit, she had never demonized Helen to the boys. But she had lived in mortal fear that the boys would one day arrive home, announcing that they liked Helen better.

Just the way that Jim had once announced he liked Helen better.

It took a moment for Ann to realize that Chance was in distress. He dropped his plate on the floor, where it broke in half, and the mussel shells scattered everywhere. Ann jumped out of the way. Then she saw Chance clutching at his throat; he was puffing up, turning the color of raw meat.

"Help!" Ann shouted. She spun around, hoping to find Jim,

but behind her was a stout, bald man with square glasses and a bullfrog neck. "Help him!"

A commotion ensued. Chance sank to his knees. The man behind Ann rushed to his side.

"We need an EpiPen!" he shouted. "He's having an allergic reaction!"

Ann snatched her phone out of her purse and dialed 911. She said, "Nantucket Yacht Club, nineteen-year-old male, severe allergic reaction. Please send an ambulance! His throat is closing!"

Chance was clawing at his neck, gasping for air in a way that made it look like he was drowning right in front of them. He sought out Ann's face; his eyes were bulging. Ann was hot with panic. She was shaking, she thought, *My God, what if he dies?* But then her mothering instincts kicked in. She knelt beside him.

"I've called an ambulance, Chance," she said. "Help is coming."

One of the club's managers shot through the kitchen's double doors holding a first aid kit, from which he pulled an EpiPen. He stabbed Chance in the thigh.

Suddenly Jim was there. "Jesus Christ!" he said. "What the hell?"

"He ate a mussel," Ann said. "He must be allergic. He swelled right up." It had reminded Ann of the scene from *Charlie and the Chocolate Factory* where Violet turns into a blueberry and the Oompa-Loompas roll her away.

And then Ann saw a flash of yellow.

"Chancey!" Helen screamed.

The epinephrine seemed to help. Chance's color didn't improve, but neither did it deepen, and he was still forcing wheezing breaths in and out. A crowd gathered, and urgent queries of

What happened? and *Who is it?* circulated. Ann heard someone say, "It's Stuart's stepbrother," then someone else say, "It's the other woman's son." Ann turned around and to no one in particular said, "His name is Chance Graham, and he's the groom's half brother."

Jim and the yacht club manager kept imploring people to back up so that Chance could have some air. Helen was kneeling by Chance's head, smoothing his hair, patting his mottled cheeks. She seemed elegant and glamorous, even on her knees. She looked up at Ann. "What did he eat?" she demanded.

The question was nearly accusatory, as though *Ann* were somehow to blame. She felt like the wicked stepmother who had given him a poison apple.

"He ate a mussel," Ann said.

Helen returned her attention to Chance, and Ann felt a creeping sense of shame. Chance had said he'd never eaten a mussel before, and Ann had said, *They're yummy, you'll love them.* She hadn't *told* him to eat it; he had tried it of his own volition. But she also hadn't given him a warning about allergies. She hadn't even *considered* allergies. Hadn't Chance been allergic to milk as a child? Ann thought she recalled hearing that, but she wasn't positive. He wasn't *her* child. But lots of people were allergic to shellfish. Should she have warned him instead of encouraging him?

The paramedics stormed in, all black uniforms and squawking police scanners. The lead paramedic was a woman in her twenties with wide hips and a brown ponytail. "What'd he eat?"

"A mussel," Helen said.

There was talk and fussing, another shot of something, an oxygen mask. They lifted Chance onto a gurney.

Helen said, "May I ride in the ambulance?"

"You're his mother?" the paramedic asked.

"And I'm his father," Jim said. Jim and Helen were now standing side by side, unified in their roles as Chance's parents.

"No family in the ambulance. You can follow us to the hospital."

"Oh, please," Helen said. "He's only a teenager. Please let me come in the ambulance."

"Sorry, ma'am," the paramedic said. They whisked Chance down the hall and out the front doors.

Helen gazed at Jim—in her heels, she was nearly as tall as he was—and burst into tears. Ann watched Jim fight what must have been a dozen conflicting emotions. Did he want to comfort her? Ann wondered.

He patted her shoulder. "He'll be fine," Jim said.

"We have to go to the hospital," Helen said. "Can I get a ride with y'all?"

"Okay," Jim said. He took Ann by the shoulder. "Let's go."

Ann hesitated. An old, dark emotion bubbled up in her, as thick and viscous as tar. She didn't want to go anywhere with Jim and Helen. She would be an outsider; *she* wasn't Chance's mother. She loved Chance and was sick with worry, but she didn't belong at the hospital with Jim and Helen. However, she didn't want Jim and Helen to go without her, either. She couldn't decide what to do. It was an impossible situation.

Suddenly Stuart and Ryan and H.W. were upon her. "Mom?" Ryan said. He circled his arm around her shoulders.

Stuart said, "Is he going to be *okay?*"

Jim said, "Your mother and I are going to the hospital with Helen."

"Actually, I'm going to stay here," Ann said. To Jim she said, "You go. Please keep me posted."

"What?" Jim said.

Helen shifted from foot to foot. "Can we please leave?"

"Go," Ann said. She gave Jim's arm a push.

"Would you stop acting like a child?" he whispered.

"I need to stay here," Ann said. "It's the rehearsal dinner. It's Stuart's wedding." These words sounded reasonable to her ears, but *was* she acting like a child? She didn't want to be a third wheel with Jim and Helen. She didn't want to have to watch them together in their roles as Mom and Dad. She hated them both at that moment; she hated what they'd done to her. She couldn't believe that she had somehow thought having Helen at the wedding would be a healing experience. It was turning out to be the opposite of healing.

"Ann," Jim said. "Please come. I need you."

Ann smiled her senatorial smile. "I'm going to represent here. You go, and let me know how he's doing." She took Ryan's arm and headed back into the party.

Ryan put his hand on her lower back and whispered in her ear, "Well done, Mother. As always."

Ann fixed herself a plate of food and went to sit with the Lewises, the Cohens, and the Shelbys. On the way, she stopped at each table—most of them filled with people she didn't know—and reassured everyone that Chance would be fine, he was on his way to the hospital to get checked out. As a politician, Ann had spent her career managing crises; the soothing smiles and words and gestures came naturally to her. She wouldn't let herself think about Helen and Jim side by side in the front seat of the rental car, or about how Helen's intoxicating perfume would linger there for Ann and Jim to smell every time they opened the door and climbed in.

Violet, you're turning violet. All the nights that Ann had read *Charlie and the Chocolate Factory* to her boys, Jim had been living in Brightleaf Square making love to the woman he was now driving to the hospital.

Ann closed her eyes against the vision, but all she saw was yellow.

Ann sat next to Olivia, who squeezed the heck out of Ann's forearm but said nothing except "I'm sure he'll be fine."

"Of course he'll be fine," Ann said. She beamed vacantly at her friends, all of whom were wearing plastic bibs and attacking their lobsters. The conversation turned to allergic reactions that people had witnessed or merely heard of secondhand—a man going comatose over his bowl of New England clam chowder, a fifteen-year-old girl dying because she kissed her boyfriend, who had eaten peanut butter for lunch. Meanwhile, in the background, the orchestra played "Mack the Knife" and "Fly Me to the Moon." Couples danced. Stuart and Jenna got up to dance, and there was a smattering of applause. Those two made such a sweet, earnest, clean-cut, wholesome, good-looking couple. Thank God Stuart had broken up with She Who Shall Not Be Named. When Ann used to gaze upon Stuart and Crissy Pine, she had had visions of expensive vacations and overindulged children; she imagined Stuart trapped in a soulless McMansion with a perpetually unhappy wife. Stuart and Jenna's union would be meaningful and strong; they would live with a social conscience, serve on nonprofit boards, and be role models, envied by their friends and neighbors.

Ann picked at a boiled red-skinned potato. Yes, it all looked good from here, but who knew what would happen.

The Cohens got up to dance, and Ann buttered a roll that she had no intention of eating. She checked her cell phone: nothing. Jim and Helen would be at the hospital by now. They would be sitting in the waiting room together, awaiting news. People who saw them would think they were a couple.

Tap on the shoulder. Jethro.

"Dance with me," he said.

"I don't feel up to it," Ann said.

"You have to," Jethro said. "You need to show these northerners you didn't bring me along as chattel."

Ann made a face. "Please spare me the self-deprecating black humor." But Ann then admitted she was powerless to resist Jethro under any circumstances. "Only you," she said.

She accepted his hand and followed him to the dance floor, where he swung her expertly around. Ann and Jim had taken dance lessons right after getting married the second time; it was one of the things they'd made an effort to do together, along with couples Bible study, and antiquing in Asheville, and trout fishing on the Eno River in a flat-bottomed rowboat Jim had bought. They had been happy the second time. Happy until thirty minutes ago. Now Ann could feel herself cracking inside, a ravine opening up.

The song ended. She and Jethro clapped. She kissed his cheek. Ryan had told Ann and Jim that he was gay during Thanksgiving break of his freshman year in college. Ann would say she had handled it well. It wasn't exactly her wish for him, only because she feared his life would be difficult—and of course there was the issue of grandchildren. Jim had taken the news in stride. He had said, "I'm in no position to judge you, son. But for crying out loud, be careful." Ann hadn't been able to predict then how she would adore her son's future boyfriend. She felt even closer to Jethro than she did to Jenna.

She looked at him frankly. "I shouldn't have invited Helen to this fucking wedding."

He grinned, and Ann spied his two overlapping front teeth, and she imagined him as an adolescent in Cabrini-Green, saving his money to buy copies of *Esquire* and *GQ.* "I love you, Annie," he said.

She hugged him. "I love you, too," she said. "Never leave us."

That was a wonderful moment, perhaps Ann's favorite moment of the wedding weekend so far. She wondered what everyone else made of their clan—Ryan with his black boyfriend, Jim with the wife, the mistress-ex-wife, and the love child. Ann stopped at the Carmichael table, where Doug was sitting with Pauline and Pauline's daughter, who was a carbon copy of Pauline, but thirty years younger. The three of them looked perfectly miserable.

Ann remembered Pauline's words and her hot cashew breath. *Do you ever feel like maybe your marriage isn't exactly what you thought it was?*

"Great party!" Ann said.

Doug looked at his watch. The band launched into a Neil Diamond song, and some of the younger people got up to dance.

Jethro escorted Ann back to her table, where she checked her phone. Nothing.

Olivia said, "Eat something, please, Ann."

"I can't," Ann said.

Olivia gave her a knowing look, a look Ann might last have seen twenty years earlier when Jim first left and Ann dropped to ninety-seven pounds.

"I'm going for a little walk," Ann said.

"Want company?" Olivia asked.

Ann shook her head. She put on her wrap and headed out the back doors across the patio and down the brick walk that cut between swaths of green lawn.

Ann imagined the scene at the hospital. Helen and Jim would

be standing hip to hip at the admitting desk, answering questions about Chance.

Date of birth?

April 3, 1994.

Ann remembered the day well. It had been Easter Sunday, and Ann had dutifully gone through all the motions. She had insisted the three boys wear navy blazers, and she'd ironed their khaki pants. They had attended Immaculate Conception; she had smiled and greeted everyone, despite what she knew people were saying about her.

Ann Graham, state senator, her husband ran off with one of the women from their wine-tasting group, he got the woman pregnant…Then there's Donald Morganblue, who's sure to take her senate seat, he's been campaigning like crazy…

Ann had cooked all her special Easter dishes: a honey-baked ham and corn pudding and herbed popovers. The boys devoured the meal, but Ann had simply stared at her food. Jim had especially loved her popovers, and she wondered if he was missing them. Missing her.

The phone call had come at seven o'clock that evening, as Ann was doing the dishes and wrapping up the leftovers and listening to the boys roughhouse in the den. They were high on sugar after so many chocolate bunnies.

"Hello?" Ann had said.

"Ann?" It was Jim calling. The sound of his voice still caused her heart to shimmy with anticipation. She continued to wait for the phone call where he said he was coming back to her.

"Hi," she said. "Happy Easter." She was always civil on the phone. Despite all her anger and pain, she couldn't bring herself to hate the man. She was doomed to love him.

"Easter?" Jim said.

"Yes, Jim," Ann said. "It's Easter." Could he really not know this? Helen was a philistine, that had been proved, but had she brainwashed Jim as well?

He said, "I'm calling to tell the boys that they have a new brother. Chance Oppenheimer Graham, eight pounds, eight ounces, twenty-three inches long. Twenty-three inches, can you believe that?"

Ann had started to sob, and then she hung up the phone. She couldn't believe Jim had just delivered the news so blithely. Did he not remember when it was *she* in the delivery room—the first time when Stuart's heartbeat had dropped dramatically after the doctors gave Ann a shot of Pitocin. The second time when she had popped out not one baby boy but two. Nine pounds, two ounces; six pounds, five ounces; five pounds, fourteen ounces. Stuart had been twenty inches long, the twins each nineteen.

Jim hadn't realized it was Easter because Helen was in labor and had then delivered a baby. Jim had another son. A new family.

Chance, Ann thought. It was a bizarre name, not to mention unsuitable. That baby hadn't been born by chance. That baby had been in Helen's plans for a long time.

Ann heard the strains of the band playing "Witchcraft," and she decided to head back in, find the boys, and enjoy the party. This was Stuart's rehearsal dinner; she wouldn't spend it moping.

She danced like a woman who didn't have a care—first with Ryan, then H.W., then Devon Shelby, and then, finally, Stuart. She went to the ladies' room to freshen up and emerged just in time to see Jim, Helen, and Chance coming around the corner. The three of them looked like they had just shared a joke; Helen was laughing. Ann had an urge to fill her pockets with rocks and drown herself in the harbor — but Jim saw her. "Ann! Ann, we're back!"

Ann let them approach her. She looked only at Chance. "You okay, sweetie?"

"Yeah," he said shyly. "Sorry about that."

"It's not your fault," Ann said. "You didn't know."

"But we know now," Jim said. "No shellfish for him, ever again."

"I could have died," Chance said.

"But you didn't die," Ann said. "Though I'm sure it was terrifying."

"Terrrrrrrrrifying!" Helen sang out. "And now Chance is hungry. He's *starving!* Can y'all get him a hamburger?"

Ann thought, *Do I look like a short-order cook?* Because Chance was going to be okay, Ann could now let her ungenerous thoughts float to the surface: she hated Helen, she wanted to stab Helen in the heart with her stiletto heel, the day of Chance's birth had been one of the worst days of Ann's life. She resented that she had been forced to witness Jim and Helen fussing over *their* son when this weekend was supposed to be about Jim and Ann and *their* son. Ann was a strong woman, but Jim Graham was her kryptonite. When he'd come back to her, crawling on his hands and knees, begging for her forgiveness, she should have kicked him in the teeth. But she had only felt love and gratitude. She was a saint, not a queen. Helen was a queen: imperious, demanding, entitled. Asking Ann to rustle up a hamburger. Why don't *you* find him a hamburger? Ann thought. *He's your son!* Ann should never, ever, ever have invited Helen to the wedding. What had she been thinking? She had been thinking that she wanted that thank-you, goddamn it. And while she was at it, a big fat apology would be nice.

Ann said, "A hamburger? Why, yes, of course." She cast her

eyes about the room for a server, someone to ask. Where was Ford from Colgate when you needed him? Ann saw Olivia staring at her, eyes about to pop out of her head and land in her ramekin of melted butter; she saw Pauline Carmichael throw back a healthy slug of chardonnay. She saw Jethro blow her a kiss. Ann decided she would find Chance a hamburger. She would make that happen.

THE NOTEBOOK, PAGE 37

The Rehearsal Dinner

The rehearsal dinner is normally the responsibility of the groom's family, and there is no reason for me to believe anything will be different in your case. However, assuming your Intelligent, Sensitive Groom-to-Be hasn't spent every summer of his life growing up on Nantucket, here are my thoughts on the perfect rehearsal dinner.

Offer up the Yacht Club. We both know there isn't a more picturesque location on the island. Start with passed hors d'oeuvres on the patio, then segue into a classic clambake buffet (make sure the corn is sourced locally from Moors End Farm). Hire a band. I'm going to suggest ONLY STANDARDS here because this will please the older guests. You can have your "Honky Tonk Woman" and "Electric Slide" at the reception. Serve blueberry cobbler for dessert. End at 10 p.m. Resist the urge to go to the Chicken Box afterwards (now I really do sound like a mother)! You want to be well rested for your big day.

MARGOT

No Edge.

The Nantucket Yacht Club was one of the last places on earth with a pay phone, and Margot was tempted to use it. Call Edge's cell phone, find out exactly what was going on.

She was distracted from thoughts of Edge, however, when Stuart's brother Chance went into full-blown anaphylactic shock. Margot was pretty far from the center of the action, but she quickly ascertained that Chance had eaten a mussel and his throat had started to close. Someone on the yacht club staff produced an EpiPen, the paramedics showed up, Chance was taken to Cottage Hospital, and Stuart's father and the woman in the yellow dress—who, it turned out, was *Chance's mother*—followed in their car.

Chance's mother was here. That was pretty interesting.

A hush followed, as tended to happen after unforeseen emergencies, but once it was determined that Chance would be all right, people returned to what they had been doing before. Ordering cocktails! Hitting the buffet line! Margot procured herself a glass of white wine and a plate of food. She knew she should mingle; she should catch up with her mother's cousins, or with Jenna's fellow teachers from Little Minds—but she just didn't feel up to it tonight. She wanted to eat with someone easy and familiar.

There was a seat next to Ryan and the black boyfriend. That would be good conversation, but Margot would be sitting with Ryan the following night. There were empty seats on either side of Pauline and Rhonda—but no, never.

Then Margot saw Beanie flagging her down. Perfect—except for the fact that Kevin would soon appear. But beggars couldn't be choosers. Margot sat with Beanie.

Beanie said, "Didn't Nick and Finn come with you?"

"No," Margot said. "They showed up really late, and they needed to shower and change, so I left without them. They walked here, I guess."

"I haven't seen either of them," Beanie said.

Margot scanned the room. "You're kidding," she said. "What time is it?"

"Quarter to eight," Beanie said.

Margot attacked her lobster, ripping the body apart, pulling the meat from the tail, cracking the claws, and dumping the empty shells in the bowl in the middle of the table. The clambake at the yacht club had been her mother's suggestion. Margot understood the reasoning behind it — it was a regional specialty, extravagant yet casual. But it was a mess! All these southerners were dressed up. They might not feel like fighting with their dinner.

Margot dipped a lobster claw in drawn butter. Mmmmm. Well, there was no arguing with that.

Nick and Finn, she thought. Still at large. There was only one thing to assume, but even Margot couldn't go there. Nick wouldn't. He just *wouldn't.* He had a moral rip cord. He would pull it.

Margot managed to get all the way through her lobster and eat half an ear of corn before Kevin appeared, hovering over Beanie's left shoulder.

He said, "Come on, we have to sit with Dad."

"What?" Beanie said. "I'm sitting here."

"I know, but you have to move. Dad wants us to sit with him."

"I'm sitting with Margot," Beanie said. "And I'm halfway through my meal, honey. Just sit here, with us."

"Dad wants us over there," Kevin said. He pointed to the table where Doug was sitting with Pauline and Rhonda.

Margot threw her crumpled, butter-soaked napkin onto her plate. "It's okay," she said to Beanie. "You can go. I'm done."

Kevin said, "I'm sure you're welcome, too. I think Dad really wants his family around. This is hard for him."

Margot barked out a laugh. "Yes, Kev, I know it's hard for him. It's hard for all of us."

"But especially hard for Dad," Kevin said.

Margot gave her brother an incredulous look, which he pretended not to see. She loved how Kevin was now taking the whole family's emotional temperature and triaging them. *But especially hard for Dad.* What about Jenna, who was getting married tomorrow without their mother present? What about Margot, who was trying to serve as daughter and sister and surrogate mother? What about poor Pauline—now there was a phrase Margot had never expected to utter—who had to witness all the Beth Carmichael worship and be a good sport about it? And meanwhile her husband was about to divorce her.

Margot pushed her chair away from the table. She said, "I'm going to the ladies' room. Excuse me."

Margot stood at the sinks, washing the lobster juices from her hands. It was probably better that Edge wasn't here, she thought. There was enough drama transpiring as it was. Margot couldn't imagine having to deal with seeing Edge but not being with him, with having to ignore him, with having to pretend in front of her father and everyone else that they were just casual family friends. Edge had been right: Margot couldn't handle it.

The toilet flushed inside one of the stalls, and Jenna stepped out. When Margot saw her sister in the mirror, she grinned. She felt like she hadn't seen Jenna in weeks.

"Hey!" Margot said. "That dress is foxy."

Jenna's rehearsal dinner dress was one place where Jenna and Margot had blatantly disregarded their mother's advice in the Notebook. Beth Carmichael had suggested something conservative—a linen sheath, or a flowered print.

"Linen sheaths and flowered prints are what I wear to work," Jenna said. "I want something sexier!"

Margot and Jenna had shopped for a dress in SoHo, and Margot had to admit that it had been almost the best part of the wedding preparations, probably because the task was infused with a sense of lawlessness. They were defying the Notebook!

They found the peach dress at the Rebecca Taylor boutique. It was a backless halter dress with delicate petals embellishing the short skirt. Jenna had a perfect body, and the dress showed it off.

Jenna did not smile back at Margot. Instead she opened her straw clutch purse and took out lip gloss. "What is going on with Dad?" she said.

Margot grabbed fifteen paper towels in a nervous flurry. "Dad?" she said.

Jenna leaned toward the mirror and dabbed at her lips with the wand. "I know you know," she said. "Please just tell me."

"I'm not sure what you're talking about," Margot said.

"Don't bullshit me!" Jenna cried, waving the gloss in one hand and the wand in the other like an irate orchestra conductor. "I'm sick of it!"

"Sick of what?" Margot said.

"Of you and Kevin and Nick always *keeping* things from me. Trying to *protect* me. I'm twenty-nine years old; I can handle it, Margot. Just please tell me what the hell is going on with Dad."

Now was the moment in the family wedding saga when Margot had to weigh her loyalties. But she still had one more chance to stall.

"I think he's feeling melancholy about tomorrow," Margot said. "Giving away his little girl, throwing this wedding without

Mom. I suggested he finally read the last page of the Notebook. Do you know if he did that?"

"Margot," Jenna said.

"What?"

"Tell me."

Margot studied herself and her sister in the mirror, and Jenna did the same.

Sisters, Margot thought. Eleven years between them, but still, there was no bond closer than sisters.

"He asked me not to tell anyone," Margot said.

"Tell me anyway."

Margot sighed. The yacht club ladies' room wasn't a great place to tell a secret. And yet it had been in this very bathroom that Margot had told her mother she was pregnant. It was during the Commodore's Ball, Labor Day weekend, 2000, at the end of Margot's second summer of dating Drum. Drum's father had set up an internship for him at Sony, but Drum had decided to turn it down. He wanted to go back out to Aspen to ski one more time, he said. Margot had just accepted an entry-level position with Miller-Sawtooth; she was headed to adult life in the city. It looked like a breakup was imminent.

But then Margot had started feeling funny: tired, dizzy, nauseous. She had abruptly left the table during the Commodore's Ball after being served a tomato filled with crab salad. And her mother, sensing something wrong, had followed Margot into the ladies' room and had crowded into the stall with her and held her hair while Margot hurled.

Margot, teary eyed, had stared into the pukey toilet water and said, "I think I'm pregnant."

Beth had said, "Yes, I think you are."

Whoa. Margot sensed her mother's presence so strongly at

that moment that she steadied herself with both hands on the cool porcelain edge of the sink.

Looking at Jenna in the mirror—so much easier than looking at her directly—Margot said, "Dad is going to ask Pauline for a divorce."

Jenna closed her eyes and bowed her head. "Please tell me you're kidding."

"Um, no," Margot said. "Not kidding. He said he doesn't love her. I think...I think he's just still really in love with Mom."

Jenna's eyes filled with tears, and Margot became confused. Did Jenna have a strong alliance with Pauline that Margot didn't know about? Did Jenna *love* Pauline? Pauline was fine, she was okay, on a good day she could be sort of fun—at Halloween, she dressed up as a witch to give the children of Silvermine candy bars—but Margot had no attachment to Pauline, and she assumed her siblings didn't, either.

"Hey," Margot said, patting Jenna's back.

"It's just..." Jenna said.

The door to the ladies' room flew open, so that music floated in. The band was playing *more* Sinatra—"I've Got the World on a String" (her mother's suggestion of "only standards" had been obeyed). By now, Margot guessed, the blueberry cobbler had been served. She glanced up to see who was coming in.

For the sake of poetry, Margot half expected to find Rhonda, or possibly even Pauline herself, entering, so she was taken aback to see...Finn.

Finn wore a silver Herve Leger bandage dress, which Margot knew to cost fifteen hundred dollars. Finn's hair was a mess, and she appeared flushed. Her cheeks were bright red with sunburn, and her eyes were shining and manic.

Margot thought, *Oh, God, no. He didn't.*

"Hi!" Finn said. She was glowing. She would have glowed with a paper bag over her head.

He did.

Jenna spun around so quickly that her skirt flared; it was like a Solid Gold dance move, and Margot would have laughed had it not been for Jenna's tone of voice. In twenty-nine years of knowing her sister, Margot had never heard Jenna speak sharply to anyone, but now her voice was a glinting dagger.

"Where the hell have you been?"

Finn gnawed her lower lip, and Margot could tell she was trying not to burst out in an explosion of bubbles and rose petals.

Jenna looked at an imaginary watch. "It's eight thirty. You were supposed to be at the church for the rehearsal at five. Three and a half hours ago. Where have you been?"

"Um..." Finn said.

"You're my *best friend!*" Jenna cried. "I needed you with me. When you needed me last night, what did I do?"

Silence from Finn, who now looked appropriately contrite.

"I went home with you!" Jenna shouted. "I left my *own* bachelorette party, which Margot had been planning for *months*. I went home and let you cry on my shoulder about what an asshole Scott is. Oh—and he *is* an asshole!"

Margot watched her sister with near-anthropological interest. She was watching the first-ever fight between Jenna and Finn. Jenna could be a spitfire. Who knew?

Finn's face dissolved. She was going to revert to type and cry. This Margot could have predicted, and she further predicted that, upon seeing Finn's tears, Jenna would relent and apologize for her tone. But instead Jenna grew fiercer.

"Answer me," Jenna said. "Where were you?"

"With Nick," Finn said. "Paddleboarding at the beach, then

trying to get home from the beach." Here she flicked her eyes at Margot. "Then we took showers and got dressed at home, then came right here."

No, Margot thought. It had not taken two hours for them to shower, dress, and walk the half mile over here.

"Did something happen?" Jenna asked. "Did something happen between you and Nick?"

Margot couldn't bear to hear the answer. She didn't want Finn to admit the truth, and she didn't want to hear her lie. Margot put up a hand. "I'm leaving," she said. "You two can finish this in peace."

"Thank you," Finn whispered.

As Margot pushed open the door to leave, she heard Jenna say, "Tell me the *truth!*"

Outside, in the corridor, Margot surveyed the happenings in the rest of the club. It was, from the look of things, a lovely party. The band was playing "One for My Baby (and One More for the Road)." Margot's father was dancing with Beanie, Kevin was dancing with Rhonda, Ryan's boyfriend was dancing with Pauline. Nick was standing in the doorway of the kitchen, eating what appeared to be a club sandwich off a paper plate. Unlike Finn, Nick was not radiating ecstasy and moonbeams. He seemed his usual nonchalant, nonplussed self, maybe even a little subdued. Perhaps he was bummed because he'd missed the lobster buffet, or perhaps he was suffering guilty pangs about the sex acts he had just performed with the newly married childhood neighbor girl.

But who was Margot kidding? Nick didn't suffer guilty pangs. Margot had to get out of there.

You can't tell me you wouldn't love an opportunity to vent your frustration with your family to a friendly acquaintance.

Goddamned Griff, Homecoming King, was right. She would love.

Margot told herself that the Boarding House was on her way home. She told herself that she would just poke her head in, and if Griff wasn't instantly visible, she would leave.

She stepped into the welcoming energy of the Boarding House bar; the air smelled like roasting garlic and warm bread and expensive perfume. The lighting was low, the good-looking patrons were exuding a happy buzz, and "You Can't Always Get What You Want" was playing.

Ha! Margot thought. Got that right.

She stepped up to the bar, where there was one leather stool available. She didn't see Griff, and she considered leaving. But the barstool looked comfortable; it would be nice, maybe, to just sit and have a drink by herself. She was lonely nearly all the time, but so seldom alone.

She ordered a martini. She tried not to appear self-conscious, although the word described her exactly. She was conscious of herself sitting alone, sipping a stronger drink than she should be having at this hour, waiting for . . .

A tap on the shoulder.

She turned around. Griff.

"You came," he said. He sounded full of boyish wonder at that moment, as if discovering the presence of Santa Claus on Christmas morning.

Margot sipped her martini. She would not let him rattle her. She would be her genuine self. But she was struck by the ocean of colors contained in his eyes; she felt as if she might drown in them.

"It was on my way home," Margot said.

He was wearing a white button-down shirt and jeans and a navy blazer. He now sported three-day scruff, which was even sexier than two-day scruff.

"You came to see me," Griff said. "Admit it, you did."

There was the smug confidence that Margot had expected. She juggled a dozen possible replies in her head, but then she settled on the truth. "You were right," she said. "This morning."

Griff's eyes widened. "About what?"

"I *would love* an opportunity to vent my frustrations with my family to a kindly stranger. I would like to detail the many ways they are destroying my spirit."

Griff held up open palms. "By all means," he said. "Detail away."

"Have you ever lost anyone?" she asked.

Griff said, "You mean, other than when my wife walked out?"

Margot said, "Yes. I mean, has anyone close to you died?"

Griff said, "My younger brother. Highway accident. I was twenty-five, and he was twenty-one."

Margot stopped for a second. She thought, My siblings, they drive me insane, I despise two out of the three of them right now. But what if one of them died? Impossible to imagine; they were her brothers, her sister. She couldn't go on without them. "Oh," she said. "Wow. That's awful. I'm so sorry."

Griff nodded. "This isn't supposed to be about me. This is supposed to be about you."

Margot said, "You're a good guy, right?"

Griff shrugged. "My daughter seems to think so, but she's only twelve, so what does she know?"

Margot's guilt kept her silent. She thought about how painfully ironic it was that the one person she had really and truly wronged this year was the very same person she was now about to confide in. Griff would hate her if he knew what she'd done. He would be right to hate her. She should go. She couldn't sit and tell him things with this insidious secret gnawing at her, but she couldn't confess, either.

He said, "Have *you* ever lost anyone?"

"My mother," Margot said. "Seven years ago, to ovarian cancer."

She could feel his eyes on her face, but she couldn't look at him.

Margot said, "My mother left a notebook behind for my sister filled with instructions for this wedding. She wrote them down because she knew she wouldn't be around to see it."

Griff pinched the bridge of his nose. "Oh, man," he said. "That's tough."

"Tough," Margot agreed.

The song changed to "Watching the Detectives." Griff tapped his thigh. "You like Costello?" he asked.

Margot nodded. "Love him."

"She's filing her nails while they're dragging the lake," he quoted.

Her favorite line.

She said, "My father remarried a woman named Pauline. Nice woman. I have no complaints except that she's not my mother. They've been married five years. This morning, as I was driving my dad to Sankaty, he told me he's going to ask Pauline for a divorce."

"Because…" Griff said.

Then, together, they said, "Because she's not my/your mother."

Margot thought, *This guy gets it.*

She said, "I also have two brothers. There's Kevin, who is eleven months younger than me, but who acts like he's older. He's got this superiority thing, he's always right, always in charge." She stopped herself. Since Griff had lost his brother, it might be in poor taste to complain about her own brother. She said, "What was your brother like?"

"This isn't about me, remember."

"Just tell me," Margot said.

Griff sighed. "Well, he was rebellious. He rode a motorcycle, he had a bunch of tattoos, he started smoking in middle school, and drinking in high school. But here's the thing: he was brilliant, went to MIT for three semesters, then took a semester off and went to mechanics' school to learn how to fix classic muscle cars, Plymouth Barracudas, Shelby Cobras, Corvette Stingrays." Griff took a sip of his drink and a deep breath. "And he could play the piano by ear. At my grandparents' fiftieth wedding anniversary, he had everybody singing until long after midnight."

The song changed to "Lawyers, Guns and Money."

Margot said, "You like Zevon?"

"I went home with a waitress," he quoted. "The way I always do."

"How was I to know...she was with the Russians, too," she said. Again, her favorite line.

She said, "Then there's my brother Nick, the lothario. Loves women, and can't seem to exercise any restraint."

Griff nodded. "Familiar with the type."

Margot wasn't sure why Nick's behavior surprised her. He had always been like this. He had taken two girls to the senior prom. He had run through entire sororities at Penn State. Margot had heard a rumor that he slept with one of his law school professors. But Finn? Why Finn? There were plenty of single women at the wedding—any of Jenna's hippie-dippy teacher friends, or he could have had a reprise with Autumn.

"So tonight..." Margot said, but she trailed off. She didn't feel like talking about what Nick had done that night.

"Tonight, what?" Griff said.

Margot said, "My ten-year-old, Carson, barely passed the fourth grade. And my daughter, Ellie, is a hoarder."

Griff laughed. He had a very nice laugh, she remembered now.

She said, "Remind me of your kids' names. I know you told me, but I haven't been blessed with your memory." Many times a candidate would include a line on his or her résumé that said something like *Married fourteen years, devoted mother of four.* And Margot would always tell them to scratch it. Everyone loved their kids, and half of everyone loved their spouse. It didn't belong on a résumé, and it shouldn't be discussed with a potential employer unless it directly affected the candidate's work history—as it had in Griff's case.

He said, "My daughter, Colby, twelve, thinks I hung the moon. Sons Ethan and Tanner, ages ten and eight, think Robinson Cano hung the moon. I don't see them nearly enough. Every other weekend."

Margot said, "Mine fly to California the last weekend of every month to see their father. Who informed me two days ago that he is getting married again to a Pilates instructor named Lily."

Griff rattled the ice in his glass. He was drinking something and Coke, maybe bourbon like all the southerners at the rehearsal dinner, and Margot thought for a second about how good he might taste if she kissed him, sweet and caramelish. She chastised herself for thinking about kissing Griffin Wheatley, Homecoming King, and then she admitted to herself that she had been thinking about kissing him ever since she saw him on the ferry.

Griff said, "My ex-wife, Cynthia, is due to give birth in a few weeks. To Jasper's baby."

Margot finished her drink and waited for her eyes to cross. Griff's wife had fallen in love with his best friend, Jasper, who was also his direct boss, which explained Griff's sudden departure from the Masterson Group and was the reason why Margot met him in the first place. Griff hadn't wanted to tell Drew Carver or the rest of the top brass at Tricom about Jasper and his ex-wife. Margot understood: candidates never wanted to share the messy ways that their personal lives intersected with their professional lives. But it hadn't mattered; Tricom had wanted him for the job... until.

She said, "That. Totally. Sucks."

"Precisely," Griff said. He flagged the bartender for the check. "You should really get home. It's late."

Margot straightened her spine with what she hoped was a graceful, yoga-like movement. The alcohol, rather than making the edges of things soft and hazy, had turned her field of vision clear and sharp. Was Griff trying to get rid of her? Had she *bored* him? Did her problems seem petty and obvious, standard fare for an educated, upper-middle-class white woman of a certain age? Her children were healthy, she had a job, money, friends. She was divorced. So what? She had lost her mother. So what? Everyone lost his or her mother eventually. There were people in this world with real problems. There were children in the cancer ward, there were men in Bangladesh being paid twelve or fifteen cents a day to dismantle old cruise liners for scrap metal, there were millions of people across America who had to work the third shift. Margot had no reason to complain.

"You're right," she said. "I should go." She collected her wrap and her purse and plunked thirty dollars on the bar, which Griff pushed back at her.

"Please," he said. "My treat."

"Absolutely not," she said.

"I insist," he said.

She reclaimed her money and said, "Well, thank you for the drinks. And thank you for listening." He had been attentive, he hadn't tried to offer platitudes or advice. He had been a capital L Listener. Every family wedding, Margot realized, needed a Listener.

"My pleasure," Griff said.

Margot slid off the leather barstool. She felt even more conflicted than when she had walked in here. On top of her other avalanche of emotions was regret about having to leave Griffin Wheatley, Homecoming King.

Griff said, "Margot, are you dating anyone?"

She said, "Oh, sort of." Then she laughed because those three words had to represent a situation so complex she couldn't begin to explain it.

He said, "I figured I had some kind of competition, but I wasn't sure what form it took."

He walked her home, holding her arm as she crossed the cobblestones of Main Street. As they walked up Orange, Margot began to wonder about the rest of her family. Would they be home? Would they be awake? Margot had, essentially, vanished, and her phone didn't work, so no one would have been able to reach her. She couldn't believe how liberating it was to be untethered.

The next thing she knew, she and Griff were standing on the sidewalk a few doors down from her house. There was a fat gibbous moon above them, and the clock tower of the Unitarian Church was illuminated.

Margot said, "Really, I can't thank you enough..."

Griff put his hands on either side of her neck and held her like that for a second, then he kissed her softly on the lips. Then again, then again, more urgently, then there was tongue, and a flood of desire. Margot was breathless. She thought, This is the best first kiss I've ever had, and this is the worst first kiss precisely because of how good it is, because once he finds out what I did, he will never kiss me again. Therefore she had to be greedy now. Margot kissed him and kissed him, tongue, lips, hands, hair, she pulled on him, she could not get *enough*. She thought, *Edge who?* Kissing Edge had never felt like this. Kissing Edge had been like kissing an old man, sometimes their teeth clicked, sometimes his breath was sour. And yet Edge had such a stranglehold on her, he held her captive, so much so that she had been willing, eager even, to wrong this man right here. It was the secret of Edge that was addictive, it was his beautifully cut suits and his expensive watch. It was the fact that he should rightfully treat Margot like treasure, but he treated her carelessly, and the more carelessly he treated her, the more obsessed she became.

Griff pulled away, and Margot thought, *No!* She worried that he wasn't enjoying the kissing as much as she was. Was insane desire and electricity like this ever one-sided?

He said, "I have a confession to make."

She believed he was about to admit to a girlfriend, or even a fiancée, although his pursuit of her had been zealous to say the very least. She thought, *I don't care if he is married or engaged or if he's been dating someone a year or three months or a week.*

"What?" she said.

He said, "I've had a crush on you since the first second I saw you."

Her feet in her silver heels turned icy. They were suddenly so cold that they hurt; she couldn't move her toes.

"From the minute you first shook my hand," he said. "I thought you were so pretty then. But pretty was the least of it. You were smart and capable, and...so tough on me. You asked the most exacting questions. It was a turn-on. I couldn't ask you for your number then, obviously. I thought about calling you at work after I'd been signed off, but I wasn't sure if…well, I thought it might be awkward for you. I didn't expect to ever see you again, especially not on the ferry to Nantucket."

"Oh," she said. She flooded with shame, with panic. *Smart, capable, tough…exacting questions…a turn-on.* Jesus!

"And please don't worry about the outcome of all of that," Griff said. "I'm sure the other guy was a better match."

Margot said, "I…I can't talk about it."

"Of course not," Griff said. "Obviously. I'm sorry."

I'm sorry! Margot thought.

He said, "Can I see you tomorrow?"

Tomorrow? Margot thought. Tomorrow was the wedding. She would be busy all day and night, and Edge was coming. She had liked kissing Griff, she had liked it a lot, but she hated herself for what she'd done. Griff was such a good guy. Margot had always thought of herself as a good guy…until that phone call with Drew Carver, when she had become a not-good guy. Margot could never confess to it. But she also couldn't see Griff again, or kiss him again, *without* confessing to it.

"No," she said. "I'm sorry."

"No?" he said. "But…"

She waved good-bye and hurried down the street toward her family's house, thinking again that some nights had good karma and some nights were cursed, and for a few moments, tonight had seemed like the former, but it had ended up the latter.

And as if Margot needed further proof of this, when she approached the house, she saw Jenna sitting on the top step by the front door, which no one but the mailman ever used. Jenna had her face in her hands. She was crying.

THE NOTEBOOK, PAGE 26

The Bridal Bouquet

I love flowers, this you know. One summer during college, I worked for a florist on Seventy-seventh Street called Stems— it's long gone—doing deliveries, and later, simple arrangements. Stems had a beautiful built-in flower cooler with huge oak and glass doors, and I would take any opportunity I could to step inside that cooler and inhale the scent. If there is a heaven, it had better resemble the walk-in cooler at Stems, filled with roses, lilies, dahlias, and gerbera daisies in rainbow colors.

Bridal bouquet: Limelight hydrangeas, white peonies (tight, not blooming), lush white roses, jade roses, jade lisianthus, green hypericum. This combination will give a rounded, sumptuous effect with a perfect balance of white and green shades.

Bridesmaids: White hydrangeas and jade roses. Tie those up with matching green ribbon.

Please note that I've avoided adding Asiatic lilies, calla lilies and orchids. These flowers are too structured, too citified—they cannot coexist with the softness of the peonies. Trust me.

DOUG

In the master bedroom, in the king bed, Pauline reached for him. Her hands, with nails newly painted the color of brewing storm clouds, wrapped around his biceps. She pulled herself in close and breathed in his ear. Then the flat of her palm ran down his bare chest, over the softer flesh at his belly, and across the front of his boxers. Nothing.

This wasn't unusual. Doug was getting older, and he didn't always snap to attention the way he used to. He had considered seeing Dr. Fraker and getting a prescription, but that seemed like an admission of defeat. The only way he'd been able to sustain an erection with Pauline recently was to imagine her with Russell Stern from the Wee Burn Country Club. This was twisted, Doug knew—fantasizing about his wife with another man. And it couldn't be any other man, either; it couldn't be Arthur Tonelli or George Clooney. It had to be Russell Stern. Doug worried that he was somehow attracted to Russell Stern. Perhaps this was an indication of a latent homosexual urge? But further pondering brought Doug to the conclusion that he had been most attracted to Pauline when he'd suspected that Russell Stern was pursuing her. It had increased Pauline's desirability. That Pauline and Russell Stern had once been a couple made it even better. Sometimes Doug fantasized about Pauline in her short, pleated cheerleader skirt and Russell in football pads taking her from behind in what he imagined to be the fetid air of the New Canaan High School locker room.

But that vision wasn't working tonight. Nothing would work tonight. Nothing, Doug thought sadly, would work ever again. His sex life with Pauline was over.

He gathered her wandering hand in both of his and squeezed it. He wanted to be kind to her, but so often, kind was mistaken for patronizing.

"Pauline," he said.

"It's okay," she said. "I understand, I get it, it's only natural that you'd be thinking of her."

"Thinking of whom?"

"Beth."

"I wasn't thinking of Beth."

Pauline rolled over on her side so that her back was to him. "Of course you were."

He wanted to say, *Don't tell me what I was or was not thinking about. You aren't a mind reader.* But Doug didn't want to pick a fight. He didn't want to act like any of his clients. People going through a divorce faced heightened emotion every single day. Just last week, Doug had received an e-mail in which the subject line read "Rough Morning." The message consisted of a detailed description of how contentious the before-school routine in the Blahblahblah household had become. Mom and Dad both lived in the same apartment building, and little Sophie and slightly older Daniel were shuttled up and down on the elevator in search of clean clothes, breakfast, and homework while Mom and Dad screamed profanities at each other on their cell phones. Doug had read and answered a thousand such e-mails; he had a front-row seat for every imaginable variety of domestic discord. He loathed the thought of anyone — another lawyer, a therapist, or Rhonda — being privy to the inner workings of his relationship with Pauline. He just wanted the marriage to quietly go away. He wanted it to be a soap bubble he could pop with his finger.

"I wasn't thinking of Beth," Doug whispered.

"What were you thinking of, then?" Pauline asked.

He didn't answer. Pauline's insistence that he was thinking of Beth led him to think of Beth. He thought about their wedding, which had been held in New York City. The ceremony at St. James' on Seventy-first Street, the reception at the Quilted Giraffe, wedding night at the Pierre Hotel, where they had arrived, giddy and exhausted, at three in the morning, after a late-night excursion to Chinatown because Beth had been so busy talking and having her picture taken at the reception that she hadn't eaten a thing, and she found herself with an insane craving for soup dumplings.

Doug remembered sitting across the tiny, soy-sticky table holding Beth's hand as she slurped her soup dumplings. She was still in her white dress. The old Chinese women fussed over her; they petted her hair, they admired her ring. Doug remembered wanting to shoo them away like flies.

On the way back to the Pierre, Doug had asked Beth how many children she thought they should have.

"Four," she said. "Two boys and two girls."

That had seemed like a tall order to Doug, but all he'd wanted at that moment, and every moment after, was to make Beth happy.

"You got it," he'd said.

In the next instant, Doug had watched all the traffic lights on Park Avenue, as far as he could see, turn green at once. It had been a moment of electrifying synchronicity.

The last page of the Notebook, he wondered. What did it say?

THE NOTEBOOK, PAGE 40

Dinner Menu

*Beef, but not tenderloin. Something more flavorful. Ribeye?
    New York Strip?*
*Fish, not chicken. Swordfish, maybe, or striped bass, but only
    if you can get it locally from Bill Sandole at East Coast
    Seafood.*

Baked potatoes with toppings — good cheddar, sour cream,
crispy bacon, snipped chives. When I am gone, one of the
things I will miss the most is a loaded baked potato.
Grilled or pan-roasted vegetables, not boiled.
Warm snowflake rolls.
A really good salad, sourced from Pumpkin Pond Farm.
Make it different from what people expect. Make it better.

ANN

She looked good," Ann said. "Don't you think she looked good?"

"Who?" Jim said. He was standing in front of the mirror, tugging at his necktie.

"Helen," Ann said. "She looked beautiful, better than ever." Ann hated saying the words, but they were true, goddamn it. They were true. Ann decided she would be the one to say them so the thought was out in the open and not festering in Jim's brain. Ann was scared. She was terrified that Helen would steal Jim away again.

Jim approached Ann with open arms and pressed her against his chest. He ran his hands up and down her back in that way she loved. He smelled like melted butter.

"How was it at the hospital?" Ann asked.

"What do you mean?" Jim said.

Ann pulled away. "Did you sit with her in the waiting room?"

"I sat in the waiting room and she sat in the waiting room," Jim said. "Was I *with* her? No, not really."

"Did you sit next to her? ' Ann asked.

Jim sighed. "Yes," he said. "More accurately, she sat next to me. I couldn't very well get up and move. That would have been awfully rude."

Ann could not clear the color yellow from her field of vision. "What did you two talk about?"

"We barely spoke at all," Jim said. "A little bit about Chance. We both marveled that his allergy to shellfish had escaped our notice for nineteen years."

Ann did not love the phrases "we both marveled" or "escaped our notice."

"I felt like Helen was blaming me because I was with Chance when he ate the mussel," Ann said.

"Don't be ridiculous," Jim said. "It wasn't your fault. It wasn't anyone's fault."

Ann sat on the edge of the bed and kicked her flats off into the room. She felt small and insignificant and ugly. Helen Oppenheimer had been making her feel that way for twenty years, since the wine-tasting group, since the hot air balloon ride. Ann was incensed by the image of Jim and Helen side by side in the hospital waiting room. It was too reminiscent of Jim in the hospital on that Easter Sunday, crowing to Ann over the phone about how large and healthy his newborn son was.

Ann said, "Did you talk about anything else?"

Jim said, "Not really. I read *Sports Illustrated*. Helen was texting."

"Who was she texting, I wonder?" Ann said. "The younger lover?"

"No," Jim said. "They broke up."

"They broke *up?*" Ann said. "How do you know this?"

"She told me," Jim said. He whipped his belt out of the loops, removed his pants, and tossed them unfolded into the gaping mouth of his suitcase. Ann, of course, had placed all her clothes in drawers, neatly folded, except for the things she had to hang, which were in the closet. Neat Ann, Catholic school Ann, Saint Ann.

"She told you when?" Ann said.

"In the car ride," Jim said. "I asked her how Brad was doing, and she said they'd split. She got tired of him, she said."

"*She* got tired of *him?*" Ann said. The lover Brad was ten years Helen's junior, he was a successful doctor, and *she* got tired of *him?* Ann didn't like this one bit. Helen was single, she was free, and everyone, especially Ann, knew that Helen didn't do well alone. "And she told you this? In the car?"

"Ann," Jim said. "If you wanted to know what Helen and I talked about, you should have come along to the hospital. I wanted you to come. I was practically begging you."

"It was Stuart's rehearsal dinner!" Ann said. She was starting to hit her upper register, which was never a good sign. She took a moment to regroup, but the vodka martinis were wringing out her brain like wet laundry. For twenty years she had been a reasonable woman when dealing with Jim and his situation. But not tonight. "Stuart is *my* son, and he's getting married tomorrow! I didn't feel like I should miss his rehearsal dinner because Chance got sick. Chance…isn't *my son, Jim.* He's your son, and he's Helen's son."

"Please calm down, Ann," Jim said. "You're absolutely right."

"I *know* I'm absolutely right!" Ann said. She walked over to Jim and automatically turned her back because she needed him to unzip her dress. He did so, and then he helped to slip it from her shoulders, but she batted him away. The dress dropped to the floor in a pink puddle, and she left it there. She pulled on the white waffled robe over her bra and panties. "I hate her."

"Ann…"

"I. Hate. Her."

"Well, then," Jim said. He paced the room as he unbuttoned his shirt. "Well, then, you shouldn't have invited her here."

Ann thought, *And you shouldn't have fucked her. And you shouldn't have knocked her up. And you shouldn't have married her.*

Inviting her had merely been a generous, considerate way of dealing with the heinous predicament Jim had put them in.

She pointed to the door. "Get out," she said.

"What?" he said.

"Get out!" Ann said. "I want you out!"

Jim took one, two, three steps in her direction, but she did not lower her finger. "I'm serious, Jim. Get out of this room. I don't want you here tonight."

"But Stuart..."

"What do you care about Stuart?" Ann said. "What do you care about any of us?"

"So let me get this straight," Jim said. "You decide for some reason unbeknownst to me or anyone else to invite Helen to this wedding. It was *your* decision, Ann Graham, and yours alone. I was dead set against it, and I think I made that clear. And now, because Helen is here and because Chance had an unforeseen allergic reaction—where, I might add, he almost died—*I* am now paying the price."

"Paying the *price?*" Ann said. Jim hadn't "paid the price" the way Ann had paid the price, not by a long shot. He had come back to Ann as contrite as a man could be; he had cried, he had sent flowers, he had attended counseling with Father Art, their parish priest, he had shown up for every one of the boys' school and sporting events with his hat in his hands begging forgiveness, he had done everything short of renting a billboard on I-80 renouncing his sins—but had he actually paid a price? Ann thought not.

She dropped her arm. "Get out," she said quietly.

"Annie?" he said.

"Please," she said.

THE NOTEBOOK, PAGE 19

The Cake

It has been my experience that people don't eat the cake, or that by the time people eat the cake, they are so drunk that they don't remember the cake. Therefore, my suggestions regarding the cake are going to be loose. You want a pretty cake; it will be featured in photos. They do a basket-weave that is very Nantuckety. Use buttercream icing—NOT FONDANT. Fondant is impossible to eat. Decorate with flowers? Sugared fruit? Ask for matching cupcakes for the kids?

My one hard-and-fast suggestion is that when you and Intelligent, Sensitive Groom-to-Be cut the cake and feed each other, you do so nicely. Maybe this shows my age, but I don't like playing around with the cake, smearing it in each other's face or hair. Yuck!

SATURDAY

MARGOT

Margot woke up in her bed, sandwiched between Ellie and Jenna. Her left arm was asleep. Downstairs, the phone was ringing.

Margot extracted herself by climbing over Ellie, who wouldn't wake up unless there was an earthquake and an ensuing tsunami. She shook out her hand in an attempt to get the blood circulating again. Outside, she noted, there was blue sky and birdsong.

I wish for you a beautiful day.

At least they had that.

Margot rushed down the stairs, nearly slipping on the next-to-last step; the treads had been worn down to a satiny finish after so many years of bare feet up and down. *I'm coming, I'm coming,* she thought. A houseful of people, and somehow she was the only one who heard the phone? Or she was the only one stupid enough to get out of bed at—she checked the clock—6:15 to answer it.

"Hello?" she said.

"Margot? It's Roger."

"Good morning, Roger," Margot said.

"You're aware, I assume, that your sister left me a voice mail at eleven thirty last night — I'm sorry I was asleep — saying that the wedding is off?"

"Yes," Margot said. "I am aware of that."

"Is the wedding off?" Roger asked.

"I'm not sure," Margot said.

"Okay," Roger said. There was a pause and a suspicious sound of exhale. Was Roger smoking? Had Jenna's phone call been the thing that sent him right to Lucky Express for a pack of Newports? "Will you let me know when you *are* sure?"

"Absolutely," Margot said. "I will absolutely let you know."

"Thank you," Roger said. "I probably don't need to add this, but... the sooner, the better. Good-bye."

Margot hung up the phone. She would never be able to fall back to sleep, so she made a pot of coffee. She said to herself, *I won't think about anything until I have my coffee and I can sit for a minute in the sun.* She would have liked to sit on the swing, but the swing was down for now. She decided instead to take her cup of coffee and the Notebook out to the bench that overlooked the harbor, the same bench where her father had proposed to her mother in 1968. Margot took in the view — Nantucket harbor scattered with sailboats, the white fence and trellis dripping with New Dawn roses. She opened the Notebook.

Invitations, wedding dress, bridesmaid dresses, dyed-to-match pumps, pearls, rehearsal dinner clambake menu (right down to the blueberry cobbler, but Margot hadn't gotten a single bite), tenting, dance floor, flowers, antique embroidered table linens, china, crystal, silver, hors d'oeuvres, wine, dinner menus, cake, favors, hotel rooms, bands versus DJs, song lists, schedule of dances, bridesmaid gifts, honeymoon locations. There were many references to their father, including the beautiful last page. And there were many references to Margot. "Margot is the most competent woman you or I will ever know. And to butcher the old song: 'Anything I can do, she can do better.'" Margot had read those lines hundreds of times; they were among her favorite lines in the Notebook. But they missed a fine distinction: Margot could do the things that Beth could do, but Margot could not be Beth. And what Jenna needed now, more than anything, was Beth.

Margot flipped through the pages to the end of the Notebook, where the ancillary material was—the list of Beth's cousins, the brochure for Caneel Bay in St. John, the name and number of the landscaper to call should the perennial bed be trampled by the tent guys, after all.

There was no mention of Cold Feet.

In composing the Notebook, their mother had left out a few things that were really important.

Tell us what to do when we feel doubt, Margot thought. *Tell us what to do when we feel anger. Tell us how to handle our sadness, Mom. We are, every one of us, paralyzed with sadness because you aren't here today, you weren't here yesterday, you won't be here tomorrow.*

When Jenna and Margot had first met with Roger, Margot had baldly stated the fact. "We are a family without our mother."

Roger had nodded in that unflappable way of his, like there was nothing they could say that could shock him, like he had seen it all before.

Jenna had then triumphantly held up the Notebook. "But we have this!"

But this, Margot thought, as she closed the Notebook and headed back to the house, wasn't enough.

*   *   *

Margot poured a cup of coffee for Jenna and added half and half and three teaspoons of sugar. Jenna, of course, drank it sweet and light, while Margot drank hers hot, bitter, and black. Up in Margot's room, Ellie was jumping on the bed, chanting, "Auntie Jenna's getting married today! Married today! Married today!"

Jenna's spot in the bed was unoccupied.

Margot said, "Eleanor, stop that this instant. That bed is ancient, and you will break it!"

Ellie launched herself off the bed and crashed onto the braided rug.

Margot said, "Well, now the whole house is awake."

Ellie said, "Can I go up and see the boys?"

"No," Margot said. "I need you to do something quiet. Get your iPod and go downstairs."

"My iPod is boring," Ellie said.

"I don't care," Margot said. "I have to talk to your Auntie Jenna."

Ellie folded her arms across her chest. She was still in her bathing suit, still salt-and-sand encrusted from yesterday's trip to the beach. The Department of Social Services was sure to arrive at any moment.

"I want to stay and listen," Ellie said.

"It's adult stuff," Margot said. There was a part of her that believed Ellie *should* stay and listen. After all, Ellie would one day grow up to be a woman. It might not be a bad idea for her to learn now, at the tender age of six, that the world was a complicated place, that other people's minds could not be read, their emotions could not be predicted, that love was fleeting and capricious, that once you thought you'd figured everything out, some-

222

thing would happen to prove you wrong. Life was a mystery, and nobody knew what happened when we died.

"I don't care," Ellie said. "I want to listen."

"Downstairs," Margot said.

"No," Ellie said.

Margot closed her eyes. She was feeling the drinks from the night before, which brought around thoughts of kissing Griff and her treachery and Edge's impending arrival. Margot's hands trembled. She set her coffee down on the dresser and sighed. "Okay, go upstairs with the boys, then."

Ellie let out a whoop, then did a pirouette across the floor. Thank God for Mme Willette's ballet class; it was the only thing keeping Ellie from turning into a wild Indian.

Margot said, "Where did Auntie Jenna go?"

Ellie said, "Bathroom."

Margot grabbed her coffee and lay back on the bed, propping herself up against the pillows. The sheets were filled with sand.

What am I going to say? she wondered.

When she'd sat next to Jenna on the front stairs the night before and asked why she was crying, Jenna had told her she was calling the wedding off.

"*What?*"

"I'm not getting married," Jenna said.

"Why not?" Margot said.

"Stuart lied to me," Jenna said.

"He *lied* to you?" Margot said. That didn't sound like Stuart. Stuart was as square a peg as had ever lived. He hadn't even wanted a bachelor party. What man didn't want a bachelor party? Drum Sr.'s bachelor party in Cabo had included more people than had attended their wedding and had lasted longer than their honeymoon.

Jenna's lower lip trembled, and she sucked it in the way she used to when she was a little girl. "He was engaged before," she said.

"What?" Margot said.

"To Crissy Pine," Jenna said. "His girlfriend from college. He was engaged to her for *five weeks!* Helen told me, Helen who used to be his stepmother. The woman in the yellow dress tonight."

Margot's brain felt like it was going to short-circuit. She didn't know how to process this information. "Five weeks isn't very long, Jenna. Five weeks is nothing. It's negligible."

"He lied to me!" Jenna said. "He was engaged before! He never *told me!*"

"You found this out from Helen?" Margot said. "Chance's mother?"

"It was the first time I ever met her," Jenna said. "She and Stuart aren't close; he was shocked his mother invited her. But nearly the first thing Helen said to me was that she was glad things worked out for Stuart *this time.* And I must have made a confused face because then she said, 'Well, you know about his broken engagement to Crissy Pine?' And I said no, and she leaned in conspiratorially, like we were *girlfriends,* and she said, 'Stuart was engaged to Crissy Pine for five weeks, and after he broke it off, she refused to return his great-grandmother's diamond ring.'" Jenna was in full-blown tears now. "He gave her his *great-grandmother's ring!*"

Margot blinked. Why couldn't people keep their mouths shut? What did Helen think would be gained by breaking this news to Jenna the evening before her wedding? Did it give her some awful sense of accomplishment?

Margot said, "Helen is an iffy source. She might be lying. Or exaggerating."

"I confronted Stuart!" Jenna said. "He admitted it was true. He proposed to Crissy, he gave her his great-grandmother's ring, he broke it off five weeks later, and she was so mad that she never gave the ring back. She still has it!"

She sold it on eBay, Margot thought.

She said, "Why didn't he ever tell you?"

"He wanted to protect me, he said! He didn't think I needed to know, he said! He knew it was a mistake the second he asked Crissy, he said! He only proposed because she was nagging him, and so he asked her to get her to stop."

Oh, dear, thought Margot.

"I'm sure he *did* want to protect you," Margot said. "As some-one who knows you nearly better than anyone else, I can say that you are a hard person to give bad news. You're an idealist; you believe in the goodness of your fellow man beyond the point where the rest of us would have given up. Of course he didn't want to tell you. Stuart has done nothing over the course of your entire relationship except try to make you happy. He bought a hybrid for you! He registered Democrat for you! Honey, trust me, this isn't a deal breaker."

Jenna sniffed.

"Jenna," Margot said. "This *isn't* a deal breaker."

"The rest of Stuart's family has always been so *weird* about Crissy," Jenna said. "No one ever talks about her. There are fam-ily pictures in the Graham house with Crissy in them, but Ann cut out black ovals and pasted them over Crissy's face!"

Margot couldn't keep from smiling at this. She wondered if Drum's mother, Greta, had covered *her* face with black ovals—say, in the photos of Drum Jr.'s christening.

"It's not funny!" Jenna said. "We bumped into her once, at

Newark airport. She was going one way on the moving sidewalk, and we were going the other way, and she called out Stuart's name and he turned and I turned, and she flipped Stuart off. She gave him the *finger!* She was pretty — dark hair, pale skin, sort of Spanish looking — and I was like, Who was that and what was THAT all about? Who on earth would flip Stuart the bird? My wonderful, kind Stuart, the man everyone adores and admires? I said, 'Um. Do you KNOW that girl? ' He clearly didn't want to tell me, but then he admitted it was Crissy. And I dragged him to the airport bar and we ordered margaritas and I demanded that he tell me what exactly had happened with Crissy. And all he would say was that in his mind he liked to pretend she had never existed."

Margot nodded. If everyone told their stories about ex-boyfriends, ex-girlfriends, ex-fiancés, ex-fiancées, ex-husbands, or ex-wives — or those they had to cross paths with either physically or emotionally — there would be millions and millions of chapters. It was a fraught topic, put mildly.

"You've had serious relationships before," Margot said. "What about Jason? You *loved* Jason. You basically gave yourself an eating disorder and put yourself in the student infirmary because of Jason. Have you ever admitted that to Stuart?"

"I didn't have an eating disorder," Jenna said.

"When he broke up with you the first time, you went on a hunger strike!" Margot said. "Do I have to wake up Autumn to corroborate? You lived on toast and vodka."

"Ever since Stuart proposed, you've been urging me to reconsider," Jenna said. "You told me everyone gets divorced. You told me that love *dies.*" Jenna blinked, tears fell. Her makeup was a mess; there were black smudges on the skirt of her peach dress. She had been using her dress as a Kleenex. "And you're right!

Love does die, people do change, everyone is unfaithful, vows do get broken, betrayal is real. Stuart Graham, who I thought was *beyond reproach,* lied to me about being engaged to someone else."

"Stuart gets a pass on this one," Margot said. "Forgive him."

"That's *my* decision," Jenna said, "and I've made it. I am not marrying Stuart tomorrow."

With that, she spun on the balls of her bare feet and walked inside.

Margot had remained planted on the step, her elbows on her knees. She took off her silver heels and wiggled her toes. Jenna needed time to cool down and a chance to come to her senses. She needed sleep.

The funny thing, Margot realized, was that she had won the argument. *Love dies.* But she didn't like it one bit.

Jenna was taking a long time in the bathroom. Margot got out of bed and checked down the hall. The bathroom was dark and unoccupied. No Jenna. Shit, Margot thought. She really wanted to have a talk with her before the house sprang to life.

The door to Jenna's room, which she was sharing with Finn and Autumn, was closed tight, as were the doors to the master bedroom and Kevin's room. Footsteps from upstairs—the kids— but that was to be expected.

Margot headed back down to the kitchen; she needed more coffee. And she should eat something. Maybe she and Jenna could walk down the street to the Bake Shop to pick up dough-nuts. They had time. Margot ran through the day's schedule in her head. If Jenna could find it in her heart to forgive Stuart for doing what any kind-but-flawed groom-to-be might do (lie by omission about a long-past, ill-advised, super-brief engagement), the following would take place:

The bridesmaids and Jenna were due at RJ Miller for hair at eleven.

The caterers were coming at noon.

The florist was dropping off the bouquets at two.

The photographer was coming at three.

The musicians—two violinists and a cellist—were arriving at the church at four.

The Model A Ford, which was owned and driven by Roger's son, Vince, was arriving at the house at four thirty to pick up the girls. Then it was showtime. Church at 4:45. The parents would be seated—Pauline first, then Ann and Jim.

The processional would begin at five o'clock. Roger had been eminently clear: he could abide anything but a delayed start to the ceremony. If Jenna or anyone else in the wedding party caused the musicians and the guests and Reverend Marlowe to wait, Roger would levy a ten thousand dollar fine.

He had delivered this news with his usual poker face, though Margot was certain he was kidding.

Margot entered the kitchen expecting to find Jenna. But there, crushed into a corner of the breakfast nook, were Nick and Finn. Nick had his arms around Finn, and his face was in her hair.

"Jesus Christ!" Margot said, mostly out of shock, but partially out of disgust, too.

"Marge," Nick said in a world-weary voice that made him sound exactly like Kevin. "Please mind your own business."

Margot stared at the two of them. The sight of them together was *profoundly* disturbing. It was incestuous! Finn had been a part of the Carmichael family for twenty-five years; she had been at the house all the time—at the table for Sunday dinner, around the tree on Christmas morning. She had gone on vacation with them to Disney World; Margot and Kevin and Nick had ridden Space Mountain a total of eleven times while Jenna and Finn had donned blue Cinderella dresses so that Beth could take them to the castle for breakfast with the princesses.

Now Nick and Finn were having a love thing. And Finn was *married.* They all realized this, right? Both Margot and Nick had attended the Sullivan-Walker wedding last October. Nick had been Margot's ersatz date, until he hooked up with the chesty, frizzy-haired bartender. They all remembered that too, right?

"Where's Jenna?" Margot asked, unable to say anything more.

"No idea," Nick murmured. He was running his hand up and down Finn's bare, sunburned arm in a way that struck Margot as very tender, especially for Nick.

"I don't know what the two of you think you're doing," Margot said, "but I assure you, it's a bad idea."

"Shut up, Marge," Nick said. "You know nothing about it."

I don't want to know anything about it! she thought. What she wouldn't give to be blind, deaf, and dumb, or so self-absorbed with her own excellent love life that she couldn't summon the energy to care about anyone else's.

She said, "Finn, is Jenna up in your room?"

"No," Finn said. She wasn't able to meet Margot's eyes, the little minx.

"Is *Autumn* in your room?" Margot asked, knowing the answer even as she asked the question.

"No," Finn said. "She went back to the groomsmen's house with H.W."

Margot nodded. So Nick and Finn had shared Jenna's room, which was why Jenna had crawled into bed with Margot and Ellie. Autumn had gone home with H.W. This was FINE because both Autumn and H.W. were SINGLE. Everyone did understand the difference, *right?*

"Good for Autumn," Margot said. She left Nick and Finn in the kitchen and trudged back up the stairs to Jenna's room.

In the hallway, she bumped into her father, who had showered and dressed. He was wearing cutoff jean shorts, circa 1975, and an orange-and-navy striped T-shirt that made him look like Ernie from *Sesame Street*. Margot nearly commented on the awful outfit, but he already looked morose.

"Hi, sweetie," Doug said. "How's everything going?"

Margot took a measured breath. She was tempted to tell him that he was going to lose over a hundred thousand dollars in wedding expenses because Stuart hadn't been able to come clean to Jenna about his past.

Margot gave her father a tight smile. He was, most likely, headed down to the kitchen. What would he say when he saw Nick with Finn? Would he even *get* it?

"Everything's fine," Margot said.

Doug descended the stairs, and Margot turned the knob to Jenna's room — no knocking, sorry, this had grown too urgent to worry about manners — and stepped in. The room was dim and empty. Jenna's bed was mussed, but the trundle bed was neatly made. Margot saw sunlight around the edges of the balcony doors, which she opened, thinking she would find Jenna sitting on the deck, drinking her sweet, light coffee, overlooking the stage set for her beautiful wedding.

Nope.

Margot stood on the balcony alone, taking in the pointed top of the tent with its fluttering green and white ribbons, and Alfie's artificially raised limb. Margot recalled when her most pressing worry had been about rain.

She recalled when her most pressing worries had been about herself: Edge, her drowned phone, the reappearance of Griff in her life.

She stomped upstairs to the attic. The six kids were in the middle of a world-class pillow fight; feathers fell like giant flakes of snow, and Brock, the youngest of Kevin's sons, was crying. Margot collared Drum Jr.

"Have you seen Auntie Jenna?"

"No," he said. He frowned contritely. "I'm sorry about the mess."

Feathers could be cleaned up. New pillows (foam) could be purchased. Brock would stop crying in a minute or two; he, like Ellie, was a tough little kid.

Margot dashed back downstairs. She caught Beanie on her way to the bathroom. Beanie was wearing a pair of men's white cotton pajamas with her own monogram on the pocket.

"Have you seen Jenna?" Margot asked.

Beanie shook her head. She said, in a froggy voice, "Is there coffee?"

"Downstairs," Margot said.

Beanie entered the bathroom. The only room Margot hadn't checked was the guest room, where Rhonda was staying. What were the chances that Jenna was in with *Rhonda?* Should Margot check? Of course, she had to check. But at that instant, the guest room door opened and Rhonda stepped out, wearing running shorts and a jog bra, which showed off her perfect, if slightly orange, six-pack abs.

Margot said, "You haven't seen Jenna, have you?"

Rhonda said, "No, why? Is she missing? Is she, like, the runaway bride?"

"No," Margot said. "No, no."

"Do you want me to help you look for her?" Rhonda asked. She pulled her dark hair into a ponytail. "I'm happy to help."

Rhonda was nice, Margot decided. She was, Margot realized—perhaps for the first time ever—her *stepsister.* But probably not for much longer.

"I'm good," Margot said, flying down the stairs. "But thanks for offering! Enjoy your run!"

To avoid the kitchen—Nick, Finn, her father—Margot cut through the formal dining room, where the table was laden with hotel pans and serving pieces for the reception. The grandfather and grandmother clocks announced the hour in symphony. Seven. Margot popped out the little-used rear west door, wedged between the powder room and the laundry, to the backyard.

Margot checked the proposal bench, where she had been sitting a short while ago—empty. Then she entered the tent, which looked even more like a fairy-tale woodland now that the sun was dappling in. Margot searched among the tables and chairs, looking for her sister. Was she *hiding* in there somewhere? Margot peered up the center pole, where she had imagined her mother's spirit hovering.

No Jenna.

Out the back of the tent, past the as-yet-unmolested perennial bed, to the driveway. All cars present and accounted for. Out to the front sidewalk, where Margot could just barely discern the ghost of her and Griff kissing. It was so early that the street was quiet; there wasn't a soul around, which was one of the things Margot loved about Nantucket. In Manhattan, there was no such thing as a quiet street.

No Jenna.

She was gone.

THE NOTEBOOK, PAGE 21

Band or DJ

Band! Preferably one that can play both "At Last," by Etta James, AND "China Grove," by the Doobie Brothers.

ANN

She woke up sprawled across the massive, soft, luxurious hotel bed alone. She lifted her head. Hangover. And her eyes burned. She had fallen asleep crying.

"Jim?" she said. Her voice was as dry as crackers. Jim had pulled on khaki pants and a polo shirt and had left when she asked, clicking the door shut behind him. Ann figured he went down to have a drink at the bar, then slipped back upstairs after she was asleep.

But he wasn't in the room.

"Jim?" she said. She checked the bathroom—there was enough room in the Jacuzzi for three people to sleep comfortably—but it was empty. She checked the walk-in closet and opened the door to the balcony.

No Jim.

Her head started to throb, and her breathing became shallow. She had lost H.W. once, when he was nine years old, at the North Carolina State Fair in Raleigh. Ann had had all three boys in tow; they were headed to the ag tent to see the biggest pumpkin and the prettiest tomatoes and to taste prize-winning hush puppies and dilled green beans. But Ann had stopped to talk to one of her constituents, and at some point during the conversation, H.W. had wandered off. He was missing for seventy-four minutes before Ann and the state fair security officers found him in the Village of Yesteryear, watching a woman in colonial garb weaving cloth on a loom. Ann had spent those seventy-four minutes in a purple panic; it had felt like someone had flipped her upside down and was shaking her.

She felt similarly now. Maybe Jim had come back up to the room to sleep, and maybe he'd left again. Maybe he was down in the restaurant having coffee and reading the paper. But no, Ann didn't think he'd been back. There had been no imprint of his body on the bed; she had definitely slept alone.

She brushed her teeth, washed her face, took some aspirin, put on the outfit she had planned especially for today—a cherry red gingham A-line skirt and a scalloped-neck white T-shirt and a pair of red Jack Rogers sandals that pinched between her toes, but which she'd seen nearly half a dozen woman on Nantucket wearing. Her outfit was too cheerful for the amount of anxiety she was experiencing.

Where was he? Where had he gone?

She checked her cell phone, now showing a dangerously low 12 percent battery. Nothing from Jim, only a text from Olivia that said, *Party was wonderful. Madame X can go fuck herself.*

Typical Olivia.

Where would Jim have gone? Ann racked her brain. She was a problem solver; she would figure it out. The Lewises and the Cohens and the Shelbys were all staying at the Brant Point Inn, which was a bed-and-breakfast. None of them would have had space to accommodate Jim in their rooms.

Had he imposed on the Carmichaels and slept on their sofa?

God, Ann hoped not. How would that look, the father of the groom kicked out of his hotel room? Ann couldn't believe she had ordered him out. But she had been angry last night, angrier than she could ever remember being in all these years. Jim had been right: it was Ann's fault that Helen was here.

Then a ghastly thought encroached: Had Jim gone to spend the night with Helen? Had more transpired between them at the hospital than he'd admitted? They had looked pretty chummy upon returning to the yacht club.

Ann raced into the bathroom. She was going to be sick. Her body was in rejection mode, just as it had been twenty years earlier. For weeks after the hot air balloon ride, she had been unable to keep her meals down.

She retched into the toilet. Of all the things for the mother of the groom to be doing on the morning of her son's wedding.

One day, of course, Chance would get married, and Ann would be subjected to the humiliating sight of Helen and Jim as "Chance's parents" again. She had successfully avoided attending Chance's graduation from the Baylor School because Ann had a senatorial session she couldn't miss. But Chance would graduate from Sewanee in a few years. There would be the baptisms of Chance's future children and then those children's graduations and weddings.

Ann would never be rid of Helen. They were tethered together forever.

Ann rinsed her mouth and made a cursory attempt at applying makeup, although she had a salon appointment for hair and makeup that afternoon. As she was applying mascara, staring bug eyed and purse lipped at herself in the mirror, she realized that Jim must have gone and stayed with the boys.

She snapped up her purse and, filled with a cool wind of relief, dashed out the door.

* * *

Jim had taken their rental car—it was no longer parked in the lot across the street—and so Ann was stuck taking a taxi. This was okay; she didn't know her way around anyway, and she might have popped a tire bouncing over the cobblestones. She had the address of the house Stuart had rented for himself and his groomsmen. She had all the important wedding information written down. Catholic schoolgirl Ann, organized Ann.

To the taxi driver, she said, "130 Surfside Road, please."

The taxi negotiated the streets of town, including a bucking and bouncing trip up Main Street, and Ann ogled the impressive homes built by whaling fortunes in the 1800s. She would have loved to be out strolling this morning, peeking in the pocket gardens, admiring transom windows, and reading the plaques that named the original owners of the houses. *Barzillai R. Burdett, Boatbuilder, 1846.*

Instead of tracking down Jim.

So far the wedding weekend had been distinguished by Ann doing things, regretting them, then attempting to undo them. Looking at her behavior here, no one would believe that she had effectively served the city and county of Durham, representing 1.2 million of the state's most educated and erudite citizens, for twenty-four years. As the taxi headed out of town, the houses grew farther apart. They passed a cemetery; then the land opened up, and there were pine trees, some low-lying scrub, the insistent smell of the ocean. A bike path bordered the road on one side—families pedaled to the beach, there were joggers and dog walkers and a group of kids sharing a skateboard. Then the taxi signaled and pulled down a sandy driveway. Back among the pine trees was a two-story cottage with front dormer windows and gray shingles. Two cars were parked out front, but neither was their rental car.

"This is it?" Ann said. "You're sure?" She checked the piece of paper from her purse. "130 Surfside Road."

The taxi driver was about twenty years old; he wore a blue button-down oxford shirt and Ray-Ban aviators and appeared to be the identical twin of Ford from Colgate, their waiter at the yacht club.

"Yes, ma'am," he said. He wrote something on his clipboard. "This is 130."

Ann climbed out of the cab, paid the kid an astronomical fare of twenty-five dollars (the same-length ride anywhere in the Research Triangle would have been seven dollars), and then felt utterly abandoned as the cab backed out of the driveway.

Ann walked to the front door, the damn Jack Rogers sandals torturing the tender spot between her first two toes, and knocked.

A moment later, H.W. answered.

Henry William, named after Ann's father. Ann was nearly as happy to see him now as she had been when he turned up at the fairgrounds seventeen years earlier.

"Hi, Mom," he said.

Of her three boys, H.W. was the least complicated. As a child, Ann and Jim had nicknamed him "Pup," short for "puppy," because he was just about that easy to please. Whereas Stuart was the dutiful firstborn and Ryan was the emotionally complex aesthete, all H.W. needed was to be run, fed, and put to bed. The occasional pat on the head.

"Hi, honey," Ann said. "Is your father here?"

"Dad?" H.W. said. He turned around and peered into the house. "Hey, is Dad here?"

"No," a voice said. Ryan appeared, smelling of aftershave, his hair damp. "Hi, Mom."

Ann stepped into the rental house. It reeked of mold and

cigarettes and beer. On the coffee table, she spied a dirty ashtray and empty bottles of Stella and plastic cups with quarters lying in the bottom. There was a sad-looking tweedy green sofa and a recliner in mustard yellow vinyl and a clock on the wall meant to look like a ship's wheel. On the walls hung some truly atrocious nautical paintings. *SportsCenter* was muted on the big flat-screen TV, which looked as unlikely as a spaceship in the middle of the living room.

"Dad's not here?" she asked Ryan.

"No," he said.

"He hasn't been here at all? Last night? This morning?"

"No," Ryan said. He cocked his head. "Mom?"

Ann deflected his concern. She nodded at the walls. "Nice place," she said.

"It's like we've been beamed back thirty years to a time-share decorated by Carol Brady after the divorce and meth addiction," Ryan said. "Jethro wants to burn it down solely in the name of good taste."

"Yeah, I'll bet," Ann said. On the far wall was a Thomas Kinkade print.

"But we drank and smoked like naughty schoolchildren," Ryan said. "Went to bed so blotto that the plastic venetian blinds in the windows seemed whimsical."

At that moment, Chance came down the stairs, wearing only boxer shorts. He was so long and lean and pale that seeing him in only underwear seemed indecent. Ann averted her eyes.

"Hey, Senator," Chance said.

"Hi," Ann said. "How are you feeling, sweetie?"

He shrugged. "Okay, I guess," he said. "I can breathe."

"Good," Ann said. She had thought Jim would be here, he wasn't here, that was bad, that was awful, and now she had to explain, or make up a story. Helen, she thought. Where was Helen staying? Did she dare ask Chance?

Suddenly she felt hands on her shoulders.

"Hey, beautiful lady," Jethro said. He kissed the top of her head.

"Hey," Ann bleated. She felt like a little lost lamb. To avoid further questioning, she gave herself a tour of the house. She stumbled through a doorway into the kitchen. A young woman was sitting at the rectangular Formica table, smoking a cigarette. She was wearing an oversized N.C. State T-shirt, and not much else. It was H.W. 's T-shirt. And then Ann got it.

"Oh," she said. "Hello. I'm Ann Graham."

The woman stood immediately, setting her cigarette in a half clamshell that served as an ashtray, and held out her hand. "Autumn Donahue," she said. She had hair the color of shiny pennies, and lovely long legs. "I'm one of the bridesmaids. I was Jenna's roommate at William and Mary."

Ann reverted to state senator mode and shook the woman's hand. "Nice to meet you, Autumn."

Ryan entered the kitchen. "I don't understand why you're looking for Dad at eight thirty in the morning."

"He got up early and went out," Ann said. "I thought he might have come here."

"You're a terrible liar," Ryan said. He eyed Jethro. "Isn't she a terrible liar?"

"Terrible," Jethro said.

"Plus, I wanted to make you all breakfast," Ann said. She opened the refrigerator, hoping her bluff hadn't just been called, and exhaled when she saw eggs and milk and butter and a hunk of aged cheddar (Ryan and Jethro must have done the shopping) and a container of blueberries and a half gallon of orange juice.

"*I'm* hungry!" Autumn said.

Ann took out a mixing bowl and cracked all the eggs; she added milk, salt and pepper, a handful of grated cheddar. She melted butter in a frying pan. She thought, *Where the hell is Jim? It's the morning of Stuart's wedding, for God's sake.* Ann felt her temper smoking and sizzling like the hot pan. And yet how could she be angry when she had asked him to leave? She had told him to get out.

A Quaalude would be nice right now, she thought.

She poured the egg mixture into the pan, popped a couple of pieces of seeded whole-grain bread into the rusty toaster, and got to work on the coffee. Starbucks, in the freezer. Thank God for small blessings.

Ryan said, "Mom, you do *not* have to do this. I'm sure you'd rather be having breakfast at your hotel."

"I'm fine!" Ann sang out. "It's the last morning I'll ever be able to do this for Stuart. Tomorrow, he'll belong to Jenna."

"Whoa!" Ryan said. "Sappy alert."

"Where is Stuart, anyway?" Ann asked.

Ryan said, "The door to his room is closed. I knocked earlier, fearing he had been asphyxiated by the synthetic bed linens, and he told me to go away." Ryan lowered his voice. "I guess he and Jenna had a spat last night concerning She Who Shall Not Be Named."

"A spat?" Ann said. A spat the night before the wedding wasn't good. A spat about She Who Shall Not Be Named wasn't good at all. Why must love be so agonizing? Ann wondered. She moved the eggs around the pan, slowly, over low heat, so they would be nice and creamy. "This reminds me of when we used to visit Stuart at the Sig Ep house. Remember when we used to do that?"

"The Sig Ep house was nicer," Ryan said.

"The Sig Ep house *was* nicer," Ann agreed, and they both laughed.

A few minutes later, Ann had managed to plate, on mismatched Fiesta ware, scrambled eggs, toast, juice, coffee, and blueberries with a little sugar. They crowded around the sad Formica table: H.W., Ryan, Jethro, Chance, and Autumn.

"We need Stuart," Ann said. "This is supposed to be for him."

"I just knocked on his door," Chance said. "He told me he'd be down in a minute."

"It'll all be gone in a minute," H.W. said, helping himself to a second piece of toast. "No grits?"

"Grits?" Ryan said. "Please don't tell me you still eat grits."

"Every day," H.W. said.

"Oh, my God," Ryan said. "My twin brother is Jeff Foxworthy."

"Well, your boyfriend is André Leon Talley," H.W. said. He grinned at Jethro. "No disrespect, man."

"None taken," Jethro said. "Love ALT."

Autumn pointed her fork at H.W. "I'm impressed you know who André Leon Talley is."

"What?" H.W. said. "I have been known to read the occasional issue of *Vogue*."

"Oh, come on," Ryan said.

"Hot women half dressed," H.W. said. He hooted and gave Chance a high five.

Ryan said, "Mom, aren't you eating?"

"Oh, no," Ann said. "I couldn't possibly."

She left the kitchen to retrieve her purse from the scratchy green sofa and to check her phone. No new messages, 3 percent battery. She stepped outside to use the last bit of juice to call Jim's cell phone. She should have called him from the taxi, but she had been *sure* he would be here, with the kids.

The phone rang and rang and rang. She got Jim's voice mail, but before Ann could leave a message, her battery died.

Where are you? Ann thought. Where the hell did you go?

Ann and Jim had joined the wine-tasting group in 1992. The invitation had come from a woman named Shell Phillips, who had recently moved to Durham from Philadelphia when her husband took a job in the physics department at Duke. Shell Phillips was a northerner, which—although the Civil War was 125 years in the past—still marked her as a potential enemy. She was from the Main Line, she said, Haverford, she said, and Ann bobbed her head, pretending to know what this meant. Shell Phillips had introduced herself to Ann at the Kroger. *Hello, Senator Graham, I've been so wanting to meet you, someone pointed you out to me the other night at the Washington Duke.*

Shell Phillips had shiny, dark hair that she wore in a bob tucked behind her ears, and a strand of pearls and pearl earrings. Clearly she was trying to fit in; Ann had heard that most northern women went to the grocery store in their yoga clothes.

Shell Phillips asked if Ann and Jim might want to join a wine-tasting group that Shell was putting together. Just a fun thing, they'd done it in Haverford, five or six couples, once a month. A different couple would be responsible for hosting each month, choosing a varietal and getting a case of different labels so that they could compare and contrast. Hors d'oeuvres to complement the wine.

Just a little social thing, Shell Phillips said. Like a cocktail party, really. We had such fun with it back home. It would be wonderful if you and your husband would join us.

Of course, Ann said. We'd love to be part of it.

She had committed without asking Jim because despite her

natural skepticism toward northerners, she thought a wine-tasting group might add some flair to their social life. She and Jim could stand to learn a little about wine; when Ann was at the Washington Duke or somewhere else for dinner, she normally defaulted and ordered a glass of white Zinfandel or the house Chablis. Shell Phillips might have assumed all southerners made their *own* wine. Any which way, Ann felt flattered that someone had sought her out for a reason that had nothing to do with local politics.

Yes, yes, yes, count them in.

There had been six couples. In addition to Ann and Jim, and Shell and her husband, Clayton Phillips, there were the Lewises, Olivia and Robert, whom Ann and Jim were already friends with, as well as three couples unfamiliar to them: the Greenes, the Fairlees, and Nathaniel and Helen Oppenheimer.

The wine-tasting group was a success from the start. They began with chardonnays at the Phillips's house, a beautiful old stone home on West Club Boulevard. It had been one of the best parties Ann had ever attended. She had drunk no fewer than eight glasses of chardonnay, and she nibbled on wonderful cheeses, and smoked salmon dip, and pâtés. (Where had Shell Phillips gotten her hands on such provisions? Charlotte, she said.) The night had ended with everyone dancing to Patsy Cline in the Phillipses' ballroom. Who knew such sophisticated fun could be had in their little town? Ann had babbled on and on in the car on the way home. It was nice to expand their circle; their social life had needed a boost. Ann had noticed the other women's outfits: both Shell Phillips and Helen Oppenheimer had looked more glamorous than Ann, who had worn a linen skirt that nearly reached her ankles. She would go shopping in Charlotte before next month's wine group.

Merlots at the Lewises'.

Sauvignon blancs at the Greenes'.

Ann was desperate to host, and she wanted to do champagnes. *Expensive choice,* Jim said. Yes, it was expensive, but that was part of the appeal. Ann bought two cases of champagne; most of it she had to special order from the bottle shop: Veuve Clicquot, Taittinger, Moët et Chandon, Perrier-Jouët, Schramsberg, Mumm, Pol Roger. Ann killed herself over the hors d'oeuvres. She toasted and seasoned macadamia nuts; she prepared phyllo triangles with three fillings. She bought five pounds of shrimp cocktail.

A thousand dollars spent, when all was said and done, though she'd never admitted that to Jim.

The night should have been a great success, but from the get-go, things were off-kilter. Helen Oppenheimer showed up alone; Nathaniel was sick, she said. Then Helen proceeded to get very drunk. But really, Ann thought, they all got very drunk. It was something about the nature of champagne, or about the tiny, delicate (insubstantial) hors d'oeuvres Ann had prepared. The evening reached a point where Helen collapsed onto Ann and Jim's sofa and said, "I've been lying to all of you. I'm sorry. Nathaniel isn't sick. We've separated."

There were expressions of shock followed by sympathy, followed by a lot of confessional talk, all of it too intimate for the nature of their group. However, Ann had willingly participated in it. She found the news of Helen's separation titillating. It turned out that Helen, who worked in the development office at Fuqua, was desperate for children. And Nathaniel, who was a curator at the North Carolina Museum of Art, refused to have any. Their sex life was a joke, Helen said. In fact, Helen suspected that Nathaniel was gay.

"It's an irreconcilable difference," Helen said. "It is THE irreconcilable difference. So I left."

Ann and the other women agreed that Helen *should* have left. Helen was young, and so beautiful. She would find somebody else. She would have children.

When the night drew to a close, Helen was . . . well, if it hadn't been for her tragic revelation, Ann might have called her a sloppy drunk. She couldn't drive herself home. Ann volunteered Jim to drive her.

Ann remembered Olivia giving her googly eyes. As in *What the hell is wrong with you?* But Ann was too drunk herself to pick up on it.

She remembered that Jim had come home whistling.

But at the time, Ann thought nothing of it. She was happy that Helen had felt close enough to the group to reveal the truth. It meant the evening had been a success. And the next day everyone called to thank Ann and tell her it was the best wine tasting yet.

Cabernets at the Fairlees'.

Finally, it was Helen's turn to host. She had moved out of the house that she had shared with Nathaniel and into one of the brand-new lofts built at Brightleaf Square. She invited everyone over for a port tasting. She would serve only desserts, she said, and cigars for the men.

Ann had been excited to go. She was dying to see what those lofts looked like, and she wanted to support Helen in her new life. It must have been difficult to stay in the wine-tasting group as the only single person among couples. But then Ryan got the chicken pox. On the Saturday of the port tasting, he had a temperature of 103 degrees and was covered in red spots. Jim had offered to stay home and let Ann go. But Ann wouldn't hear of it. She didn't really like port anyway, and Helen had made a big deal about the Cuban cigars she had gotten from a friend of hers living in Stockholm. Jim should go. Furthermore, Ryan was a mama's boy, a trait that became even more pronounced when he was sick. Ann couldn't imagine Jim staying home to deal with him.

"You go," Ann said.

"You're sure?" Jim said. "We could both stay home."

"No, no, *no!*" Ann said. "That would make it seem like we're rejecting Helen."

"It will *not* seem like we're rejecting Helen," Jim said. "It will seem like our child has the chicken pox."

"You go," Ann said. "I insist."

At the groomsmen's house, breakfast was devoured, and everyone complimented Ann's efforts in the kitchen—especially Autumn, who seemed surprisingly at ease with Ann, considering that Autumn was wearing no pants and had spent the night with Ann's son after knowing him all of six hours. Ann cleared the dishes and began washing them at the sink, until Ryan and Jethro nudged her out of the way and told her to go relax.

Relax? she thought.

She headed upstairs to find Stuart.

Ann often wondered: If Jim had stayed home to take care of Ryan with the chicken pox and Ann had gone to the port tasting at Helen's new apartment, would any of this have happened?

As it was, Jim went to Helen's party and returned home at 3:20 in the morning. Ann had fallen asleep a little after ten after giving Ryan a baking soda bath, but she opened one eye to Jim, and the clock, when he climbed into bed. He smelled unfamiliar— like cigar smoke, and something else.

In the morning, Ann asked, "How was the party?"

Jim nodded. "Yep. It was good."

In the afternoon, Olivia called. She said, "Helen Oppenheimer is trouble. She was *all over* every man at that party." She paused. "What time did Jim get home?"

"Oh," Ann said. "Not late."

The affair had started that night, or at least that was what Jim confessed later. Ann had her suspicions that something had actually happened when Jim drove Helen home after the champagne party. But Ann had continued on, blissfully unaware, throughout the spring, into the summer.

It was in July that Shell Phillips had called with the idea of hot air ballooning. It could be done near Asheville, in the western part of the state, a four-hour drive away. They would lift off at five in the evening and land just before sunset in a meadow where there would be a gourmet picnic dinner with wines to match. There was a bed-and-breakfast nearby where couples could spend the night.

"Perfect for our group," Shell said.

Ann had been thrilled by the prospect of ballooning, and she accepted right away. She wasn't sure how Jim would react. He had been moody around the house, sometimes snapping at Ann and the kids. He bought a ten-speed bicycle and started going on long rides on the weekends; sometimes he was gone for three hours. Ann thought the bike riding was probably a good thing. She said to Olivia, "He must have seen *Breaking Away* one night on TV. He's *obsessed* with the biking."

Ann started calling him "Cutter."

She worried that Jim might not want to go on an all-day ballooning adventure with the wine-tasting group. But when she asked him, he said yes right away. It was almost as if he already knew about it, Ann thought.

*   *   *

It had been so many years earlier that certain details were now lost. What did Ann remember about the hot air ballooning trip? She remembered that Jim had been quiet in the car on the way to Asheville. Normally on a ride that long, he popped in a cassette of Waylon Jennings or the Marshall Tucker Band, and he and Ann sang along, happily out of key. But on that ride, Jim had been silent. Ann asked him what the matter was, and he said tersely, "Nothing is the matter."

Jim liked to stop on the highway at Bob's Big Boy for lunch. He positively *adored* Bob's Big Boy; he always ordered the catfish sandwich and the strawberry pie. But this time, when Ann suggested stopping, he said, "Not hungry."

Ann said, "Well, what if *I'm* hungry?"

Jim shook his head and kept on driving.

Ann remembered gathering with the group in the expansive green field; she remembered her heightened sense of anticipation. Along with Ann, Helen Oppenheimer seemed the most excited. She had been positively *glowing*.

Ann remembered the gas fire, the heat, the billowing balloon, the stomach-twisting elation of lifting up off the ground. She recalled the incredible beauty of the patchwork fields below them. The farmland, the woods, the creeks, streams, and ponds below them. She filled with pride. North Carolina was the most picturesque state in the nation—and she represented it.

The basket was eight feet square. Their group was packed in snugly. Ann, at one point, found herself hip to hip with Steve Fairlee and Robert Lewis as they leaned over the edge and waved to children playing a game of Wiffle ball below. It was only bad luck that caused Ann to turn around to see how Jim was faring. She happened to catch the smallest of gestures—Jim grabbing Helen's hand and giving it a surreptitious squeeze. Ann blinked. She thought, *What?* She hoped she'd imagined it, but she knew that she hadn't. She hoped it was innocent, but she knew Jim Graham. Jim wasn't a hand grabber—or he hadn't been—with anyone except for Ann. He used to grab Ann's hand all the time: when they were dating, when they were engaged, the first few years of marriage. It was his gesture of affection; it was his love thing.

And at that moment, it all crashed down on Ann. The champagne party, the port party, Jim coming home at three in the morning, the absurdly long bike rides. He rode to Helen's loft, Ann knew it, and they fucked away the afternoon.

Ann came very close to jumping out of the basket. She would die colliding with North Carolina; her body would leave an Ann-sized-and-shaped divot, like in a Wile E. Coyote cartoon.

Instead she turned. The fire was hot enough to scorch her. She called out, "Hey, Cutter!"

Jim and Helen both looked over at her. *Guilty,* she thought. They were guilty.

Once back on the ground, Ann drank the exceptional wine Shell had selected, but ate nothing. She tried to keep up with the conversation swirling around her, but she kept drifting away. Jim— and Helen Oppenheimer. Of course, it was so obvious. Ann had been so *stupid.*

She shanghaied Olivia, pulling her away from the picnic blankets to the edge of the woods. She said, "I think my husband is having an affair with Helen."

Olivia gave her a look of sympathy. Olivia knew. Possibly everyone knew.

After the picnic was eaten and every bottle of wine consumed, they all piled into a van that drove them back to where their cars were parked. When they arrived, it was ten o'clock. The other couples were all making the short drive to the bed-and-breakfast for the night. Ann and Jim had booked a room at the B&B as well, but there was no way Ann was going to spend the night under the same roof as Helen Oppenheimer. She was certain Jim and Helen had made plans to meet in Helen's room in the middle of the night to fuck.

When Jim and Ann got into the car, Ann said, "Jim." His name sounded unfamiliar on her tongue; she had been calling him "Cutter" for weeks.

"Yes, darling?" Jim said. The wine had significantly lightened his mood, or seeing Helen had. Ann wanted to slap him.

Ann said, "You're sleeping with Helen Oppenheimer."

Jim froze with his hand on the key in the ignition. The other couples were pulling away. Helen, in the lipstick-red Miata she had bought herself upon leaving Nathaniel, was pulling away.

Jim said, "Annie..."

"Confirm or deny," Ann said. "And tell me the truth, please."

"Yes," he said.

"Are you in love with her?" Ann asked.

"Yes," he said. "I think I am."

Ann nearly swallowed her tongue. Her head swam with wine and the fumes from the balloon.

"Drive home," Ann said.

"Annie..."

"Home!" Ann said.

"She's pregnant," Jim said. "She's pregnant with my child."

Ann had started to weep, although the news didn't come as a surprise. Ann had known just from looking at Helen that she was pregnant. The glow.

Jim drove the four hours home; they arrived in Durham at two in the morning. Ann took the babysitter home, and by the time she returned, Jim had a bag packed. The very next day he moved into Brightleaf Square with Helen, and when Chance was born, he bought a house in Cary. Ann was certain he did this so that he and Helen would no longer be Ann's constituents.

It had not been Ann's intention to relive all of this on the weekend of her son's wedding. But since she'd made the ill-advised decision to invite Helen, it now seemed inevitable that this would be exactly what she was thinking about.

Ann knocked on the last door on the left, which was the room where Stuart was staying. "Sweetie?" she said. "It's Mom."

No response. She pressed her ear against the door, then tried the knob. It was unlocked, but she couldn't bring herself to open the door. One of the things she had learned when the boys were teenagers was that she should never enter their rooms uninvited.

"Stuart, honey?" she said. "I made breakfast. There's still some left, but you'd better hurry or H.W. will finish it."

No response.

"Stuart?" Ann said.

The door opened, and there stood Stuart in wrinkled madras shorts and a white undershirt. His hair was sticking up; his eyes were puffy. It had been years since Ann had seen Stuart look anything but pressed and professional. Right now, he seemed far younger than he was. Ann was again reminded of visiting Stuart at the Sig Ep house at Vanderbilt.

"Darling," she said. "Are you okay?"

He shrugged. "Jenna's upset."

Ann nodded. "I heard something about that."

"She found out about Crissy," he said.

"What *about* Crissy?" Ann said. Had Stuart *seen* She Who Shall Not Be Named? Had he suffered a Crissy relapse? Oh, God. Ann had prayed nightly that infidelity wasn't a behavior Jim had passed on to the boys. "What *about* Crissy, Stuart?"

"Just that we were...you know...engaged..." He swallowed. "And, um, that she has Grand-mère's ring."

"Oh, dear," Ann said. "You never told her that?"

Stuart shook his head. "I didn't see the point. I can't stand talking about it."

Well, yes, Ann thought; the entire family shared this sentiment.

"So she knew nothing about it?" Ann said. "Nothing at all?"

"She knew Crissy was my girlfriend. She didn't know about the engaged part. Or the ring part."

As a state senator, Ann had had plenty of lessons in damage control. She tried to assess how bad this was. Why oh why hadn't Stuart just told Jenna about Crissy on their first few dates, during the information-gathering period? The engagement had been brief, a matter of weeks. Ill conceived from the start! Ann had never uttered an "I told you so," but she had been very reluctant to hand over her grandmother's ring, even though she had always planned on giving it to the first son ready to propose. She hadn't thought Crissy Pine worthy of the ring; Ann had been certain the marriage wouldn't last. Crissy was a complainer (she sent back food in restaurants, she criticized Stuart's taste in clothing, and she mimicked his accent), and she was a spendthrift (she had a weakness for anything French—champagne, soap, perfume, antiques). Ann vividly remembered the day that Stuart broke off the engagement. He came home smiling for the first time in months, and the eczema that had been plaguing him for just as long stopped itching, he said, the instant Crissy drove away. The only problem was the ring. Stuart felt too guilty for breaking off the engagement to ask for it back.

Ann had said, *Well, it's a family heirloom, a two-and-a-half-carat diamond in a platinum Tiffany setting. It's valuable, Stuart. We sure as hell better get it back.*

But the ring had never been returned. Jim had made a gentleman's phone call to Thaddeus Pine, Crissy's father. Thaddeus had listened considerately and then called Stuart an "Indian giver." Next, Ann and Jim had contacted an attorney. They had spent nearly a third of the ring's value trying to force Crissy to return the ring, but their legal recourse was limited, and Ann's high-profile career made her hesitant to pursue the lawsuit.

Now, Ann shuddered every time she thought of Crissy Pine. Who would want to keep a diamond ring after the engagement had been broken? No one! For a while, Ann checked on eBay, hoping the ring would turn up, but it never did, leaving Ann with the disturbing vision of her grandmother's ring on Crissy's finger.

"Oh, dear," Ann said. "How upset is she?"

"Really upset," Stuart said. "Like, *really.*"

"As in…" Ann said. Suddenly she imagined the wedding weekend going up in flames as dramatic as the ones that had swallowed Atlanta in 1864. Jenna would call the wedding off; Ann would watch her marriage to Jim fail again, she would lose him to Helen *again.* It was too hideous to contemplate; Ann felt light-headed. *Quaalude!* she thought. *Please!*

The spot between her toes throbbed with pain. She hated these shoes.

"Is Dad here?" Stuart asked hopefully. "I think I need to talk to him."

"Not here," Ann said. "I don't know where he is. I threw him out of the room last night."

"You did?" Stuart said.

Ann nodded slowly and whispered, "I did."

She and Stuart were quiet for a moment. Ryan would have demanded every detail, but Stuart wouldn't ask a thing.

"You don't really need Dad," Ann said. "Maybe I could talk to Jenna." Ann was certain this was the solution. She would convince Jenna that Stuart's not disclosing the full story about a very brief engagement was a minor infraction. Minor! Ann would say, *And believe me, sweetie, I know what I'm talking about.*

"No," Stuart said. "I don't think that's a good idea."

At that moment, Ann heard new voices in the living room. Helen's voice. Most definitely Helen's voice. Ann said to Stuart, "Helen's here. I'm going downstairs."

Stuart said, "I can't deal with Helen right now. I don't care if H.W. eats my breakfast." He shut the door, then opened it a crack. "Thanks, though, Mom."

"Oh, honey," she said. "I love you so."

Ann descended to the living room. Helen had just walked in the door with a man who towered over her, which was no small feat. The man was a giant; he must have been six-nine or six-ten. He was good looking, early fifties, graying hair, wearing a pair of white Bermuda shorts embroidered with navy whales, which would have gotten him egged on any street corner south of the Mason-Dixon Line.

Helen said, "Hey, y'all! Is Chancey here? I've come to take him out for breakfast."

Chance emerged from the kitchen, still wearing only his boxers. He said, "Mama?"

"Honey, your clothes."

"Oh," he said. "Yeah. I just got up a little while ago."

"Chance," Helen said. "This is Skip Lafferty, a friend of mine from Roanoke, way back in the day. Skip has a house here on Nantucket. He's going to come with us to breakfast, then show us around the island."

Skip Lafferty offered his hand. "Nice to meet you, Chance." Then he waved at the rest of the room. "Nice to meet y'all."

Ann was so relieved, she nearly levitated. She stepped forward and offered her hand. "I'm Ann Graham," she said. "Lovely to meet you."

Chance said, "I kind of just ate breakfast. Eggs and everything."

"But sweetie," Helen said, "I told you I'd be here at nine to pick you up."

"I know," Chance said. "But I think I just want to hang here with everyone else."

Helen opened her mouth to speak just as Autumn stepped out of the kitchen. H.W. 's shirt, Ann saw now, barely covered the girl's tiny behind, and whereas ten minutes ago this might have bothered Ann, now that Autumn was displaying herself to Helen's old friend Skip Lafferty, whose eyes were popping out of his head, Ann wanted to break out in peals of delighted laughter.

Jim wasn't with Helen. Of course he wasn't! Ann felt happily like an idiot.

Autumn said, "Oops, excuse me." She winked at Skip Lafferty before scurrying up the stairs.

Chance said, "I'm not hungry. I want to stay here."

"Honeybun," Helen said. "Skip is eager to show us around. He has a restaurant picked out that serves the best corned beef hash."

"But I already ate," Chance said.

Ryan piped up. "Mom came over a little while ago, Helen, and made us all breakfast."

Jethro appeared from the kitchen with a dish towel slung over his shoulder. He said, "Those were the best eggs I've ever eaten."

Ann said, "I'm sorry, I didn't realize Chance already had breakfast plans."

Helen wrinkled her nose, maybe because her senses were assaulted by the beer-and-cigarette miasma of the house, or maybe because the circumstances were so distasteful to her. Ann, of all people, had made Chance breakfast. "Well, he did and he does, and he's going to honor them. Chance, go put clothes on, please."

"Sorry, Mama," Chance said. "I'm not going."

There was an awkward silence in the room that was so refreshing, Ann could have swum around in it for hours.

Skip Lafferty said, "It's okay, Helen. We can just go into town together, you and me."

Helen put her hands on her hips. "Chancey," she said.

"I'm nineteen, Mama," he said. "Not nine."

Helen kept her stance for another couple of seconds. H.W. burped. Ann watched Helen debate whether or not to persist with the tough-guy approach, or beg, or give up. Helen had always worn her emotions right on her face. There had been a time, after Jim had left Helen to come back to Ann, when Helen had shown up out of the blue at Ann's office at the statehouse. She had Chance with her; he was three years old, a towhead with skin so pale it looked nearly albino. That was the first time Ann had ever seen Chance in person.

Helen had been a mess — crying, trying not to cry, screeching, beseeching. "Please," she'd said. "My child is younger. I need Jim more than y'all do."

Ann had seen and recognized the particular brand of pain

Helen was feeling; she knew only too well what it felt like to be left by Jim Graham for another woman.

"I don't need him, Helen," Ann had said. "I just love him."

Now, Helen capitulated. She said, "Fine, then, stay." Her voice sounded like that of a jilted lover, or maybe that was just Ann projecting. "I'll see y'all later, at the ceremony."

If there is a ceremony, Ann thought.

Helen took Skip Lafferty's arm and turned to go, without a good-bye to anyone.

Just then, the front door opened. Margot Carmichael stepped into the living room. Her cheeks were pink, and her forehead was shiny with perspiration.

"Hey," she said. "Has anyone seen Jenna?"

THE NOTEBOOK, PAGE 32

Something old — my wedding dress???

Something new — If you wear my dress, everything else should be new. New veil (elbow length?), white satin heels (I wore a kitten heel, but I ended up kicking them off for the dancing, anyway, which the people at the Pierre frowned upon, but I was having too much fun to care), new lacy underthings, new clutch cocktail purse.

Something borrowed — Margot's makeup. She buys the good stuff. You might even let her do it for you; remember how she worked wonders with the green eye shadow.

Something blue — The sapphire earrings that Grammie wore the day she was married to Pop-Pop. Daddy is keeping them for you in a safe-deposit box at the bank.

MARGOT

She was determined to do this by herself. She would find Jenna, she would save the wedding.

She left the children with Beanie, saying she had to run some errands. Kevin, who was reading the *Times* at the kitchen table, huffed.

"Why can't your kids go with you?" he said.

"Because," Margot said. "They can't."

"It's not a problem for us to watch them," Beanie said. "They're all happier when they're together anyway."

Kevin arched his eyebrows. Margot could hear his thoughts: *Margot is outsourcing her children again.*

He said, "What errands?"

"I need to pay my cocaine dealer," Margot said.

He said, "You might try and get Ellie out of her bathing suit before you go."

"Fuck you, Kevin."

"Nice," Kevin said.

"What do you care what Ellie wears?" Margot said. "She's not your child."

"She's a girl," Beanie said. "Girls are different. Kevin doesn't understand that."

Kevin eyed Beanie over the top of his newspaper. "I don't understand that girls are different?"

"You're trying to make me feel like a bad mother," Margot said. "You're being passive-aggressive."

Kevin said, "Along with apparently not understanding that girls are 'different,' I have also never understood that term. 'Passive-aggressive.' What does that actually *mean?*"

"It means you're a jackass," Margot said. She hated acting this way; being around Kevin and Nick made her revert to twelve-year-old behavior.

Beanie pretended to search for something in the refrigerator. Margot needed to ask Kevin or Beanie for one of their cell phones—she couldn't go on this quest without a phone—but she was so pissed at Kevin that she wasn't willing to ask him for anything else.

"I won't be gone long," Margot said to Beanie, hoping this was true.

She left the house by the side door. *Thank God for Kevin!* she thought angrily. But she was glad to have avoided her father and Pauline, and Nick and Finn. Suddenly everyone was a land mine.

Margot had read all the Nancy Drew mysteries as a girl; she had waited thirty years to do some sleuthing of her own. How had Jenna traveled? All the cars were present and accounted for. Had Jenna gone by foot? If so, the only logical place to look for her was in town. She might be browsing in the stacks at Mitchell's Book Corner, or maybe she'd bought a strawberry frappe at the pharmacy and was sitting on a bench on Main Street, counting the number of Lilly Pulitzer skirts that passed her by.

Bicycle? Margot wondered. And sure enough, when she checked the shed, the padlock was hanging loose, and the door was ajar. The bikes in the shed were the bikes of their childhood, Schwinns circa 1983, all rusted and, Margot had assumed, unrideable.

But Jenna had taken a bicycle somewhere.

Where?

Well, if Jenna was dead set on canceling the wedding, there was one person she would have to talk to.

As Margot was unlocking her Land Rover, Rhonda popped out of the house with white earbuds in.

"Hey, Rhonda," Margot said.

Rhonda removed her left earbud, and Margot could hear the tinny screeching of Rihanna. "I'm going running!" she said, too loudly.

"Is there any way I could borrow your phone for an hour?" Margot asked. "I sunk mine on Thursday night, it's useless, and I really need a phone this morning." She swallowed. "Secret wedding mission."

Rhonda's face was uneasy as she regarded her phone. "I can't really run without music. And Raymond is supposed to call..."

"Oh," Margot said. "Okay, no problem." She looked at the house and sighed. She would have to go back in and ask Beanie.

Rhonda said, "Don't be like that."

"Be like what?" Margot said.

"You know like what," Rhonda said. She shoved her phone at Margot. "Just take it."

"No, no," Margot said. When she looked down at the phone, she saw that the screensaver was a picture of Rhonda and Pauline taken the night before at the Nantucket Yacht Club. They were standing in front of the giant anchor with their arms wrapped around each other. Pauline, in her blue suit, looked like Gertie Gloom, but Rhonda was smiling wide enough for the two of them, perhaps realizing that it was up to her to put forward a good face on behalf of the Tonellis. "It's okay, Rhonda. I'll ask someone else."

"You asked me," Rhonda said. "Just take it."

Margot couldn't tell if Rhonda was being passive-aggressive

(whatever that meant) or genuine. Margot didn't really have time for games or mind reading, so she accepted the phone.

"Thank you for this," she said. "I'll bring it back as soon as I'm done."

"Whenever," Rhonda said, shrugging. "Glad I could help."

Margot considered asking Rhonda to come with her. This would then become the story of a woman and the stepsister she had never appreciated and was about to lose, as they hunted down the runaway bride.

But no, Margot wanted to do this herself.

"Thanks again," Margot said.

"Good luck," Rhonda said.

Margot turned the key in the ignition. The radio was playing Elvis Costello, "Alison," and Margot thought about Griff the night before at the bar and how he had so easily identified her favorite lyrics in the other song, and she wondered what it would be like to be with someone who actually wanted to understand her, then she wondered if anyone would ever kiss her again the way Griff had kissed her, and she knew the answer was no. She was doomed to have experienced the very best kissing of her life with someone she would never kiss again.

This might have seemed like a problem if she didn't have bigger problems on her hands.

"Why?" Stuart said as he descended the stairs of the grooms-men's house, looking like death on a stick. "Is she missing?"

"What is it this morning?" Ryan said. "Everyone is going missing."

"Margot!" Ann Graham said. "I hope you're hungry. We have eggs."

"Negative on the eggs, Mom," H.W. said. "I just finished the ones left in the pan."

"If you'll excuse me." These words were spoken by Helen, Chance's mother, who was responsible for this whole mess in the first place. Margot was tempted to call Helen out right there and then, but she didn't really have time for a grand confrontation with all the Grahams watching. Helen edged past Margot out the front door, followed by a very tall man who was wearing a pair of embroidered whale shorts that he must have bought right out of the front window at Murray's Toggery.

Margot took one step into the house. She watched Helen leave, thinking, *Interloper!*

Stuart ran his hands over his bad haircut. "*Is* she missing?" he asked again. He looked green—maybe alarm, maybe nerves, maybe hangover. The house was trashed; it looked like it had hosted an all-nighter with Jim Morrison, John Belushi, and the Hells Angels.

"She went for a bike ride," Margot said. "And I need to find her. Roger has a pressing question."

All true. She congratulated herself.

"She hasn't been here," Ryan said.

Chance pulled aside one of the truly horrendous brocade drapes and said, "Thank God my mother is gone."

Now Ann Graham looked worried. "When was the last time you saw Jenna?"

"A little while ago," Margot said. She didn't want to disclose anything more. "I should go."

"Do you want me to come with you?" Stuart asked.

Margot regarded Stuart. He was pale and sick with love. If he came with her, this would become the story of Margot and the soon-to-be-jilted groom as they hunted down the runaway bride.

Margot said, "Come outside with me?"

Stuart followed Margot outside, and she could sense that Ann

Graham was antsy to join them. Margot and Stuart stood in the overgrown crabgrass of the front yard. It was warm in the sun, and Margot worried momentarily about freckles, then told herself to forget it.

"Jenna was really upset last night," Margot said. "She called Roger and canceled the wedding."

Stuart dropped his head to his chest. "Fuck," he whispered.

That was the first time Margot had ever heard the man swear. He was such a good guy. "She's upset about Crissy."

Stuart held out a hand. "Stop," he said. "I can't even stand to hear her name."

"You probably should have told her about the engagement," Margot said.

"It wasn't a big deal," Stuart said. "It only lasted a month. As soon as Crissy booked the Angus Barn for the engagement party, I broke up with her. And two weeks later, I moved to New York. I was done with her—done done done."

"It feels like a big deal to Jenna," Margot said. "She's . . . well, you know how she is."

"Sensitive," he said.

"Yes," Margot said. "And in this case, she's also jealous. She was raised differently from the rest of us. You know, Kevin and Nick and I were always fighting for our parents' attention. Always jockeying for first place. But not Jenna. She had their undivided attention."

"Are you saying she's spoiled?" Stuart said. "She's never seemed spoiled to me."

"She's not spoiled," Margot said. "But she's probably not as experienced with this kind of jealousy as another person might be."

"I didn't tell her because I didn't *want* to tell her," Stuart said.

"I just didn't want her to know. It meant nothing, it was a big fat mistake, and I wanted to pretend like it never happened."

"She feels like you lied to her," Margot said. "I understand it was a lie of omission—"

"I apologized fifty times, a hundred times. If she ever checks her phone again, she'll see I called her seventeen times last night between the hours of midnight and five. I don't know what else to do." He put his face to his hands. "If she leaves me, I'll die, Margot."

"I have to go find her," Margot said. "Let me talk to her."

"I want to go with you," Stuart said. "But I'm afraid I might mess it up even worse."

"You might," Margot said. She smiled to let him know she was kidding. "But I might, too."

Margot drove out to Surfside, searching the road for Jenna. She turned down Nonantum Avenue and headed toward Fisherman's Beach. From Rhonda's cell phone, she called Jenna's number. Jenna wouldn't answer if it was Margot, or the number of the house, but would she answer if she saw a call coming in from Rhonda? Maybe.

But no. The call was shuttled right to voice mail.

Margot paused in the parking lot at Fisherman's and walked to the landing at the top of the beach stairs. She scanned the coast to the left, then the coast to the right. No Jenna. There were only a couple of men, surfcasting at the waterline.

Margot remembered herself as a malcontented teenager, pacing this very beach with her Walkman playing "I Wanna Be Free," by the Monkees, and "Against All Odds," by Phil Collins. The beach was often shrouded in fog, which made it an even better place for soulful reflection for Margot and her adolescent woes: she hated her braces, her parents didn't understand her, and she missed Grady McLean, who was back in Connecticut working the register at Stew Leonard's.

Margot had also surfed this beach, too many times to count, with Drum Sr. He had been a bronzed surfing god back then, king of these waves. Margot had been awed by his grace and agility on the board. *Of course* she'd fallen in love with him! Every single person—man and woman, boy and girl—who had watched Drum surf had fallen in love with him. Margot had believed that the magic he demonstrated in the water, and on the ski slopes, would translate to real life. But as a landlubber, Drum Sr. had floundered. He had never been able to display the same kind of confidence or authority.

Maybe now, with his fish taco stand and Lily the Pilates instructor. Who knew.

But these were Margot's ruminations, which she had to set aside. She needed to start thinking like Jenna.

Margot checked Rhonda's phone for the time. It was nearly ten o'clock. She wondered what Roger looked like when he lost his cool. She had to move quickly.

As she turned away from the beach, she noticed someone waving at her. It was one of the surfcasters. Waving at *her?* Was there someone drowning offshore, or a shark? Margot squinted. The man was wearing a white visor.

It was Griff.

Not possible. But yes, of course. *Of course* Griff was fishing here. Had he mentioned fishing the night before? She couldn't remember. Maybe he had, and now it would look like Margot was stalking him. Maybe this would become the story where Margot and the man who had kissed her like no other man before but whom she could never kiss again because of the awful way she had wronged him would hunt down the runaway bride.

Margot waved back, but the wave was halfhearted, despite the way her whole heart felt like it was dangling from the end of Griff's line.

She hurried to her car.

Beth Carmichael had requested that her ashes be scattered in three places on Nantucket. And so, seven years earlier, Margot and her father and her siblings had taken the box of Beth's remains to the locations she'd specified. The first place Margot and her family had scattered Beth's ashes was the Brant Point Lighthouse. Brant Point was just a knuckle of land that jutted out into the harbor. The lighthouse was a white brick column with a black cap and a red beacon. It was prettiest at night or in the fog when the crimson light seemed to glow with warm promise. The lighthouse also charmed at Christmastime when the Coast Guard hung a giant evergreen wreath on it.

An old Nantucket legend said that when a visitor left the island on the ferry, she should toss two pennies overboard as the boat passed Brant Point Lighthouse. This would ensure the visitor would return one day. Beth Carmichael had been fanatical about the penny throwing. On the day that the Carmichaels departed each summer, Beth would herd all four kids to the top deck, where they would throw their pennies. Margot even remembered throwing pennies in rainstorms with punishing winds. When Margot, Kevin, and Nick were teenagers and refused to participate in the penny throwing, deeming it "lame," Beth had taken Jenna up with her to throw the pennies. Jenna had believed in the penny throwing, just as she believed in Santa Claus and the Tooth Fairy. It was Nick who said, "You know it's a bunch of baloney, right? Throw the penny, don't throw the penny, you can still come back to Nantucket. It's a free country."

But their mother would not back down from this particular superstition. She could risk certain things, but she could not risk a life without Nantucket.

Now a part of her was here forever. As Margot walked to the lighthouse, she spied bike tracks in the sand, ones that her Nancy Drew instincts told her belonged to Jenna's Schwinn. But when Margot reached the small beach in front of the lighthouse, the exact place they'd all stood when they'd scattered Beth's ashes, it was deserted. There was gravelly sand, pebbles, the overturned shell of a horseshoe crab, and one of the most arresting views on the island: the sweeping harbor, sailboats, the shore of the first point of Coatue visible a few hundred yards away across sparkling blue water.

Breathtaking.

But no Jenna.

Margot got back in the car. She checked Rhonda's phone in case Jenna had called. Nothing. It was 10:18.

Madaket was the settlement on the west coast of the island, the somewhat poor relation to Siasconset in the east. Sconset was fashionable and popular; it was home to the Sconset Market and the Sconset Café, it had the Summer House and Sankaty Head Golf Club, it had rose-covered cottages that had once been owned by the silent film stars of the 1920s.

Madaket was low-key by Nantucket standards. There was one restaurant that had changed hands a few times—in Margot's memory it had been called 27 Curves, and then the Westender, which had served a popular drink called the Madaket Mystery.

Now it was a popular Tex-Mex place called Millie's, named after an iconic but scary-looking woman who had worked for the Coast Guard named Madaket Millie.

Beth had loved Madaket; she found its simplicity pleasing. There was no flash, no cachet, very little to see except for the natural beauty of the sun setting each night and the quiet splendor of Madaket Harbor, which was small and picturesque and surrounded by eelgrass.

Margot traveled the road to Madaket slowly, searching the bike path for Jenna. There were, in fact, twenty-seven curves in the road that took one past the dump, then the trails of Ram's Pasture, then the pond where Beth used to take Margot and her siblings turtling—four sturdy sticks, a ball of string, and a pound of raw chicken equaled an afternoon of hilarity. Both Kevin and Nick had always ended up in the pond with the turtles.

Margot didn't see Jenna on the bike path. This was impossible, right? Margot tried to calculate time. If Jenna had left the house when Margot suspected she had, and if she'd stopped at Brant Point Lighthouse, then Margot would have seen Jenna on the bike path, either coming or going. There was only one way out and one way in. There were a few stands of trees and a couple of grassy knolls, but otherwise nowhere to hide.

Margot reached the parking lot of Madaket Beach. She climbed out of the car and wandered over to the wooden bridge that looked out on both Madaket Harbor and the ocean.

Madaket Mystery, Margot thought. Where is my sister?

It occurred to Margot then that maybe she was wrong. Maybe Jenna *hadn't* gone on a quest for their mother. Maybe Jenna had ridden her bike to the airport and flown back to New York.

Margot pulled out Rhonda's phone and dialed the number of the house. Five rings, six rings...there was no answering machine. The phone would just ring forever until someone picked it up. There were a dozen people in residence; *someone* had to be home. But answering the phone was one of the things the rest of the family left to Margot. How long would it take someone to realize she wasn't there?

Finally the ringing stopped. There were some muffled sounds, then a froggy "Hello?"

Margot paused. It sounded like Jenna. Had Jenna made it back? Had she possibly never left? Had she found a quiet corner of the house to hide and fallen back to sleep?

Margot said, "Jenna?"

"Um," the voice said. "No. This is Finn."

"Oh," Margot said. "This is Margot."

"Uh-huh," Finn said. "I know."

Margot said, "Is Jenna there? Is she at the house?"

"No," Finn said.

"Have you heard from her since I saw you last?" Margot asked.

"I've sent six texts and left her three voice mails," Finn said. "And I've gotten nothing back. She hates me, I think, because…"

Margot understood why Jenna might hate Finn right now. "Stop. I can't get in the middle of this," Margot said. "I'm just trying to find Jenna."

"*Find* Jenna?" Finn said. "What does that mean?"

Margot closed her eyes and inhaled through her nose. Madaket Harbor had its own smell, ripe and marshy. Margot could go back to the house and pick up Finn, and this would become the story of the sister and the shameless, irresponsible best friend hunting down the runaway bride.

That's my *decision,* Jenna had said. *And I've made it. I am not marrying Stuart tomorrow.*

"I have to go," Margot said, and she hung up.

*   *   *

She had a hard time finding a parking spot near the church. It was July; the streets were lined with Hummers and Jeeps and Land Rovers like Margot's. Margot felt a sense of indignation at all the summer visitors, even though she was one herself. She drove around and around—Centre Street, Gay Street, Quince Street, Hussey Street. She needed a spot. It was five minutes to eleven, which was the time they were due at the salon. Margot couldn't bear to think about Roger. Would he be attending to the 168 details of this wedding that needed his attention, or was he throwing darts in his garage, or was he out surfcasting?

Surfcasting, Griff, the kissing. Margot needed a parking space. She had waved back at Griff, but lamely. What would he make of that? What would he be thinking? *The one thing I miss about being married is having someone to talk to late at night, someone to tell the stupid stuff.* Did Roger have a picture of Jenna's face plastered to his dartboard? Was he trying to stick her between the eyes? He would get paid regardless; their father would lose a lot of money if Jenna canceled, but of course that was no reason to go through with the wedding. Edge was coming today, or so Doug had said, but Margot was trying not to care. Of course she did care, but that caring was buried under her concern for Jenna and her urgent desire to salvage the wedding, and her pressing need for a parking space.

In front of her, someone pulled out.

Hallelujah, praise the Lord, Margot thought. She was, after all, going to church.

The Congregational Church, otherwise known as the north church or the white spire church (as opposed to the south church, or the clock tower church, which was Unitarian) was the final place that Beth's ashes had been scattered. Beth wasn't a member of this church; she was Episcopalian and had attended St. Paul's with the rest of the family. Beth had asked for her ashes to be scattered from the Congregational Church tower because it looked out over the whole island. Doug, fearing that tossing his wife's remains from the tower window might be frowned upon by the church staff, or possibly even deemed illegal, had suggested they smuggle Beth's ashes up the stairs. They had gone at the very end of the day, after all the other tourists had vacated, and the surreptitious nature of their mission had made it feel mischievous, even fun—and the somberness of the occasion had been alleviated a bit. Margot had stuffed the box of ashes in her Fendi hobo bag, and Kevin had pried open a window at the top. Beth's remains had fallen softly, like snowflakes. Most of her ashes had landed on the church's green lawn, but Margot imagined that bits had been carried farther afield by the breeze. She lay in the treetops, on the gambrel roofs; she dusted the streets and fertilized the pocket gardens.

Margot entered the church and checked the sanctuary for Jenna. It was deserted.

The Congregationalists normally asked a volunteer to man the station by the stairway that led to the tower. But today the station was unoccupied. There was a table with a small basket and a card asking for donations of any amount. Margot had no money on her. She silently apologized as she headed up the stairs.

Up, up, up. The stairway was unventilated, and Margot grew dizzy. Those martinis, all that wine, four bites of lobster, Elvis Costello, Warren Zevon, Griff's brother killed in a highway accident. Chance's mother at the groomsmen's house at the same time as Ann Graham. Was that awkward? What was it like for Ann to see the woman whom her husband had had an affair with so many years ago? Margot would someday meet Lily the Pilates instructor; Margot would probably be invited to the wedding, since she and Drum Sr. were still friends. Margot used to love to watch Drum surf; she had been unable to resist him. All her children had his magic, if that was what it was, despite Carson's near flunking and Ellie's hoarding; they were all illuminated from within, which was a characteristic inherited from Drum, not from her. Kevin was an ass, Margot didn't know how Beanie could stand him, and yet she'd been standing him just fine since she was fourteen years old. *So there,* Margot thought. Love did last. She wondered if her father had read the last page of the Notebook. She must remind him.

Margot was huffing by the time she reached the final flight of stairs. She couldn't think about anything but the pain in her lungs. And water—she was dying of thirst.

At the top of the tower was the room with the windows. Standing at the window facing east—toward their house on Orange Street—was Jenna.

Margot gasped. She realized she hadn't actually expected to find anyone up here, perhaps least of all the person she was looking for.

"Hey," Jenna said. She sounded unsurprised and unimpressed. She was wearing the backless peach dress, which was now so bedraggled that she resembled a character from one of the stories they'd read as children—a street urchin from Dickens, Sara Crewe from *A Little Princess,* the Little Match Girl. She wore no shoes. If anyone but Margot had discovered Jenna up here, they would have called the police.

"Hey," Margot said. She tried to keep her voice tender. She wasn't positive that Jenna hadn't completely lost her mind.

"I saw you walking up the street," Jenna said. "I knew you were coming."

"I had a hard time finding a parking spot," Margot said. "Have you been here long?"

Jenna shrugged. "A little while."

Margot moved closer to Jenna. Her eyes were puffy, and her face was streaked with tears, although she wasn't crying now. She was just staring out the window, over the streets of town and the blue scoop of harbor. Margot followed her gaze. Something about this vantage point transported Margot back 150 years, to the days of Alfred Coates Hamilton and the whaling industry, when Nantucket had been responsible for most of the country's oil production. Women had stood on rooftops, scanning the horizon for the ships that their husbands or fathers or brothers were sailing on.

"I have a question," Margot said.

"What's that?" Jenna asked.

"Did you go to Brant Point?"

"Yes," Jenna said.

"And did you go to Madaket?"

"Of course," Jenna said.

"I didn't see you," Margot said. "If you had biked to Madaket, I would have seen you."

"I didn't bike," Jenna said. "I hitched a ride."

"You hitched?" Margot said. "I'm surprised anyone stopped to pick you up. You look like an Alphabet City junkie."

"Four Bulgarian guys in a red pickup," Jenna said. "It was pretty funny. They're baggers at the Stop & Shop."

"That's not funny," Margot said. "They could have taken advantage of you. Who brought you back to town?"

"The guy driving the Santos Rubbish truck."

"Really?" Margot said.

"Really," Jenna said.

"But you knew I would come looking for you, right?" Margot said. "You knew I would find you."

"I figured probably," Jenna said.

Margot gulped fresh air from the one partially open window. She was sweating, she was very, very thirsty, and Roger—who represented 150 people and over a hundred thousand dollars— was waiting for an answer one way or the other.

"Listen..." Margot said.

"No," Jenna said. "You listen."

Margot clamped her mouth shut and nodded once sharply. She hadn't known what to say next anyway.

"I thought Stuart was different," Jenna said. "I thought he was a good egg."

"Jenna," Margot said. "He *is* a good egg."

"He's just like everyone else," Jenna said. She cleared her throat, then said, "Finn slept with Nick! She told me she thinks she's fallen in *love* with him! After one afternoon on a paddleboard, she thought nothing of letting him join her in the outdoor shower, the second you walked out the door!"

Margot put up a traffic cop hand. "Please," she said. "Please don't tell me any details."

"And do you know what Finn's excuse is? Scott was unfaithful first! Scott hooked up with some waitress from Hooters on a golf trip to Tampa in April. He and Finn had only been married six months, she was thinking about trying to get pregnant, then he goes away on this golf trip with the guys, no big deal, because Scott is always going on golf trips with the guys, only this time he comes home and gives Finn the clap—and then he has to confess about the skanky waitress. Now he's in Vegas, and instead of being on his best behavior, he told Finn that all the guys were getting lap dances, and going to a private party with performing lesbians."

Margot sighed. "She was obviously bent out of shape about that on Thursday night."

"So then Nick shows up and starts paying all kinds of sweet attention to her." Jenna sniffled and wiped her nose on the neckline of her dress. Margot winced. "And Finn starts imagining they have all this *history,* she's been in love with him since she was thirteen years old and he came home from Penn State, then yesterday they had this magical day at Fat Ladies Beach, and…"

"And I left for the yacht club," Margot said. Because she was so anxious to see Edge. She should have waited for Nick and Finn. She should have stayed home and chaperoned.

"And it's Nick," Jenna said. "And apparently he just can't help himself. Doesn't matter that Finn is *married,* doesn't matter that I was her maid of honor, or that she's my bridesmaid and best friend."

"You can't let Nick's behavior or Finn's poor judgment influence you," Margot said.

"Then we have Dad and Pauline. He's sixty-four, and she's… what? Sixty-one? This was supposed to be their great second chance at love; they were supposed to grow old together. But no. Love has died there as well, and now Dad will start dating younger and younger women — your age first, then my age, then Emma Wilton's age…"

"Jenna…"

"And then we have Stuart's parents. I used to think their story was so *lovely* — at least the part where they got married for a second time. But last night, when I met Helen, I felt sick, and that was even before she opened her mouth about Stuart and Crissy Pine. She's this freaking Swedish supermodel-type woman, and she wore that look-at-me, center-of-attention dress when she was

275

lucky to be invited to the wedding at all. Ann only included her because Ann is a saint."

"Okay," Margot said, thinking, *Stupid Ann.*

"And when Chance got sick and Jim and Helen left for the hospital, it became, duh, obvious to me that Jim had *cheated* on Ann, cheated badly. He had a child with another woman!"

Margot wanted to say, *Oh, come on, that just occurred to you tonight?* What kind of Pollyanna world had Jenna been living in? But instead Margot said, "You can't let other people's failings—"

"But worst of all," Jenna said, "worst of all is you."

"Me?" Margot said. Her thoughts twirled and tumbled. How could *she* be the worst of all? Worse than *Nick?* Worse than Helen in the yellow dress? What did Jenna know about her personal life, anyway? Had Autumn told her about Edge? Had she seen Margot kissing Griff? And why would either of those things matter to Jenna?

"Of all the marriages I've ever seen, yours was my absolute favorite," Jenna said. "And you just walked away from it."

"My marriage?" Margot said. "You mean to Drum?"

"Maybe it was because of our age difference," Jenna said. "I was still in high school when you got married, and as we know, I'm a hopeless romantic."

"There was nothing romantic about when I got married," Margot said. "Hello? It was a shotgun wedding."

"You two were the coolest people I knew," Jenna said. "When you two surfed together, you were so...beautiful. Then you got pregnant and Drum took you to dinner at the Blue Bistro and he gave you the oyster that had the diamond ring in it."

"And I puked," Margot said. "I saw the ring embedded in oyster mucous and I ran to the ladies' room and threw up."

"You got that amazing apartment in the city," Jenna said.

"Drum's parents bought us the apartment," Margot said. "They picked it out, they paid for it. That's not romantic or cool, Jenna. That's mollycoddling."

"You had your job," Jenna said. "Drum watched the baby, he cooked those gourmet dinners and always had a glass of wine waiting for you when you got home. You took those great vacations to Costa Rica and Hawaii and Telluride."

"Because Drum wanted to surf," Margot said. "And he wanted to ski. I always got stuck at the hotel watching the kids."

"I wanted your life," Jenna said. She sniffled a little more. "I wanted the beautiful babies and the doorman building and the trips to exotic places. I wanted someone to love me as much as Drum loved you. He worshipped you, Margot. You were a goddess to him."

Margot snorted. It was astonishing how warped Jenna's view of her marriage was. "Please."

"I got a text from Drum yesterday, you know," Jenna said. "He said he's getting married in the fall."

Margot felt a pang of guilt. "I meant to tell you."

Jenna brushed off her dress, an exercise in futility. The dress would end up in the trash, along with Margot's stained white dress from Thursday night.

Margot thought, *We are a couple of girls without a mother.*

"So, anyway, my dream of you and Drum getting back together is over."

"Excuse me," Margot said. She decided to pull out some Taylor Swift lyrics, maybe make Jenna smile. "We were never, ever getting back together. Like ever."

The joke was lost on her. She made a face. "But you two were perfect together!"

"Honestly," Margot said. "You have no idea what you're talking about. And that's the thing about marriage. It can look perfect to people from the outside but be utterly imperfect on the inside. The reverse is true as well. No one knows what goes on in a marriage except for the two people living in it."

"I lied when I said you were the worst," Jenna said. "You weren't the worst."

Margot felt stupidly relieved. She pursed her lips; they were so dry, she feared they were going to crack.

"The worst of all..." Jenna trailed off and stared out the window. Her eyes filled. "The worst of all was Mom and Dad. At the end. I was there, watching them."

"I know," Margot said.

"You *don't* know!" Jenna said. "You don't know because you weren't around. You were living in the city with Drum and the boys. You were *working*. Kevin was in San Francisco that spring, and Nick was in D.C. I was at home with them by myself."

Yes, Margot remembered. Seven years ago, Drum Jr. had been five, and Carson only three. Margot had been desperately trying to make partner at Miller-Sawtooth, which meant not only acting like a person without two small children at home but also acting like a person whose mother was not dying an hour north in Connecticut. Margot would use the fifteen minutes she took for lunch in those days to call Beth. They talked about normal things—Drum Jr.'s kindergarten teacher, Carson's biting problem, the placements Margot was working on. Only at the end of the conversation would they address the elephant in the room. Margot would ask Beth how she was feeling; Beth would lie and say she was feeling okay, the pain was manageable, she was glad, anyway, to be finished with chemo. Anything was better than chemo. Margot would promise to come to Connecticut over the weekend and bring the kids, but more than once she had failed to do so. Drum Jr. had kinder-soccer, or Carson took a longer nap than Margot expected, or Margot sneaked back into the office for a few hours—and plans for the trip to Connecticut were dashed.

Margot knew her brothers had been busy, too. Kevin had been trying to save the Coit Tower, and Nick had just taken the job with the Nationals. They were, all three of them, inconsolable about the idea of losing Beth, but they hadn't been *right there* the way that Jenna had been. Jenna had taken a semester off from William and Mary to go home and be with Beth. She moved back in at the same time that Beth went into hospice.

"You know what?" Jenna said. She was gearing up now, her voice taking on a scary intensity that Margot almost never saw. "For most of my life, I felt like I wasn't even part of the family. It was always the three of you and Mom and Dad. When we used to sit at the dinner table, you all would be talking and arguing and I couldn't understand or keep up. The three of you would have parties or go on dates, and you would break curfew and come home with beer on your breath. One of you ended up lost after a concert at Madison Square Garden, and Mom was on the phone with the police all night."

Me, Margot thought. The Rolling Stones, the summer between junior and senior year.

"Nick crashed the car and then he got caught growing those pot plants in the attic, and Mom was certain Kevin was going to get Beanie pregnant. Mom and Dad were so consumed with keeping track of the three of you that they forgot about me."

"That's not true..."

"It *is* true. Kevin broke his leg playing lacrosse, remember, and they left me at Finn's house for three whole days."

"Well," Margot said. "We were older."

"And when you all moved out and moved on, we were like a

family again. But a different family. A family with me and Mom and Dad. We would sit down to dinner and we might talk about you, but it was like talking about relatives in Africa or China, you were so far away. Which was fine by me."

Margot made a face. What was this? Decades-old resentment about birth order?

"At the end of Mom's life, it was just the three of us again. I had a front-row seat for her death and what it did to Dad." Now her tears were flowing freely. "It was *horrible,* Margot. He loved her so much, he wanted to go with her. Hell, I wanted to go with her." Jenna yanked at her blond hair, which was still in some semblance of a bun. "Love dies. I watched love die with my own eyes. She left, we all stayed. And that, *that,* Margot, was the worst of all."

"You're right," Margot said. "Of course, you're right."

"And so now we have Finn and Nick, and Daddy and Pauline, and Jim and Ann Graham and horrible Helen, and you and Drum Sr. And as if all of that didn't make me skeptical enough, Stuart lies to me about an enormous event in his life. Enormous!"

"But it's not a deal breaker, Jenna," Margot said. "When you said that he revealed himself to be just like everyone else, you were right. He's a *human being.* He was scared to tell you about Crissy Pine. He wanted to pretend like it never happened. I'm not saying he wasn't in the wrong. He was. You deserved to know. But do not cancel the wedding over this. It isn't worth it."

"He gave her his great-grandmother's ring!" Jenna said.

"Since when do you care about things like rings?" Margot asked. "I promise you there are hundreds of thousands of diamond rings in this world that have been kept or stolen or thrown out of car windows in anger."

"I care because he gave it to *her*—something precious, a family heirloom. He loved her enough to give her that ring." Jenna sniffled. "I want him to love *me* that much."

"He *does* love you that much!" Margot said. "He loves you more than that! He loves you enough to have gone out and found a ring with ethically mined diamonds! He didn't recycle some fusty ring that belonged to his dead ancestor. He found a ring for you, one that you could love and be proud of."

Margot thought this was a point well made, and she let her words hang in the air for a moment. Then she said, "I saw him this morning. He's a mess."

"I hope he is," Jenna said.

"He is," Margot said. "He looks god-awful. He said if you leave him, he will die—and I don't think that was hyperbole."

Jenna started to cry again. "I love him so much! I've just spent the past twelve hours trying to make myself *stop* loving him. And I can't stop, I'll never be able to stop, I'm going to love him for the rest of my life! But he lied to me! It's like he's suddenly become a completely different person—a person who was engaged and chose to hide it from me."

Margot knew enough not to speak. They both stood at the window, the same one Kevin had pried open so that they could all toss handfuls of their mother's ashes out over the island she adored. The breeze coming in the window was the only thing that was keeping Margot from fainting.

She pulled Rhonda's cell phone out of her pocket and handed it to Jenna. "Call Roger," she said. "Call Roger and tell him it's definitely off."

"Okay," Jenna said. She accepted the phone and stared at the face of it for a second, and Margot thought, *She won't be able to do it.* She loves Stuart, and they will end up having a marriage like Beth and Doug's—a marriage that will be a fortress for all of them. Margot's perfect instincts told her so.

But this time, it seemed, Margot's instincts were wrong. Jenna dialed the number and held the phone to her ear. Margot had the urge to grab the phone from her sister's hand and talk to Roger herself. *The wedding is on,* Margot would say. *Jenna is just scared. She's just scared is all.*

Anyone who had listened to that laundry list of marital disasters would have been scared.

"Hello?" Jenna said.

Margot thought, *Oh, honey, please don't. It's not a deal breaker. Stuart is just like everyone else, but you and Stuart, as a couple, are different. You two are going to make it.*

She thought, *Mom? Help me?*

"Stuart?" Jenna said. "I love you, Stuart. You jerk, I love you!"

OUTTAKES

Finn Sullivan-Walker (bridesmaid): She hates me. Jenna Carmichael, who has been my best friend since we were eating graham crackers, drinking apple juice, and watching *Barney,* hates me. I went to the salon with Autumn and Rhonda at eleven o'clock. Just the three of us because Margot and Jenna were AWOL. I asked Autumn if she had heard from Jenna, and she pretended to think about it, then she admitted that no, she hadn't talked to Jenna since the party the night before. Autumn went back to the groomsmen's house with H.W., where they had wild, drunken sex, which she then described in lurid, pornographic detail to Rhonda, who lapped it up. *Tell me more, tell me more, was it love at first sight?* I thought maybe Autumn was being bitchy to me because she was jealous — she hooked up with Nick herself at Jenna's graduation from college a bunch of years ago. I tried not to care about Autumn or Rhonda or even Jenna. If being with Nick means losing Jenna, then I guess I'll have to live with that, because my feelings for Nick are overwhelming. It's like they've existed forever but I've only allowed myself to acknowledge them this weekend.

I was in the chair having my hair twisted into a chignon when Jenna and Margot walked in. Everyone in the place started to applaud. *The prodigal bride!* Frankly, I didn't understand Jenna's disappearing act. She's not usually one for drama.

I, on the other hand, am a magnet for drama. My mother always told me I was so flighty and so hard to please that she was sure I would end up married at least four times. She told me that on my wedding day, and I think that was what jinxed me.

When Jenna got to the salon, I thought she might apologize or try to make things right, but she didn't come anywhere close to my chair. She didn't look in my direction. I thought, *Fine. I don't care. I won't be your stupid bridesmaid, I won't wear the god-awful green dress, I'll go home and you never have to see or talk to me again. Find another best friend, make Autumn your best friend even though she's a documented superslut. Make Rhonda your best friend or buddy up with Francie or Chelsea or Hilly or any one of the "womyn" you teach with at Little Minds. I won't stand up for you, my spot will be blank, my place at the head table empty.*

A hand on my shoulder. The stylist.

"Honey," she said. "Why are you crying?"

Beanie (sister-in-law of the bride): I was left in charge of six kids for most of the morning, and whereas normally they're a breeze to watch—they all hang out together and make up their own games, they only come to me when they're hungry—it's no surprise that something went awry. Brock, my youngest, is serving as the ring bearer, and hence Kevin was appointed "Lord of the Rings." He was in charge of holding on to Stuart's platinum band and Jenna's platinum band embedded with fourteen ethically mined diamonds, to represent the number of months they were together before Stuart proposed. The rings were side by side on our dresser in chocolate velvet boxes. The boxes appeared to be untouched, but when Kevin opened them at two thirty this afternoon—two and a half hours before the ceremony—he found that the box with Jenna's ring was empty.

Autumn (bridesmaid): H.W. is a grown-up frat boy asshole, which makes him exactly my type. He likes to drink a beer with a shot of Jameson, which I could have predicted the second I laid eyes on him. He's a Carolina fan; he has a tattoo of a panther on his ankle. He works as a salesman for a liquor distributor in Raleigh, meaning he hangs out with bar owners and gets free tickets to everything. He plays poker every week with a group of guys he went to NC State with, and the best vacation he's ever taken, he says, was to Cancún, which he won for having the most lucrative Patrón accounts in his region. He had a girlfriend for a while but she got too clingy so he broke up with her via text message while he was in Cancún, at which point she stalked him and tried to hack into his Facebook account. All he wants this weekend is lots of sex and someone to drink and dance with. I promised him that, come Sunday at 3 p.m., he would never see or hear from me again.

Nick (brother of the bride): I never get myself into situations

I can't handle; that is a Nick Carmichael trademark. But I think Margot might actually be right this time. I think I might be in over my head. Can I have a mulligan, please?

DOUG

The photographer was due at three, and Doug knew that meant he had to be dressed in his tuxedo at two forty-five. And he had to see Jenna.

She was getting dressed with the girls. Outside Doug's bedroom door, he could hear the chatter, the talk of foundation garments and false eyelashes. Music was playing, Bob Seger's "Katmandu," which had been another of Beth's favorite songs, and he wondered if the getting-ready music had been prescribed in the Notebook, or if this was a song Jenna normally listened to.

He stood on the quiet side of the door, hesitant to open it.

Pauline was also getting ready, again sitting at his grandmother's dressing table where she didn't belong, spritzing herself with a perfume that, for the past five years, had been making Doug sneeze. It was called Illuminum White Gardenia; Pauline always wore it on special occasions. It was expensive, she bought it at Bendel's, and Doug was allergic to it. Pauline had never noticed this last fact, however.

The perfume was one more thing he would be happy to bid good-bye.

"What color am I wearing?" Pauline said.

"Excuse me?"

"Don't turn your head," Pauline said. Doug obeyed; he stared at his hand on the glass doorknob. It was the hand of an old man, he feared. "Tell me what color I'm wearing."

Blue, he thought. But no, that had been the night before. What color was the dress she had picked for the wedding? Certainly she had told him sixteen times, and possibly even modeled the dress for him.

"I don't know," he admitted.

"Because you don't look at me," Pauline said. "Or when you look at me, you see right through me."

"Pauline," he said.

"Cinnamon," she said. "I'm wearing cinnamon."

He turned to her. The dress was long and lacy—and yes, the color of cinnamon. He might have called it brown. It seemed a bit autumnal for a hot day in July, although the color looked nice with her dark hair.

"You look lovely, Pauline," he said.

She laughed unhappily, and Doug twisted the glass knob and opened the door.

The hallway was a frenzy of green. Rhonda, Autumn, Finn, Margot. Margot kissed him just as the song changed to Crosby, Stills, and Nash's "Teach Your Children." *You, who were on the road, must have a code, that you can live by.*

Definitely Beth's song list, he thought.

Margot said, "You look great, Daddy."

"Thanks," he said. "So do you. I'm looking for your sister."

Beanie appeared in the hallway in a pink polo shirt and denim skirt with a stricken look on her face. "Margot?" she said. "Can I talk to you a second?"

"Sure," Margot said. She turned to her father. "Jenna is in the attic, getting dressed."

"In the *attic?*" he said. "Where are the kids?"

"We shooed them out," Margot said. "She wanted her own space."

"Okay," he said, and up to the attic he headed.

"I'm coming up the stairs!" he called. There was no door to the attic. "I hope you're decent!"

"I'm dressed," Jenna said. "I don't know about decent."

Doug laughed.

He ascended the final three steps and entered the sweltering, cavernous attic with its nine unmade bunk beds. The room most closely resembled a cabin at sleepaway camp. For some reason, there were feathers all over the floor, as though a goose had gotten caught in the ceiling fan.

Standing in the middle of the room like a pearly column of light was Jenna.

"Oh, God, honey," Doug said.

"Do I look okay?" she asked.

It hurt to swallow, such was the lump in his throat. His baby girl, wearing Beth's dress. The attic was so hot that sweat dripped into Doug's eyes, and yet his daughter stood before him, cool and composed, beaming.

The most beautiful girl he'd ever seen.

The second most beautiful.

He had been standing at the altar at St. James' in New York City; his brother David, who died three years later of a heart attack, was next to him serving as best man. Doug had seen Beth on the arm of her father at the end of the very long aisle, and as she grew closer, he thought, *I can't believe it. I just can't believe it.*

And the thing was, their wedding day hadn't been the happiest day of their lives together. Not even close. There had been the births of the four children, there had been the day Doug made partner at Garrett, Parker, and Spence, there had been birthdays: thirtieth, fortieth, fiftieth. But none of those were the happiest day, either. When had the happiest day been? He sighed. There had been so many. There had been long summer days spent here in this house when the kids were younger—hours spent at the beach with Doug and Beth side by side in their canvas chairs as the kids played in the waves. Doug and Beth used to share a sandwich, Doug would read Ken Follett or Ludlum, Beth would needlepoint. They always took one walk together, holding hands. There were days when their biggest concern was whether to head left or right on the beach, whether to grill swordfish or a rack of ribs. They used to climb into bed at nine o'clock and lock their bedroom door and make sweet, silent love while the kids played manhunt with flashlights in the backyard.

There had been strings of shimmering silver days like that, and golden days of autumn when they bundled in sweaters and Beth made a pot of chili or a bunch of sub sandwiches and they tailgated at the Yale-Columbia game. There had been Christmases and ski weekends and trips to Paris, London, the Caribbean. There had been regular days of school and work, court for him, the hospital for Beth, where she was constantly trying to stretch the budget, there had been family dinners most every night, sometimes movies or TV or school functions or neighborhood cocktail parties where the neighbors, he was sure, would gossip after they left, asking one another if the Carmichaels could really be as happy as they looked.

Yes.

All of it, he had loved all of it.

And it had officially begun on the day he saw Beth in this dress.

"You're a vision," he said to Jenna. "Stuart is such a lucky bastard, I hate him a little right now."

"Oh, Daddy," Jenna said, and she hugged him. He rested his chin on top of her sweet-smelling head.

"My hair," she said, pulling away.

"Ah, yes," he said, admiring it. It was in some kind of complicated updo, though she had yet to set her veil. She was wearing the sapphire earrings that his own mother, Martha, had worn on the day that she married his father here at this house. They were Jenna's "something blue." What did Doug and Beth used to say when Jenna was a baby? *Wake up and show us the jewels.* Her sapphire eyes.

"If your mother could see you," he said.

"Daddy," she said, blinking rapidly. "Please don't. My makeup. And it's hot up here. We should go downstairs."

"I know," he whispered. "You're right. I'm sorry. Let's go."

"But wait, first..." Jenna opened a plastic box that was resting on the dresser and produced Doug's boutonniere. "I want to pin this for you."

Doug stared over Jenna's head into the dusty rafters as she attached the flower to his lapel. He couldn't speak. *Your father will be a cause for concern.*

"And here," she said. "Let me fix your tie." She tugged on his bow tie, her eyes appraising him, and he basked in it. He had left his tie crooked on purpose, just so she could straighten it.

THE NOTEBOOK, PAGE 29

The Registry, Part I: The Kitchen

I know you well enough to realize that you might skip over any section of this notebook titled "Registry," because material things mean little to you, and if you got married tomorrow, you would ask everyone to donate to Greenpeace or Amnesty International instead of bringing a gift. However, here is another place where you must trust me!

You and I know that Margot doesn't cook, she has a hard time with anything more elaborate than a peanut butter and jelly sandwich, and she's too busy with work to entertain—which is a pity because that apartment is begging for a dinner party. But you, my darling, are a magnificent cook. You have been whipping up healthy things like steel-cut oats with bananas, and that chicken stew. I was only able to eat a few bites, but it was delicious. The fresh dill made it.

This established, a list of items for your kitchen follows. Remember, Jenna, people are going to bring you gifts no matter what you say. Better they give you something you can use.

Crock-Pot/slow cooker
10" and 12" nonstick frying pans (All-Clad is best).
3 qt. sauté pan with lid
large cutting board, preferably Boos
knives: Do not register for a "set." Knives are too important.
You want a 10" chef's knife, a serrated bread knife, a

*hollow-edge Santoku, a sandwich knife, and two good
paring knives.*
8 qt. stock pot
immersion blender
*KitchenAid stand mixer (I've had mine 35 years, never a
problem.)*
good coffeemaker
11-cup Cuisinart food processor
tall wooden pepper mill
1 qt., 2 qt., 3 qt. saucepans with lids
colander
Le Creuset Dutch oven
large wooden salad bowl (Check at Simon Pearce.)

MARGOT

Abigail Pease, the photographer, showed up fifteen minutes early with Roger at her side. Roger looked calm; he showed no anger or frustration at having the wedding nearly canceled then resuscitated. Probably it happened all the time. Margot wanted to ask, but she was caught off guard by the appearance of the photographer. Pictures at the groomsmen's house had gone more quickly than anyone had anticipated.

"Why was that?" Margot asked.

"They were all ready to go," Abigail said. She was about fifty years old, she had long, curly blond hair, she spoke with a touch of a southern accent, and she wore Eileen Fisher to great effect.

"Most times the men take more time to get ready than the women. But these guys were in their tuxes, drinking beer and throwing the football around."

"Well, we're almost ready," Margot said. This wasn't really true. She was ready and Autumn was ready; like a good grooms-man, Autumn was drinking a beer in the backyard.

But when Margot went upstairs to check on the other two girls, she discovered that Rhonda wasn't happy with the work of the makeup artist at RJ Miller, and so she was redoing her makeup herself. This process entailed cleaning, moisturizing, and reapplying with surgical precision, which was tying up the bathroom. Finn was standing morosely in front of the full-length mirror, applying aloe to her already-peeling sunburn. Makeup was lost on Finn because she had been doing nothing but crying since they returned from the salon, though everyone was pre-tending not to notice. The crying was Finn's way of getting Jenna to pay attention to her, but Jenna wasn't taking the bait, and Mar-got was proud of her.

Then Nick ascended the stairs in his tux, having just finished with pictures, and Jenna excused herself to the third floor to fin-ish getting ready "in peace," which really meant that she wanted to get away from Finn and Nick. Finn and Nick vanished down the stairs, holding hands, and Margot hadn't seen them since.

Margot thought, There was no way Abigail Pease was going to get all four bridesmaids in the same picture frame any time this century.

Margot considered going downstairs and telling Abigail Pease this. There had been discussion of Abigail snapping candids of the bridesmaids getting ready, but what would those pictures look like? Autumn swilling a Heineken, Rhonda with foaming cleanser all over her face, Finn sobbing in Nick's arms. Abigail might take a photo of Margot fretting about any or all of the above—or she might capture the envy on Margot's face when she saw Jenna in their mother's gown. Jenna looked stunning, and whereas Margot felt a bloom of love and pride—and relief—that this was so, she was also jealous. She wished that she had had a real wedding where she might have had an opportunity to wear Beth's dress, instead of some salmon-colored chiffon number from A Pea in the Pod. She wished she had gotten married here at the Nantucket house instead of on a cliff in Antigua, where she had never been before and would never go again. She wished she had married someone different, someone better matched to grow with her.

Someone like Edge? But Margot couldn't imagine being married to Edge. To be married to Edge, history had proved, meant to one day be divorced from Edge.

Someone like Griff? Margot wondered.

Margot never made it downstairs to talk to Abigail Pease, because at that moment her father emerged from his bedroom in his tux, and Margot was distracted. And two seconds later, Beanie popped her head out of her bedroom and told Margot she needed to talk to her.

"The ring is gone," Beanie said. She held out the brown velvet box. It was empty.

"Wait," Margot said. "What do you mean?"

"The boxes were here," Beanie said. She pointed to the East-lake bureau, which matched the ornately carved twin beds that had, long ago, been the summer beds of Kevin and Nick. The beds and the dresser with the matching attached mirror were antiques that predated even Margot's grandparents. How the boys had ended up with them was another mysterious family injustice. On the dresser was the second brown velvet box, which held Stuart's wedding band. Stuart's band was there, but not Jenna's. Jenna's was embedded with fourteen ethically mined diamonds, totaling nearly two carats, and was worth twenty or thirty times what Stuart's was worth.

Had someone come into the Carmichael house and stolen the ring? The house was filled with people. Downstairs was crawling with catering staff and tent guys and, now, the production people for the band and the band members themselves.

"The boxes have been here the whole time?" Margot asked.

"The whole time. Entrusted to Kevin yesterday by Stuart."

"Your bedroom door was unlocked?"

"Oh, come on," Beanie said. "Of course. I never thought the rings were unsafe here. Would you have thought that?"

"No," Margot said. "I can't believe this. I really can't believe this." On top of everything else, she was dealing with jewelry theft? "Did you look around? It didn't fall, did it?"

"Fall?" Beanie said. The idea was preposterous. If the box had fallen, would the ring have tumbled out? No way, never—and yet a second later both Beanie, and Margot in her green bridesmaid dress, were on their hands and knees, sweeping the dusty wooden floorboards and the ridges of the braided rug with splayed fingers, looking for the ring.

They found an earring back. No ring.

Margot stood up and straightened her dress. She said, "Was anyone else in your room?"

"Not to my knowledge."

"Did you see any of the staff up here?" She really felt like Nancy Drew now, but it didn't bring the high she had been hoping for. She did *not* want to go downstairs to Roger and tell him that he had to start questioning the people slaving over this wedding reception because a diamond wedding band had gone missing. And yet a diamond wedding band had gone missing, it was worth a lot of money, five figures for sure, and they needed to find it. The only people who had been on the second floor were the family and members of the wedding party.

Family. And members of the wedding party.

Margot sat on Beanie's unmade bed. Kevin's bed, naturally, had been made with military precision.

Margot thought, *Finn? Because she was angry and hurting?*

She thought, *Autumn? Because she needed the cash?*

She thought, *Pauline? Pauline had taken the Notebook and not returned it.*

Margot tried to imagine herself approaching any one of those people about the missing ring. She could never do it. And to be honest, none of those answers felt right. Margot closed her eyes. Abigail Pease was waiting.

Family. Members of the wedding party.

And then she knew.

She hopped off the bed. "I'll be right back," she said.

In her room, she rummaged through Ellie's suitcase—nothing. She looked in the dresser drawers and the single drawer of the nightstand—nothing. She hunted in the tight, dark corners of the closet—nothing. Then she marched downstairs. Abigail Pease was perched on the arm of the sofa with her camera in her lap. She perked up when she saw Margot. "You ready?" she said, checking her watch as if to remind Margot, as if Margot didn't already *know,* that they were working with a tight schedule here.

"In one minute!" Margot sang out with false cheer.

Ellie and the boys had changed into their wedding clothes and had been placed outside on a blanket with a deck of cards, a tray of poker chips, and a bucket of spare change. Margot half expected the boys to be flinging poker chips at one another like tiddlywinks, but as she approached, she could see all five boys studying their cards.

Drum Jr. was dealing. He said, "Brian, are you gonna see him for a quarter or fold?"

Her son's knowledge of the game was frightening. Both he and Carson had spent way too many hours watching the World Series of Poker on ESPN. Oh, the guilt.

Ellie didn't have any cards. She was sitting on the edge of the blanket, stacking dimes in one pile, nickels in another.

"Eleanor?" Margot said. "Would you come here, please?"

Ellie looked up. Did she seem guilty? She appeared wary, but that wasn't quite the same thing. "I'm not getting dirty," she said.

This was true, Margot thought. The dress was still pristinely white. Until ten minutes ago, Margot's biggest concern was that Ellie would trash the dress before photographs and the walk down the aisle. All the Carmichael women were trashing their dresses this weekend.

Margot smiled tightly. "Can you come here, please, sweetie?"

Reluctantly, Ellie stood up and shuffled over to her mother.

"What?" she said.

Margot said, "I'm looking for Auntie Jenna's wedding band. It's silver and has diamonds. Do you know where it is?"

Ellie stared at the ground and shook her head.

Margot took a second to congratulate herself on her perfect instincts. "Honey, we need that ring or Auntie Jenna can't get married."

Ellie locked her hands in front of her. She shook her head so hard that her whole body trembled, like she was having a seizure.

"Ellie, where is it?"

Ellie raised her head. Her eyes were pure blazing defiance. "I don't know," she said.

Margot was left temporarily breathless. If her daughter could stare her right in the face and lie to her at age six, what would happen when she was sixteen?

"Eleanor," Margot said. "I need you to tell me where you put that ring *right now.*"

"No," Ellie said.

No: It was progress. She wasn't denying knowing where the ring was; she was just refusing to tell.

Margot said, "Honey, we need it. Auntie Jenna needs it to get married. You must help me find the ring."

"No," Ellie said.

Margot grabbed Ellie's arm and squeezed. She didn't have *time* for this! She leaned over and treated Ellie to her scary Mom whisper. "Tell me where the ring is right this instant."

"No," Ellie said.

Margot straightened. She stared up past the top of the wedding tent into Alfie's upper branches and willed herself not to cry and not to curse out her child.

Roger stuck his head out the back screen door. "Margot?" he said. "Phone for you."

What now? She stormed into the house and took the receiver from him. He said, "And as soon as you're off, I need you to gather the bridesmaids. Abigail is out front, shooting your father and Jenna right now."

"Okay," Margot said.

"We were ahead of the game," Roger said. "Now we're running behind."

"Okay," Margot said, less patiently. Roger was a slave driver. She reminded herself that this was why she loved him. Into the phone, she said, "Yes? Hello?"

"Margot? Are you okay?"

Margot plopped into a kitchen chair. Around her, the caterers buzzed like bees. It was Drum Sr. He was supposed to call every Saturday at noon his time, three o'clock eastern time, but he was often tardy. It was quarter after three now, which was pretty prompt for him, although quite frankly Margot had forgotten about his weekly call, and furthermore, she wondered why he hadn't decided to skip the call, since he knew Jenna was getting married today.

"Oh," Margot said. "Sort of."

"I tried calling your cell phone, like, forty times," he said. "Do you have it shut off?"

"I sunk it," Margot said. "I dropped it in the toilet at the Chicken Box."

"You're kidding!" Drum said. He laughed gleefully. "Wow, you must be having more fun than you even expected! Is every-body there? Kevin, Beanie, Nick, Finn, Scott...?"

"Yes, yes, yes, not Scott, he's in Vegas," Margot said. She felt a pang of longing then, longing for Drum. He had been her hus-band for ten years and her boyfriend for two summers before that. He had been a part of this family, especially close to her siblings, especially fond of Beanie, his fellow in-law, and Jenna. How did it feel to not be included in this wedding? Margot should have invited him. He should be able to see the boys in their blazers, Ellie in her white eyelet dress with the matching white sandals.

"Hey, listen," Margot said. "I could really use your help."

"Of course," Drum said. "Anything. What can I do?" His voice was so open and friendly that Margot couldn't help but think, *He is a good guy and a doting father.* There had been times in the two years since their divorce when the sound of his voice had irked her. After moving to California, he had acquired a surfer dude twang that made him sound like even more of a slacker and a bum than she already believed him to be. But right now he sounded capable and attentive; he sounded like himself. He sounded like exactly the person Margot needed.

After Ellie got off the phone with her father, she stomped into the house, and Margot trailed her at a discreet distance. From the middle drawer in the bottom row of the thirty-six tiny drawers of the apothecary chest, Ellie pulled out a plastic change purse, this one indistinguishable from the many plastic change purses that she carried in her many pocketbooks and handbags, all of them crammed with shit.

Hoarder, Margot thought. My fault. Because I divorced her father and she's afraid of giving up anything else.

From the change purse, Ellie pulled out Jenna's wedding band.

"Am I in trouble?" she asked.

Margot clenched the ring in her palm and sighed. A fifteen-thousand-dollar ring stuffed into one of the drawers of the apothecary chest, where they might not have found it for twenty years, when it would have magically appeared like a prize in a game show. Margot wanted to believe that Ellie would have handed it over of her own volition. But maybe not. Maybe it was a secret she wanted to keep safe. The poor child. "No," Margot said. "In fact, I have an idea. Follow me."

"Margot!" a voice called out. "We're waiting for you!" Margot glanced out the back screen door. Somehow Abigail Pease had lassoed Autumn, Finn, and a freshly made-up Rhonda, who were all standing in a line in the backyard, holding their bouquets. Off to the side stood Jenna and their father, with Kevin and Nick.

"One second," Margot said.

"No, not one second, Margot," Roger said. "We need you now."

"Sorry," Margot said. She led Ellie by the hand out the side door. She had spent all weekend being a daughter and a sister—and now, finally, she was going to take time to be a mother. She opened the tailgate of her Land Rover and brought out the white cardboard box from E.A.T. bakery. She lifted the hideous bow-and-paper-plate hat out of the box.

"Would you like to wear this when you walk down the aisle?" Margot asked.

"Oh, yes, Mommy!" Ellie said. She jumped up and down and her sandals crunched in the gravel and she clapped her hands. She looked less like a world-weary teenager-before-her-time and more like a six-year-old girl. "Yes, yes, yes!"

Margot placed the hat on Ellie's head and tied the ribbon under her chin.

"Very fetching," she said, and she kissed her daughter's nose.

THE NOTEBOOK, PAGE 16

Seating Arrangements

The key to seating: Everyone should feel included and important. You want each of your guests to have a friendly face at his or her table, although surprising mix-and-matches have been known to work, such as my cousin Everett and my college roommate Kay, who have now been married for seventeen years. Yes, they met at our wedding.

With the exception of divorce, infidelity, or a long-standing Hatfield-McCoy feud, anyone can be seated with anyone. Give them enough alcohol and they will enjoy themselves.

I do have strong feelings about the "Head Table." If a bridesmaid or groomsman is married or has brought a date, I believe the spouse/date should be included at the Head Table. This is a controversial stance. If your brother Nick serves as groomsman (per my suggestion on page 6), and he chooses to bring a stripper named Ricki whom he met in Atlantic City the week before as his date, should Ricki be granted a seat at the Head Table? Should Ricki be included in all of the Head Table photos?

Yes.

The reason I say this is because when your late uncle David married your aunt Lorna in Dallas the year before your father and I got married, your father served as best man and was seated at the Head Table, and I was seated across the room with Lorna's elderly aunts and her deaf, flatulent uncles. There wasn't enough alcohol in the state of Texas to make me enjoy myself at that wedding.

ANN

The wedding was on! Ann didn't have many details about how Stuart's gaffe had been fixed. All she knew was that Margot had found Jenna, Jenna had called Stuart, and they had made amends over the She Who Shall Not Be Named crisis. Or at least temporary amends, amends enough to proceed with the wedding. Ann knew from experience that Stuart and Jenna would revisit the topic of Crissy Pine again, and probably again.

Ann had butterflies as she ascended the steps of St. Paul's Church. It was beginning!

As luck would have it, the first person Ann saw in the sanctuary was Helen. Helen was wearing fuchsia, which was just another word for the hottest pink the eye could handle—and a fascinator with pink feathers.

Really? Ann thought. *A fascinator?* This wasn't a royal wedding, it wasn't Westminster Abbey, Helen wasn't British; she was from Roanoke, Virginia. The fascinator wasn't fascinating; it was absurd. Ann felt embarrassed on Helen's behalf. The pink of the dress was an assault on the senses. Ann had a hard time looking at the spectacle that was Helen, but she had a hard time *not* looking at the spectacle that was Helen.

Ann waited in the vestibule for all the guests to be seated, including the Lewises and the Cohens and the Shelbys in the middle pews of the groom's side. Then the music stopped momentarily and started up again, a new song. Ryan appeared at Ann's elbow.

"You look beautiful," he whispered.

Ann beamed. She would never say she had a favorite son, but she was very glad that she had a son who could be counted on to constantly lift her spirits, like Ryan.

"Thank you," she said. "So do you."

Pauline was escorted down the aisle by Jenna's brother, Nick. Ann waited for Pauline to be seated in the front pew on the left, and then she and Ryan stepped forward. All the assembled wedding guests turned to watch them, and this felt good to Ann. She was an important person here, the mother of the groom, and her dress was sensational if she did say so herself. It was a long sheath with cap sleeves in a beautiful shade of turquoise silk that gently ombréd into jade green around her knees. The only jewelry she wore was her dazzling new strand of pearls. She carried a small silver clutch purse that contained her lipstick and a package of tissues. She smiled at the wedding guests who turned to admire her, whether she knew them or not. She couldn't help but remember when she had been the bride and had walked down the aisle at Duke Chapel to a lineup that included Jim, his fraternity brothers, and Ann's roommates from Craven Quad. Jim had been grinning, and sweating out the shots of bourbon that he and said fraternity brothers had done only moments before the wedding. They had been so young, so innocent, and unaware that any roadblocks might lie ahead.

The second time they got married, it was just the two of them and the three boys, no trip down the aisle, but that hadn't mattered. They were older and wiser, and they were resolved. Nothing would take them down again.

Ann knew she should be basking in the moment, but she was distracted by the fuchsia. Helen's dress was another one-shouldered number that was inappropriate on a woman her age. But the problem wasn't the dress. The problem was that the scrutiny wasn't mutual. As Ann passed Helen's pew, Helen was looking at her cell phone. She was...texting. Texting in church, during a wedding! What Ann wanted, what she required, was Helen's attention on *her.*

Look at me, Ann thought. *My son is getting married. I am the last to be seated. Look at me, goddamn it.*

But no, nothing. Helen was determined to act as though Ann wasn't even present on Nantucket this weekend. To Helen, Ann might have been a complete stranger.

Ann kissed Ryan—beautiful, elegant Ryan, whose attention she never needed to seek—and sat next to Jim, who reached instantly for her hand. By the time Ann had left the groomsmen's house and made it back to the hotel, Jim was in the room. He had spent the night sleeping in the rental car, he said, and he had the backache to prove it. He had just emerged from the shower when Ann walked in, and his lower half was wrapped in a white towel. Ann had never been able to resist him in a towel or otherwise, and so she had jumped into his arms and he held her as though they'd been separated for twelve years instead of twelve hours. They said nothing, there was no reason to speak when they could read each other's minds: he was sorry, she was sorry, they had been drinking, it was an emotionally charged situation and they had to deal with it as best they could. He kissed her and slid his hands up her very cute red gingham skirt and she kicked off the painful Jack Rogers sandals and they made love on the grand expanse of their hotel bed, despite his aching back.

It was as Ann was getting dressed that Jim handed her the long, slim box from Hamilton Hill jewelers.

"What is this?" she said.

"Open it," he said. "It's your son's wedding day. You did such a good job with him, Annie, even when I wasn't around..."

"Hush," Ann said. "*We* did a good job with him."

"Open it," Jim said.

Ann opened the box, her heart knocking. If the box was from Hamilton Hill, Jim had bought this at home, planning all the while to give it to her today. And she had kicked him out!

It was a strand of pearls—a choker, which was her preferred length. And it had a sparkling diamond rondelle. Ann gasped as she fingered it.

"Do you recognize the stone?" he said.

She thought for a moment that it might be the stone from her grandmother's ring, the one Crissy Pine had walked off with.

Had Jim contacted Thaddeus Pine again and brokered a deal to get the diamond back? But when she looked more closely, she realized it was the diamond from *her* engagement ring. Her first engagement ring.

"Full circle," Jim said. "I love you, Ann."

It had been a romantic moment, more romantic by far than the day Ann had walked down the aisle to Jim thirty-three years earlier. It was more romantic because they had fought for each other, and they had survived.

THE NOTEBOOK, PAGE 30

The Registry, Part II: The Dining Room

I am finding that dying has its advantages. The biggest advantage is that everything is put into perspective. When you were twelve years old in seventh grade, you brought home a sign that you wrote in calligraphy that said, "Only Family Matters." Your father and I were struck by this lovely sentiment, and I insisted your father take the sign to his office, which he did. He's told me he looks at the sign each day and that even as he works dismantling other families, he gives thanks for ours, crazy and imperfect though it may be.

I am here now to tell you that you were wrong. Family is not the only thing that matters. There are other things: Pachelbel's Canon in D matters, and fresh-picked corn on the cob, and true friends, and the sound of the ocean, and the poems of William Carlos Williams, and the constellations in the sky, and random acts of kindness, and a garden on the day when all its flowers are at their peak. Fluffy pancakes matter and crisp clean sheets and the guitar riff in "Layla," and the way clouds look when you are above them in an airplane. Preserving the coral reef matters, and the thirty-four paintings of Johannes Vermeer matter, and kissing matters.

Whether or not you register for china, crystal, and silver does not matter. Whether or not you have a full set of Tiffany dessert forks on Thanksgiving does not matter. If you want to register for these things, by all means, go ahead. My Waterford pattern is Lismore, one of the oldest. I do remember one time when I had a harrowing day at the hospital, and Nick had a Rube Goldberg project due and needed my help, and Kevin was playing Quiet Riot at top decibel in his bedroom, and Margot was tying up the house phone, and you had been plunked by the babysitter in front of the TV for five hours, and I came home and took one of my Lismore goblets out of the cabinet. I wanted to smash it against the wall. But instead I filled it with cold white wine and for ten or so minutes I sat in the quiet of the formal living room all by myself and I drank the cold wine out of that beautiful glass crafted by some lovely Irishman, and I felt better.

It was probably the wine, not the glass, but you get my meaning. I will remember the impressive heft of the glass in my hand, and the way the cut of the crystal caught the day's last rays of sunlight, but I will not miss that glass the way I will miss the sound of the ocean, or the taste of fresh-picked corn.

MARGOT

They changed the order at the last minute, at Jenna's request. Finn first, Rhonda second, Autumn third, Margot last, followed by Brock and Ellie. Margot knew that Jenna wanted Finn as far away from her as possible.

She was the bride; she could do as she wished.

Finn, Rhonda, and Autumn processed to Pachelbel's Canon in D, played by two violins and a cello.

Before she processed, Margot checked on the children behind her. Brock held the velvet pillow with the two rings attached. Ellie had a basket of New Dawn rose petals filched from the vines that climbed the side of the house. She was wearing the silly hat, which would add comic-and-cute relief.

It was Margot's turn. She stepped forward in her dyed-to-match pumps. She thought, *Smile. Be poised.* She thought, *All this planning, all this money, for this one moment.* She thought, *I saved this wedding.* Maybe that was overstating the case, maybe Jenna would have come down from the church tower with the same conclusion on her own, but Margot liked to think that she had been the catalyst. Maybe tonight, or maybe forty years from now, Jenna would tell someone the story of how scared and hurt she had been — and how Margot had hunted her down and how the wedding had been saved.

It was amazing, really, how many thoughts could ricochet through a person's brain in the period of time it took to walk thirty feet.

Margot was halfway down the aisle when she saw Edge. Her breath caught. He was gorgeous. He wasn't gorgeous in the way Brad Pitt or Tom Brady was gorgeous; he was gorgeous in a sophisticated, graying, wealthy, powerful way. The manner in which he held himself commanded attention, along with the fine cut of his suit, the sweet, tight knot of his lavender tie. He looked tan, which was impossible because he'd been in court all week — but yes, he had color, his skin glowed with the sun.

Then Margot noticed the woman beside him, a youngish woman with red curly hair and a million freckles, the kind of freckles that Margot would do everything but sell her children to avoid. The woman wore an off-the-shoulder emerald green dress that cinched at her impossibly tiny waist. She and Edge weren't touching as Margot passed, but Margot could sense they were together. They were *together*. Edge had come to the wedding with a date, and he hadn't warned her.

Or maybe he had. There were those two text messages on her phone, and possibly others since then.

Margot kept the smile plastered on her face, but it was a chore; it felt like one of the straps of her dress had snapped and she was trying to keep the bodice from slipping. At that very moment, Abigail Pease appeared a few steps in front of Margot in the aisle and snapped her picture.

It didn't matter how good a photographer Abigail Pease was, that picture would show heartbreak.

Margot took her place at the altar, just as they had practiced at the rehearsal, but now she was trembling, and she didn't know where to look. At that moment, the church broke out in delighted gasps and muted laughter as Brock and Ellie processed. Abigail was going crazy with the camera, the hat was a stroke of genius, Ellie was both cute and composed, and Margot knew she should savor the moment because this would most likely be the only time Ellie served as a flower girl. But Margot's eyes were drilling into the back of Edge's head. Who had he brought with him?

Suddenly everyone rose.

At the back of the church stood Jenna and Doug.

Margot watched Edge touch the emerald back of the freckled redhead's dress and lean over to whisper something in her ear.

It was Rosalie, Margot realized. His paralegal. All those tedious hours of work had led to…sex on Edge's desk or in Edge's burgundy swivel chair or in the partners' lounge after hours—or all of the above. Of course, all of the above! Margot's vision started to blotch. She felt like the turtle who had long ago veered off the side of their dining room table and crashed to the ground, landing upside down. She could not right herself.

Jenna was processing down the aisle on her father's arm. Her father was holding it together better than the day before; there were no actual tears, although his expression was pained, as though his shoes were too tight. Jenna smiled beatifically, she was a Madonna, Margot couldn't remember a time when she had ever looked more beautiful. Margot checked on Stuart. His eyes were brimming with tears, and he mouthed, *I love you.*

Margot bowed her head. Edge would be looking at her and thinking…what? That she was a good, cool kid, a pretty girl, a great lay, but that it had been doomed from the start. Margot was Doug's daughter. Edge had always held a part of himself in check because of this fact. But was dating his *paralegal* any better? Rosalie, from the look of her, was ten years younger than Margot; Margot put her at twenty-eight, so she was thirty years younger than Edge. *Thirty years younger!* Men were disgusting creatures; the younger the woman they took to bed, the more powerful they felt. Or something like that. Wouldn't Doug have an issue with Edge and Rosalie together? Maybe not, maybe it was standard practice to screw the paralegals, what did Margot know? She knew nothing. Nothing at all.

Jenna and Stuart met at the altar. Doug kissed Jenna's cheek and gave her a squeeze and then leaned in to shake Stuart's hand, then pulled out a handkerchief and dabbed at his eyes. There were sniffles in the church. Doug sat next to Pauline, who was wearing a rust-colored dress that made her look like a monk.

Reverend Marlowe raised his hands and in a commanding voice said, "Dearly beloved."

Margot stood at Jenna's side, she did not faint or falter, she did not throw up, she lifted Jenna's veil and held her bouquet—and in between performing these duties, she sneaked surreptitious glances at Edge, who had put on his bifocals to read the program. Rosalie looked interested in the actual ceremony; her eyes wandered from Jenna to the groomsmen to the bridesmaids, then back to the groomsmen. Was she looking at Margot? Did she know who Margot was, beyond being Doug Carmichael's daughter? Did she know that Margot and Edge had been lovers up until—well, until today, Margot supposed, although the last time she had been with Edge was eight days earlier, and the last time she had spoken with him was Monday night. Any way you sliced it, it was clear that Edge had been cheating on Margot with his paralegal Rosalie, although it couldn't really be called cheating because Margot and Edge's relationship had no official status.

Rosalie looked at the groomsmen again.

Beanie stood at the pulpit to do her reading. She was wearing a navy sailor dress with white piping—typical Beanie. People didn't change, Margot knew this, and yet it constantly took her by surprise. People were who they were.

Beanie adjusted the microphone and cleared her throat. Margot was dying to sit down. The ceremony lasted twenty-five minutes start to finish. Margot was still an hour away from her first glass of wine.

Beanie started to read. "Love is not all: it is not meat nor drink. Nor slumber nor a roof against the rain..."

It was a beautiful poem, an appropriate choice; Margot had really adored it until this moment. Now, she defaulted to her philosophy of Love Dies. Or, in the case of her and Edge, whatever was between them had died before it became love. At least for Edge. Margot thought she felt love, but probably it belonged in another category. It was pointless obsession with a man who had never wanted her the way that she wanted him. Whatever the case, the fact was that looking at Edge sitting with Rosalie hurt. It hurt.

"I might be driven to sell your love for peace, or trade the memory of this night for food... It may well be. I do not think I would."

A stifled cry came from the pews. Margot snapped from her own thoughts at the very moment that Pauline stood up. Pauline pressed a tissue to her nose and mouth, but another sob escaped. She rustled her way to the aisle, then executed a half run, half walk in her high heels until she was at the back of the church. This caused no small disruption. Everyone murmured and whispered, and when Kevin took the pulpit to read the lyrics to "Here, There and Everywhere," nearly everyone was facing the back of the church, eyeing the door through which Pauline had disappeared.

Margot looked at her father. He was sitting with his eyes closed, no doubt wishing that he could rewind the last thirty seconds and make them go differently.

Margot thought, *Dad, do something.* But what was he to do? Chase after Pauline and miss his daughter's wedding?

Margot saw motion to her left. Rhonda stepped off the altar and hurried down the aisle in the wake of her mother.

The Tonellis, Margot thought.

The church was *really* a-chatter now. But Kevin, never one to doubt his own importance, took the microphone.

"Here, making each day of the year," he read. "Changing my life with a wave of her hand, nobody can deny that there's something there."

THE NOTEBOOK, PAGE 34

The Prenuptial Agreement

I'm not talking about a legal document. If you feel you need a pre-nup, or if Intelligent, Sensitive Groom-to-Be comes from billions of dollars and wants you to sign a pre-nup, consult your father. The kind of "pre-nup" I'm talking about are the agreements you make with Intelligent, Sensitive Groom-to-Be before you marry.

It basically all boils down to who, in the marriage, will be responsible for the following:

> *Trash*
> *Emptying dishwasher*
> *Mowing lawn*
> *Laundry*

You take two, he takes two. I suggest taking the lawn mowing. You'll recall I mowed the lawn in the sunny middle of the afternoon wearing a bikini top with my headphones on, playing "Suite: Judy Blue Eyes" as loud as it would go.

Afterwards I always had an ice-cold beer and admired my perfect lines and the deep, green smell. Do not automatically gift that slice of heaven to your husband — enjoy it for yourself!

ANN

She had always drifted in church. No matter how hard she tried to pay attention, her mind wandered. The same had been true for long sessions of the state senate. Some windbag would have the microphone, loving the sound of his own voice, and Ann would doodle or pass irreverent notes to Billy Benedict from Winston-Salem. She would think, *All the real legislating gets done in bars and good steak houses. Nobody's mind gets changed in here.*

Ann had thought it would be different with Stuart's wedding. She had thought she would hang on every word so that she could re-create it for herself and others later. This was her son getting married; it was one of those things she was meant to reflect upon on her deathbed. But as soon as Jenna walked down the aisle and kissed her father and stood by Stuart, Ann started to float away. She thought, The best part of a wedding was seeing the bride walk down the aisle. Everything else was anticlimactic. Why was that? Did anyone listen to the readings or the prayers? Did anyone listen to the minister's sermon or the vows? Did anyone care if the couple had children or miscarried, if they made their mortgage or were foreclosed on, if they stayed together or split up? People, Ann thought, were self-absorbed. They cared about themselves, and sometimes about one other person. And, of course, every mother cared about her child, that child being an extension of herself. Ann had long suspected that all human behavior boiled down to biology, and that the whole catastrophe with her and Jim and Helen could be chalked up to Helen wanting a baby and Jim following an atavistic desire to propagate the species.

"Dearly beloved," the minister said.

Ann studied the color of the bridesmaids' dresses. Such an interesting choice, that green.

Stuart was standing nice and tall, square shouldered, dignified, respectable. As the firstborn, Stuart had accepted the burden of perfection. He had never given Ann or Jim one moment of trouble; he had always been the exceptional child that every parent dreamed of.

The readings began. The love poem first, recited by the sister-in-law. It was the first and only poem Ann had ever really appreciated. She had taken a class on Frost in college and had found it boring—all snowy woods and stone fences. Helen was more of a poetry person. She had cultivated her flaky-literary dramatic persona to great effect back in Durham. Ann recalled a moment during the cabernet dinner at the Fairlee house when Helen had raised her enormous balloon glass of wine the color of blood and recited:

My nerves are turned on. I hear them like
musical instruments. Where there was silence
the drums, the strings are incurably playing. You did this.
Pure genius at work. Darling, the composer has stepped
into fire.

The table had gone silent. Ann, and she suspected everyone else, realized that Helen was reciting *something,* but no one spoke up in recognition of exactly *what.* Helen had taken a long swill of her wine and then said gleefully, "Anne Sexton!"

Jim, Ann remembered, had chuckled and raised his glass to Helen, even though Ann knew damn well that Jim Graham had no clue if Anne Sexton was a poet or a prostitute.

Now, Jim's eyes glazed over as he listened to the love poem. His head bobbled. Ann delivered a charley horse into his thigh with two knuckles. She realized he probably hadn't gotten much sleep in the rental car, but she couldn't let him *fall asleep* during his son's wedding.

Suddenly there was a noise—a whimper or a cry—and Ann's head whipped around in time to see Pauline Carmichael scurry from the church in tears.

Jim leaned over, fully alert now. "What happened?" he whispered. "What'd I miss?"

Ann wasn't sure, although she knew Pauline was unhappy, or uneasy, in her marriage. But to run from the church in the middle of the *ceremony?* Ann stared over at Doug Carmichael, wondering if he would rise and follow his wife—but he remained in the pew. Ann craned her neck in time to see Pauline burst through the back double doors, and then Ann caught sight of Helen, four pews behind her. Helen was staring dreamily at the altar; she seemed not to have noticed the dramatic disruption. Typical. Really, what did Helen Oppenheimer care about another human being's pain or disillusionment? She cared not at all. Ann considered going after Pauline herself, although that might seem strange and inappropriate. Someone else should go. At that moment, Pauline's daughter stepped out of the green ranks and hurried down the aisle.

The church broke into a rash of coughs and whispers— however, on the altar, the action continued. Jenna's brother did the next reading. It was the Beatles, and who didn't love the Beatles—but Ann drifted away again.

She thought, *Pauline.* What was the problem? Was it anything worse than what Ann herself had endured? Was Doug Carmichael having an affair? Ann recalled Pauline's words from the day before, *Do you ever feel like maybe your marriage isn't exactly what you thought it was?* Ann hated Helen, Helen was here at the wedding, ostensibly to see Chance, but really Helen had come to torment Ann with her undeniably magnetic presence. Or she had come to sink her teeth into her old Roanoke friend Skip Lafferty. Or she had come to call Ann's bluff, and she was winning, damnit. Her presence was like a hot pink poker up Ann's ass.

The vows now. Ann tried to focus. Through good and bad, in sickness and in health, till death do us part.

Ha! Ann thought. She had said those exact vows, and while she was now sitting next to the man she had said the vows to, and while she did love him very much—more, possibly, than she had loved him then—she had not known what the vows meant, or the many creative and awful ways they could be broken.

Stuart and Jenna exchanged rings—platinum band for Stuart, and platinum with diamonds for Jenna, but they could have been aluminum or plastic. Expensive rings did not guarantee a happy life together.

Ann decided she would ignore Helen in the receiving line. Helen would approach, and Ann would look right through her; she would stand like a statue, gazing over Helen's scandalously bare shoulder. She would not speak or take Helen's hand. The moment would be awkward for a second, until Helen understood that although Ann had invited Helen to the wedding, Ann despised the ground that Helen walked on.

It would be a small passive-aggressive triumph. It would be a mean-girl silent treatment victory derived straight from the sixth-grade lunchroom. Ann couldn't wait. She promised herself she would not break down, she would not buckle, she would not speak to Helen or touch Helen or offer any other indication that Helen was alive.

The minister said, "We will now observe a moment of silence to remember the bride's mother, Elizabeth Bailey Carmichael."

The church hushed. Ann bowed her head and sent a message out to Beth Carmichael, wherever she might be. *You raised a wonderful family, and a beautiful daughter. They clearly loved you very much. Good job, Beth.*

The minister raised his hands and said, "Thank you." He beamed at Stuart and Jenna. "By the power vested in me by the Commonwealth of Massachusetts, I now pronounce you man and wife. You may kiss the bride."

Stuart held the side of Jenna's head, and Stuart and Jenna kissed. The kiss, Ann thought, was very tender. People clapped, the pipe organ celebrated, and Stuart and Jenna faced the minister for the final blessing.

"Almost out of here," Jim whispered.

Ann felt a sense of elation, and she congratulated herself on an appropriate emotion. Her son was married, and she felt happy.

Jenna and Stuart—now Mr. and Mrs. Stuart Graham, another Mrs. Graham, that was odd—processed out of the church, followed by Margot and Ryan, Jenna's brother Nick and the sunburned bridesmaid whose skin looked sticky with aloe, and H.W. and Autumn—who, Ann admitted to herself, didn't look half bad together. Chance processed out at the end alone because his partner, Pauline's daughter, hadn't returned. Ann and Jim were meant to leave next. Ann stepped out into the aisle, and as she turned to face the back of the church, she saw Helen—with that bloodcurdling scream of a dress—step into the aisle, take Chance's arm, and process out of the church before Ann and Jim. Ann gripped Jim's arm, blinking furiously. How *dare* Helen presume to process out of the church with the wedding party! How dare Helen presume to process out of the church in front of Ann! Ann wanted to yank Helen's blond hair. She wanted to stop dead in the middle of the church and scream. Chance seemed unbothered by his mother's presence; maybe he was relieved not to have to walk out of the church alone. The quandary of being unexpectedly unpartnered had been solved by his mother. But Ann didn't care how Chance felt about it. Helen had crossed a line. She had inserted herself into the wedding party without qualm or hesitation, exactly the way she had inserted herself into Ann's marriage years ago.

"Can you *believe* her?" Ann whispered to Jim.

Jim didn't respond, and when Ann checked on him, his head was held high and dignified, the way it always was when he knew people were looking at him, most often when he was attending some political event with Ann. Ann had always been proud to have Jim beside her, although she'd wondered over the years if the power differential between them was the reason he'd strayed. Jim made far more money than Ann, but Ann had influence and prestige. She was the one people sought out, she was the one who was photographed and named in the newspaper. State Senator Ann Graham. Jim must have wearied of it.

They stepped out of the church into the bright, warm afternoon, and behind them someone rang the church bells. Ann and Jim followed Jenna and Stuart and the wedding party and Helen out to the front lawn, where the receiving line was to be held. Ann narrowed her eyes at Helen. Helen would not stand in the *receiving line,* would she? For the fifteenth time that weekend, Ann wished for a Quaalude.

Helen kissed Chance on the cheek and appeared to bid him farewell. Ann stepped closer so that she could hear what Helen was saying.

"I'll see y'all later, darling. I'm meeting Skip in town."

"All right," Chance said. "I'll see you at the reception."

"No, I don't think so, darling," Helen said. "Skip has invited me for dinner at the Club Car."

"Oh," Chance said. "Okay." He didn't sound like he cared one way or the other. "I'll see you tomorrow, then, I guess."

"Now, remember," Helen said. "Don't eat the crab cakes!" She laughed, kissed Chance again, and descended the concrete steps to the sidewalk without a further word to anyone. She sauntered off in a flash of shocking, hair-raising pink.

Ann stared after Helen with her mouth agape. Helen was leaving the wedding before the reception. She had RSVP'd yes; Ann knew there was a place card with Helen's name on it, and a seat for her at a table in the Carmichaels' backyard. Ann knew that $120 had been spent on behalf of Helen's expected presence at the reception. She couldn't just *walk off* to meet *Skip Lafferty!* She couldn't just *leave* like that! When Jim found out that Helen had chosen not to attend the reception, he would be relieved. He would say, *No one wanted her around, anyway.* He would expect Ann to share his feelings. Now they could eat and drink and laugh and talk and dance without worrying about Helen. It would be just as Jim had wanted it; it would be as if Ann had never invited Helen to the wedding in the first place, or as if Ann had invited Helen and Helen had declined. But Ann found herself feeling vexed. Ann had wanted Helen to see her and Jim laughing and talking and dancing; Ann had wanted Helen to feel bereft and jealous.

But instead Helen had walked off.

Wait! Ann wanted to call out. *You can't leave! I haven't had a chance to ignore you yet!*

THE NOTEBOOK, PAGE 7

Bridesmaid Dresses

Oh, the bridesmaid dresses! When I was in my twenties, I had a whole closetful of atrocious taffeta dresses — mustard yellow, Pepto-Bismol pink, and one with navy and red diagonal stripes where we all had to stand a certain way or the stripes didn't align, which made for visual confusion and caused dizziness and nausea in those who gazed upon us. There was one flowing dress in an unfortunate apricot hue that I wore when I was pregnant with Kevin that could have served as a pup tent for a family of four.

I am thinking silk shantung, sheath, nipped at the waist, maybe off-the-shoulder — simple, classic — either long with a slit to the knee or cut just above the knee. I am thinking the green of new leaves — a fresh, just-cut-grass green, a green that will echo with the delicate embroidered ivy on Grammie's antique linens, a green that will make people think of life in full bloom.

DOUG

His age was showing. It was only six o'clock, and already he was tired enough to go to sleep.

He had a decision to make. He could either go in search of Pauline, or he could fulfill his duties as the father of the bride and stand in his place in the receiving line and smile and shake hands with 150 guests. He really wasn't sure which was the right course of action. Rhonda was standing on the lawn outside the church when they all emerged, and so wherever Pauline had run off to, she had gone alone.

What would Beth want him to do? She might insist he put Jenna first at any cost. But she might remind him that Pauline was still his wife, for better or for worse, and obviously something was wrong, something that Doug had set in motion, and now was the time to deal with it.

He couldn't believe she had run from the church. If it had been Beth who had run from the church, Doug would have followed right after her.

Beth would never have run from the church.

Doug decided to ask for help. He approached Roger.

"Can I talk to you for a minute?" Doug said. Roger was standing off to the side, holding his clipboard and his pencil. He was wearing a white shirt, striped tie, and navy blazer and looked just like every other male guest at the wedding. But Roger was a quiet warrior; he exuded competence and gravitas, and Doug was confident that not only could the man deal with errant tree branches, but he could deal with disintegrating relationships, as well.

"Sure, Doug," Roger said. "What is it?"

"My wife ran out of the church," Doug said.

"Yes," Roger said. "I noticed that."

"Should I take time now to go find her and see what the matter is?" Doug asked.

"You don't have time right now," Roger said. "You have the receiving line, then photographs."

"Is Pauline supposed to be in the photographs?" Doug asked.

Roger consulted his clipboard. "Some of them," he said. "So I suggest you send someone else to go find her and bring her back here."

"Okay," Doug said. He liked the idea of passing the buck and of having this suggested and sanctioned by Roger. "I'll do that."

The logical person to fetch Pauline was Rhonda. Doug saw her, now talking on her cell phone, at the edge of the church parking lot. Was she talking to Pauline? Was she trying to convince Pauline to come back to the wedding? Doug crept up on Rhonda, not wishing to disturb her, but also hoping to eavesdrop.

He heard Rhonda say, "I want your hands on my body. I want that so badly. And then I want your tongue inside of me…"

Rhonda glanced up and saw Doug, and her expression immediately became one of horrified embarrassment. She said quickly, "I'll call you later, Beast." And she hung up.

"What?" she said to Doug.

Doug was speechless. He'd interrupted Rhonda's private conversation with…whom? Someone she called "Beast," whose hands she wanted on her body. Was it possible Rhonda had a boyfriend and Pauline didn't know about it?

Doug said, "I'm sorry, I didn't mean…" He took a step backward.

"What?" Rhonda said. Her voice was like a single slap to the face. "What do you want?"

"I thought maybe you were talking to your mother," Doug said.

"No," Rhonda said. "That was *not* my mother."

Doug took a breath; he was floundering here. "Listen, Rhonda, I wonder if you could go get your mother? She's supposed to be in the photos. Do you know where she is?"

"She's at the house," Rhonda said.

Doug noted that both Pauline and Rhonda always referred to

the Carmichael family homestead on Orange Street as "the house." Never "home."

"Can you get her?" Doug asked. "Please?" He turned around and, with a sweep of his hand, indicated the guests milling around. "I have all this…"

"She doesn't want me," Rhonda said. "She wants you."

"Yes, but—"

"Doug," Rhonda said. "I'm not going. I'm a bridesmaid. Jenna asked me to stand up for her. I want to stay here and enjoy being a part of this wedding. I'm not an errand girl. It isn't my job to clean up your mess." She blinked at him.

Doug nodded. In the five years that he had known Rhonda, she had been combative, sour, and unpleasant, and on more than one occasion, snarly and mean. But now she wasn't any of those things. Now she was right.

"I'm sorry," he said, and he walked away.

Across the lawn, Doug spied Margot. They made eye contact, and Margot hurried right over.

"Daddy," she said.

"Hey," he said, thinking, *Margot will help me.*

"Did Edge bring Rosalie as his *date?*" she asked. "Like his *date* date?"

"Oh," Doug said. He had temporarily forgotten about Edge and Rosalie, although they were a problem, or they had seemed like a problem half an hour before the ceremony, which was when Doug had first seen Edge and Rosalie together. "You know what, sweetheart, I'm not sure what's going on."

"Edge RSVP'd for *one!*" Margot said. Her cheeks pinkened and her eyes flashed. Those ice-blue eyes, they unsettled people. "He RSVP'd for one and he showed up with a *date!*"

"He told me Thursday before I left the office that he was

bringing a guest," Doug said. "And I e-mailed Roger to let him know."

"He told you on ... *Thursday?*" Margot said.

"Thursday, yes," Doug said. "At lunchtime on Thursday." It had been rather late to add a guest, but Edge was doing Doug an important favor by covering the shitshow Cranbrook case, and he had seemed keen to bring this "guest," and Doug had agreed. *Certainly,* Doug said. Doug suspected the guest was the reason for Edge's calm and focus; he always worked tougher and smarter when he was seeing someone. What Doug didn't know was that the guest was Rosalie Fitzsimmon, the firm's top paralegal, who was working alongside Edge and Doug on the shitshow Cranbrook case. Doug didn't approve of dating within the firm, although there were no specific rules against it. Now he feared that things between Edge and Rosalie would go very well or very badly, and either way, Rosalie would leave the firm, and they would lose a superlative paralegal.

"But why didn't you *tell me?*" Margot asked.

"Like I said, I told Roger," Doug said. "Roger is the wedding planner."

"Oh, for Christ's sake, Daddy," Margot said. She stormed off—and not in the direction of the receiving line where she belonged. People were still streaming out of the church, and the receiving line was marked by more Carmichael absences than presences. Jenna and Stuart were there, along with Ryan, and Jim and Ann Graham. Doug needed to take his place right now.

He horse-collared Nick because Nick was the offspring in closest proximity. Nick was already yanking at his bow tie as he talked to Finn. Finn looked as sulky as she had when she was six years old and she felt Jenna was hogging more than her share of the wading pool. Doug sensed there was something going on between his younger son and Finn, but he didn't dare ask. He didn't have room in his imagination for any more drama.

"Nick," he said. "I need a favor."

"What is it?" Nick said warily.

"Don't take your tie off yet," Doug said. "We have pictures."

"Okay," Nick said. He looked relieved, perhaps believing that not taking off his tie was the favor that was being asked of him.

"I'd like you to go get Pauline," Doug said.

"*What?*" Nick said. "No way. No...way."

Doug paused and reconsidered. Nick was exactly the wrong person to send after Pauline. Nick was a bull in an emotional china shop. He had no tact and very little patience. For all his conquests, Doug suspected that Nick actually knew very little about women. This was probably Doug's fault, but he had felt that the best way to teach his boys about how to treat a woman was to lead by example. He had always treated Beth like a goddess. He couldn't help it if Nick hadn't been paying attention.

"Can you please find Pauline and tell her it's time for photos, and her smiling presence is required?"

"I'll go with you," Finn said.

"No," Doug said. "I think it would be best if Nick went alone."

"She's *your* wife," Nick said. "You go."

"I can't," Doug said. "I have the receiving line."

"Crap," Nick said. "Where is she?"

"At home," Doug said. "You'll have to hurry because we need you in pictures."

"Jesus!" Nick said. If he were still fifteen, he might have told Doug to go stuff himself, and so it was a testament to his adulthood that Nick headed down the street without Finn. Doug had, maybe, done something right in raising him, after all.

Doug strode over to the receiving line and began to shake hands.

Hello, good to see you, yes, it was a beautiful ceremony, the church was built in 1902, the east and west windows are real Tiffany, my wife, Beth, loved those windows, yes, I'm very proud. Honestly, I couldn't be happier.

Abigail Pease, the photographer, was a no-nonsense go-getter who knew how to arrange a shot. Doug found her attractive, as well, and if he wasn't mistaken, she was flirting with him. She called him "Dougie," a nickname he deplored, but when it came out of her mouth in her southern accent, it sounded playful and sexy. (The photographer at Kevin and Beanie's wedding, so many years ago, had insisted on called Doug "Dad" and Beth "Mom," which had driven them both nuts.)

Abigail had voluminous blond curls that cascaded down her back. She was lightly tanned but wore no makeup (and no wedding ring), and her rear end looked fabulous in her palazzo pants. Doug wondered if, say, a year from now, he would have the guts to ask Abigail Pease, or someone like her, out on a date.

"Dougie, baby, I need you over here with Jenna," Abigail said.

Doug slid his arms tenderly around Jenna and gave his best smile.

"The two of you are *gorgeous*," Abigail said. "Oh, my God, the camera is *eating* you up!"

Whatever he was paying this woman, he decided, it wasn't enough.

He wondered how grossly inappropriate it was that he was lusting after the photographer while his wife was crying somewhere in a darkened room because Doug didn't love her anymore.

Bridesmaids with Jenna. Jenna and Margot. Jenna and Kevin and Beanie and their three boys. Bridesmaids with Stuart. Jenna and all the kids, including Ellie in her funny hat. Jenna with just Brock and Ellie. Stuart with Ryan and H.W. Stuart with Ryan and H.W. and the half brother with the shellfish allergy. Stuart with his parents.

It was taking forever, despite Abigail's impressive efficiency. Doug wanted a drink.

Finally Abigail turned to Doug and to Roger—Roger was so crucial to the proceedings that Doug wanted to suggest that Roger get in a photo or two—and said, "I can't take any more pictures without Nick..." She checked her list. "And Pauline."

"Pauline?" Doug said.

Abigail smiled at him. "Pauline is your wife."

She seemed to be telling him this, not asking him, and Doug felt chastened.

"Yes." He felt like he was confessing to something.

"Is she sick?" Abigail asked. "Not feeling well?"

"Not feeling well," Doug confirmed, because any way you sliced it, that was the truth. "I sent Nick to get her. They should be here any second."

He stepped to the sidewalk to take a look down the street, and there he saw Nick and Pauline, marching side by side, neither of them talking, neither of them smiling. They looked like they were going to a funeral or to the dentist for a root canal.

Doug turned to Abigail. "My wife, Beth, Jenna's mother, died seven years ago of ovarian cancer."

Abigail said, "Yes, I know. Roger told me. And Jenna showed me the Notebook. It touched me very deeply, I must say."

Doug wondered if Abigail Pease had read the last page of the Notebook. He had been meaning to do so all day; he was hoping it was something that would give him strength.

"Beth was a remarkable woman," Doug said. Now he really

felt like he was confessing something. As Pauline drew closer, Doug spoke more quickly. He wanted to get the words out before she could hear them. "I mean, she was a hospital administrator and the mother of four children, and my wife, which may or may not *sound* remarkable, but she was also one of those people that everyone gravitated to. She was the magnetic north of our family, she held us together, she made us work. Every single one of us *adored* her." He swallowed. "But especially me."

Abigail's hand rested on Doug's forearm, and her pale blue eyes were glued to his face, and suddenly whatever physical attraction Doug had felt for her evaporated. What he wanted, what he *really* wanted, he realized, was someone to listen while he talked about how much he missed Beth. He had never been able to talk to Pauline because Pauline had always been jealous of Beth's memory, and therefore unwilling to listen. But maybe if Pauline *had* listened, Doug would have been happier. Maybe, but maybe not.

"I'm sorry, Dougie," Abigail said. "Today must be difficult."

Doug nodded and stuffed his hands into the satiny pockets of his tuxedo pants. There was so much he wanted to say about how difficult the weekend had been, but there wasn't time or opportunity because Pauline was approaching. Doug watched her march up the steps. Her hair was escaping the confines of her bun, and her eye makeup had been rubbed off. Her eyes looked like small brown holes. Her chest was mottled red, and her breathing was erratic, maybe from crying, or maybe from the brisk walk.

"I'm here," she said. "Where do you want me?"

"We're going to take a Carmichael family portrait," Abigail said. "With Stuart."

Abigail called everyone together and began arranging them: Doug, Pauline, Margot, Kevin, Beanie, Nick, Jenna, Stuart, the six grandchildren, and Rhonda—they nearly forgot to include Rhonda! Doug realized then that he hadn't expected Pauline to show up. And worse than that, he had been hoping she wouldn't show up. He wanted a Carmichael family portrait that was free of Tonellis. He wanted to insist on a photograph—maybe the photograph after this photograph—that included only him and his kids and his kids' spouses and his grandchildren. Was that awful? Yes, he decided, it was awful, and as badly as he wanted it, he decided he would take the remaining pictures with Pauline standing next to him as his wife. Years from now when he reflected on this day, he would remember posing for these photographs as one of the last things he would do to make Pauline happy. He would include her now, in the center of his family, in a spot that rightly belonged to another.

"Smile, Dougie!" Abigail called out.

Doug smiled.

THE NOTEBOOK, PAGE 11

A Letter for the Matron of Honor

Dear Margot,

Hi, it's Mom! I will assume I'm talking to you here and not Finn or Autumn or some other friend that Jenna has made after I'm gone. If you and Jenna have had a falling out—if you, for example, fought over who was to inherit my copy of Rumours *signed by Mick Fleetwood and Lindsey Buckingham, or my brand-new set of gardening tools from Smith & Hawken, get over it. Kiss and make up. You,*

Margot, need to stand at your sister's side. She was there for you in Antigua, remember, and she was in the delivery suite for the birth of both boys. You are so lucky to have a sister. I only had cousins, which wasn't really the same thing.

My cousin Astrid served as my maid of honor. We were very close, but she tended to be flighty, and in the days leading up to my wedding she was hormonal and cranky and more concerned about the pimple on her chin than anything else. I was worried I had chosen the wrong person — my cousin Linda was more steadfast — but on the day of, Astrid shone brightly, I am happy to say.

Here are some thoughts on how you can help your sister on the day of the wedding:

Maintain her bouquet. Hold it for her when it needs holding. Keep track of it when she sets it down.

Have Kleenex at the ready, an emery board, dental floss, Band-Aids, tampons, eyeliner, mascara, and lipstick.

Know the schedule.

Make sure she always has a glass of champagne.

Make sure she eats! I didn't get a single bite of food at my reception at the Quilted Giraffe, something I've always regretted.

Accompany her to the ladies' room.

Tell her she's beautiful when she smiles. You both are. My beautiful girls.

MARGOT

To talk to Edge alone, Margot had to wait for Rosalie to excuse herself for the ladies' room. This turned out to be a test of endurance. Rosalie was downing glass after glass of champagne, but she hung stalwartly at Edge's side. Her bladder must have been the size of a volleyball, but as Margot watched her, she seemed untroubled. She was more attractive than she had seemed in the church, which irked Margot.

Rosalie was quick and lively; she was a woman who oozed confidence and was comfortable in her own body. Her face was freckled, but her breasts, which were pushed up and out to lovely advantage by the bodice of her dress, were all roses and cream. Margot could barely keep her eyes off Rosalie's sweet and luscious bosom, so Edge must have been mesmerized. Of course, Rosalie hadn't breast-fed three children. Rosalie had one of those sexy-gravelly voices, which was perhaps the thing Margot envied the most. She had always yearned for a sexy-gravelly voice but instead had been given a voice that sounded camp-counselor chipper on a good day, and shrill and strident on a bad day. Margot couldn't stand to hear herself recorded; she only liked her voice when she had a scratchy sore throat or had spent all night screaming at a rock concert, and her rock concert days now were few and far between. As a placement person, Margot knew how important voice was. After all, you not only had to look at someone eight to ten hours a day in the office but also had to listen to them. Rosalie had been blessed with a voice that was a cross between Anne Bancroft and Demi Moore.

Advantage Rosalie. Margot couldn't deny it.

As the maid of honor, Margot was meant to chat and socialize; she was meant to make sure that Jenna had a full glass of champagne at all times and that Jenna ate a canapé from one out of every three trays presented to her. But Margot's constant surveillance of Edge and Rosalie distracted her from these duties. He did *see* her, right? He knew she was here, he realized he couldn't spend the whole night ignoring her, he would have to explain himself.

Margot stood in line at the bar with Ryan's boyfriend, Jethro, who looked marginally less uncomfortable and out of place than he had the night before. Margot wondered if it was difficult to be openly gay, citified, and black at a WASP wedding on an island thirty miles out to sea.

She said, "What did you think of the ceremony?"

He said, "Well, it wasn't without intrigue."

Margot wondered for a second if he was talking about Edge and Rosalie—but how would Ryan's boyfriend from Chicago know about *that?* Then Margot realized Jethro was referring to Pauline's wild exodus from the church. She chastised herself for being so self-absorbed.

Margot said, "The Carmichaels are always good for some drama." She hadn't asked her father why Pauline left the church—partly because she felt she knew too much already, but mostly because she had been focused on only one thing, and that was Edge and Rosalie.

"It just as easily could have been the Graham family," Jethro said. "Trust."

Their turn at the bar came. Margot ordered three glasses of Sancerre—one for Jenna, two for herself—and then she was faced with the question of how to carry three glasses without spilling one down the front of her grasshopper green dress. Jethro offered to help, but he had three drinks himself—Ketel One and tonics for himself and Ryan, and a Heineken for Stuart.

Margot said, "Oh, I'll manage," and she held the three glasses in a balanced triangle with both hands and tottered through the grass in her dyed-to-match pumps toward Jenna, who was talking to her gaggle of young teacher friends. Margot handed off the wine and said, "You eating?"

One of the young teachers—Francie or Hilly—said, "I just made sure she had a chicken skewer."

Jenna beamed at Margot. "Isn't it beautiful?" she said. "Isn't it perfect?"

Margot took a breath and willed herself not to glance over at the proposal bench, where Edge and Rosalie were standing, talking to Kevin. Was it beautiful? Yes. The sky was brilliant blue, the sun had achieved a mellow slant, the tent was a masterpiece of natural elegance. There was a jazz combo playing now—four members of the sixteen-piece band that would start up after dinner—and the music floated on the air along with chatter and perfume. Waiters passed trays of champagne, along with chicken satay and lobster fritters and blue-cheese-stuffed figs wrapped in bacon and mini–beef Wellingtons. The local Nantucket legend, Spanky, had set up his raw bar in an old wooden dory. This was where Margot parked herself to spy on Edge. She would double-fist her wine and suck down oysters and flirt with Spanky—all the while, her surveillance camera would be trained on Edge and Rosalie. They were still talking to Kevin and might remain there all evening. Kevin never shut up.

Margot ate three oysters. She was joined, temporarily, by Stuart's father, Jim, who attacked the pile of jumbo shrimp rather indecorously.

Jim said, "Hell of a party."

Margot faked a smile and slurped another oyster. "Mmmhmmm." No other response seemed to be required of her, thank God. She needed Jim Graham to stay right where he was, shielding Margot and keeping her safe from any conversation that might cause her to miss her chance with Edge.

Rosalie's glass was empty, Margot could see, as was Edge's. But then the girl with the champagne came by, and Rosalie accepted a glass with a smile, and Margot read Edge's lips as he ordered a Scotch.

Margot's heart cracked open a little bit more. Margot kept a bottle of Glenmorangie in her liquor cabinet at home for the evenings when Edge stopped by.

Rosalie had a steel-reinforced bladder. She outlasted Margot; Margot had to go. She bypassed the elegant portable bathrooms set up in a discreet corner of the yard beyond Alfie, and instead went into the house and headed up the stairs to her own bathroom.

On the second floor, Margot heard voices, then a rhythmic banging. Margot stopped. The noise was coming from Jenna's room. Finn and Nick. Margot nearly shouted at the top of her lungs. GROSS! But she refrained, slamming the door to the bathroom to make her point instead.

She hiked up the skirt of her grasshopper green dress and peed, holding her forehead in her hands. The banging continued against the wall behind her, and she heard Finn cry out in ecstasy, and Margot thought, *All right, I've had enough.* She washed her hands and stared at her reflection in the dingy medicine cabinet mirror.

I've had enough!

But she wasn't sure what that meant, and she didn't know what to do.

Suddenly she heard her mother's voice. She knew it was her mother's voice and not her mimicking her mother's voice because Margot did not like what the voice said.

It said, *Get back out there, honey. Pronto.*

*   *   *

A glass bell sounded: dinner was served. Everyone sat except for the wedding party; they lined up so that they could be introduced by the bandleader and then take their places at the head table. Everyone in the wedding party had been asked to divulge one "interesting thing" about themselves to be read aloud by the bandleader. Margot was introduced as follows:

And now, ladies and gentlemen, put your hands together for our maid of honor, who has taken surfing vacations on four continents—Margot...Carmichael!

Polite applause. Margot wasn't crazy about the surfing vacation answer because all those vacations had been taken with Drum Sr., and at least half the people in this tent knew it. But the word *interesting* had presented a challenge because the things that filled Margot's days—work placing executives in major corporations, raising three kids as a single parent, conducting a clandestine relationship with her father's law partner—weren't interesting. Margot would have liked to have said that she played classical guitar or spoke five languages, but neither was true. The fact was, she didn't do anything out of the ordinary, she didn't have any skills—except for surfing. And although her surfing had always been eclipsed by Drum Sr.'s surfing, she had ridden waves in Bali and Uruguay and La Jolla and the north shore of Oahu and the frigid waters of South Africa. There was a picture hanging in her father's office of Margot in her wet suit with her dark hair slicked back and her face tanned—somehow the Asian sun had not brought out her freckles—crouched on her board in the tube of a left-hand break off the tiny Balinese island of Nusa Lembongan. Edge had once admitted to being captivated by that picture of Margot, even before the two of them started seeing each other.

You look powerful, dangerous almost, like a jaguar ready to pounce, Edge had said. *It's incredibly sexy.*

That had been one reason why Margot chose to mention the surfing. She had wanted Edge to recall that picture of her.

Margot sauntered across the dance floor like a game show contestant toward her seat, thinking, *Smile brightly! Don't trip! Shoulders back, head high!*

She couldn't help herself. She sneaked a look at Edge, who was sitting next to Rosalie at her father's table.

He winked.

Margot made it to the life preserver of her seat as the bandleader introduced "Our best man—who scored a perfect sixteen hundred on his SATs and still didn't get into Princeton—Ryan Connelly Graham!"

Margot thought, *He winked!* She didn't know whether to be thrilled or indignant. Indignant, she thought. How dare he wink! But thrilled won out. He had noticed her!

Then a thought broke through Margot's despair. Maybe Edge had brought Rosalie to this wedding as a front to throw Doug off their trail. Margot felt sweet relief, followed by a glimmer of actual happiness. Of course that was why Edge had winked at her like a conspirator. He must have assumed she knew that was why he'd brought Rosalie. Rosalie was a straw candidate. Margot wondered where they were staying. Had they gotten two rooms? Oh, please, Margot thought. Please let that be the case. Please let this be a huge misunderstanding on her part.

She drank red wine with dinner. Did she eat? She and Jenna had set up no fewer than six tastings to come up with the menu of field greens with dried cherries, goat cheese, and candied pecans, the choice of seared rib eye or grilled swordfish, the baked potato with choice of decadent toppings, the pan-roasted asparagus with lemon and mint—and yet Margot could only recall eating single perfectly toasted salty-sweet pecan and one bite of rosy, juicy meat dragged through béarnaise sauce. Ryan was seated next to her on one side, and Jethro on the other. Ryan was a conversational dynamo, he could uphold his own side and Margot's side with minimum output from Margot, and whereas Margot flogged herself for not doing a better job—Ryan had once confided that he thought Margot had ten times the personality of Jenna—she was determined to constantly monitor the situation between Edge and Rosalie.

They seemed so happy, Margot thought, that they had to be acting. Definitely acting. This was all a game.

And then, just as the dinner plates were cleared and Ryan pulled a sheet of paper from his breast pocket on which he had written his best man's toast, Rosalie pushed back from the table and stood. Edge stood also, and for a second Margot feared they were leaving. But Edge was only standing to be polite, and the crack in Margot's heart widened. When Edge had taken Margot to dinner at Picholine, which had been the most sublime and grown-up dinner date of her life, he had stood when Margot excused herself for the ladies' room, and then stood again upon her return. It was one of the fine, old-fashioned, charming things about him—elegant manners, respect for the gender.

Of course, now Margot realized that the dinner at Picholine and the subsequent night at Edge's apartment had all been a lubricant to ease the way for him to ask Margot to betray her professional principles.

Rosalie left the tent. Edge sat back down and said something to Doug that made him laugh.

Rosalie going to the bathroom wasn't the answer, because Edge was still trapped at the table with Doug. Margot couldn't very well plop down and engage Edge in the conversation she needed to have with him with her father present.

Still, Margot rose and, at what she thought was a discreet distance, followed Rosalie out of the tent.

"Wait, Margot!" Ryan called after her.

Margot whipped around, feeling caught. "What?"

"You're going to miss my speech!" he said.

"I'll be *right back*," she promised.

She saw Rosalie leaning against Alfie's tree trunk, smoking a cigarette.

Rosalie smoked. That explained her voice. Edge had once told Margot that everyone smoked in law school as a way of handling the pressure. Edge himself had smoked in law school and had continued until his second wife, Nathalie, demanded that he quit.

Rosalie didn't yet see Margot, and this bought Margot some time to think. What should she do? She wanted to introduce herself and see if Rosalie had any reaction. Would Rosalie know that Edge and Margot were lovers? Would he have told her? Certainly not—that might cause a security breach with Doug. But maybe Edge had felt the same pressure Margot had felt earlier this weekend to just tell *someone*, and during one of their late-night prep sessions for court, he had told Rosalie.

If Rosalie *didn't* know, should Margot tell her? Or should Margot just engage Rosalie in casual conversation that would allow her to figure out if Edge and Rosalie were really dating or if they were only coworkers?

At that moment, Margot heard the distinct chime of spoon on glass, and the tent grew quiet. Ryan's speech. Margot didn't want to miss it. Any conversation with Rosalie was bound to leave her livid or in tears. Margot spun on her dyed-to-match heels and headed back toward the tent. She nearly smacked right into Edge, who was hurrying from the tent himself.

His presence shocked her. Before she could dream up a single appropriate word to say, Edge grabbed her arm.

"Margot," he said. "What are you doing?"

"Um..." she said. "I went to the bathroom?"

He stared at her.

"I was headed there, I mean. But I wanted to get back to hear the toasts."

"You followed Rosalie out," he said. "What are you *doing?*"

"Nothing," Margot said. As much as she craved his touch, she didn't like the way he was holding her arm, and she didn't like the way he had used his lawyering skills to make it seem like *she* was the one who had done something wrong. And as badly as she had wanted to talk to him, she wasn't sure how to start.

She said, as casually as possible, "So what's up with Rosalie, anyway?"

Edge lightened his grip on Margot's arm, and his face changed. It became... well, the word that popped into Margot's mind was *kind.* In all the months of their dating, Margot had never known Edge to look kind or nice or tender or gentle. He was an attorney who specialized in land mines, trapdoors, and setting his opponents up to fail. That was why his nickname was "Edge," or so he claimed. He always conveyed mental toughness; he prized courage over compassion.

This unfamiliar facial expression, she knew, was bad news.

"I texted you on Thursday," Edge said. "I asked you to call me so I could explain."

"Explain what?" Margot said, hoping what he needed to explain was that he was bringing Rosalie as his "date," to mask his passionate and burgeoning love for Margot.

"This isn't something I want to talk about here and now," he said. "Why didn't you call me?"

"I sank my phone," Margot said. "I killed it."

Edge's hand instinctively flew to the breast pocket of his suit jacket, which was where he kept his BlackBerry. The mere idea of sinking his phone would be worse to him than losing his heart.

"Listen, Margot..."

"So you're an actual couple, then?" Margot said. "You and Rosalie?"

Edge peered over Margot's shoulder, presumably watching for Rosalie.

Margot said, "She's having a cigarette. By my estimation, we have three minutes left. Tell me the truth, Edge. Are you and Rosalie together?"

"I told you you wouldn't be able to handle it," he said.

"How can I handle or not handle something when I don't even know about it!" Margot said. "When you refuse to tell me the truth! Are you and Rosalie a couple?"

"Yes."

"How long?"

He sighed. "Since January."

"Since *January?*" Margot said. Her mind flipped back through imaginary calendar pages. It was March when Edge took her to Picholine and then home to his apartment. And even then he had been screwing Rosalie? It was too hideous to contemplate.

"It started at the firm's New Year's Eve party," he said.

Oh, God. Famously, the firm of Garrett, Parker, and Spence eschewed Christmas for New Year's at the holidays. Margot had desperately wanted to attend the party. Every year it was held at Cipriani. There were oysters and caviar and good champagne.

"The New Year's Eve party!" Margot said.

"And then it's gained momentum since we started working on the Cranbrook case," Edge said.

"I don't understand," Margot said.

"I don't expect you to," Edge said.

"Why didn't you tell me in January?" Margot said. If Edge had told her in January, she would be six months past the news by now. But he had continued to see Margot, and to sleep with her. He had continued to torture her by texting her and not texting her.

"You're a beautiful girl, Margot," Edge said.

That's a beautiful girl you've got there, partner. Edge had been thirty-two years old when he'd made that comment, far younger than Margot was now. He claimed not to recall saying it, and yet here he was pulling out nearly the same phrase to placate her.

"Don't patronize me," Margot said.

"It was never going anywhere," Edge said. "You knew it and I knew it."

"You may have known it," Margot said. "But I thought maybe…"

"Maybe what?" Edge said. "That you'd become the fourth Mrs. John Edgar Desvesnes? You're too good for that, Margot."

"What about Rosalie?" Margot asked. "Is *she* too good for it?"

"Rosalie is a better match for me," Edge said.

"She's half your age," Margot said. "Maybe not even." Rosalie would want children, and maybe Edge would oblige her, maybe he would be a new father at sixty or sixty-two—then eighty years old by the time that child graduated from high school. Rosalie would have left him for the town's fire chief or the children's orthodontist by then.

"She's mature for her age," Edge said. "And very bright."

Margot breathed out her nose like a charging bull. She wasn't going to stand here while Edge enumerated Rosalie's attributes.

"You asked me for that favor in March," Margot said. "I colored outside the lines for you, Edge."

"And I appreciated it," Edge said. "Even though it didn't end up working out."

It didn't end up working out because it had been ill conceived from the get-go. "You never would have done the same for me," Margot said. She had compromised her standards for Edge because she had so desperately craved his approval, his good graces, his love. Margot had given these things to Edge too readily, she saw now. She'd left him nothing to work for, nothing to figure out. There was no mystery with Margot. From the start, she had felt like the same awkward adolescent yearning to be thought beautiful.

"You're a jerk," she said.

"That I am," Edge said.

She couldn't stand the way he was agreeing with her. It was a courtroom trick.

"Well, thank you for ruining my sister's wedding for me," she said. "I hope you're happy."

Edge said, "It was never going to work, Margot. The fact is that you're Doug Carmichael's daughter, and you know how I love and respect your father."

"Yeah," Margot said. "Just think how disappointed he's going to be when he finds out."

"He's not going to find out," Edge said. "We agreed."

"Ha!" Margot said. "What did we agree?"

"We agreed not to tell him we were together."

"So now we're no longer together," Margot said. "So now I can tell him whatever I damn well please."

Another unfamiliar expression crossed Edge's face: fear. His eyes flickered beyond Margot at the same moment that the smoky, sexy voice floated over her shoulder.

"Edge?"

And then the tent burst out in thunderous applause.

OUTTAKES

Jethro (boyfriend of the best man): There are two other black men in the tent. One is a server, Jamaican, I think. He is very black and very, very big — I heard one of the female servers call him "Jungle Gym," which sounded like a sexual nickname rather than a racist one.

The other black man is the bandleader. He has light skin and Adam Duritz dreadlocks, and he wears funky glasses with black rectangular frames. When I saw him at the outside bar I asked his name and he said, Ernie Sands. Then he said he was from Brooklyn and I said I was from Chicago, and he asked what part of Chicago and I said that now I live in Lincoln Park but that I grew up in Red Houses of Cabrini-Green. He squinted at me and said, "What you doing at this party, man?" And I said, "My boyfriend is the best man, the groom's brother." And he held his hands up like I'd pulled a gun on him and said, "Cool, man, that's cool." Then there was an awkward moment of silence.

I said, "Did you know Frederick Douglass came here in 1841 and spoke out against slavery on the front steps of the public library?"

He looked at me like I was crazy, and the bonding ended there.

Ann (mother of the groom): I ordered the rib eye, as did the Lewises and the Cohens, but the Shelbys got the swordfish and they say they wished they'd ordered the fried chicken, even though fried chicken wasn't a choice. I said, "Wait until tomorrow, you will taste the best fried chicken ever, served with honey pecan butter." Devon Shelby said, "Amen to that," and went to get himself another bourbon.

Out of a sense of duty, I spent a few minutes talking to Maisy, Jim's sister, who insisted on wearing one of her prairie dresses, which turned her into someone whom everyone else at the wedding wanted to avoid at all costs. I could practically hear the Carmichael side wondering, *Who invited Laura Ingalls Wilder? Did she arrive in her Conestoga wagon?* Maisy had approached me, something she doesn't like to do, and said, "Where's Helen?" And I said, "Helen had a dinner date." And Maisy said, "Who with?" And I said, "With one of her old flings from Roanoke." Maisy made a sour-pickle pucker face of disapproval—whether at me for using the term *fling* or at the thought of Helen having such relationships with men (there were many, we all knew it), I wasn't sure. Maisy said, "Well, why didn't she tell *me?*" And I said, not unkindly, "Oh, Maisy, who knows, it's Helen." And Maisy nodded along, as if she understood perfectly.

Ryan (best man): Perhaps you missed my toast. Your loss! I was funny and charming and appropriate and hugely complimentary of Stuart and Jenna's union, and I took out my veiled joke about She Who Shall Not Be Named because that boat had been rocked—and righted—already. I could have posed thorny questions about why Stuart and Jenna, but not me and Jethro? Really: why a man and a woman, but not a man and a man, or a woman and a woman? I could have referenced Chick-fil-A, a place I will never eat again, despite the fact that I love their coleslaw. The main reason I kept myself in check is because I didn't want to embarrass or upset my mother. That woman has been through enough this weekend, thanks to the horrible drama queen Helen Oppenheimer. The last thing my mother needed was for me to make GAY a political issue. All weekend, she has been introducing Jethro as my "boyfriend," and she makes it sound wholesome and normal, like Jethro is the person I take to the drive-in and then later out for milk shakes. So the GAY issue has been sensitively treated. I had wanted the punch line of the toast to be me saying how happy I was that Stuart was marrying Jenna because I had waited a long time for there to be another girl in the family.

But Jethro vetoed it. He can be prudish that way.

DOUG

The band played "The First Man You Remember," from *Aspects of Love,* and Doug took Jenna into his arms and danced with her alone in the spotlight while everyone else looked on. *I want to be the first man you remember, I want to be the last one you forget, I want to be the one you always turn to, I want to be the one you won't regret.* Doug recalled sitting in the third row orchestra of the darkened Broadhurst Theatre on Broadway watching *Aspects* with Beth and Jenna. Doug had held Jenna's ten-year-old hand during the song, and Beth had whispered over the top of Jenna's blond head, "You'll have to dance with her to this song at her wedding."

Now here they were. Jenna's blond head rested against the front of Doug's tuxedo shirt, and she said, "Oh, Daddy, thank you. Thank you for everything."

Doug felt himself choking up once again. He was unable to speak, but if he had been able to speak, he would have said, *I wish I could give you even more. I wish I could wave a magic wand that would ensure that you and Stuart are as happy as...*

Instead he squeezed her tighter. Stuart and his mother had joined them on the dance floor and were spinning in circles. Those two could really dance; it was lovely to watch.

Then, all too soon, the song changed to "One," by U2, which was a song Stuart and Jenna had picked, and Doug realized it was time to hand Jenna over. Jenna and Stuart danced alone while Doug stood at the edge of the dance floor feeling bereft. Then Ann Graham led Jim Graham to the dance floor, and Doug knew he should dance with Pauline, but when he turned, the person his eyes settled on was Margot. Margot was sitting at the head table with tears streaming down her face. Tears? Doug had to check to make sure. Yes, Margot was crying. Doug walked over and offered his hand.

"Dance with me?" he said.

She followed him to the dance floor, and a murmur went through the tent.

"What's wrong, sweetie?" Doug asked.

"Oh, Daddy," she said into his ear. "There's something I have to tell you."

It took her two and a half songs to tell the whole story. She was weeping and trembling, and Doug held on to her, rigid with anger. *Edge and Margot.* Doug heard about the chance meeting outside Ellie's dance class and the "dates" that followed. They were sleeping together. Doug knew there had been someone in Edge's life, and he knew that Edge hadn't wanted to tell him who it was. Because it was Doug's daughter. Doug wasn't going to lie—the thought of the two of them together made him physically ill. The cherrystone clams and the phyllo triangles filled with Brie and pear and the three vodka tonics churned in his stomach and threatened to come back up. Doug had always thought of Edge as a sort of uncle to his kids. He and Beth had toyed with asking Edge to be Jenna's *godfather;* they had only decided against it because Edge had no religion to speak of.

He was godless. Lawless. He had no morals, no scruples, no guiding principles. He was a shark in the courtroom and a great guy to golf with, and Doug had loved him like a brother—but this. This!

Margot described what Edge had asked her to do at work. Doug couldn't believe it—he couldn't believe Edge had asked, and he couldn't believe Margot had agreed. It was an egregious lapse in judgment.

What had Margot been *thinking?*

Well, she said tearily, she had been thinking that she loved him. And then, Rosalie.

Doug had already believed that Edge bringing Rosalie to the wedding was ill-advised, but now it seemed downright cruel. Other couples danced around Margot and Doug—Kevin and Beanie, H.W. and Autumn, Finn and Nick, Ryan and Rhonda, and at least a dozen couples Doug didn't know, although they all seemed to be having fun. Pauline was sitting at their table, where Ann and Jim Graham had joined her. Doug was grateful; he couldn't think about Pauline right now. He scanned the tent for Edge. He and Rosalie were admiring the cake in the corner.

Shit, the cake.

Doug passed Margot off to Ryan, and Rhonda went to sit with her mother and the Grahams. Doug strode over to Roger. "How long until they cut the cake?"

Roger checked his watch. "Eighteen minutes," he said.

"Perfect," Doug said.

Edge saw him coming, and for a second Doug thought he might try to run. He ought to run, Doug thought. He couldn't ever remember being this angry.

Edge held his palms up. "Doug," he said. "Wait."

Doug grabbed Edge's forearm. "Rosalie," he said. "Will you please excuse us?"

Rosalie nodded once sharply, and for an instant the three of them resumed their in-office personae: two partners and a paralegal. "Yes," she said, ducking deferentially out of the way. "Of course."

Doug pulled Edge out a flap in the back of the tent into the driveway, where they stood between Margot's Land Rover and Doug's Jaguar. It was dark and fairly quiet, although the caterers hustled in and out of the house, letting the back screen door slam each time. The noise seemed to startle Edge.

"You're jumpy," Doug said.

"Are you going to shoot me?" Edge said. "Throw me in the Jag, fill my pockets with stones, dump me in the harbor?"

"It's not funny, Edge," Doug said.

"I know it's not, Doug," Edge said.

"It's my daughter."

"What did she tell you?" Edge said.

"Everything," Doug said. "She told me everything."

"I'm sure she blew things out of proportion," Edge said. "If there's one thing we've learned in this business, it's that there are three sides to every story, right? You'll hear me out?"

"She didn't blow anything out of proportion," Doug said. "She didn't exaggerate, she didn't lie. Margot is as quality a human being as exists on this planet. She is smart and capable and strong. But—and you'll appreciate this because you have Audrey—she is my daughter. She is my *daughter,* Edge."

"I realize that," Edge said. He ran his fingers through his clipped silver hair, then rattled his watch on his wrist. "I never meant for you to find out."

"You put your disgusting hands on her," Doug said. Edge had been married three times, and there had been dozens of women on the in-between. He was a player. Doug had always secretly admired this about him, if only because it was novel to Doug. It had been fun to sit down after a round of golf and a couple of beers and maybe a shot or two of good tequila and listen to Edge tell stories about the stewardess in first class on his flight to London or the gorgeous Filipino sisters who worked at the dry cleaners. There had been relationships with clients, too—Nathalie the most notable—but others as well. There had been that delivery girl from FedEx; there had been a first-year associate from a rival firm. There was Rosalie.

"Doug, you have to listen to me. I know you think I was some kind of predator. But believe me when I say, Margot came after *me*. She pursued *me*. There were texts from her day and night, sometimes so many texts I couldn't answer them all. I tried to keep it casual, but Margot constantly pressed for more."

"Yes, I know," Doug said. "She got sucked in, she said. She fell for you, Edge, and you took advantage of that."

"I never promised her anything," Edge said.

"What about the favor you asked of her?"

Edge tilted his head. "Which favor?"

"You know damn well which favor. The favor you asked her to do at work," Doug said.

"I wanted to see if she could help Seth out," Edge said. "He was having a god-awful time, and she was in a position to save him. All I did was ask. She could have refused."

"She said you took her to Picholine," Doug said. "Plied her with good champagne and an expensive bottle of wine, and then you asked her to stay over at your apartment for the first time ever. It was intoxicating for her, she thought the two of you were finally getting serious. Of course after a night like that, she would have done anything you asked. You knew exactly how to play it." Doug cracked his knuckles; he wanted to sock Edge right in the mouth. This kind of violent urge was foreign to Doug. Despite the thrill he got from beating someone verbally in the court-room, he had never wanted to hurt anyone physically, much less his own partner, his closest friend. "You're no better than the creeps we see in the office."

"Come on, Doug."

"I'm not even angry about the relationship," Doug said. "If it had worked out, if the two of you made each other happy, I mean, I might have been a little uneasy at first, but I would have gotten over it. But the fact that you disrespected my daughter, that you used her, that you two-timed her with Rosalie, that you brought Rosalie *here* without telling Margot about it, that you *hurt* her, Edge, you hurt my daughter: that I cannot excuse."

"Doug," Edge said. "I'm sorry."

"You're not sorry," Doug said. "You have preyed on women for the thirty years that I've known you, and I didn't judge you. I let you go about your business. I watched you divorce Mary Lee and marry Nathalie and divorce Nathalie and marry Suki, and divorce Suki. I stood by your side, I gave you good counsel, I was your friend. But today your victim is my child, and you're lucky I don't beat the crap out of you right here and now."

"So are you telling me you've never hurt a woman before?" Edge asked. "You've never broken anyone's heart? What's up with you and Pauline, anyway? That was a pretty dramatic exit from the church. Want to tell me what that was about?"

Doug narrowed his eyes at Edge. He was one of the finest law-yers Doug knew, so a cross-examination shouldn't surprise him. And yet Doug was taken aback. Obviously everyone at the cere-mony had seen Pauline leave in tears, but Doug had assumed they would let it remain a private matter. He knew why Pauline had run from the church. He was as transparent to her as a piece of glass; she realized he didn't love her anymore and that, possibly, he had never loved her.

Doug took a deep breath. *Beth,* he thought. She had died and left him to flounder through the rest of his life.

How to answer Edge? How to differentiate himself? Yes, he had hurt Pauline a little already, and he was about to hurt her a lot more. His affection for her, his desire to be with her, his stockpile of patience and goodwill, his *like* of her—intense as it was at times—was depleted. His emotional reservoir, where Pauline was concerned, was empty. This happened between husbands and wives every single day in every country in the world. How many hundreds of times had Doug heard a husband or wife say, "I don't have a reason. I am just done." And Doug, and Edge, and every divorce attorney worth his or her salt, would accept that answer without judgment. After all, human beings couldn't control how they felt. If they could, everyone would most certainly decide to stay madly in love their whole lives.

"I don't want to talk about Pauline," Doug said. "This isn't about Pauline."

"I never said it was about Pauline," Edge said. "I just wondered if you had ever hurt anyone."

"Well, I never lied to anyone," Doug said. "I never cheated on anyone. I never led a woman on."

"I wonder about that," Edge said.

Doug ground his molars together. "I want you off this property in five minutes. No. Less than five minutes."

"What?" Edge said. "You're throwing me out?"

"I want you and Rosalie to leave immediately."

"I can't believe this," Edge said. "I can't believe you're throwing me out."

"She's my daughter, Edge," Doug said. "And you hurt her."

"What if the roles were reversed?" Edge said. "Margot is young and beautiful. What if she had hurt me? She might have, you know, and I would have had to live with it. Every relationship comes with risks."

"You would have been fine," Doug said. "You always are. Now get out."

"Thirty years of friendship," Edge said.

"Only family matters," Doug said, and he headed back into the tent.

A few minutes later, Stuart and Jenna cut the cake, they fed each other nicely (as Beth had suggested in the Notebook; Beth strongly disapproved of shenanigans with the cake), and then it was time for Jenna to throw the bouquet. Doug watched Margot gather up the single women—Autumn and Rhonda and all of Jenna's schoolteacher friends. Doug wanted Margot to catch the bouquet. He wanted to see Margot meet someone worthy of her in a way that neither Drum Sr. nor Edge was worthy.

When she had come to the end of her story about Edge, she had said, *I don't believe in love, Daddy. I just don't believe in it.*

And Doug had said, *What about your mother and me? We were in love until the day she died. I'm in love with her still.*

I guess what I mean is that I don't believe in love for me, Margot said. *Some people are lucky that way—you and Mom, Kevin and Beanie, Stuart and Jenna—but I'm not.*

Oh, honey, Doug had said. He wanted to refute what she said, but he knew the truth. He had seen families broken and children caught in the crossfire. He had facilitated the dissolution of households and corporations and dynasties. He had brought about thousands of endings. Some of those stories continued on in a happier way—every Christmas he received dozens of cards from clients who had remarried. But not everyone ended up this way, of course. Doug had a client who had married and divorced five times. Some people tried and tried but could not succeed at love. Was Margot one of those people? God, he hoped not.

Catch the bouquet, he thought.

The bandleader had some kind of corny procedure to follow as the girls assumed the ready position. They looked like the offensive line for the New York Giants. Jenna turned her back and raised her arms over her head and flung the flowers through the air.

There was a great burst of animated laughter. It seemed that, out of nowhere, Stuart's brother, Ryan, the best man, had appeared and caught the bouquet. He held it up in a triumphant fist, and everyone cheered. Then Ryan pulled his boyfriend up from his chair and kissed him on the lips and the band launched into "Celebrate," by Kool & the Gang.

And Doug thought, *Unexpected twist there. But okay, why not?*

He found Margot a few minutes later, licking thick white buttercream off her forefinger.

"That was so great," she said. "Ryan."

Doug said, "I had a talk with Edge. I asked him to leave."

Margot pressed her pretty lips together, and her ice-blue eyes filled with tears. "Thank you, Daddy."

"I know you're forty years old," he said. "But as long as I'm alive, I'm here to take care of you."

Margot set down her cake plate and gave him a hug. When they separated, she wiped her eyes and said, "And now there's someone I need to apologize to."

"Yes," Doug said, as he scanned the tent for Pauline. "Me, too."

THE NOTEBOOK, PAGE 40

Thank-You Notes

When you order the invitations, you should order the same number of corresponding cards (white or ivory, with the same seashell or sand dollar on top, blank) to use as thank-you notes for your gifts. Try, try, try to send them promptly, the same day the gift arrives if possible, and add at least one personal line to each card. Your Intelligent, Sensitive Groom-to-Be should share this responsibility, but honestly, honey, I have yet to meet a man who can write a decent thank-you note.

For example, from Kevin we got one of the precious cards Beanie had ordered, and across it, in nearly illegible penmanship, he wrote THANKS FOR THE CASH! Love, Kev.

I thought then that marriage must have lightened our Kevin up. But his frivolity was short-lived.

I kept the card, however, as proof. I have it still.

MARGOT

Back up in her bedroom, Margot riffled through the cocktail purse she had taken to the Galley on Thursday night. Ellie was passed out cold on the bed, still in her dress and the silly paper plate hat, although she had shed her sandals, so that Margot could see the black bottoms of her daughter's feet. As badly as Margot needed to find what she was looking for, she could not resist any of her children when they were sleeping. She hovered over Ellie, marveling at the perfect features of her face and the flawlessness of her skin. When she bent down to kiss Ellie's lips, she smelled frosting. Probably, Ellie had had nothing to eat tonight *but* frosting. Margot carefully removed the hat so that the paper plate would not be crushed by Ellie's nighttime thrashings. She pulled the bedsheets up to Ellie's chin.

She thought, *Go to hell, Edge Desvesnes. This is the real thing right here.*

Griff's card was exactly where she thought it would be, tucked in her cocktail purse next to her dead phone. Unable to help herself, Margot pressed the phone's buttons, hoping it would spring back to life, the way certain human beings had been known to do, even after being declared dead.

But no. The phone was torched, fried, useless. Somewhere in its now-silent plastic-and-metal depths lurked the two unread messages from Edge. Which would have said something like *Please call me. I need to speak to you about this weekend.*

Margot was caught in a wave of sadness that nearly pulled her under. Fifteen months of her life, wasted, all that energy squandered on someone who was never in the game to begin with. A part of her yearned to lie down next to Ellie and cry herself to sleep. *Rosalie is a better match for me.* The New Year's Eve party. While Edge and Rosalie were kissing at that party, Margot was picking popcorn kernels out of her teeth, watching the ball drop on TV. All those nights when Margot had waited for Edge to respond to her texts, moving from room to room in her apartment, thinking that maybe it was her phone's cell reception that was the problem, Rosalie and Edge were at the office "working together" on the shitshow Cranbrook case. Twenty-eight years old. Sexy gravelly voice.

Margot pinched Griff's business card between two fingers. She had to do this.

There were two phones in the house. One was hanging on the wall in the kitchen. One was on the nightstand in the master bedroom. This was a holdover from Margot's teen years. When Margot and Kevin and Nick were teenagers, they were forced to make all plans on the phone in the kitchen, right smack in the middle of the action, where everyone could hear. Margot had preferred talking to her friends or boyfriends in the privacy of her parents' bedroom, though this was frowned upon. The phone in her parents' bedroom was basically only there to serve as a late-night hotline. The police called to say that they had broken up a party at Dionis and had a Carmichael child in custody (Nick). A daughter called to say she'd be late for curfew (Margot). A son's girlfriend called to see if he was home because it was late and she hadn't heard from him (Beanie).

Now that the master bedroom was occupied by Doug and Pauline, that phone was really off-limits, so Margot had no choice but to call Griff from the phone in the kitchen. It was as mortifying as it had been as a teenager. The kitchen was filled with catering staff, who were all trying to clean up while simultaneously preparing the late-night offerings for the after-party: potato chips and dip, pretzels with honey mustard, pigs in a blanket, White Castle burgers, and the fixings for s'mores, which would be cooked over the bonfire in the backyard, which Roger and his crew were now setting up beyond the proposal bench, at the edge of the bluff. Under the tent, the band played "Two Tickets to Paradise" and "Buttercup." Margot was sure most guests were still lighting up the dance floor—but for her, this wedding was over.

She dialed Griff's number and plugged her ear. She could

barely hear the phone ringing. She thought she heard Griff answer, but after a second or two, she realized she'd gotten his voice mail. His recording was talking to her.

She hung up the phone. She had bumped into Griff so many times by accident that she hadn't anticipated having a problem finding him.

When she dialed again, he picked up on the first ring. "Hello?"

"Griff?" she said. "It's Margot."

"Who?" he said.

"Margot," she said, feeling like an imbecile. "Margot Carmichael."

"Oh," he said. "Hold on." Margot could hear bar noises—music, and people laughing. He was probably sitting at the Boarding House, talking to some sexy blond advertising executive, telling her he missed having someone to talk to at night, someone to tell the stupid stuff. Since he didn't believe in love anymore, anyone would do.

Suddenly Griff's voice was clear and strong. "Hey?" he said. "Margot?"

"Hi," she said.

"Sorry, I just had to step out. What's up?"

Margot said, "Where are you? Are you someplace I could meet you?"

"I'm at the Boarding House," he said.

Margot and her perfect instincts. She was probably right about the blonde, as well. "Are you busy? I don't want to interrupt."

"Not busy," Griff said. "Nothing to interrupt."

Margot felt a surge of relief and something sort of like happiness, even though what she was about to do was going to suck eggs.

"I'm coming down there," Margot said. "I'm at my house, I'm leaving now."

"No," Griff said. "I'll come to you."

"I'll come to you," Margot said. "I'm leaving right this second." She heard the oven timer beep, and one of the caterers moved her gently aside so he could slide out a hotel pan of fragrant sweet-and-spicy pecans. When Margot and Jenna had pored over the after-party menu selection, Margot had imagined herself sitting around the fire pit with her sister and her brothers, munching on those yummy pecans and washing them back with an ice cold Cisco brew from the keg. She had imagined the guitar player singing "Goodbye Yellow Brick Road." She had imagined a peaceful ending to a drama-free wedding. She had not imagined anything like what was now happening, but oh, well. Margot hung up the phone and took a handful of warm pecans for the road.

She bumped into Griff on Main Street. Margot thought, *Men never listen! I said I would come to him!* But it was nice to have someone meet her halfway for a change.

He grinned. "Nice dress," he said.

She was still wearing the grasshopper green. She should have changed, she realized—but after she told him what she had to tell him, it wasn't going to matter what she was wearing.

He touched her arm. "What's wrong?" he said.

"Can we sit?" she said.

"Sure," he said. He led her to the bench in front of Mitchell's Book Corner. The shopwindows up and down the street were lit, but there were only a few pedestrians out, and the occasional taxi rumbling up the cobblestones, taking people home to their beds, Margot supposed, or to the Chicken Box to dance.

She said, "There's something I have to tell you."

"Okay," he said.

When Griff had first come into Miller-Sawtooth as a candidate for the head of product development at Tricom, the applicant pool had been unparalleled by anything Margot could remember seeing in her whole career. The slate she had compiled was all Princeton undergrad and Harvard Business School; everyone was a potential superstar. Margot had overseen all the interviews; she had been the one, along with the associate principal, Bev Callahan, and with occasional consult from Harry Fry, the firm's managing partner, to winnow the group down to five, and then to three candidates, which she sent to Tricom.

Griff had looked good. He had fourteen years' experience at a comparable company called the Masterson Group, although with an unexpected, abrupt departure. He had attended the University of Maryland as an undergrad, then Wharton, and there had been a curious gap—when, he explained, he'd spent two years on the PGA tour. All of this was very good, *including* the gap—Harry Fry *loved* golfers, and Griff told a charmingly self-effacing story about rooming with Matt Kuchar and Steve Stricker and the hazing he'd had to endure. (They had made him drink warm beer that they'd run through the dishwasher.) Griff presented *very* well in person. The whole room was nodding at Griff, eating his words up. Harry had loved him, Bev had loved him, Margot had loved him.

Margot was known as a shrewd reader of résumés. In his first interview, she had said, "You mention here that you were homecoming king at Maryland?"

"Yeah," Griff said. "I was."

"That's so cool," Bev Callahan said. "Was that, like, voted on?"

"Voted on, yes," Griff said. "Secret ballot. Juniors and seniors eligible, so chances were about one in eight thousand."

"Wow!" Bev had said. Bev, Margot knew, had been on the

kick line in high school, and although she was a very serious professional, she was prone to this kind of gushing.

Margot put a check mark next to "Homecoming King." And after that first interview, she called Griff and told him to strike it from his résumé.

"It makes you sound shallow," she said.

"I wasn't sure," Griff said. "I figured it would either be something fun to talk about in the interview, or it would make me look like a tool."

"The latter," Margot said. "Get rid of it."

The other front-runner for the job was a man named Seth LeBreux, who came from New Orleans — Tulane, LSU Business School. Seth had a Cajun accent that everyone loved, and he'd been with BellSouth for a decade and had pulled New Orleans through post-Katrina hell. He left BellSouth in 2007, however, and invested in a trio of restaurants in the French Quarter that had failed. And so, he said, he decided it was time to give up the gumbo and go back to IT.

Seth LeBreux was Edge's nephew.

Margot didn't know this, however, until Edge took her to dinner at Picholine. At that dinner, she and Edge had been seated in an intimate, cozy corner of the restaurant. Immediately when they sat down, champagne appeared. He then ordered house-made burrata cheese with heirloom tomatoes, and a wild mushroom risotto. He knew his way around the menu; Terrance Brennan was a friend, he said.

When Edge had invited Margot to dinner a few days earlier, he'd told her that he wanted her to spend the night with him. She couldn't believe it. She had checked back with him twice. *You're sure?*

Of course, he said.

Margot had gotten Kitty, her afternoon babysitter, to spend the night with the kids.

During the first course of dinner, Edge held her hand. At one point, he leaned over and gave her a long, lingering kiss. In public! Every sexual and romantic cliché happened at once— Margot swooned, her stomach dropped, her knees turned to water.

It was more than an hour later—after several glasses of Malbec and entrées of day boat lobster for her and suckling pig for him—that Edge cleared his throat and brought up the subject of Seth LeBreux, his nephew, his sister's only child, a good kid, a kid Edge had looked out for since his sister's husband died in Vietnam in 1974. A kid who was like a son to Edge. And Seth had had such a hard time with his restaurant ventures, why he'd ever left BellSouth no one could say except that Seth had a dream of running a restaurant empire, maybe he'd watched too much Emeril, who knew, but it hadn't worked out for him. He'd lost his shirt.

Edge had been the one to encourage Seth to come north. Start over in New York.

Seth LeBreux, Edge said again, in conclusion, as if Margot might have missed his name the first time.

Margot had held a bite of butter-poached lobster suspended over her plate.

She said, her voice barely a whisper, "Edge, you know I can't..."

And he said, "Oh, I know, I know, I'm not *asking* you for anything. I would never do that. He just mentioned Miller-Sawtooth, and I wondered if he'd encountered you, and he said—"

"Yes," Margot said. "Yes, that's my placement. Tricom."

"So," Edge said.

Margot had set her food down, unable to eat anything else. Edge poured her another glass of Malbec. He said, "I shouldn't have brought it up. I feel like an ass. Can we forget I mentioned it?"

Yes, Margot agreed this was for the best. She excused herself for the ladies' room, where she spent a good, long time staring at herself in the mirror, trying to convince herself to walk right out of the restaurant. Fuck Edge Desvesnes. Margot wasn't a moron; she saw what he was doing. Seth LeBreux had that Cajun accent—quite frankly, that was the best thing going for him, that and his tear-jerking stories about post-Katrina, which to Margot had sounded a bit too crafted. He was one of the top three candidates, but he was also, in Margot's mind, the maverick. He'd been out of the industry for six years, and a string of failed restaurants didn't say much about his management skills or his imaginative problem solving.

Walk out the door, Margot thought. She felt like a suckling pig, one that had been spit-roasted to Edge's liking. He had set her up. *Get in a cab, go home, change your phone number.*

But she was too weak. She went back to the table, drank her wine and then a glass of port with the apricot tarte tatin that Edge ordered for them to share, and when she slid into the back of a taxi, it was with Edge. They sped uptown to his apartment, and there Edge took his time with her. It was, by far, the best lovemaking of their relationship; it was almost as if he hadn't been trying before. Later, he brought her a robe and a glass of ice water, and he rubbed her back until she fell asleep.

In the morning, she was up and out, but she felt like the issue of Seth LeBreux needed addressing, so she said, as she kissed Edge good-bye at the door, "It's in the client's hands now, but I'll see what I can do for Seth."

"Thank you, Margot," Edge said. "You don't know what it would mean to me."

*   *   *

Margot didn't explain all of this to Griff, however. What she said was: "The guy I was dating, a man I thought I was falling in love with...his nephew was a competing candidate for that Tricom job."

Griff stared at her levelly. She loved the complexity of his eyes, but she couldn't let herself get distracted.

She said, "Tricom loved you, you know they loved you."

"Yes," he said. "I thought I was in. I thought it was fit and finish. I thought I was their guy. And then out of nowhere...I got signed off."

Margot said, "I threw you under the bus so that Seth would get the job."

Griff said, "You're kidding."

"Oh, God," Margot said. "I wish I was."

The final slate of three for the Tricom job had been Griff, Seth, and a woman named Nanette Kim. Nanette Kim was phenomenally brilliant (Georgetown, Harvard Business School, fifteen years at AT&T, she had a ten out of ten on her handshake, she was a woman, and she was Asian). Margot couldn't *not* send her. But Margot also knew that Drew Carver, the CEO of Tricom, was as chauvinistic a human being as had ever been born, and Margot knew the new hire was going to be a man. It would be Griff or Seth.

Drew and his team at Tricom were leaning toward Griff, and Margot couldn't blame them. Seth wasn't going to win on his own merits; she was going to have to cut Griff down.

Margot had thought Drew might have concerns about Griff's abrupt departure from the Masterson Group. Griff had been adamant in only saying it was for "personal reasons." He didn't want Drew or anyone at Tricom to know about his wife's affair or the baby. Margot had been prepared to explain the situation to

Drew sotto voce if the issue arose. But Drew had been content with "personal reasons."

However, in the final phone call, the one where Margot suspected Drew would be offering the job to Griff, Drew said, "I do have some concerns that maybe this guy lacks gravitas. The golfing, the partying. Maybe the frat boy in him is a bit too pronounced."

Margot had been shocked by this statement. Drew Carver, like Harry Fry, was known to love the golfers, the partiers, the fraternity presidents, the captains of the hockey team. Drew Carver was giving Margot an opening. She could slip right through to the dark side undetected.

"Well, I wasn't going to mention this before," Margot said. "But now that you bring it up..."

"Yes?" Drew said.

"In his original résumé, he listed that he had been voted homecoming king at Maryland. And I thought the same thing, Drew. I thought, What kind of person lists that as an *achievement* on a professional résumé twenty years after the fact? I told him to strike it, and he did, but the fact that he chose to list it initially shows questionable judgment, I think. I mean, really, *homecoming king?*"

"Oh," Drew said. There was a long pause, then he said, "Yes. Thank you for letting me know."

And with those words, Margot knew that Griff was out and Seth was, most likely, in. She could call Edge that very night and tell him that she'd worked her magic. She had single-handedly landed Seth LeBreux a job he didn't deserve.

"You were the better candidate," Margot said. "And I stole that job from you."

"You did," Griff said. "You *did*. God, I can't believe it."

"I did," Margot said. "Professionally, it was abominable. I hate myself for it."

Griff tented his hands and bowed his head. "Jesus," he said. A string of seconds passed, then he said, "And you did it for some *guy?* Some guy you thought you were falling in love with?"

"Yes," Margot whispered.

"You know what that makes you?" he asked.

"A tool," she said. "It makes me a tool."

Griff stood up and stared at the brick facade of the Pacific National Bank. Nantucket was an old place; no doubt endless dramas had taken place on Main Street, countless treacheries, and here was one more. What Margot had done was monumentally bad. Bad, bad, bad.

"I liked you," Griff said. "I wanted to be impressive and win that job for *you*. And then, when I got signed off and you weren't the one who did it, I was *relieved*. Because I didn't want to have to see you after I'd been cut."

"I didn't do the signing off because I couldn't face you," Margot said. She had made Bev do the signing off for Griff, and Bev hadn't wanted to do it, either. She had been incredulous that Tricom passed over Griff. She kept saying, *It just doesn't make sense.*

"So the other guy got hired, then?" Griff said.

"No, actually," Margot said. "They hired Nanette Kim. She lasted six weeks, then declared that Tricom was a hostile workplace for women and minorities. I tried to come back to you — I did, Griff — but you had already signed with Blankstar."

Griff nodded. "Nice," he said. He turned and started walking down the street. "I'll see you around, Margot."

Margot squeezed her hands together and watched his figure recede down the street. She was dying to follow him; she was scrambling for the words that would make him forgive her. But those words didn't exist. He had made one small tactical error—he had given Margot something to ridicule—and Margot had turned it into a deal breaker to advance her own romantic agenda.

If Griff wanted to, he could call Miller-Sawtooth and speak to Harry Fry and relay the details of their conversation. Margot wouldn't get fired, but she might get disciplined. She almost *wanted* Griff to call, she wanted to be punished, she wanted him to get even—but she knew he wouldn't. He was too good a guy. And he had just done the exact thing she'd feared and walked out of her life, which felt like punishment enough.

Margot rose from the bench. Her feet, in her dyed-to-match pumps, were aching, and she slid the shoes off. Some nights had good karma and some nights were cursed, and this night had been cursed from the beginning.

The whole weekend had been cursed. Margot, with her perfect instincts, had been right to dread it.

As she turned the corner onto Orange Street, she saw a figure walking toward her—a man, alone, and she filled with dread. Not possible. But yes.

He called out, "Margot?"

She knew she should walk past him, but he stopped, and instinctively she did, too.

"Have you seen Rosalie?" he asked.

"No," she said.

"Your father kicked us out of the wedding," Edge said. "Rosalie was mortified. She doesn't get it, and I can't explain it to her. She thinks Doug kicked us out because he doesn't approve of her and me."

"Oh," Margot said. She was close enough to Edge to smell him. He was wearing Aventus; she would know the scent anywhere. Margot couldn't believe it. He was wearing the scent she'd bought for him — finally! — but he was wearing it for Rosalie. Edge was a cheese rat, but Margot was too worn out to fight with him. "Why don't you just tell Rosalie the truth?" she said. "Tell her about me."

"I can't," he said. "She'll leave me. Of course, after tonight, she might leave me anyway." He gave Margot a weak smile, and Margot was surprised that he didn't seem more concerned, but that was how Edge was with women — easy come, easy go. If Rosalie left, he would meet someone else, perhaps someone even younger and more inappropriate, whom he would marry and then divorce. Margot was fortunate to have escaped getting in any deeper. In her head she knew this, and she wondered if someday her heart might follow.

"See you, Edge," she said. She leaned in and gave John Edgar Desvesnes III, her fifty-nine-year-old sometime lover, a kiss good-bye, which really was exactly that, and then she walked barefoot up the street toward home.

THE NOTEBOOK, PAGE 39

The Video

Back when Daddy and I were married, there was no such thing as videotaping a wedding. Some people we knew did home movies, but my mother thought this was in poor taste. I haven't often agreed with my mother, but I am tempted to here. Do I love the idea of some guy with a video camera following your every move over the course of your wedding weekend? Not really. Do I think you'll ever pull the video out to watch with Intelligent, Sensitive Groom-to-Be on your anniversary, or inflict it on friends? No, I don't. But there is a part of me now, as I'm lying in bed and I feel my body and mind slipping away, that would love nothing more than to have the chance to watch my wedding again.

I would love to see how young Daddy and I look.

And how happy.

DOUG

He found Pauline lying in bed reading the Notebook. She was still in the cinnamon-colored dress, although she'd kicked off her shoes. She was on top of the covers on Doug's side of the bed, and she was crying.

Doug had noticed Pauline missing after the throwing of the bouquet, but at that point, the traditional portion of the festivities was winding down, and many of Doug's friends and Beth's cousins were leaving, and Doug had to put in face time to say goodbye and remind everyone about the brunch in the morning. The band was still playing—Etta James's "At Last," and Al Green's "Let's Stay Together." These songs were thorns in Doug's side. He couldn't very well dance to them with Pauline, and yet he most certainly owed Pauline a dance. He hadn't danced with her once all night.

Pauline was no longer at the table, nor elsewhere in the tent that he could see. He nearly asked Rhonda if she had seen Pauline, but he didn't want to call attention to the fact that he had

lost track of her once again. Roger and his crew were transition-
ing from the traditional wedding to the after-party. The lead
singer of the band was staying on to play an acoustic set. The
after-party was really for the young people, and so Doug figured
it was okay for him to leave the cleanup to Roger and the caterers
and go in search of Pauline.

He had expected to find her in bed. He had *not* expected her
to be reading the Notebook.

"Really?" he said.

"What does it matter now?" she said. "The wedding is over."

Well, yes, that was true, the wedding was over—Doug acknowl-
edged this with equal parts relief and melancholy. He found
himself hoping that Nick did end up getting married someday,
because there was nothing Doug relished as much as having his
family together, despite all the attendant malarkey.

To Pauline, he said, "Right, the wedding is over. Why again
with the Notebook?"

" 'Your father will be a cause for concern,' " Pauline read.

Doug put a hand up. "Pauline, stop."

" 'Even if your father has Another Wife, I want you to do those
things. Do them for me, please.' "

"Pauline." Doug wondered if she had read the last page of the
Notebook. He was tempted to ask her to hand it over so that he
could read it himself, but he sensed this was exactly the wrong
time.

Pauline was gazing at him with tears streaming down her face.
"How is this supposed to make me feel?"

"It isn't supposed to make you feel *any* way," he said. "It wasn't
meant for you. It was meant for Jenna."

"It was like Beth knew that whoever came along after her
wasn't going to be good enough." Pauline turned the page of the

Notebook so violently that Doug feared she might rip it. "Wasn't going to be as good as she was."

"Pauline."

"I just want you to admit it, Douglas," Pauline said. "You don't love me as much as you loved her, and you never will."

"I wasn't looking to replace Beth," Doug said. "That was never my intention."

"What *was* your intention, then?" Pauline asked. "A little sex? A little fun? We took *vows,* Douglas, just like Jenna and Stuart did today. We pledged the same things they did, in sickness and in health, until death do us part. I meant those vows, but you didn't. You just went through the motions — but why? Why did you marry me? We should have just continued dating if you didn't want to give this relationship the same time and energy that you gave your first marriage." Pauline set the Notebook down and sat up in bed. "That was what crystallized for me while we were sitting in that church. You never treated our marriage the way you treated your marriage to Beth. Beth was your real and true love; I was just someone you met afterwards. I was a coda, an afterthought, a person on your arm, a warm body in the bed so you didn't have to sleep alone."

Doug sighed. He could hear voices outside, Jenna's voice above all the others, asking everyone to gather around the campfire.

Before Doug had walked Jenna down the aisle, she said, "I love him so much, Daddy. I never want to be away from him. You know that song that Mom liked with the line 'If I could choose a place to die, it would be in your arms'?"

" 'Bell Bottom Blues,' " Doug said. "Derek and the Dominos."

"Well, that's how I feel about Stuart."

Doug nodded. Jenna was the only one of the kids who had

inherited Beth's appreciation of the rock anthem. "Good. That's the way you're supposed to feel, honey."

But that wasn't how Doug felt about Pauline—now, or ever.

"You're right," he said to Pauline. "The things you say are all at least partially correct. I felt so strongly about Beth that it wasn't fair of me to marry you or anyone else. And I'm sorry for that."

"Sorry?" Pauline said. "You're *sorry?*"

"It wasn't fair to you," Doug said.

"You're *damn right* it wasn't fair," Pauline said. "I married you because I was in love with you. I married you because I wanted to be in a good relationship, one that succeeded. You, more than anyone, *knew* how I needed that. You knew what I endured with Arthur, you knew I deserved better, and you promised to deliver."

Doug said, "I promised to do the best that I could. I promised I would give you everything I was able. I'm sorry if it isn't enough."

"*Damn right* it isn't enough," Pauline said. "It isn't even *close* to enough. I want a divorce."

"What?" Doug said.

"I want a divorce," Pauline said.

"Oh," Doug said. He thought, *What is happening here?* Was it what he *thought* was happening, or was it some kind of confusing trap? He stood very still, afraid to move an inch or whisper a word. He didn't have to be the bad guy? Pauline had read his mind and done exactly as he wished? She had asked for a divorce? Was it really going to be this easy? "All right. We can start the process when we get home, then."

He heard Pauline sob, but he turned and left the room before she could speak. He didn't want her to take it back. He didn't want her to give him one last chance.

*   *   *

Outside, the fire raged. Roger had done a beautiful job building a fire pit, and people sat in a circle in beach chairs and on blankets. Jenna and Stuart had changed out of their wedding clothes into matching T-shirts that said *Just Married*. Rhonda was still in her bridesmaid dress; she was talking to Ryan and his boyfriend. Autumn was cozied up with the other twin brother on a blanket, and Finn was nestled in Nick's lap in the scoop of a Sleepy Hollow chair. Doug stared at Finn and Nick, wondering what exactly he was seeing. If Doug wasn't mistaken, he and Pauline had attended Finn's wedding in October. Had something happened between Finn and Scott *already?* It seemed like just yesterday that Bud Sullivan was joking about how relieved he was to get Finn off his payroll. Scott Walker wasn't here, Doug had realized that, but he thought that was because Scott had a commitment elsewhere. Doug couldn't tell if Nick and Finn were actually canoodling or only horsing around. He hoped for the latter. When he'd thought earlier that he wanted Nick to get married, he had not been thinking of Finn. No, that would never work. Doug had thirty-five years of professional experience telling him that.

Doug took a handful of potato chips and strolled over to talk to Jenna and Stuart.

"This is nice," Doug said. The bandleader had a guitar and started to strum the first chords of "Helplessly Hoping," by Crosby, Stills, and Nash.

Jenna gazed up at Doug. "Have you seen Margot? I'm worried about her."

"Not since the bouquet," Doug said.

Jenna motioned for Doug to come closer, so he crouched by her chair. "Drum Sr. is getting married again in the fall," Jenna said. "I think Margot might be shaken up about it."

Drum Sr. getting married? That meant Margot would be getting *him* off the payroll—no more palimony. Margot could only feel happy about that, right? If Margot seemed upset, it would be because of Edge. But maybe Jenna didn't know about Edge. Was this possible? Theirs was a family where it was arduous to keep track of who confided what to whom. Doug was grateful for all he knew, and even more grateful for what he didn't know.

"I'm sure she's fine, honey," Doug said. "She'll probably be here any minute."

"I don't want her to miss this," Jenna said. "We planned this part together."

It was comforting: the fire, the snacks, the guitar, and the singing. Doug poured himself a beer from the keg, and as he took the first sip, he realized he felt younger and lighter than he had in years.

He sat in one of the last empty chairs. He wanted to move closer to Jenna and Stuart—they were all the way over on the opposite side of the circle—but he figured it was now time to start giving his little girl and her new husband some space.

"I'm going to make a s'more," he said. "Would someone hand me a stick?"

Beanie passed Doug a stick and the bag of marshmallows. But before Doug could skewer his marshmallow, someone shoved the back of his shoulder, and he inadvertently kicked his beer over. He turned to see Pauline, her face lit a raging orange. She held the Notebook in front of Doug's face, and for a second he thought she was going to smack him with it.

But instead she tossed it into the fire.

"No!" Doug said. He leaped to his feet and reached out to save it, but the fire was too big and hungry. The pages of the Notebook were swallowed in a burst of white light.

There was a confused murmur around the fire. Had anyone understood what just happened? Pauline dashed for the house. Doug wanted to chase her down and demand an explanation. What the hell was she *thinking?* What had she just *done?* He collapsed into his chair; his legs felt heavy and useless. As he stared into the fire, his eyes blurred with tears.

Your father will be a cause for concern.

Doug pinched the bridge of his nose. The wedding was over. Really over. Beth's precious words, gone up in smoke. In a way, it felt like losing her all over again. And he had never gotten to read the last page.

Doug pushed himself to his feet and walked around the circle to check on Jenna. Had she seen what happened?

No—she was curled up in Stuart's lap with her pretty blond head resting on his chest. She was singing along with the guitar player: *They are one person, they are two alone, they are three together, they are for each other.* Her face was serene, as though everything was right with the world.

THE NOTEBOOK, PAGE 43

The Honeymoon

I really wanted to go to Europe—Italy or London—but we didn't have the money and your father was studying for the bar. And so your father chose St. John because it didn't require a passport, it was tropical, and because we could camp there. It was cheap.

I was skeptical about his choice at first because it wasn't what I had imagined I wanted, but I fell in love with the place the second the ferry pulled into Cruz Bay. St. John has a magic and a uniqueness, just like Nantucket. It is 70 percent national park, and it is breathtaking.

Daddy and I stayed at the Maho Bay campground, where we lived in a rustic cabin. We heated water in a large black bladder and took what we called sun showers. We rented a kayak. Daddy paddled and I lay across the front like Cleopatra. We hiked through the ruins of the old Danish sugar plantations. We snorkeled with rays and sea turtles, we encountered wild donkeys walking along the side of the road, we gazed at the stars from the beach, we drank rum punch.

Daddy and I returned to St. John on our twenty-fifth anniversary. We stayed at Caneel Bay, and we ate lobster every night. We rented a nice new Jeep. We did the island like people who had money, but we were no more or less happy than we had been the first time. It was exactly the same. All that mattered was that we were together.

SUNDAY

ANN

Beau—the White Elephant bartender, originally from Charleston—made the best whiskey sours Ann had ever tasted. She drank one down as she oversaw the preparations for the brunch, and doing so put her in an excellent mood. It was a sparkling, sunny day, and the open-sided tent on the front lawn of the White Elephant had resplendent views of the harbor. Under the tent were two long tables swathed in white linen, each with twenty-four seats, and eight arrangements of luscious, multicolored hothouse roses in round cut-crystal bowls. The waiters had chilled two cases of good champagne (Pommery, a favorite since the wine-tasting group). The orange juice, Ann had been assured, was freshly squeezed, pressed by the tiny hands of industrious elves all night long—or so joked Confederate Beau, who couldn't have been more beguiling. Ann was wearing a white lace sundress and her new pearl choker; she could now wear white without worrying about competing with the bride.

The buffet included standard brunch fare—fruit salad served in a carved-out watermelon, Danish, bagels and muffins, as well as bacon, hash browns, and home fries, eggs Benedict with Canadian bacon, spinach, or lobster, and an omelet station. In addition were Ann's regional specialties: barbecue from Bullock's, fried chicken, collard greens, hush puppies, coleslaw, regular grits and cheesy grits. Later they would bring out banana pudding, a bourbon pecan pie, and red velvet cake.

The Dixieland band—five men in their sixties, two with white handlebar mustaches, all five wearing peppermint-striped shirts, suspenders, and straw boaters—were tuning up. There was a small dance floor. Ann was a little disappointed that only fifty people had RSVP'd—she had been hoping for eighty to a hundred—but the right people would be here. All the groomsmen were coming, all the Carmichaels, and Maisy and Sam, and all of Ann and Jim's friends from Durham.

And Helen was coming—or at least Ann believed she was coming. She had RSVP'd yes, although that seemed to have a fluid definition for Helen. She clearly thought it was okay to say she would be in attendance and then not show. Her place at dinner the night before had sat empty, although no one had missed her, with the possible exception of Maisy—and so Ann figured it was probably a wise decision Helen had made, despite its rudeness. And Jim had been right: Ann was far happier without Helen under the tent. Ann didn't know if she should wish for Helen to show today or not. "Not show" would be the obvious answer—let Helen loll around in bed with Skip Lafferty all morning—but a part of Ann still wanted to prove something to Helen. This was Ann's party—and look how lovely it was!

Ann and Jim stood together in the middle of the tent, and she hugged him tight, and he kissed the top of her head. The band played "Georgia." They were, for the moment, the only guests at their party, and they swayed to the music. It was perfect right now. Too bad she couldn't stop time and have it stay just like this.

*   *   *

Forty-five minutes later, the band was in full swing. They were playing "Riverboat Shuffle," and the whiskey sours and Lynchburg Lemonades were flowing freely. When Jenna and Stuart entered the tent—looking fresh faced and completely reenergized, as though they'd slept for ten hours then awoken and gone for a bracing swim in the ocean (although Ann knew this couldn't have been the case)—Stuart led his new wife right onto the dance floor and swung her expertly around to "When the Saints Go Marching In." Everyone burst into applause. Because it was a buffet, people could get up and move around, switch seats if they wanted to, stand at the edge of the dance floor and tap their toes, then go out and dance to a few numbers. Yes, everyone complained about being tired and hung over, but this seemed to add to the conviviality of the gathering rather than detract from it.

"Hair of the dog!" Robert Lewis said as he toasted Ann with his bourbon.

"*Great* party!" Autumn said. She and H.W. were attached at the hip. Ann watched H.W. fetch Autumn a plate of barbecue, saying, "You have to try this. It's from the most famous smoke pit in Carolina." He actually went so far as to feed Autumn the first bite, and Ann had to look away.

Ann hadn't eaten yet; she was too busy talking and laughing, and then taking a quiet minute to observe and appreciate. Doug Carmichael seemed subdued, and Ann didn't see Pauline anywhere. She approached Doug and said, "Thank you so much for last night. It was magnificent."

Doug smiled and raised his drink. "They're great kids, they deserve the best."

Ann touched her glass to his own. "Is Pauline coming?"

Doug cast his eyes down at his plate, which held a gnawed chicken leg, the crusts of an English muffin, and a smear of ketchup. "Pauline headed home," he said. "There were some things she had to do back in Connecticut."

"Oh," Ann said. She had the urge to sit next to Doug and see if she could get him to open up—why had Pauline run from the church? Was everything okay? After all, Doug and Pauline were now Ann's family; someday they would all be grandparents to the same children. But Ann was a politician, not a therapist; in conversation, she had always been a surface glider rather than a deep digger.

As Ann was wondering what to say next to Doug Carmichael, she saw Helen walk into the party.

Helen. Jaw-dropping, impossible-to-miss Helen was wearing a fire-engine red strapless patio dress that flowed in one shocking column from her breasts to the ground. Her hair was tousled and wavy, as though she had just come from the beach. She was on the arm of Skip Lafferty, who was wearing a navy blazer and a red bow tie that matched Helen's dress. The two of them were so tall and so striking that nearly everyone turned to gawk at them. There was a lull in the tent, then the band launched into "A Good Man Is Hard to Find."

"Excuse me," Ann said to Doug. "I have to go say hello."

Ann marched over to Helen and Skip. She knew she should wait until Jim was beside her, but there wasn't time. She was the hostess of this party; she would greet her guests. It was, of course, unspeakably rude that Helen had brought Skip with her when she'd only RSVP'd for one—but at this point, Ann had ceased to be surprised at the woman's lack of breeding. When Ann got home, she was going to secretly send Helen a copy of Emily Post in an unmarked envelope.

"Hello, Helen," Ann said. She held out a hand, but Helen

insisted on bending down to execute the ludicrous European double-cheek kiss. There was a slit to the knee in Helen's patio dress, and Ann caught a glimpse of the red patent leather platform sandals Helen was wearing, which added at least three inches to her already formidable height. Ann was so much shorter, she felt like a child. Why would someone who was already so tall wear platform shoes? She liked lording her height over everyone else, Ann supposed, and Skip Lafferty was such a sideshow giant, she could wear whatever shoes she wanted. Ann offered her hand to Skip. "Skip, I'm Ann Graham. We met briefly yesterday morning."

Skip shook her hand and smiled. "Yes, I remember. Hello again. Thank you for including me."

"Oh, you're welcome," Ann said. She turned toward the party, thinking, *Honestly, the nerve of the woman!* In one corner of the tent, she could see Olivia Lewis and Jim both eyeballing her. "Well, it's a buffet, so get a drink and help yourself. Enjoy the music."

Skip took in the scene and rubbed his hands together. He looked delighted to have scored this invitation, and Ann felt a small ping of gratitude. Then Skip said, "Oh, look, there's Kevin Carmichael! I hired his company to help me with a building project in St. Louis last year. Hold on, Helen, I'll be right back." Skip beelined for Kevin, leaving Helen and Ann standing alone.

Ann thought, *Oh, God, I have to get away.* But walking off now and leaving Helen would be impolite, and Ann refused to stoop to Helen's level. A waiter with a tray of champagne approached, and both Helen and Ann accepted a glass.

"That's funny," Ann said. "That Skip knows Kevin. What are the chances?"

"Who?" Helen said.

"Kevin Carmichael?" Ann said. "Jenna's brother?"

Helen nodded distractedly, and Ann couldn't be sure that Helen even knew who Jenna was.

"Jenna," Ann said. "The bride."

"Yes, I know," Helen said. "I met Jenna on Friday night at the rehearsal dinner." She smiled at Ann, and Ann was cheered to see that Helen had a smudge of red lipstick on her front tooth. "I'm afraid I threw her for a loop."

At first Ann thought Helen meant that Helen's presence threw Jenna for a loop, just as it had been throwing Ann for a loop all weekend. But then she wondered if Helen meant something else. "Threw her for a loop? How?"

"I accidentally mentioned Stuart's first fiancée," Helen said.

"Criss—." Ann swallowed. Her ears were ringing, and the band suddenly seemed too loud. What was Helen saying? "You were the one who told her about Crissy Pine?"

"Obviously I assumed she already *knew*," Helen said. "I mean, my God, Ann, she was about to marry Stuart and she didn't know that he'd been engaged before? He'd never *told* her?"

"It certainly wasn't *your* place to tell her!" Ann said. "I don't think you realize what kind of fiasco you caused. Jenna nearly canceled the wedding. She nearly *left* him!"

Helen sniffed. "Well, it's better that it's out in the open," she said. "Stuart didn't want to get married with *that* skeleton in his closet." Helen's red dress made her look like a she-devil. Evil incarnate.

"What do you even know about it?" Ann asked. "Stuart isn't your son."

"I heard the whole story from Jim," Helen said. "I do ask him about the other kids; I always have. We are all one family, Ann, like it or not."

Ann was rendered speechless. She squared herself in front of Helen. "You know what, Helen?"

Helen sipped her champagne. Her eyes were now fixed on Skip Lafferty, who was deep in conversation with Kevin Carmichael. Skip's hand was resting on Kevin's shoulder, and it was for this reason that Ann noticed Skip's wedding band.

He's married! she thought.

"What?" Helen said.

"I should never have invited you to this wedding," Ann said. "I don't know why I did. I guess I wanted to prove that I was the bigger person, I wanted to show myself that I had moved beyond what happened twenty years ago. I could offer an olive branch, I could invite you here. But the fact of the matter is, we are *not* all one family. You destroyed *my* family. You're responsible for the worst catastrophe of my life."

"Y'all can blame me," Helen said, "but I wasn't acting alone. I didn't get pregnant alone."

"I have made my peace with Jim," Ann said. "But I find that I simply cannot make peace with you."

"I could never believe you took Jim back," Helen said. "It seemed pitiful to me. You're a smart woman, Ann, and halfway attractive. You wield actual power in certain circles. You could have met someone else. You could have done better."

"That's where you and I differ," Ann said. "For me, there is no one better. My life has always been about loving Jim."

Helen opened her mouth to speak, but Ann was done listening. Ann walked away, leaving Helen and her lipstick-smudged teeth. Ann tapped Skip Lafferty on the shoulder, interrupting his conversation with Kevin Carmichael.

"I need to warn you about Helen," Ann said. She leaned in closer to Skip's ear. "She's a pit viper."

Skip smiled at Ann uncertainly; he might not have heard what she said over the strains of "The Entertainer," but Ann didn't care. Another woman might have repeated herself, another woman might have screamed at Helen, or called her a bitch or a whore, another woman might have made a snarky comment about the bright colors Helen had worn all weekend and the way they echoed the natural bright colors of poisonous snakes, and venomous frogs, fish, and spiders, another woman might have thrown a drink or accidentally "spilled" a plate of cheesy grits all over Helen's red patent leather platform sandals. Another woman might have heard the phrase "halfway attractive" and made a scene, but not Ann. Saint Ann, Catholic schoolgirl Ann, state senator Ann. Ann had gotten the chance today to say what she'd wanted to say, and that was enough.

Jim approached her and took her in his arms. "You okay?" he said.

"Wonderful," Ann said.

"I would marry you again, you know," Jim said. "Again and again and again, every day of our lives I would marry you, Annie."

The band launched into "Ain't Misbehavin'."

"Let's dance," Ann said.

THE NOTEBOOK, PAGE 42

The Wedding Night

Ha! Only kidding, sweetie pie! I'm sure you'll do just fine without your mother's input here!

MARGOT

All she had left to survive was the brunch. Then, at three o'clock, she would drive the Land Rover up the ramp of the ferry, the wedding weekend would be over, and she could get down to the business of putting her life back together.

Edge gone.

Griff gone.

Jenna married.

Her mother still dead.

Margot wouldn't even be able to cry about these things in peace during the two-hour boat ride as she had planned, because now her father was driving home with them.

Pauline had thrown the Notebook into the bonfire, and it had gone up in flames. Margot had just accepted this as the final devastation of the weekend—until Jenna told them that Stuart really *was* the Intelligent, Sensitive Groom Beth had predicted. Stuart had scanned the Notebook, page by page, into his computer—so Beth's words in Beth's handwriting would be preserved digitally forever. Doug would finally be able to read the last page of the Notebook.

Pauline had spent the night in the guest room with Rhonda, and at the crack of dawn, she drove Doug's Jaguar onto the early morning ferry. She was going home alone. Doug was planning to stay at the Marriott in Stamford until he found a place in the city.

Splitsville.

Rhonda, however, had remained at the Carmichael house. She had gotten up early to run, she'd made a pot of coffee, and by the time Margot and her twice-broken heart stumbled downstairs, Rhonda was home, sweaty and breathless.

She had seemed sheepish. "I'm sorry about my mother," she said.

Margot poured herself a cup of coffee, hot and black; the more bitter it tasted this morning, the better. "It's nobody's fault," Margot said. This had long been Doug's party line in regard to 95 percent of the divorces he saw. "Things happen, people change, there's no point placing blame."

Rhonda nodded but looked unconvinced.

Margot said, "We should go out together sometime. Drinks or dinner or something. I'd love to meet Raymond."

"Would you?" Rhonda said, brightening. "How about Thursday night? Are you free Thursday night? You could meet Raymond and me at Swine."

Margot had been thinking of some vague future date, but she was charmed by Rhonda's enthusiasm. "I am free Thursday," she said. "And I've been dying to go to Swine."

It was a date, then. Margot hoped that by Thursday the excruciating pain she felt about Edge and Rosalie, and, oddly, the even worse pain she felt from watching Griff walk away, would have subsided to a point where she could be halfway decent company. It seemed an awful irony that she and Rhonda would become friends now that their parents were separating. And yet Margot was happy to have gotten at least one positive thing from the weekend.

She grabbed a glass of champagne from the tray and stood in the buffet line with Ryan and Jethro, who both looked beyond haggard. Waves of alcohol fumes emanated off of Ryan that even the heady scent of Aventus couldn't disguise.

Aventus. Damn Edge.

Ryan and Jethro told Margot they had stayed up until four in the morning doing Patrón shots with the bandleader, whose name was Ernie Sands. They had gotten into a long, discursive conversation about *Moby-Dick,* and Ryan had started calling Jethro "Daggoo."

"Daggoo and I might come back to Nantucket next summer," Ryan said.

Jethro said, "Yeah, we might get married ourselves."

Margot clapped her hands and mustered what she hoped passed for enthusiasm, but the thought of anyone else getting married—even people as ideally suited for each other as Ryan and Jethro—depressed her.

Ryan said, "You look worse than I feel. We brought copies of the *Times* and the *News and Observer* so everyone could see the wedding announcements. You want to be the first one? We're sitting over there."

"I would," Margot said. "But I have to talk to my mother's cousins. I've been putting it off all weekend."

Margot fixed a plate of things she didn't normally allow herself to eat—fried chicken, hash browns, and a big scoop of cheesy grits topped with barbecue. What did it matter if she weighed five hundred pounds? No one had loved her when she was thin.

She sought out Everett and Kay Bailey, her mother's favorite cousins. It was a sign of devotion to her mother that Margot did this. She had always loved Ev and Kay, but the whole "catching up" thing was the last way Margot wanted to spend her time at this brunch.

They were, of course, delighted when Margot sat with them.

"Oh, what a wonderful surprise," Kay said. "Here's Margot! Where are the kids?"

"Back at the house," Margot said. "With their cousins and a babysitter." *Playing their iDevices,* she thought. *Eating cake for breakfast.*

Margot hadn't seen Ev and Kay since her mother's funeral seven years earlier, so there was a lot to discuss. Like her divorce from Drum Sr.

"He's getting married again," Margot said. "To a Pilates instructor named Lily." *A woman I had never heard of until three days ago.* She ate a few huge forkfuls of barbecue and grits.

Was Margot dating anyone? "No, nobody special." *Unless you count the fifteen months I spent in a nebulous haze of sex and unrequited texting with my father's law partner.*

And how about work? It sounded as though she'd had quite the meteoric rise up through the ranks at Miller-Sawtooth. "Work is good," Margot said. "I love my job." Work had always been Margot's ace in the hole. The rest of her life might be falling apart, but work—promotion, esteem, salary—had always been gangbusters. Or at least it had been until Griff. The first event of Griff was bad enough, but the reappearance of Griff had been exponentially worse. She had liked Griff months ago and regretted her actions, but over the course of the weekend, he had revealed himself to be even kinder, funnier, cooler, and more genuine than he had seemed previously. And he had liked her! He thought she was pretty! And smart! And tough and discerning! (The ultimate compliments, in her line of work.) And she had picked him off like a sniper. She had been ruthless and unethical; she had blown, blown, *blown* it!

Maybe the expression on her face gave away that work was a sore subject.

"Your dad seems good," Ev said.

"Good?" Margot said. "Yep, he's good." *As long as he doesn't end up as a permanent denizen on my pull-out couch.* More than anything, Margot hoped he didn't default and go back to Pauline just because he couldn't face life as a singleton.

"And your brothers?" Kay asked.

"Kevin is Kevin," Margot said. "Out slaying dragons, making the world a safer place for humanity." She and Ev and Kay all pivoted in their seats to observe Kevin and Beanie, arm in arm at the bar—where, Margot knew, Kevin would order a light beer and Beanie would get a V8 with nothing in it.

"And Nick," Margot said. What the hell could she say about Nick that wouldn't make Ev and Kay's hair stand on end? At that moment, he was dancing with Finn to "Am I Blue?" The two of them looked like they had been welded together; Nick's chin was on Finn's head, her face smushed into his chest, her eyes closed. Their feet were barely shuffling. Margot watched them for a moment with awe and horror. They had spent the night together in Jenna's room—Autumn had once again repaired to the groomsmen's house with H.W., and Jenna and Stuart had spent their wedding night in the cottage at the Cliffside Beach Club. No one had said a word about Nick and Finn cohabiting in the family home—not her father, not Kevin, and not Margot herself. She wasn't the moral police, they were both consenting adults, infidelity wasn't against the law. But come on!

Jenna and Finn still weren't speaking. They might never speak again, even if Nick and Finn ended up getting married someday.

Married! Margot barked out an unhappy laugh. Ev and Kay smiled at her as if to ask what was funny, and Margot rummaged for a neutral statement to make about Nick.

But at that moment, something happened. Margot saw a man enter the tent. Handsome guy, broad shoulders, bowlegged walk. Margot's mouth dropped open.

No way, she thought. *Oh, my God, no way.*

"Excuse me a second," she said to Ev and Kay.

She bumbled with her chair and her drink, which she had wisely decided to bring with her. She needed to get a better look.

Oh, my God, yes.

The man who had entered the tent was Scott Walker.

Inwardly, Margot squealed. She watched Scott Walker approach Nick and Finn on the dance floor. The band continued to play, but Nick and Finn stopped dead and separated, although Nick still had a hold of one of Finn's sunburned arms.

Margot thought, *Jesus, Nick, let go!*

She thought, *Scott is going to punch him.*

Finn's face was the face of someone who saw dead people. She looked *petrified.*

There were words, spoken by Scott, but Margot couldn't hear them over the strains of "Everybody Loves My Baby." Then Nick said something, and Margot hoped he was pulling out the charms that had, heretofore in his life, kept him alive and out of prison. Finn said nothing; she barely blinked.

Scott took Finn by the other arm. For a second, both Nick and Scott had a hold of Finn like they were engaged in a tug-of-war, and Margot thought, *Everybody loves my baby, indeed!* She wanted to know why Finn had men fighting over her wimpy, lying, cheating ass. It was neither fair nor just. Then Nick let go, and Scott led Finn out of the tent and down by the dock, where they stood and talked. They were fifty yards away, but still in full view of everyone.

Jenna appeared at Margot's side.

Margot said, "I cannot believe this is happening. Can you believe this is happening?"

Jenna said, "I called him."

The foghorn sounded. The ferry pushed forward off the dock. Margot and Doug sat in the front seat of the Land Rover, and the three kids with their iDevices were in the back. Ellie was wearing her flower girl dress; she had spilled Hawaiian Punch down the front, and the back was covered with grass stains, but that hardly mattered now.

The wedding was over.

"Forget the Marriott in Stamford," Doug said. "I'm going to pack up my things, deal with some issues at the office, and come back up here next weekend. In fact, I'm going to stay all summer."

"All *summer?*" Margot said. "You're kidding me."

"Not kidding," he said. "I'll go to the beach. I'll golf at Sankaty. Why not? Edge can take care of things at the office."

Margot nodded once sharply, in a way that she hoped conveyed that she did not want to talk about Edge. She was, however, insanely jealous at the thought of her father spending the entire summer on Nantucket. Because despite how weird and difficult the weekend had been, she didn't want to leave the island. It physically pained her. As the ferry lumbered toward Hyannis, her heart broke a third time.

Which reminded her.

"I'm going up," Margot said. "Who's coming with me? Ellie?"

Ellie shook her head.

"Come on, you said you would."

"I changed my mind."

"Boys?" Margot said.

"No!" In chorus.

She sighed and felt impending tears. Her mother had never had a problem getting Margot and her siblings to do her bidding when they were this age. Margot and Kevin and Nick hadn't been allowed to rebel until they were teenagers.

But maybe that was revisionist history. Maybe Margot just liked to believe that she had been an obedient daughter now because her mother was dead and Margot couldn't bear to imagine that she'd given her mother a moment of trouble. Any which way, she wasn't going to fight with her children; she wasn't going to force them upstairs.

She said, "Fine, then, I'll go alone."

Doug leaned back in his seat. "I'd go with you, honey, but I'm beat."

Margot got out of the car and climbed to the upper deck. She felt better with the air and the horizon, although Nantucket Sound was as flat as a mirror and the ferry wasn't rocking at all. Margot stood out in the sun, without SPF 90, without a hat. What did it matter if she weighed five hundred pounds, what did it matter if she detonated into five million freckles?

She pulled two pennies out of her wallet, and as the ferry passed Brant Point Lighthouse, she tossed them into the sea. Her throw was lame; the pennies barely cleared the bottom deck. If either of her brothers had been present, they would have told her she threw like a girl. Margot checked to make sure no one had seen her. She heard footsteps. Someone was coming up behind her.

Margot thought it was her father, who would forgive her a bad throw and a whole lot more.

He sidled up next to her and rested his arms on the railing. Margot turned.

White visor.

Not her father.

Griff said, "Do you happen to have two pennies I could borrow?"

Margot felt like her heart was dropping off the side of the boat. She fished two more pennies out of her wallet and handed them to Griffin Wheatley, Homecoming King.

Griff grinned. He said, "I figure you owe me at least that." He took the pennies and threw them so far they nearly landed on shore.

Margot said, "Very impressive."

Griff said, "So they gave the job to Nanette Kim. I met her, you know, at the Starbucks on the first floor of Tricom's building. She approached me, actually. She went to college with the woman that Jasper ditched when he married my wife. Anyway, Nanette Kim was extremely cool and smart as hell. She deserved that job."

As badly as Margot wanted to be let off the hook, she couldn't let him do it. "*You* deserved that job," she said. "They liked *you.*"

"Nanette Kim left after six weeks because it was a hostile environment for women and minorities," Griff said.

"I'll point out," Margot said, "that you're neither a woman nor a minority."

"But do you really think I would want to work at a place that is hostile toward women and minorities?" Griff said. He ran his hand over what was now his very, very appealing four-day scruff. "I wasn't voted homecoming king for no reason. I'm a good guy, Margot. And I think you did me a favor by signing me off."

Margot shook her head. "I wasn't a good guy, though, Griff. I mean, I *am* a good person, in my heart. But what I did was… despicable."

"I'm happy at Blankstar," Griff said. "Really happy. It's the right place for me."

"Good," Margot said. "I kept checking on you, you know. I Googled you first thing every morning until I found out you'd gotten a job."

"Did you?" he said.

"I did."

"You didn't have to tell me the truth," Griff said. "I never would have known. Never."

"Yes," Margot said. "I realize that."

"So why did you?" Griff asked.

Why did she? Well, because she was her mother's daughter and her father's daughter, and because she was the mother of three young and growing souls. She could feed them takeout every night, she could leave them for hours with Kitty, the afternoon babysitter, but ultimately the person who was responsible for installing their moral compass was her. It was okay to mess up—to set a scorching-hot pan directly on a soft pine table and mar it forever, to file for divorce when she was no longer in love and had exhausted every hope, to become utterly infatuated with the wrong person and then commit what was essentially a crime of passion—but she had to own it.

How to explain this to Griff? She couldn't possibly.

"I don't know why I told you," she said.

Griff took her chin and turned her face toward him. "But I do know," he said.

Margot thought he was going to kiss her. He was going to kiss her, and this painful, difficult wedding weekend was going to get the kind of movie star ending that Margot could never have dreamed of. But instead Griff let his hand drop to the railing, and he stared out at the water.

"I don't believe in love," he said.

"Me either," Margot said.

"And I'm never getting married again."

"Me either," Margot said.

Griff stood up straight and adjusted his visor. He looked at Margot, and she became transfixed by his blue-and-green kaleidoscope eyes. It was a genetic anomaly, and Margot wondered if *heterochromia iridum* came with any benefits. Did he see things differently? Did it lend him a sixth sense that enabled him to guess people's favorite lyrics? Did it allow him to be generous of spirit even when he'd been wronged?

"I want you to call me," Griff said. "Tonight, after you get home and settled, when you're climbing into bed, as late as you want. Okay? I'll answer, I promise."

Margot nodded. "I'll tell you the stupid stuff," she said.

"All of it," he said.

"Okay," Margot agreed.

As Griff walked away, he spun around. "Thanks for the pennies," he said. He squinted off the side of the boat. "You know, I can't wait to come back here."

Margot followed his gaze to the coastline of the island, the place where she had wandered the beach as a soulful teenager, where she had partied with her brothers and sneaked in the back doors of bars, where she had met Drum Sr., where she had discovered she was pregnant, where her mother's spirit shone like the sun on every surface. It was the island where Margot wanted to rest her weary bones when this exquisite, tremendous, and endlessly confounding life was through. It was home.

"Me either," Margot said.

THE NOTEBOOK, THE LAST PAGE

Happily Ever After

There is no doubt in my mind that, whether you've followed my advice or ignored it, you had a glorious, memorable wedding. A wedding is one thing, sweet Jenna, and a marriage is quite another. I know there are writers and psychologists and talk-show hosts and "experts" out there who claim they can give you the secret to a long, happy marriage. I assure you, they know nothing. Your father has seen every possible permutation of marriage, separation, and divorce, and he will be the first to tell you—and here I wholeheartedly agree—that half of all marriages will end and half will endure and there is no telling which is which. I am grateful for all the blessings I have been given, especially you and Margot and Nicholas and Kevin, my strong, bright, beautiful children. But my family begins and ends with your father, Douglas Carmichael, who has sustained me for thirty-five years with his devotion and infinite kindness. He did two things for me every single day of our marriage: he made me laugh, and he was my friend.

How lucky, how very lucky, I have been.

OUTTAKES

The New York Times
Carmichael-Graham

Jennifer Bailey Carmichael, daughter of Douglas Carmichael of Silvermine, CT, and the late Elizabeth Bailey Carmichael, married Stuart James Graham, son of James and Ann Graham of Durham, NC, yesterday on Nantucket Island, Massachusetts. The Reverend Harvey Marlowe officiated at St. Paul's Episcopal Church.

Ms. Carmichael, 29, is the lead teacher at Little Minds Preschool in Manhattan. She is a graduate of the College of William and Mary.

The bride's father is the managing partner at Garrett, Parker, and Spence, a family law practice in Manhattan.

The groom, 30, is a food and beverage analyst for Morgan Stanley. He is a graduate of Vanderbilt University, where he graduated summa cum laude. He received an M.B.A. from Columbia.

The groom's father is a vice president at GlaxoSmithKline in Research Triangle Park, North Carolina, and the groom's mother has served as a state senator in North Carolina for twenty-four years.

Ryan Graham (best man): Wow, the wedding announcement states all the facts, but it actually tells you *nothing*.

Nick Carmichael (brother of the bride): Normally, I break hearts like it's my cool second job. But this weekend, I had a girl swiped right out from under me, which has never happened before. It took a minute for me to realize that she hadn't belonged to me in the first place. It felt like she belonged to me because I have known her for so long—longer than Scott Walker, by the way—but only by a couple of decades. Finn had always been Jenna's little friend, but then, this weekend, she became someone else. Had I fallen in *love* with her? Man, I don't know if I would go that far, though I felt something crazy and unfamiliar. But then I've heard weddings can do that. They can bring out the romantic in anyone.

H. W. Graham (brother of the groom): Her flight was at three o'clock and mine was at quarter to four so we decided to go to the airport together. We had gotten a pretty good glow on at the brunch, and since we had time at the airport, we sat at the bar and did a couple of tequila shots. She had been saying the whole weekend that she knew guys like me and that I didn't have to worry, there were no strings attached. Once she got on her plane for Myrtle Beach, I would never see or hear from her again. So it took a little convincing for me to get her number. We can text, I said. I'll hit you on Facebook, stuff like that. Plus, I go to Pawleys all the time to golf (this wasn't strictly true, though I had been there once), so I can come see you. I can come to your res-taurant. She said, It's a free country. Then her plane was called and I kissed her good-bye and I watched her copper hair disap-pear through the gate at security, and I'm embarrassed to admit what I did next. I got on my computer and MapQuested the dis-tance between Raleigh and Murrells Inlet. One hundred and eighty-seven miles, three hours and thirty-four minutes. Piece of cake. I'm going next weekend.

Carson Bain (nephew of the bride): My mother says that as soon as we get back to New York I have to start seeing a tutor *three times a week!*

Douglas Carmichael (father of the bride): By my calculations, the wedding cost me between a hundred and seventy and a hundred and eighty thousand dollars. If Beth were alive, she would *kill* me for telling you that. She would also insist that I add that it was worth every penny. Which it was.

Roger (wedding planner): We all know what Tolstoy wrote about happy families being alike but unhappy families being unhappy in their own fashion. I am not Russian and I am not a novelist, and a hundred and fifty years from now, no one will be quoting me—but that's not going to keep me from saying what I think. What I think is that every family is happy in their own fashion, and every family is unhappy in their own fashion. Every family is both functional and dysfunctional. The Carmichaels and the Grahams weren't my easiest clients, nor were they my most difficult—not by a long shot. But they stood out. The first time Jenna and Margot came into my office and told me that they had lost their mother but she had left a Notebook behind, I thought, *Now this is going to be interesting.* And it was.

The thing Beth Carmichael wanted for her daughter more than anything was a beautiful day. I have to say, I have worked on over a hundred and seventy-five weddings—some in the driving rain and wind, some in a fug of unbearable heat and humidity, one in a blizzard (in April!)—and they have all, every single one of them, been beautiful days.

But especially this one.

Jenna Carmichael Graham (newlywed): Weddings are a big deal. You might think I would have realized this before yesterday, but I didn't. It was only as I stood on the altar of the church with Stuart and my family and Stuart's brothers and my best friends and Reverend Marlowe, and I looked out at all the faces of the people I loved who loved me back and wished the best for me, that I understood. Love is scary! Taking a vow to love someone through sickness and health, for richer for poorer, *forsaking all others, until death do us part,* is the most terrifying experience a person can have. Why pretend any differently?

ACKNOWLEDGMENTS

Everyone loves a wedding!

Phyllis Frielich was unbelievable in her willingness to go over every possible detail of the Carmichael-Graham nuptials with me. She was filled with wonderful, creative ideas, and the bridal bouquet is her vision, along with many other details.

The Boston wedding planner Michelle Ciccarella and her cohorts Jackie Parker and Michelle Reid were the ones who got my gears moving, back in the fall of 2011. Thank you, ladies! Four Seasons forever!

Deborah Briggs Bennett, who is a friend so close she's family, gave me the lowdown on the world of executive placement. I could never have written this book without her help. She also provided the inspiration for the section titled "The Registry, Part II: The Dining Room" and the answer to the timeless question "Does the twelfth Tiffany dessert fork matter?"

Renaissance man Andrew M. Porter, Esq., was my go-to guy on the profession of Douglas Carmichael and John Edgar Desvesnes III, as well as serving as my Civil War expert.

I will again crib the words of Anne Sexton to describe my editor at Little, Brown, Reagan Arthur: "Pure genius at work." There's really nothing else I can say. Reagan is always, always right—and I have seven books to prove it. The ways in which she made this book better are too numerous to name.

The other wizards and goddesses at Little, Brown who have made me the happiest author in America are: Michael Pietsch, Heather Fain, Terry Adams, Michelle Aielli, Marlena Bittner, Justin Levine, Sarah Murphy, and the most magnificent David Young.

My agenting team of Michael Carlisle and David Forrer at Inkwell Management are truly and forever my champions and my darlings.

Sarah Cutler, you were a dream; thank God I found you.

In memoriam to my first "biggest fan," Nora Jaksic, mother of the gallant and divine Jimmy Jaksic. Nora will always live in my heart as the ultimate Blue Bistro fan.

As ever, I want to acknowledge my family, my friends, and my fellow football/basketball/baseball mothers. You all know who you are and how you make my life rich, interesting, and worthwhile. You tolerate me screaming from the sidelines and the bleachers—and for this I can't thank you enough.

This novel is for my grandparents Clarence and Ruth Huling, who would have been married for seventy years on June 19, 2013. This book was meant to be published in honor of their anniversary. My grandfather Clarence W. Huling Jr. died before he could see this book published. And so, to my grandmother Ruth Francis Huling, I would like to say this: Thank you, Gramma, for showing me what love is supposed to look like. You allow me to believe.